Praise

Our Homes

Longlisted for the Scotiabank Giller Prize for Fiction • A *Globe and Mail* Best Book of the Year • A *National Post* Top Ten Book of the Year • A CBC Best Canadian Fiction Book of the Year

"True to its title, *Our Homesick Songs* is filled with music. The lyrical language is met with literal accordions, violins and songs passed through generations, sung by parents and children and even mermaids (a phenomenon in which they all believe). The town is filled with magic, and so is Hooper's writing. *Our Homesick Songs* is a eulogy to not just a town but a lifestyle—one built on waves, and winds, and fish, and folklore."
—*The New York Times*

"Warm-hearted and winsomely imaginative." —*The Sunday Times* (UK)

"A lovely homage to Newfoundland culture, a story about storytellers told with a beguiling simplicity. Lovely and lyrical . . . Hooper's work brims with mermaids and music and memory, as any good Newfoundland story must, and there is no shortage of eccentric characters." —*Toronto Star*

"After gaining worldwide success with her first novel, *Etta and Otto and Russell and James*, which was translated into over two dozen languages, Albertan Emma Hooper now places the musicality of her pen in the service of a marvellous tale on the edge of a dream, borne by an imagination that is both vivid and enchanting. . . . A novel of great beauty."
—*Le Devoir*

"A haunting fable about the transformative power of hope." —*Booklist* (starred review)

"[Emma Hooper] has recreated the demise of the fishery on the one hand, and explored the persistence of folk memory on the other. . . . [She] has constructed such an authentic sense of place from such a distant shore. In Hooper's hands Newfoundland has become a kind of Narnia, or Never-Never Land, a place that we believe in." —*The Irish Times*

WE SHOULD NOT BE AFRAID OF THE SKY

EMMA HOOPER

PENGUIN

an imprint of Penguin Canada,
a division of Penguin Random House Canada Limited

First published in Penguin Canada hardcover, 2022

Published in this edition, 2023

1 2 3 4 5 6 7 8 9 10

LIBRARY AND ARCHIVES CANADA CATALOGUING IN PUBLICATION

Title: We should not be afraid of the sky / Emma Hooper.
Names: Hooper, Emma, author.
Description: Previously published: Toronto: Penguin Canada, 2022.
Identifiers: Canadiana 20210309032 | ISBN 9780735232761 (softcover)
Classification: LCC PS8615.O5157 W4 2023 | DDC C813/.6—dc23

Cover and book design by Lisa Jager
Cover images: (lady) Trasteverina, ballando il saltarello by Pinelli, Bartolomeo. Courtesy of
The New York Public Library; (lemons) © channarongsds / Adobe Stock

Printed in the United States of America

www.penguinrandomhouse.ca

Penguin
Random House
PENGUIN CANADA

EKH, sister.

We lose a good deal, perhaps, of the benefit we might derive from the Saints' lives, by not considering them to have shared, after all, the same flesh and blood that we are of.

REV. W. H. ANDERSEN, "SS. Perpetua, Felicitas, and their Companions, Martyrs at Carthage, A.D. 203," 1880

St. Quiteria . . . The Bollandists pronounce her story to be utterly fabulous.

AGNES B. C. DUNBAR, *A Dictionary of Saintly Women*, 1904

The various accounts of [Saint] Quiteria's life, miracles and martyrdom share many factors, yet . . . discrepancies.

KATHARINE D. SCHERFF, "Saint Quiteria: An Investigation of a Saint's Developing Iconography throughout Medieval Spain," 2014

2

MARINA

Oh
    said our mother
        Oh no
            Oh no no no no no.
                She said it nine times
                    No no no no no no no no no.

                    Once for each tiny red head, once for each tiny
                    open mouth.

I don't blame her. I don't, we don't. She never wanted to be a mother. She didn't even want to marry. Not that there was a choice, in those things. Not that she'd had a choice.

Quiteria was first. The eldest, by two minutes. Momentarily loved and wanted before the rest came.

I was next.

She would have been okay with that, I think. With two. Quiteria and me. Twins, just twins, normal. Precious. Loveable. She and us, a little team.
    But not nine.
    Nine isn't a team. Not with her on it. Nine is deafening. Nine is impossible, is wave after wave of her life ending. Not hers anymore.

Like the contractions that gripped her and ripped her and held her and didn't stop, even when they were supposed to, didn't stop, wave after wave of little doors closing inside her with every chopped cord. Each first gasp at life was a bit of her ending.

Nine is not a team; nine is a swarm.

Nine is animal.

She shut her eyes and opened them and we were still there. It took almost every female servant in the house to hold us. Waiting, watching her. Now what? Now what, madam, mother?

She shut her eyes and opened them and we were still there, again, so she beckoned Cyllia, the most experienced maidservant, the hardest, towards her.

Cyllia gave the baby she was holding to the water girl, who was already holding two others, and walked over and bent down and pushed her veil away from her ear so my mother could turn and lean close and whisper, because all she could do was whisper, we'd made her into such a ghost, flat, empty. She whispered and none of the others in the room,

not the midwife

not the priestess

not the water girl

not the cook

not the cook's girl

only Cyllia and us babies, brand new, ears ready to hear anything, everything, ready for our mother, could hear her ghost-words:

Please, Cyllia, please.

Cyllia nodded, careful not to let her face touch our mother's. That would be too much, even now.

There was blood on everything. On everyone.

Please, Cyllia, please, she said. The water, she said. The stream.

Then a beat. Then, for a moment, silence.

Then Cyllia whispered,

Drown?

Quieter than the tiny push of our heartbeats.

Our mother had no words left. She moved her head, down a little, up a little, down again. Yes.

I don't blame her. I don't. Maybe I would have done the same.

Cyllia nodded again, pulled her veil back into place, stood up, and sent the cook's girl to go get four baskets. Then she put us in those baskets, living babies in three and the two who didn't live, Eumelia, Genebra, just names, in the other, and tucked us in with cloth, the cleanest that could be found in a house that had just given birth nine times. She left the priestess to watch our mother, eyes closed now, maybe breathing maybe not breathing, dismissed the midwife and other servants, and, balancing two baskets on each arm, set off down the stairs, out the door, and on into the trees, to the water that ran between them.

It was so hot that day. Early in the season but already so hot and everything smelled of lemons, this new fruit, this brand-new fruit, the trees hanging low with it, the juice bursting out onto her feet when Cyllia stepped on windfall, everything smelled so sweet when she got out there, into this orchard, to the stream that ran through the orchard now but would be only a trickle by April and gone completely by June, this predawn orchard of insects and juice and birds, so sweet and the sun almost up, the sweetness even louder than our crying, so heavy, so sweet that Cyllia, four baskets, nine babies, seven still alive, seven still trying, stopped at the stream's edge and breathed, in-out, and hesitated.

Babies died all the time. Died of poxes, of hot and loud fevers, of quiet and slow chills, of just being born. She herself had lost three. Her mistress had lost two already, one at almost five years old, almost not a baby anymore. And one that had come out almost dead, and then dead.

Cyllia hesitated.

Babies died all the time. Like her first two, both gone at once. Freezing fever so they were unable to speak or see or do anything but hold her hand and hold each other's hands.

The smell, the forest, was so sweet. The promise of fruit was all around. A summer of fruit. A future of fruit.

Cyllia hesitated and we wailed. We were red and purple and blue. We were starving. We were half crazy with it.

She set down the baskets and dug two small holes with her bare hands just off the stream bed, where the soil was softest. She put Eumelia and Genebra, our sisters, the ones already gone, in the holes, one hole each, small enough to be rabbit holes, small enough to be nothing. She covered them with lemon-scented soil. She packed it down. She didn't mark it. She washed her hands in the stream, and then, with the first morning sun pushing its way to her through the leaves, the branches, the fruit, the fruit, the fruit, she reached up and picked a lemon, one of the first lemons.

This is what Cyllia told me, when we met again, twelve years later.

Were you looking for guidance? I asked her. For a sign?

I was looking for a snack, she answered.

She peeled the lemon, she told me. Pith under nails, oil between fingers. This strange fruit. Still new to her. It fell open: nine segments.

She did love her mistress, she did love her work. But there were nine segments. That can't have been luck. That was a sign, a message.

She split the segments apart and put one in each of our mouths. Just the right size, just the right shape. One by one we stopped crying. The segments bobbed up and down as we sucked, draining the juice little by little, absorbing the sour-sweet. Cyllia dropped two segments into the stream for the lost babies and then reached up and got another lemon, a whole one, for herself. She ate it in the new morning quiet.

—⁂—

We survived. Most of us survived. It's important to know that. For a while anyway, a good while. We lived and fought and fought and lived and then we died. Or almost. Because we can't really die, not really, right? We step up to death or death steps up to us, and whispers, Ready? And we whisper back, Ready, and then we jump, we both jump, right? We all jump, eventually.

We, the seven still-alive babies, finished the lemon segments, and the dry, floppy, empty pith drooped over our cheeks and our chins. Cyllia peeled them off our faces, sticky, wet, rolled them together into a ball, and tucked them into a pocket. Some of us cried, some of us slept, some of us stared up fuzzily at the sky or just listened fuzzily to the stream bumping past roots and rocks, a familiar, bodily sound. A comfort.

Cyllia picked another fruit, peeled it, counted the segments—nine again—divided and distributed them among us all, with two in the stream for Eumelia, for Genebra. She was stalling. Anyway, drowning seven infants would take time. She wouldn't be expected back for a while.

It occurred to her on the fourth lemon that this probably counted as stealing. It occurred to her on the fifth one that this was probably the least of her offences. She went through seven pieces of fruit until we were all asleep, our breathing synchronized and tiny against the sound of the water, our baskets stinking of sweet baby pee. Cyllia lay down between the baskets, her bare feet dangling into the stream. It was cool, it wouldn't be an unpleasant way to die, in there, it would be better than pox. Better than fever. She fell asleep thinking,

It would be better.

She kept that first ball of lemon pith for years, she told me. She kept it in her pocket until it disintegrated, rubbed away into the fabric itself. She'd reach down to it, feel its long-dry ridges until she forgot she was doing it, or why.

Seven babies!

Cyllia woke up again. So did five babies.

SEVEN! said the girl again, louder now, over the crying.

Cyllia went to stand and found that she was standing in the stream. Water almost to her knees. YES, she said. NINE, she said. HELLO. THERE WERE NINE, NOW SEVEN. SEVEN BABIES, YES.

THEY ARE YOURS?

NO.

THEY ARE HUNGRY?

YES.

THEY NEED MILK.

YES. BUT I DON'T HAVE ANY.

I DO.

The girl sat down on the bank next to a basket. She lifted out a baby. An awake one. A crying one. Gema. She pulled her tunic loose and revealed a breast and put the baby to it. Come on, she said, quieter. This will do, come on.

Gema opened her mouth but angled it wrong. Come on. She tried again. Come on, come on. And again. And then Gema was on and her eyes went big and then closed and her body went from red and rigid to soft, baby soft, again. She drank.

I have a one-year-old at home, said the girl. And I feed my dead neighbour's child too. I have milk for the whole country. For the whole of Rome.

For seven? asked Cyllia. A new option had presented itself. She allowed it in.

Well . . . said the girl. No. Maybe two?

You'll take two?

Take? Who's talking about take? I said feed, she said.

Yes, but if nobody else could, if nobody would.

They are orphans?

Yes, said Cyllia. Maybe lying, maybe not.

And all sisters and brothers?

All sisters. All of them.

Oh, said the girl. Oh, oh, oh.

Maybe, said Cyllia,

And you? said the girl. You can't take any?

I have no milk. And a master who won't allow it.

The girl looked at Gema at her breast, and at Germana, who'd latched on to the other side, easy as anything. Then she looked to the others, then to the stream. Oh, she said. Oh, I see.

Please, said Cyllia. She picked me up from the basket nearest her. I started to cry. Please, she said.

Okay, said the girl. I know some women. I know some other women. If I go, will you be here when I get back?

The babies will be here, said Cyllia. The babies will be fine.

The girl fed us all, at least a little each, taking great gulps of water from the stream for herself in between, before going. I'll be right back, she said. I'll be as quick as I can.

After she'd gone, Cyllia wondered what her mistress would be expecting as proof. What, if anything, she could use as proof. We were newborn babies, unclothed, unadorned. There would have been nothing to bring back, nothing to show. So she brought nothing. She just left. Back through the trees and then the grass and then along the path and then up the road, back to the house.

She was halfway up the path, almost at the road, when she realized that, maybe, her mistress hadn't been talking about drowning us. The water. The stream. Maybe her mistress had been talking about herself.

It didn't matter anyway. Our mother was dead by the time Cyllia got back to the house.

We were brand new; we didn't know how to mourn, or that we should. We only knew hunger, we only knew each other, and that as soon as we went from being one, one pregnancy, one belly, to nine—removed, divided—we became able to be alone, we became able to be afraid.

The girl came back. Back to the stream, back to us. She brought four other peasant women. Together they lifted us into the water, washed us clean, and lifted us to their milk. A woman with hair already going sky white took Liberata and Basilissa together, since they were already in a basket together, since she herself had been born with, and lost, a twin.

Two others, both of whom were pregnant, took a baby each. The plan was to tell their husbands they'd had their babies early, out working in the trees. Then wild carrot could deal with their own bellies, hopefully, and they could escape labour, at least this once. One took Quiteria and one took Vitoria.

The girl took Gema and Germana, the first two she'd nursed. Her milk was good, but it wouldn't last much longer, not with children who could walk already, who could eat olives and spit out pits already. By nursing these orphans, she could hold off another pregnancy, maybe; she could buy some time, hopefully.

And, anyway, when the time came, if the time came, extra mouths could be sold as slaves. They could always be sold, for example, to the commander's big house, through the tree and the grass, along the path and up the road. Lots of work there, all those rooms to keep warm or cool or light or dark, fighting the sun the way the rich do. Not to mention all these new trees. Everyone around here, peasants or slaves, worked on those trees, nursing and picking and packing and delivering the new yellow fruit up to that house. They paid everyone's way, these new trees, with fruit as bright as the sun.

A girl called Honoria took me, just me. She was young then, the youngest of them. She had lost her own first child only a week before. There was still blood on her tunic, still a basket by her bed. She lowered me into it singing childhood songs she hadn't yet outgrown herself.

So they took us away and we lived and grew and Cyllia collected up all the oil- and blood-stained things from the big house and when our father came home from the wilds, from standing just far enough away from the barbarian hordes with his own hordes to make sure they would continue to stay far enough away, when he got home, finally, and asked the first slave he met, the little boy who looked after the dogs, asked him about his new child, who should probably have been born by now, and his wife, who should be mostly, at least, recovered, the boy, who did not speak much Latin, said one of the only phrases he did know:

The dogs are all home and well, sir.

And my wife? And our new child, due to come four weeks ago?

Sir, the dogs are all home and well.

The boy looked down at the small red stones between his bare feet. Hot like fire. The dogs, he said.

Are you crying?

The dogs are—

Boy, are you? My father got down off his horse, put his hands on this tiny slave's shoulders, crouched in close. Are you crying? Is my wife all right? Is the . . .

Sir, said one of my father's convoy, stepping up from behind.

My father was crying now too. Child, the child, this time, is the child . . .

The dogs are—

Sir, said Cyllia, who had come out to meet the convoy. Sir.

She walked towards them, the wool and linen stained and out before her. We waited, she said. We waited for your command to take it to Juno, to the temple.

The boy ran away, two dogs followed.

Cassia? said our father, as if he'd only just remembered his wife's name again, as if it had been years. His convoy, horses, dogs, men, food, perfumes, gifts, a few new slaves in clothing strange, stretched out behind him, down the road. Cassia? he said.

This is how I picture it, anyway. Cyllia didn't tell me this bit in so much detail. But she did say our father wasn't a cruel commander, wasn't a cruel man. The rumours are good. The rumours are that he could have struck that dog boy, but he didn't. That he should have taken the wool and the linen, all our mother's clothes and the birthing things, to Athena's temple and burnt them there, or had Cyllia do it. But he didn't. That he folded them up and put them away, back where they'd always belonged before. Where they still belonged. He wasn't a cruel man.

~

Hello, Marina, my new mother whispered to me as she carried me down the stream, down, down to the village tucked in by the orchard, my new home.

My mother, this adoptive mother, never had any more children. Something had broken during her first birth. Something broken in the baby, which meant it couldn't last, and something broken in her, which meant her body wouldn't do that again, knew better, maybe. All the houses where my other sisters went and grew were full of children, bodies, noise, but mine stayed quiet, just us three, always us three, my new mother, her weary, older husband, and me. I lived in that dark, cool, quiet one-room house and the years slipped by gentle in olive oil and lemons.

I

QUITERIA

I run and my sisters follow. I run and my sisters run. I jump and they jump. I say, QUITERIA IS THE GODDESS OF EVERYTHING AND I PROMISE TO GIVE HER ALL MY LEMONS, and they shrug, they say okay, they reach out their half-full baskets with their skinny arms and I say, No, no, no, I'm kidding, just kidding, keep your stupid fruit, and they laugh and say, No, no, no, we're kidding, we're just kidding too.

We're all the same size, all exactly, exactly the same, but I feel bigger. I am bigger. And sometimes this is helpful and sometimes it's not. Sometimes it means I have to carry more; it's a given, expected. It means that when someone says, What next? Now what do we do? everyone turns to me, everyone else is quiet.

Seven years after we were born and thirteen years before we died, I climbed up into a lemon tree and my six sisters followed, one tree each, all in a row. Up in those scrawny trees we picked lemons, tossing them down into the baskets our fathers had left underneath. Our mothers were at home, inside, sucking juice straight from bruised or browned fruit and nursing their babies. They had to do it there, inside, because inside was the only place shaded enough to keep the babies from crying hot murder. Baby eyes are too new, too soft for the kind of sun that shone there; they couldn't be opened in the full daylight until at least four months after birth, six months for some.

Except for me, except for my sisters after me. We were different. We were born with everything too bright, too full, inside and out, and anyway, hadn't had anyone to hold us, to nurse us, except for that white-hot sun, so we hadn't needed shady protection in early life, so we'd opened our eyes wide from day one, and me the widest of all.

Now what? said Marina. All her lemons were gone. Picked. Basketed.
Jump, I said. Do it.
Really? From way up—
I'll do it if you do it.
Really?
Really. And Liberata and Basil and Germana and Gema and Vitoria. All of us at the same time.
Okay? they said, all the way down the line and back up again.
Okay, all the way down, all the way back.
Okay, I said. Ready?
One,
Two,
Three—
I jumped. Everyone jumped. Everyone landed. Everyone grabbed lemons out of everyone else's baskets and pierced them with their teeth and ran with them, squirting juice in the direction of everyone else's eyes, and if you got it in your eyes you lost but if you got it in your mouth you won.

And that's how it was, mostly.

＊

I knew we were sisters, we all knew, even though we lived with different families. Same eyes same nose same knees same hair same skin, our adoptive parents couldn't have hidden it from us even if they'd wanted to. But they didn't want to, they didn't care, really, so long as we worked as hard as their real kids and didn't eat any more than them.

And I knew how things worked, generally, that we didn't keep the fruit we picked, that we weren't supposed to steal them or bite them or squirt them into each other's eyes. That the lemons, and the trees, and everything, really, except fruit too withered or brown or bug-full to be much good to anyone, belonged, technically, to the big house. That we weren't slaves, weren't we lucky we weren't slaves? But I knew, also, that all the fruit, all the animals, all the people, technically, really, belonged to it, to them.

Not to them, not to that house, to Rome, corrected my father. The commander is just the representative, the ambassador to Rome.

Does being Rome itself or an ambassador to Rome change how many lemons we give away and how many we keep? I asked.

No, but, said my father.

My mother, carrying a pile of filthy laundry taller than her, interrupted, And does having our very own *ambassador* to Rome make the sun any less goddamn hot, the fly-riddled babies any less sickly? She spoke, muffled, through the pile.

No, said my father. But we are protected.

From . . . ? I began.

We are fucked, said my mother, over her shoulder, already halfway down to the more-mud-than-water stream. But hey ho, she said, on we go.

And I knew, too, how soldiers and rich visitors would come down, sometimes, from that house to the village, to look at the trees and smell the blossoms and run their hands along the trunks and take fruit. How they'd come down later, sometimes, and find and take a girl, or boy, older than us but not by much, who, like the lemons, had no choice but to go with them, for a while. Then the girl, or boy, would come back, usually. Sometimes there'd be another new baby after that, sometimes not.

I knew nothing good came from that house, only that good things were taken there and sent back empty or rotten. And I knew it was my job, just me, mine, to keep my sisters from it, to protect them, all of us.

⁓

One morning just after we turned eight, there was a parade. An army was coming home from somewhere via the village and making a big deal of it. Marina and I were on caterpillar-killing duty, and since the bugs would always crawl towards the light, we were up in the trees' farthest, thinnest branches, the branches that barely held us, scanning and feeling for fuzzy green movement in the flowers and on the leaves, looking for things to crush, to kill.

We were up there, hunting, crushing, killing, when we heard the drums.

Listen, said Marina. She had a caterpillar in her hand, between two fingers. It lifted its head up and around, stretching, escaping.

It sounded like a war.

It sounds like a party, said Marina. She dropped the caterpillar and it fell down, bounced off a leaf, then landed in the soft bed of an early flower. We pulled ourselves up, sticking our heads out through the leaves like caterpillars, and looked towards the sound.

There were soldiers, armour reflecting the sun like a new kind of weapon, and there were captives, barbarians, walking behind them, tied arm to arm to arm like a human garland. There were drummers and horn players, though only the drummers were playing.

They must save the horns for extra-special things, said Marina. Like weddings.

Like battle, I thought.

Some of the soldiers were on horses, also shining, and, in the very middle of it all, there was one man with the brightest, reddest cloak and the tallest, whitest horse. A beautiful, terrifying horse.

The commander, said Marina. Almost a whisper. And her heart beat so loud I could hear it.

The commander, I repeated, whispered. And my heart beat so loud she could hear it.

Gema and Germana, sisters three and four, died not long after that. The flowers on the trees had just struggled into lemons and then they died. Lots of kids were sick that summer, and adults too, and pretty much all the babies. It was too hot. Too hot for lemons, too hot for dogs or caterpillars or us, though the dogs didn't die, or the caterpillars, except the ones we killed, because they got to live outside. Animals are lucky that way. It was hot outside, too hot, but worse inside, where the air didn't move and the heat pulsed from the walls. Small houses or big houses, they're all just traps for people. For girls.

But it's safe inside, said Marina.

Safe is the opposite of alive, I said.

One morning before Gema and Germana died but after they got sick, I jumped out of my tree and went to try to save them.

I went to the house they shared with their adoptive father and adoptive mother and five adoptive siblings.

Their eldest adoptive sister was there, just outside the door, nursing a baby in one arm and banging out a dirty sick-cloth with the other.

What? she said. The baby got distracted from its feed and looked at me. Then it couldn't find the nipple again and started to cry.

I'm here to bring Gema and Germana out, I said. Out into the air. To get better.

Their fake sister stopped banging the cloth. She looked at me: nobody's real daughter. They're sleeping, she said, then starting banging the cloth again, a grey-green cloth that hadn't always been grey-green.

I can help lift them out, I said. I'm strong.

The end of the cloth whipped back and hit the baby in the leg. It cried louder.

They are sleeping, said the fake sister. She turned her head down, away from me, and tried to reposition the baby, but by then it had forgotten it was crying for milk and was just crying because it was crying, and didn't want the milk.

It was loud, but the kind of loud it always was, there, the kind you could learn to listen around. And if you did, if you listened past it, past that crying baby, past the banging cloth, past the buzz of flies around the cloth, past the general noise of dogs and kids and bugs, if you listened around all that, you could hear, I could hear, from inside the house, Gema's and Germana's frayed breath, each inhale a difficult question, each exhale a relief, an answer, and you could hear, I could hear, running over that, like water in the stream when there was water in the stream, the soft continuous murmur of their mother, their adoptive mother, as she tended them. She whispered and whispered and whispered, without pause, without break, on and on like a rope, like her daughters couldn't let go so long as they had something to listen to, her voice to hold on to.

Go away, said the sister with the baby. Go home, Quiteria.

So I did, leaving Gema and Germana inside, in the hot and the dark.

So they died, confined, and we were down to five.

We went up the mountain. Basil and Liberata and Vitoria and Marina and I, the still-alive sisters. Everyone else was home sleeping through the hottest bit of day, or trying to, so we didn't have to work just then. As we climbed we sent rocks rolling down behind us, our bare toes curling around roots and digging into dry dirt for grip.

We stood in a circle, facing each other, and, because we weren't sure what else to do, we held hands. I thought we should make some kind of sacrifice, but where would we have gotten the wine for that, let alone any animal? So instead, we just broke some tough grey-green leaves off a low bush and made a little pile in the middle of us all. The waves of heat blurred our faces, erased them.

Maybe we should make promises, said Basil. Two each, one for each lost sister. We could close our eyes, she said, all of us close our eyes and make two promises.

Everyone looked at me. Yeah? said Marina.

Yeah, I said, sure. That sounds good.

In our heads or out loud? asked Basil, who had been first up the hill, not even out of breath. Who had made it up with enough time to climb onto a rock and jump off six times before the rest of us arrived.

Everyone waited, quiet.

It doesn't matter, I guess, I said. They'll hear or not hear the same either way.

So? said Marina.

So, quiet, I said. Let's do quiet.

So everyone was quiet, fingers intertwined, sticky with sweat, and whispered brushstrokes of promises that sounded, to everyone else, like faraway birds.

I promise, I whispered, to stay big, even when I feel small. I promise to stay big enough to lift my sisters, always, to carry them.

And I felt, as I said it, a lifting in my chest, a pulling away from earth and everything else too hot to touch.

Was that praying? Marina asked, later, walking back to the orchard. She had a scratch up the side of her arm where she'd fallen climbing down and a little jewel of blood clung to it, dried.

I don't know, I said. Maybe?

5

LIBERATA

Hi! I'm Liberata.

You know that, though, I guess. You know that because you read it, probably, right up there. Like, right before I said it. So I didn't need to say it. But, too late. I did.

Thanks, anyway, for reading it again. And for sticking around. I know I'm not a famous one. I know I'm not one of the main ones. I would guess you picked up this book ready to read about famous saints, even if only slightly famous, like a tiny tiny bit famous, like . . . like that mouse we had in the village that would ride around on top of the goats, famous like that. But I'm not even that famous, not like that mouse, not like Quiteria or Marina or Vitoria, even. But you're reading anyway, so that's great, that's super. That's really nice. And because of that, and because I like you, I'll tell you something. I'll tell you something nobody knows. Not Quiteria, not Marina, not even Gema. Not anyone but me. Ready? Okay. I'll tell you.

When I was a kid, normal and smooth-skinned like my sisters, every year on the night before my birthday, I'd go to sleep me and I'd wake up someone else. I'd be them until they died, and then I'd wake up again and be me again, me on the morning of my birthday. I'd be older and they'd be dead. This happened every year, *every year*, until I almost died myself, freezing and burning at once, so loud and so so so quiet, both at once.

They were always good people, the people I became. Not just good like we were good, like trying not to step on babies or eating only your share of bread, not even soaking up a little more oil with your chunk than you should and making it look like an accident because that kind of thing can easily happen as an accident, who knows how dry your bit of bread was, maybe very very dry, so it soaks up not just your allowed amount of oil but also your sister's and maybe even a bit or all of your fake siblings' too; these people weren't just good enough to never do that. They were really good. So good that it glowed inside them, inside me, when I was them. So good that, when I was them, I could hold my breath and hold on to that goodness and have it lift me right up, off the ground.

And even though they were almost always older than me, the people I became, they were also always younger, much, much younger, because they'd been born years and years and years after me. Years in numbers that seem impossible, 300, 1179, 1663 . . .

And here's the thing: I didn't just do it in dreams, in those birthday dreams. By the time I got to my seventh birthday, I'd figured out that every now and then, in real life, I could get that same goodness glow, not just from not hitting a baby when it bit my leg or not stealing the water that was meant for the goat, but from something a lot bigger, deeper, like when Gema and I almost fell all the way down the canyon but caught and lifted each other back up and out so that we didn't even know who had fallen and who had helped and when we got back to the top our hearts were beating beating beating and we were laughing, though also crying, a bit, and I felt it then, I felt it and I knew it and I held my breath, held on to it, and for a beat, just one small beat, I was up, I was off the ground, the cool of the air on the bottom of my feet, free from the hot hard dirt.

And then I wondered if the back of my head looked like the back of Gema's head and I fell back down.

Gema didn't see. It didn't last very long that first time. It never did, really. But I got better at controlling it, at least, at catching the glow right at the very beginning and pressing myself into it, my breath, my thoughts, my heart, so that it grew and grew and became directable.

Not controllable, quite, but directable, a bit. Like a big ram or a stupid baby. I got better at not being distracted, and that helped. That helps.

My first birthday was my first dream. The first of these other-life dreams and also the first dream I ever had, that I remembered, anyway. A baby's life is all kind of one big dream anyway, isn't it? A fog of light and hunger and dark and thirst and sound and shapes and mothers.

I fell asleep on the last night of being no-age and had my first dream. I dreamt of hunger. Terrible, unending, devil hunger. I dreamt of eighteen years of hunger, always the same no matter how much milk I took; I dreamt of nursing and nursing and nursing and nursing and nursing and nursing and nursing, and then, finally, my mother, on whom I was nursing that whole time, those whole eighteen years, looked down at me, into my starving face, and the good of her filled me so fast that all the milk rose up in me and I opened my mouth and woke up, one year old, and covered in my own sick.

At two, a band of shining dancing half-people-half-birds came and lifted me up, but without touching me, just by dancing and laughing and inviting me up with them, to laugh, to dance.

And at three, I could talk to plants, though only edible ones, not poisonous, and sing and sing until I was as high up as my own notes.

And, on my fourth birthday, I had a dog head. But a person body. A big person body, a really big adult-man one. A thirsty one, again. I was out for a walk, looking for water in a place with trees so tall and thick that the sky was green, not blue. Everything was green and alive and moving; bugs all over the place. It was a great place to walk, and my legs were so long, so much longer than usual, that, for a while, I forgot my thirst and just enjoyed walking, taking huge steps right over things, bushes and fallen trees and all sorts. Once the fun of that wore off a bit, I remembered my dry throat and I went back to looking for water, with my eyes, like normal, and with my nose, because I had that dog head and could smell in all colours and shapes and sizes. There were all the bugs, but bugs are mostly crunchy and dry, without much fluid of any kind; and lots of plants too, but I needed more water than plants could hold. So I looked and I sniffed and I looked and I sniffed and I walked around in huge steps until I found a scent to follow, a blue bright scent through all this green, a round bright wash of scent that drew me on and on and on until, at last, I came to a river, fast as light, wide as my arms again and again and again, ten times over, the smell at its banks so full and beautiful I almost rose up, already, right there.

But then I remembered my thirst, and that stopped the flying, and I knelt down to drink, at last drink, and was trying to decide if I should drink like a person, from cupped hands, or like a dog, just with my tongue, when I heard a baby, a human baby, crying somewhere really close by.

The smell of the river was so loud, I guess, that I hadn't noticed the baby before. I stopped thinking about drinking. I hesitated. Why was there a baby out here, in this wild forest-y place? Was it lost? Forgotten? And why was it crying? Was a scorpion biting it? I wasn't afraid of scorpions, not anymore, not since Gema had put one under my tunic, even though she claims not to have, and I was so angry that I just picked it up in my bare hand and threw it at her. Or maybe the baby was thirsty, like me. Whatever it was, it wasn't happy. I knew unhappy babies; our mom had loads. And I knew how flimsy they were; anything could hurt them, kill them: a scorpion, a cough, a chill, a burn. So even though I was still thirsty, thirstier even, right by all that water, I turned away from the river and listened and smelled my way to that baby.

It was a boy baby. All naked and red and screaming beside some tall spiky grass plant. It was sitting up. It smelled like baby. Mammal babies all share a smell, I now knew. A smell that meant: Help me. Stay with me. That meant: Don't eat me. It must have been that age when it could sit up but not move around. It saw me and stopped crying and stared instead, maybe because of my dog head.

Hey, I said. Hey, baby, don't cry. Even though it wasn't, anymore. Are you thirsty? I asked. Are you hot? Did something bite you?

The baby sighed. No, no, it said. Which surprised me, because I didn't actually expect it to be able to answer. Or sigh, even, really.

I just need across, it said. But there's no way across.

Across?

The water.

The river?

Yes, the river water. But there's no bridge and no boat.

I wasn't sure a bridge or a boat would help, really, since the baby was just a baby, but I didn't say that. Instead I looked back to the river, wide and fast, and then down at my adult-man legs, tall and strong; probably tall and strong enough, even if I couldn't fly, had to walk, to ford, and I said,

Okay, no problem. I think I can take you.

That'd be great, said the baby. Really, really great. Wonderful. But first, you're thirsty, right? it asked. Don't you need to drink?

Yes, I said. I do, that's true.

You're really, incredibly, almost-dead-from-it thirsty, but you came to find me first, said the baby. That was really nice of you. Look, he said. I'm not in a huge rush. Why don't you have a drink, a really big drink first, and then take me across, after that?

Okay, I said. Sounds good.

So I left the baby there, since it said I could and I couldn't see anything poisonous or fierce near to it, and I went back to the river. By now my thirst was so strong that I couldn't bother with hands; I just knelt down and lowered my head and lapped up the water in big wonderful tonguefuls. I drank and drank and the water tasted like light when you first open your eyes in the morning. I drank and drank and drank so much that the water level went down and the current calmed and I thought: Well, even if I couldn't before, I can definitely cross that now, even carrying a baby.

When I got back the baby was still just sitting there, quietly playing with its toes. Okay, baby, I said. Let's go. I put my hands, which were human hands, not dog hands, under its armpits and hoisted it up.

I had lifted babies before, loads of them, my own fake little brothers and sisters and all the other little kids who were always crawling around the grove; Quiteria's baby sister, who always tried to escape down to the stream; Gema and Germana's brother, who would scream and scream whenever he was left alone in their hut, which he usually was; and all the others. They ranged from tiny, lighter than a lizard, to really bulky and round, heavier than a pregnant goat. I'd lifted babies who were heavy, very heavy, all the time. But they were nothing like this baby. This baby by the river. Even though I was a full-grown dog-man, and even though it looked tiny, underfed in fact, this baby weighed more than anything I had ever lifted, not just babies. Heavier than goats, than lemon boxes, than my own self. Pulling it up was like pulling up an old-old tree, roots and all, with just your hands. I did it, I lifted the baby, but it almost crushed me.

I put it up on my shoulders and took a deep breath. Closed and opened my eyes to try to find balance. Geez, I said.

Sorry, said the baby.

Not your fault, I said. I managed to take a step, then two, towards the river. Even though it was lower now, and calmer, I was starting to doubt I'd be able to make it across after all, not with all that weight. I stepped forward, one foot into the water, and my leg sank heavy fast into the silt and the mud, and my balance faltered. I let go of the baby's legs and thrust my arms out, trying to break my, our, fall and I said,

My—

and the baby cried out and grabbed hard onto the fur of my head, pushing its face down and in and

and the smell of it, of its head, of its skin, of its little baby sweetness, pureness, its roundness, its fullness, like fruit, like life, like

sisters, I said. Like my sisters when we were all just babies, were all just smell to each other and that was all and that was everything and

and

and

and

and my foot pulled up, out of the muck as easy as anything. And kept going, up and up, and the other foot too, and all the rest of me, and the baby on my shoulders; we rose up, out of the water, over the water, and all the way across the river, and then came down again, gentle, careful, on the other side.

The baby climbed off my shoulders and down my back all by itself. There, it said. I knew you could.

Then it kissed my legs, once each, just beneath the knee, and crawled off, behind some bushes and away.

That dog-head version of me didn't die for a very long time, even though it almost died lots of times. Usually, almost always, flying can get you out of dying situations, especially when people don't expect you to be able to fly. In the end, I died because my dog head got cut off, which was sad, but also okay, because it was always a bit hard, having to be both. So they cut me in two, and I died, and then I woke up and was four years old.

And then I was a man who would fly whenever I heard music, whether I wanted to or not, uncontrollably, up and up until the music stopped or I couldn't hear it anymore and then I ate some bad bread and died and woke up and was five.

And then I was a girl so beautiful that people died just from looking at me, which made me sad, so I'd ask them not to be dead and they'd come back to life, just for me, but then one man got so angry at my beauty, because beauty can do that, which is strange, which doesn't seem right, that instead of him dying he thought I should die and he stabbed my neck so my blood, as beautiful as me, poured out and out in beautiful red ribbons and then I died and woke up and was six.

And then a boy tried to kick my mother, so I made his foot fall off, and all the toes fall off the foot too. Then he apologized, so I flew the toes back onto his foot and flew his foot back onto his leg, the right way around and everything. Then I got sick and tried living up in a tree to make it better but it didn't and I died and a million children cried and then I woke up and was seven.

And then I had some people build me a tall plinth out of stones piled on top of each other, which they did for me because I was so nice and so good and because they were nice and good too and once they were done I flew up to the top and lived there, because it felt good to be so close to the sky and because I had learned to talk to the sun, so I wasn't lonely. People brought me baskets of food or jugs of water and I flew them up to me and ate and drank and then flew them back down again, carefully, so as not to hit anyone's head. People also brought me messages for the sun, which I passed along, just casually, while the sun and

I were talking, and the sun didn't mind and neither did I. Then the sun wondered if I could get a bit closer so it could hear me better, so I asked the people to build me a taller plinth and they did. And then another one, and then another, until I was so high that I could just whisper and the sun could hear. The people down below, on the ground, couldn't hear me anymore, but that was okay, because they still kept sending up baskets and jugs, only now they'd include their prayers in the baskets too, written down for me to read out to the sun. And between them and the sun and the stars, which didn't talk but shone in a rhythmic kind of way that I could see, now, from up there, was like talking, between all that I was happy, very happy, up there. And I stayed up there and stayed happy until I was very old and then I curled up one day, like a very old dog, and let the sun and the stars sing to me until I died. And then I woke up and was eight.

And then the village got sick.

It wasn't my birthday; I wasn't someone else; I wasn't filled with light or love or goodness; I was just me, just normal, and everyone was sick. Not me, but everyone else, almost everyone. My sisters Gema and Germana were sick. The village, the country, the empire—all sick.

They fevered; they laid down; they slept; I slept; we all slept; I woke up, and they didn't. I woke up after a dreamless sleep and my sisters Gema and Germana had died, for real, in real life and I was cut in two for real.

Even though I'd seen lots of death and dying in all my dreams, and had died myself, in them, loads of times, eight times, this was different. This was how it should have felt, back when I had the dog head and they cut me in two, but back then it had been okay, and every other time too, so far, like my body was saving up the pain, storing it away, and then Gema and Germana died and it all broke loose, broke free, all at once, and I was cut in two for real. Every day. Every breath. The dull-toothed, slow-moving blade working its way farther and farther and farther and farther and farther and farther and farther, every day, every breath. Half of me there, alive, and half of me gone, with them. I closed my eyes and it tore me; I opened them and it tore me.

And the sun shone and the trees grew and the flies that Germana hated because they'd fly into her eyes all the time, more than into anyone else's for some reason, were still flying around, into other people's eyes instead. Nothing else stopped, nothing else changed.

And every now and then I'd be like them too. Like the sun and the trees and the flies. I'd accidentally let myself fall asleep, like before, or I'd let Basil make me laugh, like before, and, for a second, I'd forget the saw; I'd just be me, still whole, like always.

And then I'd remember. Sharp as the first time, I'd remember. And it would cut me through, again, again, and I'd swear, again, never, never to relax into sleep or laughter, never to be whole again so I'd never have to be recut again. I worked alone as much as I could; I put stones in my bed.

My mother was watching. My mother who, before everyone got sick, would sometimes put lemon peels in her mouth and smile wide so her teeth looked even more yellow than her few actual teeth.

My mother was watching and, after two months, said,

Liberata, here.

She held out a piece of rabbit leather, left over from an animal we'd caught and eaten a few weeks before. Tie it around your ankle, she said.

I took it and tried to tie it but couldn't do it myself, so she put down the baby she had in one arm, not ours, someone else's, bent down, and tied it on for me. She tied it just a bit too tight, so it dug in a tiny bit every time I moved.

Feel that? she asked.

Yes, I said.

Good, she said. You always will. Every step.

The baby had crawled away and found a thistle on the ground, was trying to eat it. My mother straightened, went to the baby, scooped it back up. She stuck her finger into its mouth and flicked the thistle out onto the ground.

Now take those rocks out of the bed, okay? she said.

It wasn't just my bed. I shared it with Basil and one bigger kid and one smaller. Okay, I said.

Okay, she said. Good.

She hoisted the baby up a bit higher on her hip and walked away, back to the orchard. I watched her go and counted the leather bands on her ankles, three on one side and five on the other.

There was a spot out behind the houses that no one really went to because the trees were old and dead and the ground was mostly ants. I didn't mind, though, because although they did bite others, like Gema and Germana before and Marina and Basil and even Quiteria, sometimes, now, the ants never bit me. Afternoons, when everyone else was sleeping, I'd go out there and I'd lie down and I'd close my eyes but I wouldn't sleep. I'd think about the time Gema and I were falling down in the canyon and I'd let the pulse of the sun on my skin glow warm and golden and bright and full and I'd whisper songs to it, to Gema and Germana, happy love songs the adults sang, sometimes, out at night burning up diseased branches, drunk enough to remember how to be happy, and gentle lullaby songs they sang, sometimes, at night when everything was quiet enough, finally, to remember how to be gentle. I'd let in the sun and whisper-sing to my sisters and to the sun, until it would pull me towards it, like in my dreams. I'd rise up and the ants would run around in the shadow I left on the ground.

I never went very high that way, just a finger or two. Sometimes I'd squish the ants on my way back down, especially when I got wobbly and lost control and came down fast, and I felt bad about that, but not too bad, because there were so many ants and they all seemed identical anyway. I'd sit up and wait until the okay ones carried the squished ones away before I lay back down and tried again.

I'd do it again and again until I was so tired and empty-feeling that I had to sleep for real, there on the ground with the ants all around but not ever biting me or going in my nose. I slept deep, heavy and dreamless.

Then, one night, I ate dinner, porridge, lemon juice, water, the same as always, and it didn't feel right in me. I excused myself and went behind a bush, like to pee, and threw it all up again. I covered the sick with some leaves and went back to dinner like everything was normal.

Then, the next morning, a baby went to gnaw on my fingers and pulled away, sudden, betrayed. My skin was too hot, burning. He looked at me like he knew; something was bubbling up, was coming.

And then the sickness was out, sweeping round again, like a double season of leaf moth, and this time it got in me, and grew.

And then it was the night before my ninth birthday, all our ninth birthdays. And since I was sick, quite sick by then, I was asleep most of the time, day and night asleep, but when that night came, in that sleep, I had a dream. I dreamt I was me. I was just me, Liberata, and I was almost nine years old and I was standing up somewhere high, but I wasn't scared, not scared at all. And everyone was there, everyone. Even dogs. Even horses. And Quiteria and Marina and Basil and Vitoria. Even Gema. Even Germana. And we all held hands, and I took a big breath to shout, shout out how happy I was, to shout as loud as I could, but then, suddenly, the sun said,

Sh.

The sun said,

Quiet, Liberata. Save your breath.

Sh, sh, sh, it said. Save your breath, save yourself. Quiet, Liberata.

So I didn't shout. I stayed quiet, quiet enough that the fish, cool and silver, that had recently landed on my forehead wasn't scared away. Quiet enough that it stayed, coiled in on itself, round, and pulled my heat up, up, away.

And wasn't the sun bright? Wasn't the fish cool? If you're quiet, if you listen, isn't the starlight just like music? Isn't it? Isn't it?

6

BASIL

Look at this, whispered sick-sister Liberata. Watch this.

She was lying down on the ground in the freckled light between two almost-dead lemon trees. It was cleaning day and bed-straw was being changed, so she couldn't be lying down inside. I was her water-bringer. Running to the stream and back, to the stream and back, bringing her cup after cup after cup of brownish water. It was really hot, so I was also taking breaks, sometimes. Sometimes I was taking short breaks and lying down near to her but not touching, because that would just make us both hotter. That's what I was doing just then, when she whispered. Both of us were lying on the ground, outside, on the far side of the houses from the healthy trees, just in case.

My eyes were closed, but I was awake. Without opening them, I whispered, What? Look at what?

Me, whispered Liberata. Look at me. Watch carefully.

I sighed. Opened my eyes even though the sun burnt them like snakebite.

She closed her own eyes.

Not fair, I thought.

She took a deep breath and held it. Then she squeezed her eyes even more closed, smiled, let the air out in one big puff and, as she did, rose up, her whole body up, three fingers, maybe a hand, off the ground, like a long branch being lifted away at clearing time. Except no one else was there; no one was lifting. Then she opened her eyes and looked over to me and flopped back down onto the ground.

Ow, she said. See?

I closed my eyes again. We're sick. I said. Feverish. Seeing things.

Both of us?

Maybe. Sure.

No, she said. It's not fever. I've squished ants, real ones.

Yeah? My eyes were closed again. Does it hurt? I asked.

The ants?

No, you.

It definitely hurts the ants. Sometimes landing hurts me. The rest doesn't.

Does it feel good then, nice?

I don't know, she said. Not exactly.

I reached down, brushed some ants off my ankle.

It feels like drinking water, she said, after not drinking for a very long time.

But I've brought you loads of water, I said.

Not like that. Different water.

Teach me? I said.

Tomorrow, she said. I'm tired now.

Gema and Germana had already died then. And loads of other people, kids, babies, grown-ups. She would die too. I knew it. Her eyes were closed. The ants were running all around her but not on her, never quite touching her. I closed my eyes. Then opened them again. I looked straight up, right up at the burning sun. Not her, I said. I didn't squint or look away.

Balance, said the sun.

Not her, I said.

It was my first real prayer.

I

QUITERIA

Not much more than a year after Gema and Germana died, before we were ten years old, even, I led everyone up the mountain again. It was the time of year when all the lizards were out. They watched lazily, half-dead, until you came just close enough, then they'd bolt like magic, like they were never there at all. Only Basil could ever catch them, though we all tried.

I can't, whispered Liberata. I can't do it. Trying to reach up, but slipping. Trying to find her breath, but losing it again and again in shallow panic.

She'd been sick too. She was only just, only barely, recovered. Her face and hands and feet were a scarred map of where the disease had been and gone. I reached out and grabbed her wrists, I boosted, helped, hauled her up, across the steepest bits, up.

Thank you, she whispered, looking down, not at me. Her voice was always a whisper, now. Thank you, Quiteria.

Another sister, Vitoria, was leaving. She wasn't dead, or dying, just leaving with her fake sisters and brother to go work somewhere else.

Should we make promises? asked Marina.

I'm not dead, said Vitoria. Not yet.

So we didn't make promises. Instead we just stood there, and everyone else looked at me, waiting, my still-alive sisters, the lizards, the sun. I squeezed my hands into fists and felt the sweat on my palms. Don't go, I said.

I won't, said Vitoria.

Marina and Liberata cried. The lizards watched, half-dead, all stone except their eyes.

But she did go. Of course. Vitoria left and we were down to four.

~

Once, around that time, Marina told me something. She told me that our father, our real father, was rich and famous and important and lived in a huge house, in *the* huge house, just there, just up the hill, full of food and water and clean clothes and beds, and that, one day, he would come down and rescue us from our hot hungry life in the orchard. One day, she said, soon.

You're a liar, I said.

I'm not, she said.

You are, I said. You are you are you are.

Usually Marina couldn't lie to a lizard, to a fly. Once she'd jumped out of a tree and landed on a pile of lemons and had crushed half of them, useless now, and her father had come along and seen the squashed pile and said, Who did this? Who would do this?

And she didn't lie. Didn't even try to.

A wild pig, I would have said. I chased it, I chased it away before it got the whole pile, I would have said, easy.

But she didn't. Me, she said. Just like that. Me.

You? he said, and looked more sad than angry. Though she still got beaten for it.

Marina wouldn't lie to a lizard, to a fly, to her father, but she'd lied to me. I knew it. Sometimes the closest things are the things you need to push away hardest.

~

Time passed. We got older. When soldiers and other big-house visitors came down to the orchard and village, they looked at us, sometimes.

They passed us by, like too-green fruit, but they looked, they started to look.

I found a windfall branch walking home one night, a good sturdy one, and brought it back to my house. I took a small pruning knife, and while the kids and adults slept and the babies cried, I carved the branch down: a smooth, straight handle, a sharp pointed end. Small enough to fit under my tunic, big enough to matter. I tied it around my hips like a sword, and carried on, out in the orchard, up in the trees, back in the dark house. I carried on and waited for something to happen.

Then, when we were eleven, something did.

Basil and I were up in the branches looking for yellow-leaf, and Marina and Liberata were down on the ground, making little trenches around each tree and patting chicken waste into them. We were tall enough, now, to reach a lot of the leaves, and lemons, when there were lemons, from the ground, but the fertilizer smelled terrible, so it was better for Basil and me up high, away. That's why, that's how, we saw the soldier first.

Oh! said Basil. Then she clapped a hand over her own mouth. Oh! said her eyes.

They usually came in groups, two or more, but this one came alone, Cyllius came alone. From up there, in the branches, we watched him walk along the rows of trees, towards us and away, towards and away, impatient, lost, until, finally, he got to the row where we were. He looked down the row at us, at me, and I looked at him, I didn't look away, and for a second, that's all we did. He looked at me and I looked at him and his confusion, his impatience, fell away. He was young. He was just seventeen then. Barely old enough to wear the uniform; barely broad enough to hold it on. He looked at me and I looked at him and then he blinked, we blinked, and, at the same time, exactly,

he straightened up and stepped forward, towards us,

and

I reached down and curled my fingers, still young enough to be soft, to feel the rough grain, around my spear, ready.

On the ground, Marina and Liberata kept working, digging, patting, facing back towards the village, oblivious. Squashed down, hiding flat against her branch like a caterpillar, Basil looked at me. Oh, said her silent mouth. Oh, oh, oh.

The soldier walked closer, saw Marina and Liberata, then stopped, stayed like that, watching them dig and pat, dig and pat, for more than twenty breaths, for longer than was comfortable. I knew he'd seen me. I knew he had. But he didn't look up again, not once. I stayed totally still. There were knots and twigs poking into me. There were bugs crawling up my tunic.

Then he moved. Stepped, decided, towards Marina. He'd chosen Marina.

In one movement, one breath, I grew huge inside; I pushed branches and leaves out of the way with my left hand, and, with my right, aimed and flung my spear. I aimed for his chest, for his heart.

I missed. But I did hit him. I hit him in the leg, in his bare calf. He shouted, swore, looked down at his leg and swore again at the blood that was starting to drip, not a huge amount, but some, enough. His eyes brown like the wild rabbits we sometimes chased, sometimes ate. I'd get better at hitting him later, soon, but this was good enough for now, for then.

Basil gasped and pushed herself up, away from her branch; said, Oh, out loud this time. Oh, oh, oh, and before I could stop her, she'd jumped down from our tree and started to run, run away. The soldier ran after her.

Oh! said Marina as they ran past.

Oh! whispered Liberata.

No! I said. No! jumping down, picking up my spear, running after them both.

He ran well for someone whose leg had just been speared. I need to make them bigger, I thought.

Basil ran well too; she was fast already, could have outrun him already, but she kept turning back to us, checking on us, which slowed her down and made her feet tangle and trip and, so, Cyllius, the soldier, caught her. He held her hands and tied them with rope. Then he tied her feet too, just in case, and picked her up and threw her over his back like a sack of lemons and carried her away, out of the orchard, just walking now. I could have caught him then, caught him easily, but Marina and Liberata stopped me, held me back. No, they said, no, Quiteria, no.

Yes, I said.

No, they said.

Please, I said.

Please, they said.

And then he was gone, out of sight, and Basil with him.

We waited for her to come back. Usually they come back, the girls, or boys, after a couple of hours, sometimes even less. If they came back at all, it was usually after a couple of hours. But Basil didn't. The sun went high and hot and then started to slide down again and she didn't come back.

He's keeping her, whispered Liberata.

No, said Marina.

Or has killed her then, said Liberata. He's killed her.

No, said Marina. No, no.

We need to go, I said. We need to go find out.

They'll kill us all, said Liberata.

They won't kill us, said Marina.

Or worse, said Liberata.

She's alone, I said. We need to go.

If she's alive, said Liberata.

She's alive, said Marina.

She's alone, repeated Liberata.

Apart from Gema and Germana, who were dead by then anyway, Liberata and Basil were the only sisters, real sisters, who got to live together. Liberata had a little rock in her hand; she kept opening and closing her fist around it. Open, shut. Open, shut. Okay, she said. I'll go.

Marina pulled at the frayed, greyed ribbon bracelet she always wore. Okay? I said.

She pulled again and a little string came off it in her hand. Okay, she said, looking down at it, not at me.

Apart from my spear we didn't have any real weapons, so we gathered sharp stones and sticks instead. We took the pruning knife.

We can't, said Marina. It's stealing.

It's borrowing, I said. We'll bring it back.

I'll make sure, Marina, whispered Liberata. I'll make sure we bring everything back.

The soldier's leg had dripped blood onto the dirt, rust-red on rust-grey. We followed it, speckled and easy as freckles, sticks tied under our tunics, stones in our hands, between the trees to the path, up the path to the track, up the track to the road, and then up the road, up and up and up towards the big house. We followed it even though we knew, we all knew, that we were going to the big house. We followed it because that way, we didn't have to say out loud what we all knew. We followed it until we could see the house, sun-white and lemon-full.

Well? said Marina, looking at me. She'd already put down her stick and her rock.

Liberata put hers down too. Picked them up again.

The house had a gate and the gate was closed. A porter stood beside it, rocking a little as he hummed to himself. There was nothing but dirt and rock between us, so the tune tumbled down to us clear and light. A song about donkeys.

Well? said Marina.

I knew the song, my mother sang that song.

There are other ways in, I said. There are always other ways in. There will be windows along the side wall, you don't have a house this fancy without windows. And maybe no porters, no guards there.

Liberata picked up Marina's weapons and handed them back to her. One stick and one rock. They looked very small. Here, she said. You can have this too. She gave her the pruning knife.

Marina worried her ribbon. I don't want—

Come on, I said. We'll run to the wall in three . . . two . . .

One, said Liberata, quiet.

And then we, all three, ran.

We made it without being grabbed or stabbed or killed or seen, even. The guard didn't stop singing, swaying. We spread ourselves against the wall, lizards. The stone was hot, almost burning at first, until it spread all the way across and through us so we were just as hot as it and couldn't feel it anymore. We stayed like that, up against it, heart-beats louder than footsteps, and crept around and all I could think, as we crept, as I crept along that hard hot wall away from the village and the huts and everything expected, known, everything laid out in straight, uncomplicated lines, as I moved away from that and towards I had no idea what, all I could think was, Yes,

Yes,

Yes,

Yes.

This, I thought but didn't say. This, Marina, is praying.

We took turns looking into each window as we came to it, a quick head up and then down again. We added up what we saw between us, made a scene:

A courtyard

A few chairs

A fat person sleeping

A thin person stirring brine

Two women weaving

No children

No soldiers,

as we worked our way around, around:

Some lazy chickens

Two slaves hanging up washing

An abandoned bowl of grapes, wasted,

and then:

A soldier. Our soldier.

I almost didn't see him because he was sitting down, on the ground. I didn't think of soldiers as sitting down. They marched. Or fought, or died. They should be either standing up, or, if dead, lying down. But this one, Cyllius, who I didn't know was Cyllius yet, was sitting, on the ground, just outside a small shed, blocking the door. He was drawing in the dirt with his sword, swirls, faces, crosses. His leg was bandaged. He looked bored. He looked no more intimidating than one of our fake brothers, back in the village.

There were no windows in the shed-cell. No way to see in, to see if Basil was in there, and, if she was, to see if she was okay, alive, alone.

We sat with our backs against the wall. Marina put down her weapons again. Liberata kept turning around and looking at the window, then back to us, then the window, then us.

Okay, I said. Okay, how about this?

Because there are things you can do when you look just the same as other people, as three other people, who look just the same as you.

Okay, I said. Here's the plan.

You're sure? said Marina.

Be careful, said Liberata.

They put their hands together and boosted me up to the window. I squeezed through and dropped down, quiet as a night spider, then walked, casual, normal, one arm swinging, the other one tucked into the folds of my tunic, fingers around my spear. I walked out and around, right past the soldier, towards the grapes.

He looked up, and then down again, back to the fish he was drawing. Then up again. Wait, he said. Hey! He stood. A real soldier again.

You're not supposed to be out! he said. How did you get out? You need to not be out, you need to . . .

There are things you can do when you all look the same.

I kept walking, casual, not running, to the grapes. Just getting some grapes, I said. Just hungry.

And the rope? he said. How did you get out of the rope?

Bit it, I said. I told you, I'm hungry.

He walked towards me, but slowly, moving away from the shed. Behind him I saw Marina push through the window, then Liberata. Now that she was strong again, she was the best at climbing. She never needed boosts up into trees, or anything else.

Do you want some grapes too? I asked. Want to share?

The soldier looked at the fruit, at me. He motioned behind him but didn't look. You need to get back in there, he said.

Behind him Liberata went into the cell and Marina followed, pruning knife clutched close.

I know, I know, I said. I will. I'm just hungry. I'm starving. Us farm kids don't get to eat on Wednesdays, you know, I said.

What? he said. Really?

Or Fridays or Mondays.

But, he said . . . Says who? I mean, the commander would never . . .

Says the store cupboard, I said. Doesn't matter what the commander says when that's empty.

Marina and Liberata were still in the shed. No sound, nothing.

Really? he said. You really don't eat? Anything?

Since he hadn't stopped me yet, I took a grape. It was old but still sweet. Yep, I said. So I'm pretty hungry today. And Mondays and Fridays. I took three more grapes, put them all in my mouth at once. Proving my point. Have some, I said, through the pulp and juice.

Um, no thanks, said Cyllius. I ate today. I eat on Wednesdays.

Lucky you, I said, and took three more. Marina and Liberata were out now, were running back to the window, and Basil was with them, ropes gone. Liberata was lifting her up to the window, through.

The soldier reached me. He put his hand on my arm, my grape arm, my casual arm. Firm, fast.

Then Marina, up,

Okay, he said. We'll tell the commander about that. About eating every day. We can tell him about the farm kids, I'm sure he'll care, I'm sure he'll help. But for now, I need you to get back in there. I need you—

And Marina through.

—to go back now, he said. Back in there. Just for now, okay? Until the commander gets here. Until I, or he, says you can.

He won't, I said, mouth still full. The grapes were good, they were so good. He won't help. He knows. He already knows. He must know.

No, said Cyllius, not much older than us, not so much older. No, I'm sure he—

Just two more, I said. Just two more grapes and I'll go back, back in there.

Liberata was scrambling, pulling herself up on nothing but bare wall, up.

Two more, so I don't die of hunger, I said. In there, in the cell. It would smell. I would smell, in this heat.

The soldier sighed. Geez, he said. You won't. His hand was still there, tight, on my arm. I could feel it for days after. I can still feel it. Not in, like, four hours, you won't, he said.

And Liberata pushed herself through.

You won't starve, he said. Not now and not—

But he didn't finish because then, just then, the last bit of Liberata disappeared through the window, and, mouth still full, I swung myself around at him, to him, and brought the full weight of me and my momentum together into my spear, and rammed it, hard, deep, into his hand, the hand on my arm.

His skin was fairer, softer, than mine.

His eyes snapped on like he was waking up. He pulled his hurt hand back and reached for his own sword, automatic, and I ducked under it, under and away.

I ran straight at the chickens, which scattered and panicked and ran towards him, between his legs, tripping him up, slowing him down. I ran past the slaves, the washing, the weaving, the brine, right to the front gate, I wasn't as good as Liberata at climbing, I couldn't get up to the window myself, so it was the front gate or nothing for me.

The soldier shook off the chickens, stepped on one, maybe killed it, angry now, really angry; he ran for me sword out.

The front gate wasn't locked, but it was heavy, I pulled and pulled and . . .

The others, the slaves doing the washing and weaving, the one stirring brine, the sleeping person who didn't look like a slave, who looked more important, were all up now, were watching.

Help! said the soldier. Help! Get her!

The washing slave looked blank for a moment, then afraid, then started running too, towards me. The brine slave ran the other way, away. The non-slave blinked, watched, confused.

I got the gate open, just enough, a crack, wide enough for me but not for them, and I slipped through. I ran past the guard—facing the other way, not expecting to guard out instead of in—down the road and away, down and down and away, away. I laughed. I couldn't stop laughing.

We met by the dry stream, as planned.

Oh, said Marina, hands on knees, catching breath. Oh, oh, oh. She had a smudge across her face and a cut on her arm, up, near the shoulder, even though she hadn't had to do any real fighting, or running, even.

I can't believe, whispered Liberata. I can't believe we did that.

I can, said Basil.

She told us the soldier didn't touch her, not any more than he had to to tie her up and carry her, anyway. She told us he took her to that cell and told her to wait there and that was all.

Wait for what? we asked.

I don't know, she said. I thought maybe you'd know.

We all shook our identical heads. No. Nobody knew. Not even me.

Back home, I cleaned Marina's cut with lemon juice and she winced and tried not to cry.

It was fun, though, I said. It was pretty fun, wasn't it, Marina?

The juice and dirt dripped off her arm, together. I don't know, she said. I don't know.

⁓

The fruit grew fat and we picked it off the branches and the ground and then it was gone and then we counted the fruitless days in hunger and slept and killed animals and counted and slept and then the buds came, again, and blossomed and the smell filled everything like storm water and they turned to fruit and grew big and full and we tended them and picked them, and, even though we weren't allowed, we squeezed them and ate them, and the seasons swung around and around and around in heat and hunger and, even so, even in hunger and heat, we grew and grew and grew.

I knew, of course, that he knew. That the soldier, Cyllius, knew where we were, where we worked and lived, and that he could, if he wanted, come back. I sharpened more sticks; I collected more pointed stones. I waited, I hoped.

⁓

One day in spring, my mother died. My adoptive mother. She had had so many babies, six by then, that nobody even considered that it could still kill her, everyone just continuing about their business when her groans came again. All the other babies had been fine, a few groans, a few screams, and then a new baby and, soon enough, everybody back to normal with just a little bit less food, less space, more noise.

But this one was different, this seventh baby. It was sideways, wrong, and there was nothing we could do but all we always did and nothing she could do but groan and scream and nothing the baby could do because it was stuck like that, sideways, and just a baby, so she died, they both did. But before she did, just a little before, when I was bringing the cleanest cloth I could find in the village, which wasn't all that clean, because all the really clean cloth had already been used and soiled, but was as clean as I could find, when I was bringing the cloth to her and the women with her, she, my mother, between wrenching, pointless contractions, looked at me, right at me, and said,

Don't bother.

Don't bother? I said.

With this. Don't bother with any of this, Quiteria. If you can. I'd say avoid it, if you can.

I was twelve years old.

She died a few hours after that, and there was no clean cloth left anywhere for miles, and every woman who wasn't in the house with her was down scrubbing scrubbing scrubbing in the muddy stream.

~

It took half a day's work to get her buried; it took half a day to bury anyone, apart from the babies, who just needed tiny holes, barely any earth moved.

When it came time to put the coins on her eyes we, of course, as always, didn't have any, so my father just put some flat pebbles on instead.

It's okay, whispered Liberata. I think they'll still let her across the Styx, down there, I think they have to.

I think it's all crap anyway, I said. Stories for kids and idiots.

I think, said Marina, as quiet as Liberata, I like to think that this means she'll get to go in it, right into the water, instead of across it. Down gentle like a river pebble. That the luckiest, the best, the women, the children, they get to stay in it, to swim.

She held my hand as we walked away, to the trees. We'd all have to work through high heat now, no time for a break, best part of day already gone.

~⁂~

Then Cyllius came back.

It was early. My father had just taken the full baskets from the day before's picking and had walked off, up the road, like he always did. He had two babies strapped to him, front and back. The other, older babies stayed by the huts and chased chickens and ate bugs and dirt. I didn't say goodbye to him or the babies, and he didn't say goodbye to me, just handed me my flask of water for the day and told me not to rip my tunic again. The babies said nothing. One was sleeping and one was staring at a bird.

That was all, for me and them. I never wanted to be there, in that hut, but, still, it would have been nice to say goodbye. It would have been something, something like a thank you.

I heard the soldiers before I, before we, saw them. They spoke in high Latin, different from us, more space between their words, more sharp edges. We were walking out through biting clouds of morning fly towards the stretch of trees we'd be in that day, me up front, then Basil and Liberata, then Marina in the back, like always. I stopped, so everyone stopped. I turn around and, without making a sound, mouthed,

Run?

No, Marina shook her head.

I thought maybe she hadn't understood, or didn't know what we were hearing. We need to run, I said out loud, but quiet, still quiet. Soldiers.

I know, she said. But maybe it's important.

Or maybe, I said, they'll kill us.

What? whispered Liberata.

What? said Basil.

Marina and I turned and looked up the road, so they turned and looked up the road, and then, there, we all saw the same thing, the same armour shimmering perfect down towards us.

Run? whispered Liberata.

Run, said Basil.

We have to? said Marina.

We have to, I said.

So she ran. So we all did, up, away. And when her tunic caught on some thorn and ripped I pulled her through it and when she tripped on loose rock I held out my hands to stop her hitting the ground and we ran, all of us, away, and we ran and my heart glowed and beat like the sun.

~

We ran until Liberata stopped at the base of a wild lemon tree and threw up. Then we stopped. The glint and voices of the soldiers were long gone. Nothing but the buzz of insects and the pull of our own breath, nothing but the brown bush and the red dirt and the one bony tree. Without the stream or fertilizer it wasn't doing well, but it did have a few green-grey fruit, it was still trying. There was a low apron of thorn around its base: a good spot to be invisible, or almost. As good as any.

Basil cleared a space of pebbles and thorns and lay down, face up to the sky. Liberata, recovered, pulled herself up into the tree and threw fruit down to us. Marina and I stepped together over and behind the thorn brush apron. We sat down and I bit into a lemon from Liberata and sucked out its juice. I'd left my flask at home, in the hut where my father had laid it, so these lemons were all we had. Marina held hers in her hand but didn't bite it yet, didn't drink. She was crouched, poking her head up just a tiny bit over the top of the brush, watching.

Do you see them? I asked. Do you see anything?

Nothing, she said. No one.

We were thirteen years old. Legs and arms longer than made sense, a fierce new something coiled precarious tight inside. We were like the stars that came out that night, endless, forever and everything, rolling and spreading and shining like the sea.

~

We took turns sleeping and not sleeping, watching and not watching. We picked only the lemons that were ready and saved the smaller ones, let them grow. We took turns ducking out, away, to find things to eat, bugs or plants, mostly, or to suck morning water from grass stalks and the base of aloe. It was gone by the time the sun was up. We were a long way from the stream, from any running water we knew of, but we had everything else we needed. If we could find water, enough water, and a way to transport and share it, we could stay forever, I thought. I hoped.

And do what? whispered Marina. We were awake. Basil and Liberata were asleep.

And do whatever we want.

I want to go home, she said.

We can't, I said. You know we can't.

Maybe they just want to tell us something. The soldiers. Or help us. Maybe they're bringing us something.

It's the same one, Marina. He's there. Did you see? The same one.

I saw, said Marina. She broke off a dry branch of brush. Pushed her thumb against its thorns one at a time, testing.

With more soldiers. With weapons, I said. When have they ever come to bring us something? To help us? I said. They took Basil, remember? They come and they take, Marina.

She pushed her thumb on a thorn. Then another, then another, round and round. I'm thirsty, she said.

We added water-searcher to our list of shared jobs. One person could sleep, one could look out, one could forage for food, and one could go farther, more carefully, to try to find water. This person got first pick from our weapons store.

Basil went first, since she was the faster runner and since she wanted to. She took two small, sharp stones.

That's all? I said.

That's all, she said. Anything more will weigh me down. I won't be able to run properly, or carry much water.

If you find it, I said.

If I find it.

I handed her the bladder Marina had had around her neck when we ran away, the kind we all had, were all supposed to carry with us and drink from when we worked, the kind we almost all forgot or lost or couldn't be bothered with almost every day. Marina's was the only one we had; she was the only one who had remembered, had bothered. It would hold a bit, if not a huge amount. Something. Basil took the bladder and ran off, and because it was my turn and I was ready, I fell asleep.

When I woke up again it was dark and she was back and she had two bladders and a clay pot, all full. She had water.

We drank, we drank and drank. We drank it all and the hot, sharp grip of thirst relaxed and then we could think, could talk. We lay on the patch of dirt between the tree and the brush, all of us awake at once for the first time in days. There usually weren't any clouds, but I remember seeing some, then. I remember watching their edges blur and change and glow as they passed over the moon. Thank you, Basil, I said, although I'd already said it.

She was lying beside me, to my right. She had a bladder in her hands and was fiddling with its strings, weaving them between her fingers. Sure, she said. No problem.

Where did you find it?

Find what?

The water, the stream or well or whatever?

Basil unwound a string, started again. I don't remember, she said.

You don't remember?

A stream, somewhere.

Where?

I don't remember. Away from here, a bit.

How far?

An hour running? Maybe two?

Which way?

I don't remember.

You started off that way, I pointed over her head, east. Did it come from there?

No . . . I curled around. I turned a lot.

But you found your way back?

Yes, that was easy. Back up to the tree, to the brush.

But the water, the stream—

Quiteria, said Basil. I don't remember.

Will you find it again?

I don't know.

Can you find it again?

I don't know.

Basil, can't you—

She doesn't know, Quiteria, whispered Liberata. She said she doesn't know.

Then nobody said anything. There was just the slightest bit of wind in the sickly tree's leaves that we could see but not feel. The clouds were gone. Blown away.

What about the soldiers? asked Marina. Did you see them?

No, said Basil. I thought I might have heard them, off that way, towards those other hills. But I'm not sure at all. I don't know.

Marina and I both sat up and looked towards those other hills. Nothing but dirt and brush and dark. In the morning, I promised myself, I'll look again, for the shining of armour against the light.

What about the pot? I said. Liberata had it, now empty, and was turning it over, squinting at the faded details. Where did you find the extra bladder and the pot? I asked.

I just found them, said Basil. Just on the ground, rolled under some purple heath.

Maybe dropped by a soldier, said Marina.

Probably dropped by a soldier, said Basil.

She was crying. Dark spots on the dusty stone.

Are you crying? I asked.

No, she said.

Don't, I said. I'm not mad that you can't remember where you found the things, the water, I said. Even though I was.

I'm just cold, she said.

But it wasn't cold. It never was.

My mother is pregnant again, she said.

How long?

Five months now, I guess. Around that.

She'll be okay, whispered Liberata. She always is.

Marina said nothing. We were all looking straight up, not at each other, at the vast sweep of nothing in the sky.

It's not really cold, I said.

I put one of my hands on the other, testing. My skin was warm like stone in the sun.

I put my hand on one of Basil's. It was cooler, but not much. Liberata reached over and put her hand on top of mine. Marina moved herself over so she could reach too.

Basil said nothing. She put her other hand on top of all of ours, on top of hers, heavy.

~ↄє~

I had my first mother dream there, out under the non-shade of that tree's skinny reach. My mother, my adoptive mother, was trudging down to the stream with an armful of blood-red cloth, her own birthing cloth.

But you, I said. But you need to be back in there, in the village. Surely you need to be back there, having your baby.

Somebody has to do this, she said. It has to be done, so somebody has to do it. And the water ran red and thick around her ankles.

~ↄє~

We looked for water, we looked for food, we looked for soldiers, and the days went on round and round and round again and the sun was hot and dry and strong, maybe stronger than us, maybe, but it was also beautiful and made the lemons grow and made waves in the air that we could watch when we had nothing to do and nothing to say and everything was golden and moving and I sharpened sticks for us all with the pruning knife. I sharpened stick after stick after stick.

~ↄє~

I was asleep when the soldiers came. Sleep is a long reach for me, always, the dropping away, the letting go; it sometimes takes me hours and hours, and when I do, when I finally let myself fall, I kick and jerk, Marina says; a fly passes by and I jolt, I'm back. Sleep is shallow for me, sleep is rare, but, still, I was asleep when the soldiers finally found us, when Cyllius came. We all were. We were tired with thirst and sun and were, all of us, asleep.

I don't know who was supposed to be on watch. Not me, even though it was always me, really.

I was asleep, and then a jolt, a crush in my chest, and I wasn't. Just like before, like always, I heard them. I heard them first. I opened my eyes and the light was white hot and more blinding than dark, so I shut them again, and felt down, automatic, into my tunic for my spear. I found it, inhaled, and listened to the breathing around me, counted it, one two three, three breaths, three sisters, all there, still, all safe. Then I listened again, past that, to the soldiers' boots, their man-heavy footfalls. They weren't talking this time. They must have known we were there. They were staying quiet on purpose; they thought they were quiet.

I exhaled and opened my eyes again, slowly this time. I drew myself up just barely above the brush, just high enough to see. I found a sharp stone in my pocket with the hand that didn't have the spear, inhaled again, and, even though I was empty with sleeplessness, with thirst, was hollow and light as summer straw, I stood. I jumped.

I drew blood from two of them, Cyllius and one other, and knocked another one down. I had him down and was on his chest and could have smashed his eyes in, hard rock into liquid eyes, gone, blind like the sun, forever, but a sister screamed and I turned and he pushed me over and held me down and that was that. It was Marina, sitting up. It was Marina who screamed, No! Quiteria! No! No!

You screamed at me, I'd say to her later, clean, fed. You stopped me.

I screamed *for* you, she'd say, draped in white, shining like Venus. To save you.

They tied us up, wrists behind our backs.

Someone else take that one, said a soldier, not Cyllius, gesturing at Liberata. I don't want to touch that one, he said.

We walked, bound and herded like goats, down the mountain, me in the front and then the rest. We walked past the village, along the goat trails, until we joined the road, then up, up, up, to the big house. And, because I was in front, I couldn't see any of my sisters' faces. I couldn't hold anyone's hand.

—✕—

The soldiers took us to a part of the house that only had women in it and then they left, because they weren't women.

With our hands still bound, the women there, the slaves Claudia and Vernica and Bea, cut away our tunics and cut our hair; they brought water and harsh soap and scrubbed away the grime and the dirt of outside, washed away the lemon oil, the insect grit, and the soldier blood; they brought water and harsh soap and washed away our old lives.

There was one woman, in finer clothes and with hair like the waves of the sun all shining and twisted and coiled onto her head, who sat away, apart, and watched. You should call her mother, said one of the washing slaves.

We'd never seen a woman like this. Men and slaves came and went from the big house, passed through the village, sometimes, but women, rich women, never. She looked fragile, shatterable, like a pot too precious to ever be used, to be useful.

Don't call me mother, she said. Please.

They braided and coiled what was left of our hair up like hers and it stung and pulled and I wondered if hers did too. She didn't look like her head hurt.

But maybe you get used to it, after a while, I said, later, to Basil.

Maybe, she said, the fingers of both her hands pushed up into her braids.

They untied our hands, slipped us into new perfect-white tunics, then retied them again.

Beautiful, whispered Marina, looking down at herself.

It will have to do, said the slave.

The tunic felt like nothing. My old tunic, my only other tunic, was rough wool, always present, heavy against the skin. This one was woven and fine and felt like nothing. A blade would cut right through it like water, like air.

It's so light, whispered Marina. We could probably fly if we wanted.

They gave us water, which I took, and food, which I didn't, and led us to a room with four windows that were narrow and long like desert grass and too high to reach, even standing on a bed. There was more water, a jug and four glasses on a small table, and four separate beds, one each. None of us had ever had our own bed before. It will be so cold, I thought, sleeping alone. It will be impossible.

They untied our hands again, this time for real, and said,

You'll meet him tomorrow. He's been away, but will be back, and will meet with you tomorrow.

Then they locked the door and left.

Who? whispered Liberata. Who will meet us tomorrow?

Basil shrugged.

You know, I said. You know who.

I don't, said Liberata. The soldier, maybe? Again?

Basil shrugged, poured out water for us all.

The commander, said Marina, glowing in stripes of moonlight. The commander will meet us.

You screamed at me, I said. You stopped me.

I screamed for you, she said, shining like Venus.

I pulled the strange suffocating cloths off one of the beds, and the cushion too, pointless since the beds were for lying on, not sitting on, and lay down. I scanned the ceiling for cracks, for faults. I closed my eyes. But she's too young to be our mother, I thought, and fell into lonely black sleep.

Morning light narrow and long, like desert grass, and I woke.

On the little table there was now bread and even more water. The slaves must have been back, but I didn't hear them, I didn't wake. They were good, very good, at being quiet, at being there and not there at once: a practiced, honed skill.

In the bed next to me, Marina was still asleep. Her foot was sticking out of her bedclothes towards me, brown and red with scratches and sun. All of her looked small, breakable. That's what I look like, I thought. When I'm asleep, I look just like that, exactly.

Then the woman came. Julia-don't-call-me-mother came.

She knocked on the door. Hello? she said. Is this the right door? Hello?

Marina, who must have been awake already, actually, who always was the best at faking, jumped up, out of her bed, and stumbled to the door. Yes, she said. Yes, yes. She knelt down and looked through the lock hole. Yes, Mother, she said. Yes, we're here.

Basil and Liberata woke. Sat up.

Don't call me mother, said the woman. Please.

Okay, said Marina.

Can you let me in? said the woman.

No, said Marina.

There was a moment of silence. No? said the woman. And then, Please? I won't hurt you. I'm unarmed and . . . weak. Pretty weak.

Basil, meanwhile, had got up and got to the bread. She divided it in four and, silently, handed it out among us. We took a few bites and then hid the rest up our sleeves.

No, said Marina, with a full mouth. She swallowed, started again. No, she said. It's not that we don't want to, it's that we can't. It's locked. We can't let you in. You have to use a key.

Oh, said the woman.

But then you can come in, added Marina, after a beat. With a key, if you want. We don't mind, she said. She looked up, around at us. Liberata nodded. Basil shrugged. Yes, said Marina, it's okay. You can let yourself in. It's fine with us.

Tell her there's no bread left, I whispered.

But there's no bread left, she added. Sorry.

Or water, said Basil, taking the bottle and squeezing it down between her bed and the wall.

Or water, said Marina. Sorry.

There was another moment of silence; we could hear the woman moving on the other side of the door. Then she was back. I don't have a key, she said.

You don't have a key?

No.

Oh. Marina looked to us, then back to the door, then to us, then the door.

Where are the slaves? the woman asked.

Not in here, said Marina. Somewhere else.

We don't know, Liberata whispered.

We don't know, said Marina.

A sigh. A bit more movement, and then the woman said, Well, fuck. We heard her sit down. On the floor, presumably. Are you all there? she asked. All four?

Yes, said Marina.

Yes, said Liberata and Basil.

Okay, said the woman. Well, I brought you some olives. But they'll hardly fit through the keyhole, will they. She sighed again. Look, she said, and we could hear that her mouth was full, that she was chewing. I just wanted to apologize, for earlier, for seeming cold, maybe, when Bea and Vernica and Claudia, the slaves, I mean, were introducing me.

Basil and Liberata knelt down next to Marina, one on either side, all three facing the door. I stood behind.

It's okay, said Marina. You didn't.

It's just, said the woman. I'm not your mother. I'm not anyone's mother. And so you calling me that is like calling a dog a goat. There's nothing wrong with being a goat, or with being a dog, either, really, but it doesn't make sense to call one the other, or the other the other, right?

No, said Marina. That's true.

But I don't have a problem with you. If it were up to me I wouldn't have this stupid door locked, for example, said the woman. More chewing.

So, said Marina. What should we call you? If not mother?

Julia, said the woman, said Julia. Just Julia.

Marina smiled. Julia, she said, quietly.

Julia? said Basil, to the door.

Yes? said Julia.

If you're not our mother, who is?

You don't know? said Julia.

No, said Basil.

A silence. Not even chewing.

Or . . . your father? asked Julia.

No, said Basil.

Julia exhaled. A long, heavy breath. Okay, she said. Listen.

So we did. And I, even I, leaned in.

Okay, said Julia, through the keyhole. Here's how it is: Your mother is dead. Your father is not.

And I looked at Marina, who was looking at me. I opened my mouth. She shook her head: No.

There were nine of you, said Julia. All identical. In the very beginning, there were nine.

Nine? said Basil. Not seven?

No, said Julia. Nine. Two who didn't survive the birth, seven who did. Nine. Altogether, there were nine.

And it was like hearing a song you forgot you knew; it was like finding your mother's hand in the dark.

There were nine of you, said Julia. At first. Not four, not seven, nine.

And something opened in the room, something like a song or a hand, and we four, we all together, thought the same thing, we all thought: I knew, I know.

Julia went on. She talked and talked, the nine, the birth, the river, the village, and we said nothing, to her or to each other, just looked straight ahead at the little hole in the heavy door, chunks of bread soft with sweat pressed against our arms up our sleeves.

Not that I was there, she said, finally. I came later, much later. I'm just a new wife, a third wife. She paused, chewed. But then again, she said. The commander wasn't there either. If you consider that, then really I know about as much as he does.

How did you find out? asked Marina. Both of you? She'd leaned right into the door so her nose was almost touching.

A soldier, said Julia. He told me. Told us. Not very long ago, actually. You think you're surprised? Think of the commander, think of that. This soldier telling him all this. He knew all along, I guess, she said.

Will they kill him? asked Marina.

He was just a kid, said Julia, back then, when it all happened. So I don't think . . . She stopped, changed her mind. I don't know, she said. I hope not. She spit out a pit and it rang when it hit the bowl or the floor, a single dull bell.

Anyway, the commander sent men to get you as soon as he found out, she continued. As soon as the soldier told him. But then you fought and ran, fair enough, so they had to chase you, and then when they did catch you, finally, you tried to run again, so they had to lock you in here, or in there, I guess. Although like I said, I think that's fairly unnecessary, locking you in now, at this point, now that you're all washed and with your hair done. I don't think that's sending a very welcoming message. She paused. It's not what I would have done, anyway, she said.

She took a big breath in and then out again. We heard the sound of a bowl set down against the hard floor.

And now I've eaten all your olives, she said.

Why didn't they tell us? asked Basil. The soldiers, why didn't they tell us why they wanted us? Why did they have swords and spears?

Well, they needed them, didn't they? You with your rocks and your sticks. And anyway, that's what soldiers are for, all that swords-and-spears business, not for talking.

I nodded, even though she couldn't see.

So, she said. To summarize, he, the commander, thought you were dead. He thought you were just one baby, not nine, and you were dead, like his wife, his first wife, and didn't ask any more questions. So he left and didn't come back for a long, long, time.

Do you think he's happy now? whispered Liberata. Do you think he's glad that he is, actually, still a father, after all?

What? said Julia. I didn't hear that.

Do you think he's happy? said Marina.

I think . . . said Julia. That he's confused.

Confused happy or confused sad?

Just confused, she said. And then, No, no, confused happy, I think. I'm sure.

We heard shuffling, like she was standing up, getting ready to go. Oh, she said, then more shuffling, back down. I almost forgot. I'm meant to give you these.

There was a pause.

We can't see, I said.

It's necklaces, she said. One each, one for each of you. He wanted me to give them to you.

They're from him? asked Marina.

Yes, well, he gave them to me to give to you.

He didn't want to give them to us himself?

No, well, I don't have any children, she said. Well, what I mean is that it's usually from the mother. It's usually the mother who gives them, officially.

She pushed the first one partway through the keyhole. Marina carefully lifted the bit that dangled through and pulled it across to us. Gold, with a little moon, also gold. Worth more than anything any of us had ever seen, let alone touched.

You don't have to wear them if you don't want to, said Julia.

She pushed all four of them through. Marina and Basil and Liberata put them on. She was just starting the last one, mine, when the slaves came back to let us out for breakfast; they waited until she was finished before opening the door. I pulled mine through and in, rolled it around itself, and put it in my pocket, away. Then the slaves opened the door and came in and refixed our hair and got us properly dressed while Julia watched. Hi, she said.

Hi, said Marina, and smiled.

After a while, one of the slaves, Vernica, said, Okay, well, that's the best we can do.

Then they took our hands and led us, all together, to meet our father.

―∾―

They stood us in a line, one two three four.

I'm sorry, said our father.

I was away, he said. I didn't know. I'm sorry.

He turned to look at Julia, who had gone to sit in a big fancy chair next to his big fancy chair.

Aren't they like her? he said.

Yes, she said. The same.

I thought, he said.

I know, she said.

He turned back, towards Marina. I thought, he said.

I know, said Marina.

He put both his hands up against his face and rubbed up and down. We watched him. The soldiers either side of him watched him. The slaves either side of us watched him. Julia watched us. No one said anything. From one window I could hear chickens out in the yard; from another a dog. Finally, he stopped and said, through his hands,

It's nice to meet you.

Before dinner, the slaves brought us bowls of cut lemon in water.

Soup, whispered Liberata.

Not soup, said Bea, Julia's slave. Not for eating. For washing. Hands in, rinse, rub, and then you'll smell lovely.

But, then, who eats them? asked Basil. After that?

Eats what?

The lemons? Who gets to eat them?

Oh no, said Bea. Nobody. Nobody eats them. She pushed a bowl away from her, towards us.

Nobody, echoed the other slaves, Vernica and Claudia, and I could tell, from the way their mouths tightened after the word, from the way they pushed the bowls out and away, that they did, that they all did.

That evening I ate and ate and ate, new foods, strange foods, wonderful foods: a dried but not dry fruit the size of twenty raisins with seeds like sweet sand; meat that wasn't rabbit or insect, that was so moist you could drink from it, suck the liquid right out; milk mixed with leaves and spice so potent it warmed your mouth and throat even if the milk was cold and warmed your blood too, and pumped your heart like you had been asleep, half asleep, your whole life until then, so that you felt you could, if you wanted to, if you had to, jump over the table and grab a soldier's sword and grab your sisters' hands and run, out and away, run and run and run. That milk smelled like nothing I'd ever had before, so intense it was almost painful.

I don't want to run, said Marina.

It was that night, after dinner, before sleep. Our door was unlocked and the soldiers had gone back to whatever soldiers normally do, and the slaves didn't care, not really. We could, I said.

I don't know, whispered Liberata. I'm tired. Tired right now for sleep and tired of being hungry and thirsty and hot and filthy and afraid all the time.

And alive, I said. And free.

Well, said Liberata, yes . . .

We could take things and run, I said. We could take dogs, even. And food and water this time, and maybe some real weapons from the soldiers, and these necklaces, probably real gold, and a chicken, maybe, a chicken that could eat bugs and give us eggs, eat the bugs we don't want to eat and turn them into eggs we do want to eat, we could run, run now.

I don't want to run, said Marina.

I don't know, said Liberata.

Basil was sitting back, arms folded, leaning against the wall at the far end of her bed with her eyes closed. I'm so full, she said. I am so, so, full.

Marina laughed. Me too, she said. I couldn't run even if I wanted to, even if I needed to.

Liberata smiled. Never been so full, she whispered. Like a pot full of water. If I tried to run, everything would just slosh out.

Let's talk about it in the morning, said Marina. Please? She lay back onto her bed and slowly moved her arms up and down across the soft bedding, the way we used to make angels in the dirt, only now there was no dirt, anywhere, none.

Yep, perfect, Basil said, without opening her eyes.

Perfect, whispered Liberata, and she lay down too.

My sisters, in their white tunics and their complicated hair and their golden pendants that reflected their faces flushed with food and candle-light and wine and milk, were happy. So I should have been happy too. So I didn't say anything else, just closed my eyes too.

Later, once I could hear Liberata and Basil and the slaves out in the hall sleeping, everyone but Marina and me, I said, You knew, about this, about all of this, long, long, ago.

Yes, said Marina. I tried to tell you.

And you weren't angry? I said. Back then?

No, she said.

You didn't hate him for not coming earlier, when we were sick, when we were burning up, when we needed him?

No, she said. I didn't.

That's gutless, I said.

That's hope, she said.

We stayed for four years. We didn't run for four years.

I dreamt of my mother again that night. I dreamt of my mother almost every night after that. I'd wake with dream pieces, whole or shattered like clay against stone, a word, a face forgotten.

I dreamt, that night, that my mother was tired. I'm tired, she said to me, in the dream. And that was all.

Another night I dreamt that she was carrying the skinniest goat.

Another night that she knocked her elbow on a box.

That's all. Nothing big or strange. Just small, normal dreams about my mother. And then I'd wake, in that huge high bed, alone.

The first day we were free to come and go as we wanted, I got up before the others so no one could follow me, walked out to the courtyard already busy with animals and slaves, and pushed three empty lemon crates to the back wall. Nobody blinked, nobody cared. I used them as steps, first up onto one, then onto a stack of two. From there I could reach the window; I could pull myself up and out. There was no guard at the back. I dropped down on the other side, outside, and went to find the soldier.

It was easy to find them, to find him. Although their camp had been set up discreetly out of sight from the house, it wasn't out of earshot. You could hear the clangs and calls and shouts and songs clear through, from sun-up to dark. I walked from the early morning shade of one tall scrub bush to the next, following that sound. I walked one thousand and seventeen steps, and then I could see it: rows and rows of every-coloured triangles, tents. I walked another three hundred and six steps and then I could see men, walking and sitting and talking around and between the tents, all uniformed and the same, all well-fed and rested. The closest one was sitting on a rock, his face tilted up towards the sun, his eyes closed. I went to him.

Hello, I said.

He opened one eye, squinted. Hello, princess, he said.

I raised an eyebrow.

He raised an eyebrow.

I'm looking for a soldier, I said.

Well, good luck, he said. That's me.

No, I said. Not you. Another one.

He lowered his eyebrow. Hm, he said. He gestured loosely towards the tents. Take your pick, he said. In that case.

No, I said. Not any soldier. A specific soldier.

He opened both eyes and swung his legs around on the rock to face me full on. Ah, he said. I see. Well. Which one?

His name is Cyllius, I said. Julia told me his name is Cyllius.

Ah, he said. Of course, of course.

He pointed me to the fourth tent in the second row. A green tent, with a blue tent to the left of it and a red tent to the right.

But be quick, he said. It'll be time for wake-up-run-and-stab prac-tice soon, and we don't get our mid-morning snack until after that, so he won't want to be late, to hold things up. Even for a Royal Daughter.

I'm not royal, I said.

Close enough, he said. Anyway, you know nobody can touch you, right? You know there would be literal death to pay if any one of us touched you, even if you wanted it, right?

Of course, I said. I should hope so.

And you still want to go to that tent, princess?

I'm not a princess, I said. And yes, I do.

He shrugged and turned away again, back up onto the rock, face back up to the sun. Okay, then, he said. Fair enough.

I left him and walked up between tents yellow and red and blue and green and yellow and red and blue and green, ignoring the soldiers I passed, who, for the most part, tried to look like they were ignoring me.

The fourth tent from the end of the second row was exactly the same as all the others. A little triangle, too small, it seemed, to hold any normal-sized person, let alone a soldier. It was too flimsy to knock on, just floppy skin, so I slapped my open hand against it instead. Soldier? I said. Hello?

Yes, hello, said the soldier. You can't come in.

Oh, I said.

Then there was silence. Then scuffling.

So you come out, I said.

Not now, not yet.

Yes now. Please.

Marina?

Quiteria.

A sigh. There was more scuffling; small lumps rose and disappeared again in the tent skin, and then, finally, he pushed his head out, no real door, just loose flaps. He didn't have his helmet on and his lemon-juice-yellow hair flopped weird and limp to one side, but it was him, Cyllius. Okay, he said. I'm out, Quiteria-who-is-not-Marina.

You're going to teach me to fight, I said. Like, properly.

I am?

Yes.

And the commander is all right with that?

Sure. Yes, I said.

He sighed. Seems like a bad idea, he said.

Seems like a great idea, I said. A command, even.

And you're sure your father is okay with it?

Yes.

And Julia?

Julia's okay with whatever.

That's true.

She ate all our olives.

I'm sorry.

There are more. Loads, here. So, you're going to teach me?

Not now, I've got—

I know, wake-up-run-and-stab practice.

Yes. Exactly, he said. He took in a big breath of air and then let it out all at once, looking at me. He was still mostly inside his tent, only his head sticking out. Okay, Quiteria, he said. Okay. Come tomorrow, earlier.

I nodded.

But not here, he said. Come meet me at the arena.

I looked around. Rocks, shrubs, sun, a rainbow of tents. The arena? I said.

Yeah, he said. The arena. He pointed to a circle, or almost-circle, of chipped and dishevelled rocks out past the end of the camp.

There? I said.

Yes, there, he said. The arena.

Okay, perfect, I said. Tomorrow, two hours before this, at the arena.

In the arena, he said. One hour before this.

Okay, I said, and smiled.

Okay, he said, and pulled his head back away, in.

That night my mother put a hand on my shoulder and shook. Not so hard it hurt, but hard enough. Wake up, she said. You need to wake up. But I didn't, I couldn't. The night pushed heavy and hard against my arms, my legs, my chest, and even though I could hear her, see her, feel her, I slept, on and on and on.

Cyllius didn't let me use his sword at first. At first he didn't really let me do anything.

You came, he said. Everything was the fragile blue of before sunrise. He was standing exactly in the middle of the six stones that made up the arena, kicking all the smaller rocks into a pile. His sandals were a bit too small for his feet and his heels hung out over the back, dark with wear. Better not to have sandals, I thought.

I figured you'd probably just sleep, he said. That you wouldn't actually come.

I came, I said. Of course.

Hm. He scanned the ground, no more loose rocks, everything neat in the small pile he'd made. All right, he said, motioning just behind it. We can sit down here.

Sit?

Yes, sit, he said.

I'm not a kid, I said.

You're thirteen, he said. So actually, you are. But that's not why we're sitting.

But I—

Sit, Quiteria. Or else I'm going back to bed.

So I sat. So did he. He picked up two pebbles out of his pile. The first thing to learn, he said, when learning how to fight, is how to not be in a fight.

But, I said. That's not—

I didn't say not attacking, he said. I said not fighting. That's why, he said, the first and most important thing we'll learn is good aim. He smiled, finally, and his face was the first sun of morning, the sun before it remembered to turn hot, turn mean. He handed me one of the pebbles. Yes? he said.

Yes, I said.

Every day after that, I'd wake from my dreams, my mother spitting out lemon seeds, my mother looking for a lost spoon, my mother leaning heavy against a wall, I'd pull myself out of the darkness, and I'd go out in the breakable early blue, I'd go to Cyllius.

He didn't let me stand for three weeks. We sat and threw pebbles, first for precision, then force, then distance. Then precision and force, then force and distance, then distance and precision. Then all three at once. I wanted to practise by aiming at tents and soldiers; he had me aim at stones and plants. Then, on my fourteenth birthday, he let me stand. Okay, he said. Today is your lucky day, kid.

You're not that much older than us, than me, I said.

I am, he said.

You're not.

I am.

I'm fourteen now.

Oh, I know, everyone knows. There's that big parade later. We have to wear full gear, even though it's hotter than scorpion sting today. And then, the commander's promised, well, according to Lucas, anyway, that we'll get double meat, to make up for it. And double wine too, maybe.

Oh, I said. I didn't know that.

It's a surprise, said Cyllius.

Oh, I said.

Anyway, said Cyllius. I'm twenty. So I am. Older. That much older.

Do we have to go to the parade? I asked. Do I?

Cyllius shrugged. It's a surprise, he said.

I'll stay here. I'll hide out here all day, just keep training.

He shrugged again. As you wish, he said. All parades are basically the same anyway, right?

I shrugged back. I'd seen just that one parade before, ever, as far away and alien as ants.

Now, he said, back to work. He reached for his belt. Instead of his sword, there were sticks in it, two sword-length pointed sticks. He handed me one. Happy birthday, Quiteria, he said.

My childhood measured out in pointed sticks.

Basil cornered me on my way to the toilet that night, before bed. You missed the parade, she said.

Yes, sorry. Was it fun?

That's not the point.

Neither of us said anything for a while. We walked past a sleeping dog and three chickens. I'm surprised the dog doesn't eat the chickens, I said. She doesn't even try.

Do you think we'll ever go home? asked Basil.

Home?

Home. Back to our families and the trees. Back to our normal life.

I don't know, I said. Even though I knew.

More silence. Another chicken, sleeping. She doesn't even try, I said.

They were there, said Basil.

Who?

Our families, said Basil. Our old, real, families, from before. They were at the parade, they were part of it.

They were?

They were.

All of them?

All of them.

Even mine?

Your father, yes. The commander invited them, as a surprise for us, then pushed as much food as he could at them at the feast after.

Did they look happy?

They looked scared.

We'd reached the toilet but didn't go in.

Basil found a crack in the wall's stone and looked at it, not me. Julia, our not-mom, says he loves us like crazy, she said. But that's stupid.

She did?

It's stupid, she repeated. You can't love people you don't even know. People you just met. Even family, right? We're just kids, in a world filthy with kids.

Parents are strange, I said.

Sometimes, she said. Not always. She put her hand up against the wall, covered the crack.

Was Marina there? I asked. At the parade? Did she go?

Of course she did, said Basil. She stood next to Julia the whole time. She held her hand.

Basil took her hand off the wall. Pressed it against her other one, palm to palm. Anyway, she said. I'm going to pee. She walked away and left me by the wall, the crack, alone.

—✳—

Every morning I went, alone, and met Cyllius at the arena, unless the army was away, which was about half the time. When they were away,

I would still go, by myself, and practise by myself, imagining I was away with them, with him, in battle, beside or in front of him, strong and fierce, more than the barbarians, more than any other soldier there.

One of those mornings, when the army was away, I was practising with rocks. I would throw one hard enough to knock over another rock, then I would run fast and quiet between the arena stones up to a big spiky cardoon that I'd stab with my stick-sword, in-out, without getting pricked, then jump up onto a stone and stab the plant again, this time from above. My tunic was rolled up at the sleeves and my sandals were off, next to the pile of throwing rocks. After all that I'd jump down and start over again, throw run stab jump stab jump, and again, and again. I'd done five times around when Liberata showed up, stepped out from between two stones. I was up on another, about to stab the plant.

Geez, she whispered.

I froze, mid-strike. What? I said.

Intense, she whispered.

Well, I said. Life is intense.

Yeah, she whispered. Still. She walked across the arena, went to pat the cardoon's purple blossom, to console it, then remembered it had thorns and stepped back again.

Anyway, she whispered. She climbed onto the boulder next to mine. Hi.

Hi, I said. How did you find me? How did you know I was here?

Well, she whispered, because you're always here. So I assumed.

You knew that? That I come here?

Yeah. I see you coming back along that path from here, every day; I see you from up in the cork oak.

The stick was getting heavy in my hand. I put it down by my feet and let it roll off the side of the stone and onto the ground, just a stick beside a bunch of other rocks and sticks.

Do the others know too? I asked.

I don't know, said Liberata. Maybe. Do you want them to know?

I looked at the stick on the ground, at my thorn-raw hands. I sat down, legs skinny over the side of the boulder. No, I said. I don't.

Okay, she said.

Anyway, I said. I'm busy here, as you know. So . . . why are you here? Did you want to learn fighting too?

No, she whispered. I don't. Thanks. She sat down and drew her legs up under her, cross-legged, and balanced, like magic, on the narrow rounded top of her stone. Basil's off running, she said. And Marina's weaving with Julia, like always, and I'm bored, so I thought I'd come find you. See what you were doing. That's all.

Does Marina go every day?

Yep, every day.

With Julia?

Yep.

Even though it's boring?

It's really boring. Still, yep, she goes.

I thrust my sword arm out, forgetting I didn't have my stick-sword anymore, and the cardoon stabbed me back, a dry grey-green spine into the side of my wrist. Ow, I said.

Are you okay? Liberata asked. She leaned over towards me.

Don't, I said. You'll fall.

I won't, she said. But she straightened back up anyway. Anyhow, she said. I'll go now. It's almost time to eat.

It's always time to eat or almost time to eat here, I said.

She shrugged, uncrossing her legs.

Wait, I said. I'll come with you.

One, she said.

Two, we both said.

Three, we both said.

And then, at the same time, we jumped.

And then I landed.

And then, a beat after I landed, she landed.

I looked down at her feet. They looked just like mine. No sandals.

Sometimes it works and sometimes it doesn't, she said. Lunch? she said.

Why would you want to fly? asked my mother that night.

Why would you not want to? I said. Think of how much easier it would be to pick lemons.

She was combing my hair with her fingers, straight and long, pulling from my scalp all the way out and down. Her own hair was different, curly, thick. Think of how much easier it would be to fall, she said.

❧

I practised jumping off rocks for two hours the next day. Over and over. But all I could do was land, heavy, hard, normal. I couldn't do it. Without her, by myself, I couldn't do it, I never could.

❧

Cyllius came back and we trained together; he left again and I trained alone.

Before leaving, though, this time, he gave me a bundle, a sloppy bundle of cloth.

I'm not doing your laundry, I said. I'm not doing anyone's laundry, ever again.

Unwrap it, he said, holding it out to me. Then he pulled it back. Actually, wait, he said. He looked around. Just tents and stones and sun and sky and that one sad cardoon plant. Everything else still sleeping. Okay, he said, and held it out again.

It was heavy, heavier than just cloth. I unwound the layers and, inside, found a small sword.

It's a small sword, he said.

Yes, I said.

Just a small one, he said. And not one of ours, it's a barbarian one.

You stole it? Or killed one and took it?

I bought it, said Cyllius.

From someone who stole it? I asked. Killed and stole?

No, said Cyllius. From a barbarian. Who sold it to me.

Oh, I said. I looked down at the sword a little more closely. It had a ridge down the middle that Cyllius's didn't, and a darker handle, softer, not shiny. It's beautiful, I said.

I'll get in a lot of trouble if anyone finds out, he said.

I know.

So much trouble.

I know.

Then we were quiet. I tried handing him back the wrapping cloth, but he motioned with his hand: No, keep it. So I wrapped the sword up again, carefully, slowly. I passed it from one hand to the other, feeling the weight, the balance. I love it, I said.

I know, he said, and smiled. Morning sun. Just don't kill anything other than the plant, he said. At least not until I get back.

Then he left again. Away for four hundred and seventy-six days.

~

And they eat babies, said Marina. And dogs. And baby dogs.

And goats? whispered Liberata.

And goats too, said Marina.

But that's normal, I said. We eat goats. Everybody eats goats.

But they steal them, the goats they eat, said Liberata. Right?

Right, said Marina. They steal them and they pull out their hairs one by one while they're still alive, the goats, I mean.

We were in bed. It was dark and we were full of food and Cyllius and his army had been away for one hundred and forty-five days and Marina was telling Liberata and me about barbarians. Basil was already asleep.

Why? I said. Why would they do that? Seems like a lot of work for no reason.

Because they think it makes the meat more tender. Even though it actually doesn't.

That's pretty cruel, said Liberata.

That's pretty stupid, I said.

And they take all those hairs and the women stick them to their faces with stonecrop juice so they look more like men, said Marina. So they look fierce. She was down under her blanket, showing only from the chin up like some kind of oracle.

Liberata ran her hand up and down her face slowly, tracing her scars. And the goat? she asked.

They don't stick anything to the goat.

No, what happens to the goat? After it's been plucked.

It gets cold, I imagine, I said.

It does, said Marina. She sighed deeply. It gets colder and colder, with no hair, until it dies from it, usually at night, and then they eat it.

It's not that cold, I said. It's never that cold.

Not here, obviously. Elsewhere. North. Where it is cold. That cold.

And the dogs? asked Liberata.

Oh, the dogs! said Marina. The dogs! They—

Please, said Basil, who wasn't asleep anymore. Please, please, please shut up. Shut up and sleep. All of you. Please.

No one said anything, then.

Slow and heavy, sleep filled the silence between us, and everyone else fell into it, easy. It was dark. There, in that room, where there was no star or moon or firefly-light, nothing, it was dark, so dark. I closed my eyes and opened them and it was the same. Black. My heart pushed out, up, against it, beat, beat, beat. I could be anywhere. I could be alone.

Marina? I whispered towards the bed next to mine, trying to keep my voice steady, normal.

No response.

Marina? A bit louder, a bit faster.

She made a noise. A little hum.

Are you awake?

She hummed again and rolled over so she was facing me. I couldn't see her, but I could feel the new heat of her breath.

Are you awake? I repeated.

Breath out, in.

Marina, I, I . . .

It's okay, mumbled Marina. I'm here, I'm here.

It's dark, I said.

Breath in, out. I'm here, said Marina.

She reached out across the gap between our beds and found my hand. She took it in hers and we made a bridge. I'm here.

Feeling is like seeing, a little bit, like light, and so, with her hand in mine, warm, felt, I breathed in and out and in and out and didn't feel the strangeness of the lonely bed under me, the darkness pressing down, anymore, I lifted up, away, and we fell asleep together, like that, both together.

~

When Cyllius had been gone for two hundred and four days, I was with everyone, eating figs at lunch, and was trying to crack each seed with my teeth, separating them with my tongue and pushing them one at a time up and out to get crunched, like little bones. I had just managed to get a particularly slippery, tricky seed when Julia turned away from Marina on her other side, to me, and said, So, why don't you ever come weave with us, Quiteria? Everyone else does it at least a little, a bit of weaving or even just some basic spinning. She looked around for help, support. Right? she said. We have fun?

Liberata caught my eye for a beat, then smiled and said, Sure, sure we do.

I crunched my seed. Swallowed. Thanks, Julia, I said. I'm sure you do. I've just got other things I need to do right now, maybe soon, though.

Of course, said Julia. Hopefully soon. She took a bite of her own fig. She chewed, swallowed. It can be important, she said. Later in life. For girls, for women. It can be an important thing to know, is all.

Weaving, she means, said Marina, poking her head around Julia's far side. She always sat next to Julia.

I know, I said.

A slave topped up my wine, even though I hadn't had a sip of it yet, and put a hand gently, briefly, on my shoulder. Then she took it, and the decanter, away.

Okay, well, just know you're invited, said Julia.

Okay, I said. Thanks. I pushed my wine aside and reached for another fig. Thanks, Julia, I said.

~

Could be worse, said my mother. She was trying to put a diaper-cloth on a baby. It squirmed and thrashed and rolled away, so she had to pin it down with a firm, fierce arm across its chest. A lot worse, she said, and the baby kicked kicked kicked kicked.

~

When Cyllius had been away for three hundred and seventy-one days I'd got up early, before the sun, as always, and was coming back to the house after training alone. I'd hidden my sword, as always, under the thickest, dampest bit of goat straw, where the smell would keep anyone from looking, or even approaching, and I was going to get something to eat when I met Julia coming the other way, face as crumpled and grey as the straw. She had a bit of bread in her hand.

Quiteria, she said. Your hair.

Yes? I said.

It looks a bit . . . broken, she said.

I put a hand to my head, patted. A braid had fallen out of its coil, so I stuffed it back into itself as a temporary measure.

There, I said. Better?

Hm, said Julia. Her eyes were glassy like those on the dead chicken heads the cook left behind the kitchen, sometimes.

Where are you going? I asked. Not lunch?

I'm ill. I'm going back to bed.

With some bread?

With some bread.

So, not weaving today? I asked.

Her eyes cleared for a second and she looked at me, her face slightly less grey. Were you going to come today? she asked.

Maybe, I said. Probably not, honestly.

Oh.

I mean, I said. No point me going if you're ill, right? But maybe another time. Maybe soon.

She smiled, sighed. Okay, she said. Maybe.

Then she continued walking, back to her room and bed.

The next day, Julia wasn't there before or during lunch, and none of the bread was missing, so I took an extra piece. I ate my own, plus a plateful of figs, followed by a plate of cheese, followed by another plate of figs, then went to find her.

Your hair, she said. It's broken again.

She was in bed. Eyes closed.

It's intentional, I said. I like it like this.

She raised an eyebrow, which was an impressive thing to do with your eyes closed. No, it's not, she said. And no, you don't.

You can't even see it.

I can. It's the braid on the left-hand side and it's uncoiled and hanging crooked down over your ear like a dead fish. I can see it.

Okay, I said. Fine. I walked over to her. Bea, the slave who was always near her these days, was near her, on a chair by the bed. The only chair in the room. She clutched a piece of parchment from which she'd been reading to Julia: poetry. She stood.

Oh, no, I said.

It's okay, she said. I need to go get some food anyway.

For Julia? I said.

For me, she said.

She knew I wasn't hungry, said Julia, after she'd left. That I didn't want any food.

The bread was bulky and warm in my pocket, making my hip bulge on one side. Not hungry at all? I said.

No. Just thirsty. Really thirsty, Quiteria. Really, really, really thirsty, all the time.

I looked around and found her cup on the little table by the bed. It was already full of water. I held it out to her, even though she could have reached herself, if she'd wanted to.

Not that kind of thirsty, she said. But thanks.

I set the cup back down. Oh, I said.

Her eyes were still closed. The room was too hot, too still. Well, I said, I was just . . .

Lots of women have babies that don't live, you know, she said. Or pregnancies that don't last, as well as those that do live, and those that do last.

Yes, I said. I know. I'd seen loads of every kind of pregnancy and baby in my old house, in the village.

But I've never had any of those, said Julia. I can be grateful, very grateful; I've never had a baby to fear losing, or a pregnancy to fear ending. Nothing. Nothing to fear at all.

Oh, I said.

She breathed in, out.

Do you have any siblings? I asked. Any sisters? Or brothers, I guess?

No, she said. Not one.

Bea came back with a bowl of porridge, so I stood up and she sat down again. Julia rolled over and pretended to be asleep. I left the bread on the table beside her still-full cup of water.

—∞—

She didn't die, anyway. Eventually Julia was back at lunch like before, eating bread and drinking water.

Then, sometimes, she'd be gone again. One day, three days, two weeks. But she always came back. And she was never ill when the commander was around, as infrequent as that was.

—∞—

We got yellow wool today, said Marina one day, at the fountain.

We were seventeen. Already seventeen. In the village, each year, each birthday, was an effort, an achievement; here time slipped by like lemon juice into water, invisible, easy.

We were seventeen. Julia was well and Cyllius was back, and we were training together every day. He was still stronger than I was and could get me down if I let him get too close, but I was quicker, was getting better at not letting him, except if I wanted him to.

After my training and lunch and nap and a bit more training again, by myself, Marina and I were both at the fountain, both washing up for dinner. Her hands were in, under, and streaks of yellow bloomed through the water when she rubbed them together. Lurid, sickly.

Are you sick? I asked. Are you okay?

Basil and Liberata were coming towards us, walking along the dirt instead of the path because the stones were too hot at this time of day. Julia and Bea followed a few steps behind, on the stones.

I'm fine, Marina said. I'm good. I'm really good. She pushed her hands down to the very bottom of the basin, yellow water up to her elbows. We got yellow wool today, she said. It's just from that.

Yellow? I said.

Yep, said Marina. The commander brought it in himself. Lots and lots and lots of it.

Yellow?

Yep.

My stomach went tight, heavy.

The colour was spreading through the water, bleeding from her hands onto mine. No, I said, or thought, or both. No, no, no.

Yellow was the colour of lots of things. It was the colour of sick babies, sick goats. The colour of cruel sun. The colour of lemons. And yellow was the colour of weddings. The colour of brides.

Basil and Liberata, my sisters, mine, were almost at the fountain now, would soon put their hands into the water too.

Yes, said Marina. She was smiling, excited. Yes. She reached out a hand, underwater, to me, and I drew back.

No.

I pulled my hands out and wiped them fast and hard on my tunic. I stood in front of Liberata and Basil, I blocked their way, I kept them dry.

When you are a child, you are owned by your father. If you are a boy child, you grow up and own yourself. If you are a girl child, you grow up and are married and owned by your husband. Then you have babies and are owned by them. And then, when you die, at last, free, at last, your grave will say, above or excluding all else,

Daughter of:
And
Wife of:
And
Mother of:

That's why. You understand? That's why I said what I did. Did what I did.

In the orchard, in the village, we would have had another four years yet, or five. Our fathers would have needed our work for as many years as they could manage, as they could squeeze out before we started to lose all semblance of girlishness, all potential. It was different, though, there in the big house, with a big father. We were already edging on old there, edging on problematic, Julia said. Marina said.

Are you sure? asked Basil. I'd pulled her and Liberata aside, away. Are you sure that's what it means? What Marina means, I mean . . . What the yellow wool means? She looked from me to Marina and Julia and Bea, over my shoulder, away but close. She looked back and forth, back and forth.

But not me, surely? whispered Liberata. Hand to her face.

But, said Basil.

But who? asked Liberata. Scars like constellations.

But we don't have to, I said.

Of course we do, said Basil. Of course we have to. That's the point. That's always been the point, in the village or here, anywhere, always. Mothers, sisters, Julia . . . There's nothing else. There's never been anything else.

Will he be kind? said Liberata, hand still up, covering half her nose, mouth.

Maybe, said Basil.

No, I said.

No, I said. No, he won't be kind, Liberata. He will marry you for the dowry, and that's all. The very generous dowry from the commander that you'll carry, you'll need, more generous than the dowry for Basil or Marina or me. He'll look at the dowry, then you, and decide that, after all, it's worth it, probably worth it. He'll take the dowry and take you, use the one up and not look at the other again, not until things run out, until things are difficult, and then he'll remember, and will look at you again and, no, no, Liberata, he won't be kind. He will hate you. And do all the things men can and will do when they hate the women they're tied to, as they do, as they always, eventually, do.

But, maybe, said Basil.

Oh, said Liberata. She lowered her hand, looked for somewhere to sit, but there was nowhere, just hot stone and grey dirt. Oh, oh.

But, said Basil.

And he'll make you stop, I said, this time to Basil, interrupting. The man who gets you. He'll make you go to temple and to the family altar and subjugate and pray and sacrifice to the gods, the old gods, and to the emperor, the human, just-human, emperor. He'll make you denounce any others, denounce your new God. He'll laugh at them and at you. He'll make you stop. He won't be Christian, Basil. He'll control where you run, what you sing. He'll make you stop.

Basil's feet, bare, rubbed the dry dirt, dug down. How do you know? she said.

Because everyone knows. Because you know, I said to Basil. And you know too, I said to Liberata.

There's nothing else, said Basil. There's never been anything else.

There is, I said. There's speed. And light. There's us, together. There's everything. There's each other. There's me.

But we—

Follow me, I said.

And there was silence. One breath. Two. Then,

How? whispered Liberata.

Run, I said.

Run? said Basil.

Run, I said. Again. One last time.

Run, said Basil.

What about Marina? whispered Liberata.

What about Marina? whispered Basil.

I'll talk to her, I said. I'll convince her. Once everything is ready.

She won't, said Basil.

She might, I said.

Soon, said Liberata. Try soon.

Yes, yes, soon. Just not yet. Soon.

Yellow was the colour of Cyllius's hair at the end of training, when the sun was full and fell through it like honey, like song.

~

We had seven weeks until the new families would come with their sons and their rings, which wasn't very long but was longer than we'd had the last time we had to run. It was long enough for some strategy, this time,

EMMA HOOPER

for some planning. I would do better this time, I told myself, I knew. For me and for all of them, I would do, would be, infallible, perfect.

~

And when I'd see our father in the halls or at meals, his face closed and confused, and he'd call me Marina, or Basil, or, sometimes, Quiteria, and he'd say, Are you well, are you okay? Are you excited?

I'd say, Yes, father, yes, I am.

~

And when I'd see Cyllius, his shadow long and light in the morning, I'd run faster, lunge harder, defend and attack and defend and attack and defend and attack until the defence was the attack, until he was confused and dizzy and off balance, and then I'd knock or pull him to the ground and hold him there, my legs against his sun-hot sides as his breath pushed them in and out, our breathing the loudest, the only sound, and I'd think, Stay, stay, stay like this, please. Stay.

And then he'd push me over, aside, and say,

Good. Okay. Again.

~

And when I saw Marina, her hands yellow, still, always, her face as open and happy as a dog's, she would look at me, waiting, and I would nod, maybe smile, sometimes smile, good, okay, and walk by. No, my head told my heart. Not yet, not yet.

~

And when I slept I saw my mother. And she was scrubbing clothes, an endless, enormous pile of clothes, scrubbing and scrubbing while I stood behind and watched and she never turned around to see me, not once, not at all.

And then the commander left, like he always did, but not for the reason he always did. He left to meet and gather the families of the men we were going to marry, to bring them back to the house, to us, so that they could, later, take us away again, with them. He went to get four brand-new sets of mothers and fathers and sons.

He took goats and wine and baskets and baskets of lemons. He took some, but not all, of his men. He didn't take Cyllius. He didn't take Julia either. He'd be gone just twenty-two days.

This meant it was time, now. While the slaves still moved slowly across the courtyards in the afternoon and the few remaining soldiers still slept in the stifling shade of their tents. The best time to move fast, I knew, was when everyone else was still moving slow.

But first I went to Cyllius. I went to him as usual, for training. But when he ran at me, lunged at me, as usual, I didn't duck and dodge and engage. Instead, I let him get me, knock me down, and when he leaned down to me, concerned, surprised, his shadow was beautifully cool on my face and I said,

Cyllius, I'm running away. Come with me.

He put out a hand; he helped me up. He waited until I had wiped the dirt off my hands and sword. Then he said, You can't.

I can, I said.

You shouldn't, he said.

I am, I said. Come with me, I said.

I can't. You know I can't.

They'd kill you? I said.

Yes, he said.

But only if they caught you, I said.

He tipped one of the big stones up, reached down and got a small round shield that was hidden underneath. Mine.

I can't, Quiteria, he said. You know. You know that. I can't run and I can't marry. I can't hurt or kill someone for my own reasons and I can't not fight if the commander says fight, and I can't get married and I can't run away, with you or anyone else. These are the rules. And there are reasons for rules.

He handed me the shield and drew his sword. There are rules, Quiteria, he said, edging towards me, just one arm up in defence. There are reasons.

Not good ones, I said. Not always. I stepped towards him, shield down.

They would kill me, he said. And maybe you too.

But, he said. But. He took a step forward. If you want it, he said, I can help you, I think. I'd like to help you. He almost never used his own shield when we were together.

Then he lunged and I lifted my shield and blocked his blow and swung my sword around, between us, ready.

After training, Cyllius put away his own sword and held out his hand; both of us were sweaty and filthy. I took it.

This way, he said, and I could feel the beat of his blood where our palms met.

He led me behind one of the biggest stones in the arena, the farthest one from the camp tents, where we couldn't be seen by soldiers or anyone else,

and my heart beat beat beat into his hand

and my chest tightened in on itself and my stomach swam

and the sun and the flies and the birds and the bugs

and my breath, our breath, stopped.

Then he let go.

Okay, he said. Look. Look at this.

He took a step away and knelt down on the dusty ground and, with a small sharp stone, made a mark, a line. Then another and another and another. When he stood up again, his knees were grey-red with dust and he'd drawn an entire world on the ground, a map.

It's far, he said.

At first I couldn't say anything. My mouth and tongue dry as the dirt on the ground, on his legs. I swallowed. And swallowed again. That's good, I said, finally. It has to be far. I want it to be far.

And you'll have to squeeze under and through this crevice here, he said. Or else go all the way around, three, four days extra. So it's best to go through, if you can. But don't get stuck.

What happens if we get stuck?

Then you'll be stuck. And it'll be dark and boring and eventually you'll starve, I guess.

We'll fit?

It's small, but you're small. Smaller than me anyway, all three of you. I think you'll fit.

Four, I said. All four of us.

Yes, he said. Right. All four.

Could you fit?

No.

He drew a bit more, adding some details: a notable plant, a dog that was often around, a bit of lewd graffiti someone had carved into a stone, and then two lines, two undulating lines, parallel, at the farther edge of the map.

There it is, he said. That's it. The river that never runs dry.

Impossible, I said.

Trust me, he said.

Never? I said.

Never, ever, ever, he said.

Then he stood and wiped his foot across the ground and erased the plant, the dog, the graffiti, the river, everything.

Now you draw it, he said.

Me?

You.

So I did. Or tried to.

Wrong, he said. He fixed it. Then he erased it again. Again, he said.

Wrong.

And again.

Wrong.

And again.

And again.

And again.

Until I was never wrong. Until I could draw and point to and describe every tree and stone and bush.

Good, he said. Finally.

Come with us, I said.

No, he said. Draw it again, he said.

—∞—

I drew the map for Basil and Liberata. Then I erased it.

Now you, I said.

Over and over.

Until they were never wrong either. Until we three could draw and point to and describe every stone and bush and stream bed and cliff. Until we didn't need to draw it anymore.

—∞—

Marina was braiding her hair, one dark strand over another, over and over and over. I found her in the courtyard fountain. Come with me? I said.

Okay, she said, letting her hair go loose, free. She stepped out and down, dripping, next to me. Our feet fell into step together like they always did.

We walked across the yard, tiles shining like water, up the crate steps and through the back window we all used, now, and down into the scrub to the dry stream. Basil and Liberata were already there, each sat on a big smooth water stone. The heat in the air between us made their faces twist and blur.

Marina went and sat with them, all lined up like the hot silent rocks they were sitting on. I stayed standing.

Come with us, I said.

I can't, she said, like I knew she would.

But, I said.

But you, she said.

Marina, I said.

Quiteria, she said.

Marina, Marina, Marina.

Quiteria, Quiteria, Quiteria.

Please, I said.

Please, she said.

Her hands clutched each other, soft, gentle, yellow. Mine were rough, chapped, red.

She went quiet and so did I, our words, our breath, crumpled in our chests.

A centipede crawled out from under a stone, sensed us, and crawled back again.

Flies circled our hair in patterns to shadow the braids and twists.

Basil and Liberata didn't say anything.

Then, finally, Marina said, You'll break his heart.

And a little fire flashed back into me: Cyllius. I looked up, at my sister. You think so?

I know so. I know it, Quiteria, said Marina.

I hope, I said. I hope so.

Will you come back? she said.

No, I said.

We'll try, said Basil, the first thing, the only thing, she said.

We didn't take hands and we didn't make promises. Because no one had died, not really.

Liberata stood, and Basil stood too. We walked back to the house together, first me, then them, leaving Marina behind. Our sister, my sister, alone on her hot dry stone.

~

Julia was at lunch the day before we left. The commander had been away for only a few days, barely over a week, but already I could see the grey rising on her face as Bea cut her meat, poured her wine.

Won't you come weave with us today? she asked.

Not today, no, I said. Not today.

You could come with me instead, I wanted to say. You could run. But I didn't say it. I ate my dates and figs and put five of each in my pockets and looked up at my sisters.

Basil?
  Basil.

Liberata?
  Liberata.

I didn't look at Marina, and she didn't look at me.

—◦—

That night I didn't dream of my mother. I didn't dream of anything. I woke up six hours before sunrise, as planned, and saw Liberata, already up, standing by the window and looking out. Her sandals were on. I bound my chest and put on my tunic. I put on my sandals because, despite my petition not to bring them at all, Basil and Liberata had made some excellent points about scorpions and night snakes.

Marina slept. She slept with full bedclothes on, every night.

I woke Basil. She bound her chest and put on her tunic and put on her sandals. Liberata came away from the window, and we three stepped careful quiet over the slaves, Vernica and Claudia, who were sleeping just outside our door like they always did. And then we left.

And Marina slept.

2

MARINA

Back

let's step back

please.

Back

before I knew any of this, back

when I knew nothing but the village, nothing but sisters and
lemons and village, back to the thirsty-simple time when Quiteria
and I were up in the branches catching caterpillars, eight years old.
Back then, there.

We were still small enough to climb up without breaking branches,
without bruising fruit or crushing flowers. The caterpillars were the
enemy, were the barbarians to the sweet walled cities of our lemons,
but I still felt bad. I didn't like this job. What did they want, really, the
caterpillars? What made them bad? They just wanted the same thing
as us, the fruit, the juice, the sugar, the food. I didn't like killing them.
I didn't like hurting herbivores.

But that was our job that day, so that's what we were doing. So that's
what we were doing when the parade came by, me up high, Quiteria a

bit lower down. The parade was soldiers and horses and slaves and music and even some flags. It was exciting. It was colour, in a life, a village, a childhood, that was only burnt brown, usually. And it was an excuse to stop killing caterpillars. So I jumped down, out of the tree, as soon as I saw, as soon as I could, and Quiteria followed me.

It was the commander coming home from the borderlands. It was our father, except I didn't know he was our father yet. The soldiers were beautiful in shining gold and the horses were all clean and brushed and calm and I wished I could reach out and touch one, just one, just for a second. I didn't, but I imagined I did, and I remembered that imaginary softness against my hand for a long time after.

Some slaves had come down from the house to the parade, to help carry things or deliver messages. I knew we were meant to pity them, be grateful we weren't one of them; no freedom, no dignity, no life, said Quiteria. Thank the gods, said my father, every day, every day. But to me they looked beautiful. Clean and tall and fed.

Nobody really noticed us, except one of them, one slave. She scanned the crowd up and down as she walked in a line with the other slaves, the rest all looking straight ahead, beautiful, tall, fed. The one stopped for a beat, a breath, when she saw Quiteria, when she saw me. She looked at us, she looked at me, and she blinked. Then she looked away, back to the parade, to a soldier she was walking towards. She said something to him, which made him turn and say something to one of the men on the horses, who nodded, first at the soldier, then at her. Then she turned around and walked back, away, back towards the big house, stopping just once to look back, at the parade, at us.

That summer

that dry hot

empty hot

fruits inside out on themselves hot

little lizards licking the corners of your mouth when you sleep for
something to drink hot summer,

that summer there were so
many
caterpillars.

They loved it hot. It was caterpillars bursting out of everything hot.
Cyllia told me, later, that our father spoke sometimes of places with
cold so intense that water turned to rocks. Cold so deep, she said he
said, that it killed people, sometimes. I didn't believe it. The idea of cold
was salvation, was Pure Good. And the caterpillars? I asked her.

They sleep, she said. They sleep through it all.

It was that summer, another high-heat day just after noon and everyone
was sleeping or being sick or both. I wasn't sick or asleep. I was alone,
lying on my back in the almost completely dry stream. I was trying to
get the trickle of it to cool one tiny bit of me at a time, this quarter-inch
of shoulder, this bit of neck, this bit of hair.

The water was running from my right temple down the side of my
right cheek when the slave appeared. It was the one from the parade,
the same one. She stopped, as she had then, and looked at me, as she
had then. Then she looked around and behind her. There was no one
there, no one anywhere, just caterpillars, but she looked again, over
both shoulders. Then she slowly lowered herself down onto the bank
beside me and put her feet into the tiny trickle coming off and around
my right side. I shouldn't be here, she said.

It's okay, I said. I don't mind.

I wanted to close my eyes, to keep the sun off them and to stop the
water running into the right one, but that seemed rude, so I kept the
left one all the way open and the right one halfway.

That's nice, she said. I didn't know if she was referring to the water
on her feet or my comment, so I didn't say anything, just smiled, which
made the water bump up and around my mouth in a new way.

She took off her sandals, put them to the side, and dug her feet into
the dust-mud. She looked at me, at my feet, tunic, neck-with-water-
running-down-it. You're Quiteria, she said. I know you. I saved you.

I opened my right eye all the way. Water and sun raced in. I squeezed it shut and sat up. No, I said, I'm Marina. I'm Quiteria's sister. One of her sisters. The stream was now hitting my tailbone, diverting around to my leg.

Oh, yes, said the slave. Of course you could be any one of you. Any of the seven . . . She stopped. There are still seven? she asked.

Yes, I said. Though some are sick.

Still, she said. Still, seven out of nine, even sick, is not bad. Not bad at all.

Nine? I said.

Remember, before this all I knew was the village. The lemons, the sun, the lizards, the caterpillars. All I knew was Basil, Liberata, Gema, Germana, Vitoria, Quiteria, and me. That we were seven, altogether. That we were orphans. That we were very

very

very

(thank the gods, thank them every day)

lucky.

And that was all.

The slave bent forward and put a hand into the trickle of stream where it hit her toes. Then she brought that hand to her face, but, of course, the water had heat-dried before her hand even reached her cheek. I shouldn't tell you, she said.

I didn't know what to say to that, so I said nothing. The sun burned my eyes.

The thing is, she said. Everyone thinks you're dead.

Despite the sun, my eyes opened themselves wider, all the way. Dead? I said.

Yes, she said. They think you and Quiteria and Vitoria and Gema and Germana and Liberata and Basilissa are dead, are all dead.

Well, I said. Some are sick . . .

Very sick? Will they die?

Um, I said. I don't know. I don't think so. I hope not. We sacrificed a dog to Apollo, the village did, the whole village, so they shouldn't die. I don't think.

I didn't tell her the dog was already sick itself. Already halfway gone. That there was nothing else, nothing healthy, to offer.

I hope not too, said the slave woman. That's the problem. I don't want, I didn't want, any of you to die.

Me neither, I said. I didn't understand why she kept talking about death, this woman. Why she still looked sad even after I'd told her we were alive, all of us, still alive. Perhaps, I thought, she's sad because even though she doesn't want us to die, we are going to die. Even though she perhaps doesn't want to kill us, she has to. Maybe we are her sacrifice. All seven of us, or just me, maybe. Her feet were old but clean, looked after. She was from the big house, after all. She might have to kill. She might have no choice.

I stood up. Bits of dirt and gravel fell from my hair. I took a small polite step away from her. I looked to see if she had a knife, or a big stone. She didn't. She had dusty hands, like me.

That's the problem, she said, and sighed.

I'm Cyllia, she said. From the big house. She wiped a dusty hand across her forehead. She sighed again, and patted the ground next to where she was sitting.

Here, she said. I won't hurt you. I never wanted to hurt you.

Did you kill the other two?

The other two?

There are seven of us, but you say there were nine. Seven plus two is nine. Did you kill those other two?

The other two babies?

Yes, the other two babies. Two sisters.

No, I didn't. They were already cold. Already gone.

But cold sounds good, I said. Cold sounds great to me.

No, said the woman. It wasn't cold like that. Not like this stream. It was a lonely cold. A having been attached and then unattached cold.

Oh, I said.

You understand? she asked.

Yes, I said, even though I didn't.

Good, she said. Good.

And then

she told me my story, our whole story, starting with our mother, our real mother, and her nine-times-over labour, our nine-times-over birth.

Oh,

she said our mother said.

Oh, oh, oh, oh, oh, oh, oh, oh, oh.

She said it nine times,

Once for each tiny red head, once for each tiny open mouth.

I listened, eyes open all the way, as it all flowed out like a much bigger, much better stream.

The story ended with the parade. I saw you there, she said. I saw you, all the same, and I knew it was you, the same ones, the babies, and that you were alive. And I was glad, glad to see that.

I saw you too, I said. And I'm glad too, to be alive.

And I wanted to come here, she continued, to tell you that. To tell you I'm sorry.

For not killing us?

No, no.

For what?

I'm not sure, she said. For secrets, maybe. Or for not coming back. For taking eight years to come back.

I eat a lot of lemons, I said. Even though we're not supposed to. That's my secret.

Cyllia gave me a ribbon. A ribbon beautiful and deep red like the almost-set sun.

Oh, I said. Oh, wow. I reached for it, then remembered how dirty my hands were, how dusty, and stopped and rubbed them on my legs. Rust-brown smears. Just for me? I asked.

Just for you, Cyllia said. She handed it to me and I took it and it was so soft, so smooth I wanted to put it against my cheek, or over my eyes, or into my mouth, but I didn't, I just held it, pushing my thumb up and down its barely-there grain, up and down. I didn't know who, which sister, I would meet here today, she said. Or if I would meet any at all. But I'm glad I've met you, Marina. This ribbon is just for you.

You don't have six more? For my sisters?

No.

I smiled.

I couldn't tell anyone that I'd seen her, that she'd visited or anything else that I knew now about us, about our father, or our mother, or the house where the lemons and the horses and the soldiers and the slaves went, that house that was our house, really.

If I told anyone, Cyllia could get in trouble. She was supposed to do something, eight years ago, and she didn't do it, and that, just that, could get her into trouble. Please, she'd said. Please, Marina, don't tell anyone, not yet. Not until I'm dead. I'm pretty old, she'd said. I'm pretty tired. I'll die soon enough. A few years, maybe.

So I couldn't tell anyone. Not until then. So I didn't. Not yet.

I didn't have any sisters or brothers in my house. I didn't have anything except a quiet old father and a tired sad mother. I didn't have anything before. Now I had something, something else. Something no one, not even my sisters, had.

We sat quietly, side by side, feet in the almost-water, for a few minutes, and then she got up and started lacing on her sandals.

I'll come back, she said. I shouldn't, but I will. When I can. I'll try again in thirty days, by this stream, at this time.

The stream will be totally dry then, I said. Gone.

It's okay, said Cyllia. I'll still come. I'll still try.

Okay, I said. Me too.

She was already turned around, already on her way when I asked, Cyllia, do you have any kids of your own?

Just one, she said, facing away, back home. Just one now. A son.
And then she walked away and was gone.

I held the ribbon to my chest, where it would stay clean and dry, and
lay back down into the water and closed my eyes all the way, and,
because I couldn't tell anyone else, I told myself the story, the whole
study of us, again and again and again, filling in lost bits, clarifying
what was unsure, until all the fuzziness of it was gone, until it was as
real and clear as anything, as water.

When it was time to get up and go back to work, back up into the trees,
I flattened the ribbon out so it was as smooth and as long as it could be
and tied it around my left wrist. I'd wear it there forever, I thought. I'd
work and sleep and climb and run in it. I'd never take it off, not myself,
not with my own hands.

I prayed that night, lying awake, pushing sleep away. Thank you, thank
you, to Diana, goddess of children, of birth, to Neptune, god of water.

Proving that she wasn't a fever dream or heat-ghost, Cyllia came back
when she said she would, thirty days later. I hid up in a tree near the
stream, near our spot. I wanted her to come, I didn't want to miss her,
but I also didn't want her to find me there, waiting. So I stayed up in
the tree and watched as she approached. She got to the stream. She
looked around. She didn't see me. She put her hands down behind her
and lowered herself down to sitting, on the bank, slowly, carefully, like
she wasn't sure when the ground would hit. I stayed in the tree, watching her there, while a caterpillar crawled all the way along the branch
I was on and disappeared, around, onto the bottom side of a leaf. I left
it alone.

Then I said, I'm here.
She looked to one side, then the other, then behind.

Here, I said.

She looked up, squinted. Up there?

Yes, I said.

I can't see you, she said. There's too much sun.

I'm here, I said.

Okay, she said. Good. Do you want to come down?

Gema and Germana died, I said.

Oh, she said. Her shoulders dropped. She spread her hands against the ground, the dry dirt. Pox? She said.

Yes, I said.

Your sisters? she said.

Yes, I said.

I'm sorry, she said. I—

We sacrificed the dog, I said. We prayed.

I know, she said. I know.

Now there are five, I said. Five of us left. I watched her hands in the dirt, I watched the top of her veiled head.

You don't have to come down, she said. But you can if you want.

Okay, I said. I didn't come down. I watched another caterpillar. I left it alone. I watched the top of her head.

Two more caterpillars went by and then she said, I brought you a doll. A grass doll.

A doll that's made of grass or a doll that looks like grass? I asked.

Made of grass, she said.

I've never had a doll, I said. And my mother doesn't have any babies.

Well, now you have one, said Cyllia.

Yes, I said.

I'll just leave it here, against the bottom of the tree, said Cyllia.

Okay, I said.

She took the doll from her pocket, reached over, and set it up against the tree. It was small, just as long as my finger, maybe.

Thank you, I said.

I'll come back in ten days, she said. I'll come to see you.

Okay, I said.

It got hotter, it got drier. The lemons pulled into themselves, into strange shapes. We didn't run as much. We did our jobs, we breathed dust, we went home to the cool shadow houses of our adoptive families. I only took my doll out of my pocket at night, laid it beside me on my mattress, smoothed its tiny grass hair.

Cyllia came back, sometimes after ten days, sometimes after thirty, sometimes after fifty, but she always came back. Sometimes she brought me food or gifts, and sometimes she brought me stories, about things going on at the big house, or about our father and where he was, about the strange and faraway corners of the empire he reached, explored, defended, and to me, the stories sounded just like the ones the village adults told about the goddesses and gods, to me, they could have been, they were, the same.

It was early in the season, not even a year after Gema and Germana died, but already there was no water left in the stream. I was lying in it anyway, like the first time. The ribbon was on my wrist; the doll was in my pocket. Flies buzzed around my face. My eyes were closed, but I could hear them, and sometimes feel them, when they got close: the tiny wind of their wings, the careful, hopeful footsteps when they'd land and walk around a bit on my nose or forehead. I didn't swat them away. I didn't move.

I felt the cool of Cyllia's shadow over me before I heard her.

Marina? she said.

Yes, I said.

It's me, she said.

Yes, I said. I know.

It's good to see you, she said. She brushed a fly from my nose. I almost stopped her, but it was hot and I was tired, really tired, and trying not to move at all. I've brought you some honey water, she said.

Liberata is sick, I said.

Cyllia was quiet then, for a while. I heard her breathe. I heard her lower herself, slowly, onto the dry bank; I felt some small bits of dirt tumble down onto my arms.

It's okay, I said.

It's not, she said. It's never okay.

I heard her shuffle over so she was right next to me. I felt her hands, big, rough, under my head, lifting it up, up until it was on her lap. I heard her uncork a bottle and felt her put it to my mouth. The rim was sweet, and cool. I drank without opening my eyes. It tasted like sun, like the light of the sun without the hurt of the heat.

There, she said. There.

I drank it all, all in one go.

There, she said.

Is it from my father? I asked.

Yes, said Cyllia. Honey water, from him. I heard her recork the bottle and put it down, off to the side. He has whole swarms of bees, hives and hives, up on the other side of the house, she said. They're the ones that come down here to the trees.

Lemon bees, I said.

Yes, said Cyllia.

Basil is afraid of bees, I said. But I'm not.

Good, said Cyllia. She put the back of one hand, big, rough, against my cheek, held it there, then took it away again. Are you sick? she said.

I'm okay, I said.

You're sure?

Yeah.

I'll come back in two days, she said.

Okay.

She lifted my head back up, put it back on the empty stream bed. I felt the tumble of dirt as she stood up again. Heard her brush and smooth her tunic where she'd sat on it.

The lemon bees are wonderful, I said. Better than normal bees. I love them.

They are, said Cyllia. Take care of them. And eat the lemons, Marina. Eat them and drink their juice, whenever you want. As much as you want.

My father says so?

He wouldn't say no, she said. He wouldn't.

And then she left. I heard her footsteps down along the stream, and then turning off onto the quieter, softer ground, and gone.

Two days later she brought the medallion. The most magical thing I had ever seen, ever held. Round, cool, metal, with the outline of a fish on it, front and back. You must touch it to your sick sister, she said. It will protect, she said. It will heal.

Is it Pluto's? I asked.

No, she said. A different god. Life, not death.

I ran away with the medal in my fist before she had a chance to push herself up again from the bank, before she said goodbye.

I ran to Liberata. She was sleeping. Everyone was sleeping. I pressed the medallion against her forehead where she was hot, hottest. I pressed too hard and left an imprint, a fish on her sleeping head, but she didn't wake up. Before I left I pressed it on Basil too, more lightly, just in case.

Out on the path between their house and mine I did myself. I pressed the medallion to my forehead, to the backs of my hands, to my wrists, to my arms, to my legs in front and my legs in back; I pressed it to my feet and then brought it back up and pressed it to my face, to my cheeks. I covered myself with the imprints of fish, little red fish everywhere.

The next time Cyllia came I was sitting up, I had my eyes open.

Everyone's okay? she asked.

Everyone's okay, I said. Liberata got better. Everyone's okay.

⸺

Everyone stayed okay, generally okay, after that. Years went by. Vitoria left, but she was okay when she did, and she promised to come back or send presents or messages or something, at least, soon. The sick and strange lemons fell away and new ones filled their places and were full and sweet and they grew big and healthy and so did we.

⸺

And Cyllia always came when she said she would.

And when I asked her, which I sometimes did, When can I tell my sisters? About you, about our father?

She would say, When I'm dead. Which won't be long now, she would say. She always said, Won't be long now.

~

And then, one day. She didn't come.

I waited by the dry stream, twelve years old, feet too big for my legs, wrist too big for my ribbon, and waited, but she didn't come.

I waited the next day, in case I'd counted wrong, somehow, but she didn't come.

She didn't come and she didn't come and she didn't come. I'd wait through the afternoon heat, and she wouldn't come, and then I'd go back to life, my other life, my ribbon now the same dull grey-brown as everything else, my grass doll broken down into a hundred dry shreds in my pocket.

~

Liberata and I were on chicken-trench duty. It was everyone's least favourite job, but for different reasons. It was Liberata's least favourite because it was a down-on-the-ground job and she wanted to be up in the trees, always. It was my least favourite because the chicken dung that we worked with, that we had to scoop into the little trench moats around each tree, smelled terrible and I was afraid the smell and the stain of it would soak into my ribbon. It was Quiteria's least favourite because she thought it was a stupid waste of time. They should just tie one chicken to the base of each tree and it would shit there and eat the caterpillars off the trunk and that would be that, all our work done, she said.

Quiteria was the only one of us who said shit.

There aren't enough chickens, though, I said.

You'd rotate them, she said. Every few days. Off these trees, onto those ones, etcetera.

Maybe falling lemons would hit and kill them, said Basil.

Then we'd eat chicken, said Quiteria. All the better.

It was Basil's least favourite job because it made everyone so grumpy.

But it was Liberata's and my turn, this time. So we were down on the ground, digging, and the others were up high, above us. I had the ribbon slid up on the top bit of my arm to keep it as far away from the dung as possible, slid right up by my armpit, where it was even tighter and turned my skin purple. I took a handful of dung from the bucket, dropped it into the trench, patted it down, and checked the ribbon. I took another handful, dropped it, patted it, checked. One tree away, Liberata was faster, less careful. We had the dung bucket positioned exactly halfway between us; we'd measured.

The ribbon was cutting into me; it hurt. I was trying to slip it a tiny bit farther down using only the back part of my hand, not my filthy fingers, when I saw the soldier.

He saw me.

I blinked. His armour was gold in the morning light. He was beautiful. Oh, I said.

He stepped towards me, one step. Is it—? he started.

And then a spear hit him in the leg. He stumbled, winced, Oh! he said. He looked at me, confused, then up, to the trees.

Oh! said the tree, said Basil in the tree. Oh no! Oh! She jumped down, out from the leaves, and started running away.

The soldier pulled the spear out of his leg; it wasn't big. It also wasn't Basil's. Basil didn't have any spears. Only one of us did, only Quiteria.

The soldier looked at Basil, running, then back to me, frozen, my hand still on my arm, on my ribbon,

It is you? he said, quickly, all one word,

isityou?

I looked at him, shining, beautiful, bleeding. I shook my head, No.

No, I said, unless—

But he had already turned away, was already gone, chasing Basil. They ran through the trees, away.

Quiteria jumped down from her leafy cover, grabbed a rock, and chased them both.

I watched her, wiped my hands on my tunic, sighed, and chased them all.

It was me, of course. Even though I didn't know that yet. He asked, istityou? and Yes, Yes, it was me, of course it was me. Even though I didn't know and he didn't know, not yet. The soldier was Cyllius, my Cyllius, and it was me he wanted, and Oh, he was beautiful.

And, still, Cyllia didn't come. And the lemons grew and fell and grew and fell. And I waited.

⁓

We got Basil back. The sun calmed down again. The stream came back again. I went and put my feet in it, waited there, every day. Nothing, nothing, nothing. First there was just enough water to slip under my arches; then enough to make mud to push my toes down into; then enough to run right over my feet, then up to the scar on my calf, then to my knees, so I had to lift my tunic or risk it getting swept away, downstream, with me in it.

I waited. I waited so long and so much that sometimes I forgot I was waiting for anything but water. The stream got so high and the year got so late that it started to turn around on itself and disappear again. When the flow was back down to my ankles again, when it didn't push against or around me anymore, I stopped waiting; I went to see Quiteria.

It's a lie, she said.

It's not, I said.

She'd been sleeping, having her too-hot-to-work nap along with the rest of her family. There were sleeping people everywhere. She had hundreds of siblings, millions. Little kids and littler kids and babies and littler babies and grandparents and parents all stuffed into the one hut. I could never sleep with that much body warmth around, with that many different breathing noises, but Quiteria could, was. I woke her and we stepped over arms and legs and babies until we were outside, then we went and sat against the back of the hut, in its bit of shade, and I told her what Cyllia had told me. I told her everything.

Oh, she said.

Up the hill, I said. To the top, to the very top.

It's a lie, she said.

And, she said, if it is true, then it's horrible. It's better if it's not true.

But it's not horrible! I said. It's great! It's wonderful! I waited, but she didn't say anything. I thought you'd think it was wonderful, I said.

I don't think it's anything, she said, finally. Because I don't think it's true. But if I did, if I did think it was true, I would think it was horrible.

She was staring down at her legs, at the night-sky pattern of scratches and scars across her legs. It was too bright to look up, at each other. I looked at her legs and then away, down at two beetles instead. They were walking in a way that meant they would, almost certainly, bump into each other very soon.

I thought you'd be happy, I said.

I am happy, she said. Just not about that. She pulled her tunic down towards her knees.

Don't tell anyone else, okay? I said. The beetles almost got to each other, but then one got diverted by a rock at the last second.

I won't, she said. What would be the point?

Just, just in case there is a point, can you promise not to? Not yet? I asked.

Yes, she said. Easy. I promise not to tell anyone something that's nothing, she said. Okay?

Okay, I said.

We sat there for a while. The beetle had made it around the rock and almost walked into the other one, but then it walked away, and then back again, and then away.

I'm starving, Quiteria said, finally. No point going back to sleep now, it's almost time to get up, she said. Let's go look for fennel to chew.

It's gross.

Yeah, but we're on shit duty this afternoon, she said. And it's less gross than that.

True.

Okay, let's go.

Okay.

I didn't know if Cyllia was dead. If she was, I could tell everyone everything, all my sisters, my mother and father. If she wasn't, I couldn't, I
wouldn't, tell anyone. But I didn't know. So I just told Quiteria, and
that was all. I just told her and worked and waited, and waited, until,
like I knew he would, eventually, the soldier, Cyllius,

    my Cyllius,

    came back.

~∾~

Cyllius blinked. Looked to the others, looked at me, he looked at me.

    We were thirteen. He was nineteen. Cyllia, his mother, was dead.

    Marina, said Quiteria, she took my hand like you would an object,
something precious you grab on the way out of a burning house, her
whisper was more animal than sister, more fear than sound.

    He'd come back with other soldiers, he'd come back with weapons.
Please, he said, with all the weight of soldiers, of weapons. Please come
with me.

    Quiteria pulled my hand; my other sisters were gone already, run-
ning. She pulled until we broke apart, fingers sweaty, slipped.

    She slipped away and I looked at him. Say something, I willed him.
Say something more. Say isityou? Say her name. Say my name.

    I held up my arm, the one with the ribbon, tattered, sun-bleached.

    Marina! called my sisters.

    I thought I would know what to do. I thought it would be, should
be, easy, obvious, like hunger and food, like water and thirst.

    I looked at him.

    But Cyllia's stories were just stories, just words, and Quiteria's fear
was real, was flesh, my flesh.

    She called me.

    And I looked away from him and I ran, with them.

~∾~

We ran away

up,

but the wrong way.
Into the hills, away from the house.

Into the hills, where the sun was closer and hotter, where the dust rose
up around our feet and covered our toes and ankles and calves with
every step, and the soldiers followed. We ran and led them away from
our homes and our families. We ran until we lost them all, the soldiers,
our homes, our families. We were thirteen years old.

We made camp by an underachieving wild lemon tree by pushing rocks
and dry branches around it into a sort of den, both camouflage and
shade. I knelt, knees in sun-softened thorn-dirt so that I could see over,
back in the direction we'd come, back towards the soldiers.

Do you see them? asked Quiteria. Do you see anything?

Nothing, I said. No one.

I sat like that, watching, while the others made plans, picked and ate
lemons, slept. I wanted to pray but didn't know who to pray to. I
watched for a signal, a sign, anything. But I saw nothing, just dust and
brush and waves of heat so thick they blurred everything.

～

One day
Two days
Three days
Four
Five
Six
Seven

And then, eight.

It was day eight, our eighth day out there under the half-tree, and we
were thirsty. The water that Basil had found was gone, and no one,
including her, could find where she'd got it from, which made Quiteria

angry and Basil embarrassed and made everyone hot and tired and slow-moving, like the bugs of high summer we'd find not-dead-dead on lemon leaves.

Their legs need water to move, Cyllia told me, once. Without it, they're stuck. They just have to sit there and wait to be brought back to life in the autumn.

Our legs were drying up. Our mouths, our eyes, our spirits were drying up. And up on the other side of the hills, just up there, was our house, our big house. The house that could be, should be, ours, where there was endless water, honey water, just there, like it was no big thing, like it was completely normal.

Sometimes, at night, Quiteria would plait my hair, her fingers smoothing and separating, strong and firm and comforting, if not gentle, and I thought, Maybe she is right. Maybe we can stay like this forever.

But other times she didn't. She wouldn't. She wouldn't do anything but look out, fierce, terrified, fist around her spear, look out, away.

Soldiers would have meat, I knew. And where there was meat there would be fire and where there was fire there would be smoke, I knew.

So after eight days, I said, I'll go. On the eighth day, I said, You rest, and I'll go tonight. I'll find water tonight.

It was easy to find him. I walked out, away from the shade and shelter of our tree, walked out and around, looking up, up at the stars, the sky, until I saw it. Smoke, light and curling in the windless sky. I followed it. It was as easy as that. No more caterpillars, no more chicken shit, no more thirst ever again; it was easy. Softness and safety. No more disease, no more death, all of us growing old, as old as Cyllia. It was easy.

I moved off the open trail and pushed my way into the dark dense branches surrounding the soldiers' camp. I made my way through until I was close enough to watch the flames reflected off their weapons silver and their shields red and gold, all in a pile to the side. Until I was close enough to make out their sitting shadows. Cyllius and three others. Quiet, eating. As alone as me.

I stood there, in that bush, for a long time. The night was soft and mild and there was enough smell of meat on the air to taste, if you closed your eyes and breathed only with your mouth, so I closed my eyes and breathed like that and felt the rich full weight of meat; I swallowed it down and let it fill me up until a slight wind picked up, and at once, it was gone.

I opened my eyes.

Cyllius was on the far side of the fire, chewing. He had a stick in one hand and was poking it into the dirt at his feet, making little dots and lines.

And they'll have the proper weapons, said another man. He spoke like us, in low dialect. And better food, probably, he said.

And wine, said another.

We have wine, said Cyllius.

Better wine.

Everyone chewed for a while, picked at bones with their teeth and fingers; one man, who had been quiet, so far, used a small fighting knife to dig out the last bits of meat from a bone much smaller than the knife itself. Until the barbarians chop off their heads, he said, half to himself.

What?

They'll have better wine to drink until the barbarians chop off their heads, said the knife solider. He put the tip to his mouth, ate something invisible off the end. I'd rather have crap wine and be sat up here babysitting than have amazing wine and have my head chopped off, he said. That's all.

Hm, said the other. Still.

Then nobody said anything and they ate in silence for a while. Someone threw a bone into the fire and it hissed and cracked and threw up a little line of smoke. I closed my eyes and breathed it in. Then I squeezed the sharpened stone I had tucked into my right hand, and stepped out from the scrub, the firelight orange and yellow and white-hot on my legs.

The soldiers sat up all at once, all at once dropped their food, reached for swords, stood up. They all at once stopped being men and became soldiers.

Hi, I said.

I'm here, I said. We're here.

We made a deal. No point capturing me then and there, when it was just me; we made a deal instead: they wouldn't capture or hurt me then, and they'd promise not to hurt anyone later, and they'd give me a bit of their rabbit and wine, and then I would tell them how to find us. Where to find us.

Make it a surprise, I said. Come the day after tomorrow, I said. In the height of the day. We'll be asleep. I'll be asleep.

They watered down my wine even more than theirs and gave me a rabbit ear to chew on. They filled my flasks with fresh water mixed with a little rabbit blood, for strength, and said, Okay. We can do that, okay. They didn't lay one hand on me; they didn't touch me.

Will you be wearing that ribbon? asked Cyllius. He motioned towards my wrist, the dark, tattered string of once-ribbon. So that I'll know which one is you?

I was next to him, by the fire. I could feel the air shift every time he lifted his hand to his face to shield his eyes from smoke. I could smell the dirt and days and wine on him.

Is your mother dead? I said.

Yes, he said. His face smoke and yellow-orange white-hot. His hair fair, like hers.

Yes, I said. I'll wear it.

～

I heard them first. We were all lying down together, bunched up in the tiny midday shade of our tree. We hadn't had enough water for more than a week now, not enough to move during this part of day, not enough to stay awake when the sun was holding us down. We curled into our too-small patches of shade like snails into shells. Quiteria was on one side of me, Liberata on the other. We made sure not to touch each other, not to spread heat. I couldn't sleep, but I couldn't look like I had any reason not to sleep, so I lay between them, eyes closed, and counted my breath, nine beats in, nine beats out, nine in, nine out, listening to nothing. To the nothing of midday: no wind, no birds, no bugs. I listened to the nothingness around my own heartbeat, to the familiar nothingness of sister breath, sister bodies. And then, far away and quiet and almost nothing, there was something; there were footsteps. I heard them first, but I kept my eyes closed, I kept counting. I reached over, found Quiteria's hand, limp with sleep, and held it. I counted one two three four five six seven eight nine. One two three four five six seven eight nine.

Oh
said Quiteria

as she woke, as she saw.

Oh no. Oh no no no no no.

At the house, they washed our hair.

Water, there, so much water, that they poured it over hair, poured it over and let it drip down down down, away away away.

When we reached the house the soldiers left us with the women slaves, none of whom was Cyllia, and these women slaves washed our hair. First with water and then with oil and soap, and then, with knives that weren't knives but were like two knives bound together, sharp and careful and precise, they cut our hair, cut off the ragged, uneven ends, cut it all straight and smooth and then braided and bound it up and I could feel air, I could feel the breeze on the back of my still-damp neck and felt, for the first time, ever, ever, cool, safe.

Would you like to eat? they asked us. A question that no one had asked before. A question that didn't make sense.

Quiteria looked at me and I looked at Quiteria.

We ate and ate, and drank and drank. We didn't speak, not to each other, not yet, not while the women were there. But Liberata was smiling, and Basil was smiling, and I looked at Quiteria and I smiled, and she drank water and put her hand to her hair, her new hair, like she was surprised by it, even though she'd had it for more than an hour now, just like the rest of us.

They took us to our room. Claudia, the slave woman with grey-silver hair and a grey-silver tunic soft as water, explained the chamber pots and pillows and blankets, gave us a jug of water and four cups, and said, You'll meet with him tomorrow. He's been away, but will be back, and will meet with you tomorrow. Then she closed the door, and left us in a safe and perfect darkness, left us to sleep in beds that were up, off the ground, four in a row, in this room that had been prepared, had been waiting.

Who? whispered Liberata. Her blanket was all the way up, over her head, so we could barely hear her. Who will we meet tomorrow?

The commander, said Quiteria. She had kicked her bedclothes to the floor, was on the bare mattress only. Of course, she said.

The linen of the blanket was warm and strange against my chest, but I left it there, skin over my skin.

The commander? said Basil. She was lying on top of her blanket instead of under it. Tall as ten men, rich as a thousand? The real commander?

Anger and wrath of a god, whispered Liberata. Muffled, quiet.

That's just a rumour, a stupid story, said Basil. To stop us stealing lemons.

Maybe it is, maybe it isn't, said Quiteria. Maybe it isn't.

I guess we'll see, I said, quietly, and the linen rubbed against my neck.

I wanted to say: Isn't this okay, Quiteria? Isn't being clean being full being safe okay? Isn't it? Isn't it good?

I wanted to say: I told you, I told you this was ours, this was us.

But I didn't. I didn't say anything more, and neither did anyone else.

We slept.

And when we woke there were pure white tunics at the ends of our beds, one each, all the same, all fine and beautiful, heart-crumplingly beautiful and for us. For the first time, there was something beautiful and for us, all of us.

Against the tunic the grime of my ribbon looked even worse, looked disgusting. I used my teeth to make a tear in its grey-black edge. I pulled until it ripped all the way across, until it fell off my wrist, and away.

~⌒~

We wore the new clothes and glided down the hall to meet our father like brides. And when he put his hand to my face, when he held it there, strong and unshaking, when he said, Marina,

I said, Yes.

~⌒~

For four years it was good. I would close my eyes at night, under my blanket, and the dark was a comfort, wrapping itself around me, soft as smoke, and I'd let myself sink into it, safe, full, knowing tomorrow would be the same: safe, full. And tomorrow and tomorrow.

That's home. Being safe is being home. Being home is being safe. Tomorrow and tomorrow and tomorrow.

It's okay? I asked Liberata one morning as the slaves were lifting, twisting, sculpting our hair into something beautiful, something better than ourselves. All, of this, it's okay, right?

I miss my family in the village, sometimes, she said, but . . .

But it's okay? It's good?

Yes. It is. I am.

I wanted to ask Quiteria, but she wasn't there. She was never there, always away, off.

I ate so many olives, so many eggs, so much meat that my cheeks filled in. Look at those, said Basil, poking them with her fingers. You're soft and round as a mushroom.

You too, I said, even though it was hard to talk with her fingers poked into my face like that. You too.

Everything filled in. Everything got soft and round. Cheeks, chests, legs, hearts, days. Sisters, fathers, soldiers.

⸺

One day, once Basil had stopped hiding food up her sleeves all the time and Quiteria had stopped talking about escape all the time, Julia, who was not our mother, real or adoptive, but was the commander's current wife, so was a sort of mother nonetheless, she, Julia, came up to me in the garden. I had hoisted myself up and into the fountain and was crouched in a ball so I could fit as much of me as possible in the water. A trickle dripped out of the carved stone mouth of a creature with a face like the sun; I'd positioned myself so it landed on the back of my neck. I did this at least once a day, for as long as I could until I heard sandals on the tiles, which meant someone coming, at which point I'd hoist myself back out again, quick and quiet as an evening lizard, and pretend I'd just been washing my face and hands like normal, like everyone else.

But Julia didn't like wearing sandals. So any time she could get away with it, she didn't. And since no one important was visiting that day and our father was gone again, back to fighting barbarians, she was barefoot. So I didn't hear her coming. The water was dripping down from the sun-mouth onto my neck, drip, drip, drip, and my legs and arms and elbows and half my torso were submerged and cool and drip drip drip and drip drip drip and then drip drip stop. Instead of water, a hand, uncalloused, long, on my neck. And then a voice:

Which one are you?

I lifted my head, turned, and water dripped down into my eyes. Ow, I said. And then, Sorry. And then, head turned back down, away from the drips, I saw her bare feet. Marina, I said. I'm Marina, ma'am.

Julia, she said.

Yes, I said.

You don't have to call me ma'am. Call me Julia.

Okay, I said.

Marina, said Julia.

Yes, ma'am? I said.

She sighed. Marina, she said, are you busy right now?

After waiting while the slaves changed my wet tunic for a dry one—we each had three tunics now—Julia led me to a space in the centre of the villa. It was thick with the smell of sheep. Clean sheep, but still, sheep. But there were no sheep there, just baskets full of clouds, and two big wooden machines. Julia put her hand on my shoulder for a beat, then took it off again, tucked it back into the endless folds of her clothes. Marina, she said, can I teach you how to spin and weave? Her face had gone pink.

There were more clouds of wool in that room, in those baskets, than there ever were real clouds in the sky. The light shone in and through them so they glowed, so they almost seemed to float.

Sure, I said. Sure, Julia. And I smiled and she smiled back.

So she taught me, and I learned.

Cloud after cloud, I'd spin all the wool in the house, and all the flax too; and then, once I was ready, I'd get it on the loom and pass the shuttle back and forth and back and forth, easy as that, easy as water, the weights knocking gently at my feet, little solid bells.

One evening, after we'd finished, locked off the cloth, tucked the shuttle away, safe, I ran into our father, the commander, in the hall. He usually wasn't in this part of the villa. He usually wasn't home at all. He was distracted, counting out something on his fingers, one-two-three-four, and then again, one-two-three-four.

Quiteria, he said.

Marina, I said.

Right, yes. Marina, he said. He looked back down to his hand, his fingers. Marina, he repeated, more softly. His tunic was frayed slightly where it met his calves. I could fix that, I thought. I could make new cloth for that. I kept my eyes down, on the frayed hem.

Well, he said. He took a breath in, then out.

Well, I said.

Well, he said, again, and moved to pass me on the right, but I was closer to the wall there and the gap was too narrow for him to pass through.

We both stepped left at the same time. We did it perfectly together, dancers.

Ha, ha, he said. Not really laughing, but making the sounds for laughing.

Then he stepped left again, and I didn't, and then he walked on, forward, past me and down the hall. I watched him. His sandals caught on the too-long edge of his tunic every few steps.

—∾—

It's okay? I asked Basil one morning as we walked together to the fountain to wash the sleep off our faces, out of our eyes. You, I mean, all this, it's okay, right? It's good?

We got to the fountain and Basil put her hands against the sun face for support and lunged down to stretch out her left calf. Sure, she said. There are certainly lots of good things about it. Undeniably. She switched sides, stretched out her right leg.

So it's for the best?

Sure, she said, pulling herself back up normal.

Okay, I said. Good. I think so too, I said. Will you come to the looms today?

No, she said. Not today. Other things to do today. She lifted her hands to her face, letting the water drip down. Tomorrow, though, I reckon, she said. I'll come see what you get up to tomorrow.

—∾—

I worked. And sometimes Julia would work too, there beside me, and sometimes she would just watch, passing me things that were out of reach when I needed them, humming tunes I didn't know. The months went by and soon I did know them, and hummed with her.

—∾—

And sometimes Basil came, and watched and worked and hummed,
    and sometimes Liberata,
      but not Quiteria, never Quiteria.

There was space, we could have made space, but Quiteria never filled it, never came.

I was finished weaving for the day. My fingers full of the pull, the twist, the spin; my fingers and wrists and hands gone stiff. I was in the fountain, on my back, with my knees up so I could fit. My head was down, in, so the water could reach between and under my braids. I pictured it curling up and around, smoke. I opened my mouth and let the water in and held it there, a fish. Or how I'd imagined a fish, since I'd never seen a live one.

I counted to ten, to twenty, to thirty, then sat up and spat the water out at the space between my knees.

Good shot, he said. He was just in his tunic. No armour or helmet or sword.

Oh, I said, and sat up all the way. Soldier.

Cyllius, he said. And you're Marina.

Yes! I said. How did you know? Most people couldn't tell us apart, me and my sisters. Our father couldn't.

Cyllius looked down to my feet; I had them positioned just over the bit where the water bubbled up into the fountain. Then he looked back at my face. A drip ran down to the end of my nose, stopped, then broke and ran down to my mouth. I licked it.

You've got distinguishing characteristics, he said.

Yeah? I said.

Yeah, he said.

So, I said. Why are you here? I didn't think they let soldiers in here, in the house or yard.

Oh, he said. He took a small step back, away. Um, no, not usually. But they let me, or I'm allowed, I guess. I always have been. But I'm not allowed to bring a sword, he said. Or not supposed to, I don't think. Unless there's an official reason.

Is there one now? An official reason?

No, said Cyllius. No, not at all.

Good, I said. Good.

Anyway, we leave tomorrow morning.

Again?

Always, he said. Maintaining the peace. Fending off hordes, maybe building a road or two, that stuff.

Oh yeah, I said.

Anyway, I'm ready, he said. I'm all packed.

Good, I said.

And I know I'll come back, I'll be fine, he said. Don't worry. I always am.

Okay, I said. Good.

All packed, all packed and ready.

Okay.

But I just thought, he said. I thought that, or wondered if, this time, before we go, I go, that, maybe, you could, well, tell me about, well, ha,

he put a hand into the water, then took it out and shook it like he was surprised by the wet,

my mother, he said. My mom. Just a bit. Just whatever you remember, if you remember much, or anything at all.

I know you were young, he said. Maybe you don't remember much of anything, and that's fine if you don't, but I was just thinking, if you did, if there was anything you might be able to tell me of it, of her, of what you remember, that you could, well, that you might.

His sentence didn't so much conclude as stop.

His tunic was clean, but you could see the outlines of stains that wouldn't wash out, burnt brown-red.

Please, he said, added.

I swung myself around so my feet and legs hung out over the side of the fountain's stone basin; I faced him. Just that? I said.

Just that, he said.

Well, of course, I said. I remember. I remember everything.

I patted the water next to me, making tiny waves.

Here, I said, sit down.

He hesitated, then hoisted himself over the stone lip and into the fountain. We were a bit squished, but he fit.

So, I said. The thing is, Cyllius, your mother was an angel.

He smiled a little, put his hand back down into the water.

No, I said. Listen. Not just like an angel. Not as good as or as sweet as an angel, I said. But an actual angel.

With wings? he said.

There are different kinds, I said.

He put his head down between his raised knees so he was looking at the water, into it. Tell me, he said. Tell me everything.

Then he left. He and my father and all the other soldiers packed up and marched off, off to the wilds where the barbarians were gnashing teeth, looking for children and dogs to hunt and feed to their own children and dogs. They left, marching with eyes and boots straight ahead and, because they didn't eat dogs or children, carts and carts and carts of provisions in a row after them. They were gone for four hundred and seventy-six days. Until I could weave faster and better than anyone in the house. Until my legs and arms stretched and made sense of my big hands and feet. Until I knew every word of every one of Julia's songs, faraway, nonsense words, everything and nothing at once.

Cyllius sat with me today, talked with me, I told Quiteria that first night, after dinner, in bed. The deepest, tightest bits of my braids were still wet with fountain water.

So? said Quiteria. He talks to everyone. He talks too much.

Does he?

Yep, everyone. All the time. Nothing remarkable about it. Nothing special.

Basil and Liberata too? They were asleep, so I couldn't ask them, so we were whispering.

And me, said Quiteria. She turned over in bed, towards the wall.

It was spring. The smell of lemon blossom drifted all the way up from the orchard, the village, up and up and up the hill the path the road the hill the wall the house, up to our long thin windows, resting heavy and thick around us as we talked, as we tried to sleep.

The next morning, before the looms, before Julia was even awake, I went to the fountain. I took off my sandals, untied and took off my purse, emptied my pockets and left everything on the still-cool stone foot of the basin. I pulled myself up, in. Lying on my back with my knees up, I took a breath as deep as the sky, if the sky were water, and let my head rest down, under.

The only sound was my heart. The only light was blurred blue.

I counted to ten. Then fifteen, then twenty. Then a hundred. Then a hundred and a hundred and a hundred and a hundred. And all the time my pulse stayed fierce, beat beat beat on and on and on, and the light blurred blue bright.

One night, one night when Cyllius and our father and all the others had been away for one hundred and forty-six days, Quiteria took a sharp breath, a breath in when she should have been sleeping. A breath too sharp for sleep.

I was awake, I was always awake. Yes? I said, quiet.

Marina? she said, even though it was obviously me, it was always me, in that bed, by her side.

Yes? I said.

Don't let me be last to fall asleep, she said. Please, she said.

It was too dark to see her. It was too dark to see anything, but I could hear her move, I could hear her reach. I reached too and found her and we matched our breath and I waited

and waited

and waited

until the pulse in her palm was slow,

was normal.

Then I said, to the darkness, to the night,

I miss you, Quiteria.

Her hand still in mine, but not holding on; her hand limp with sleep.

Cyllius came and sat with me in the water whenever the army was home. He came a lot. And when I'd told him everything I knew, every last thing I could remember, he asked me to start over.

Even though you've already heard it all? I asked. Even though I've already said it?

Yes, he said. Even though.

What about your father? I said.

Who knows, he said. Who cares, he said.

I care, I thought, but I didn't say. And when he'd gone and I'd sunk back down, my pulse beat I care, I care, I care under the water.

Instead of talking, then, mostly, before bed, I'd pray. Bring him back bring him back, I'd pray, not sure who to. I'd pray, I care, I care, I care.

⁓

Julia and I were weaving alone, just us two. Julia ran her shuttle through then paused for a second, to look at me, at mine. Then she ran it back again, then looked at me again.

I checked my tension, but it was fine; it seemed fine. I checked my threading, but it was fine. Everything was fine, everything was good, but still, she kept stopping, kept looking. I finished my own row and then I stopped and I looked back at her.

The loom weights knocked each other. Outside, the morning bugs buzzed, steady.

It's good, she said, finally.

Thank you, I said.

It's good, Marina, she said again. She reached out towards my cloth but couldn't quite touch it.

I know, I said.

Marina, she said, when you're good, when someone is really good, she can make more than just cloth. She can make pictures.

Pictures?

Yes. Of animals or plants or people or anything, really.

Like on the water jug with the woman on it? I asked. Or the wine jug, with the dogs?

Better than that, said Julia. She had her shuttle pressed between both her hands like a candle.

Better how?

Realler. More real. If you're really good, you can make a picture with thread that is just a few breaths away from something real. From life.

I threaded wool between my fingers. Then pulled it free. Then threaded it through again. Is it allowed? I asked. To capture something like that? To catch and hold and keep it? Is it safe?

Julia smiled. No, she said. That's just it, Marina. It's not safe. It's powerful, she said.

I looked at the shuttle in my hand. The same as hers. The same as always. Can you do it? I asked. Can you make pictures?

No, said Julia, I can't.

She explained the principles to me, how it should work.

If you know how it works, I said, surely you can do it yourself?

It's not the same, said Julia. Knowing and doing are not the same at all.

I started with a fish. I planned and prepared and worked at it for a week.

Oh, a dog! said Julia.

No, a fish, I said.

It's good, she said.

Its eyes are different sizes, I said. And, looking at it, I don't even think it should have two eyes, at that angle. And the tail is broken, I said.

It's good, said Julia. It's a good start.

And the slaves, Bea and Claudia, nodded.

I did another fish, with only one eye, and it was better.

Then I did a crane with a wobbly neck but a pretty good beak and legs.

Then I did two fish, swimming against a green-grey linen wave.

Then nine small ones, all in a circle, chasing each other's tails, all of them cream-white except one, which was the same blue-bright as the wool they were woven into.

A lot of fish, said Julia.

I was working, head down, on the second-last white one.

They're nice, said Julia, your fish, but maybe next time—

Next time I'm not doing a fish, I said. I'm doing a person.

Good, said Julia.

I'm doing Cyllia, I said.

Oh, said Julia. Oh. She watched me in silence while I finished with the white, switched to the blue thread, ran it through through through through through through, then switched back to the white, then back to the blue. It's just that, maybe someone a bit more, a bit less . . . She was a slave, Marina, you know that.

I'm doing Cyllia, I said, again. I ran the white thread through, switched to black for the eye, then back to white, then to blue again, through, through, through, through.

Okay, said Julia, looking at her own hands.

I did Cyllia the way she was first, stood impossible tall over our stream, smiling, feet half in water. It wasn't big compared to the tapestries Julia had described to me, tapestries that covered entire walls and contained dozens of people, gods, and animals, but it was the biggest thing I'd done, three hands by three hands. It took me weeks and weeks and weeks, during which I didn't eat lunch for fear that some bit of oil, some smear of sauce might make its way from my hands to the thread, during which I counted stitches even as I slept, dreaming in waves of thread and colour and time, during which I saw Quiteria only in the half-light of early mornings and the candle-dark of evening, during which I barely looked up from my loom, I barely saw anyone but Cyllia, Cyllia, Cyllia.

And then I finished.

The army was away, of course, so after that, I waited. I wove other things, basic wool and flax; I ate, even lunch; and I waited, listening always for the sound of men on the road. I prayed, to Abeona, to Mars. I wove, I ate, I slept, I listened, I prayed. The only time I didn't listen was when I was in the fountain, down, under, where I couldn't hear anything but myself. I wove, I ate, I slept, I listened, I prayed, and then, three fat moons later, I heard.

I let my shuttle fall and ran out, with Julia, with everyone, to see them, to meet them. Quiteria was already there, Quiteria was right in front.

The commander led the way, as always, up on his horse with soldiers on either side. Behind him were the rest, the other soldiers and carts and slaves, as always, but the line was shorter, much shorter than usual. The whole group moved slow, ragged, like the goat whose leg had become infected and weeped and withered.

The air was hot, so hot that it hurt my eyes to keep them open, to watch. I closed them, tried to remember Cyllius's face, then opened them again and looked down at the men walking towards us, still too far away to know, to recognize. Julia was on one side of me, Quiteria on the other.

When they finally made it to us, my father got down off his horse, as always, and went to Julia first, as always. He kissed her cheeks; he whispered something. Then, one at a time, he came to us and kissed us on our heads. Marina, I whispered, as he bent to me.

Marina, he whispered back. His eyes were closed. One of them, sewn shut, never opened again.

The soldiers and slaves shuffled past, each face dull with the same grey grit, each face unfamiliar, as the air got hotter and closer and hotter until, finally, third from the end, dipped into the broken lean of another soldier, was Cyllius. I let go of Quiteria's hand and lifted my own to him, but he just walked on, following the slow step of the soldiers in front.

～⁂～

He found me later, in the fountain. He tapped my knee, which was pointed up, out of the water, and I surfaced, gasped.

He smiled, but it didn't look like smiling. He stood crooked, one side crumpled against the other. There was a crust of blood dried along his hairline behind one ear. He saw me look and raised a hand to it, three fingers there, two gone. It's hot, he said. Move over.

We sat in the fountain together, squished side by side, and said nothing. Across the yard one of the dogs was asleep and one of the chickens was sitting on its back, rising up and down with its breath. We watched it.

Then he said, I've got to go to training.

Even though you just got back?

Every day. Especially when we've just got back.

Okay, I said. Of course. But I have something for you. Can I run and get it? Will you stay here? The chicken rose up, the chicken sank down.

Sorry, Marina, he said, looking at the chicken, not me. I don't have time. I'll probably be late already. He was getting up, pulling himself careful, fractured, out of the water.

Okay, I said. That's okay. I'll give it to you later.

Perfect, he said. He leaned over and kissed me on the head, just like my father did. It's nice to be home, he said, and smiled, and just for a second, just one, his smile was real, and a shine like noon sun shot up through my chest and face and down, deep to my belly and down down down. I was sixteen. We were sixteen, then, already.

We normally didn't go out after dinner, at that house. We talked a little, we washed, we talked a little more, and we slept. But that night, I did. I wrapped cloth scraps around my feet and up my legs to protect them from things that bite and held them in place with pins like we'd done back in the village. I waited until the slaves, Claudia and Vernica, left us to go eat their own late dinner, and I slipped out. Quiteria saw and opened her mouth to say something, then changed her mind and nodded. I nodded back and left, out.

Outside was cool. Cooler than it ever was when we were usually out, even in early morning. The land and brush and buildings were dark, were gone, and the sky was filled with the fixed light of stars and the moving light of fireflies, and the air was filled with the rhythm of cicadas and crickets and nightjars. I walked through it like swimming. I held the little tapestry safe under my arm.

The first I saw of the soldiers' camp was the orange glow of their fires. Beyond that were rows and rows of dark triangles: tents, all on top of, all squashing down, the plants that grew when they were away. I stopped and unrolled the tapestry. Checked it again. There were still loose threads at its edges; I should have cut more carefully. I bit off the pieces long enough and then re-rolled it as tight and smooth as I could. The fires shone and, Cyllia under my arm, I walked towards them.

The soldier on guard at the entrance wasn't Cyllius. He wasn't awake either, although still standing.

Hello, I said.

And then, Hello?

And then, HELLO?

He opened his eyes a crack, then started and opened them all the way, straightening up. Quiteria! he said. It's late! Later than usual. A lot later, no? Anyway, no problem, no problem. Just like my being a little bit tired is no problem, right? Like, maybe a problem if I actually fell asleep and wasn't doing my job, but I wouldn't do that, wasn't doing that. So no problem. No problems here, right?

Right? I said.

Right, he said. He inhaled. Exhaled. Good, he said. Thanks. I mean, right. Good.

Right, I said. Do you know where I can find Cy—

Cyllius, of course. He'll be in his tent, I'd think. You know where? Fourth from the end of the second row? Green. He's expecting you? Now?

Yes, I said. I think so.

I guess it's a good time to do your thing, really, he said. Not too hot, right? He stabbed the air like a barbarian, one, two, laughed, then noticed the strange angle of my arm, the bulge under it. What's that? he said. A weapon?

No, I said. No, it's just cloth.

Seems thick for cloth. Something wrapped up in it? Some food . . . ?

Yes, I said. Some food.

Fruit?

Yes.

Figs?

Yes.

Oh, figs. I love figs. I really love them. We don't get that kind of thing here, you know. Not often. Well. He'll be happy about that. You bringing him that. Any of us would be. Right?

Right?

Right. So. Can I have one?

Not right now.

Oh, of course, of course. I'm sorry, I shouldn't even—

But I'll bring you some another time. Next time, okay? These ones are spoken for, but I could bring you some next time.

Yeah?

Sure, yes.

Tenth tent in the first row, red, that's me. Fig deliveries accepted anytime. Just figs. Only figs. If your father, if anyone asks, it's only figs I asked for, I'm looking for. But I would take those. God, I would. Okay?

Okay.

Rufus. That's me. Tenth tent in the first row. Red Rufus.

Okay, Rufus. Red Rufus. Got it. I shifted. Moved the weight of the rolled cloth to my other arm.

Anyway, go on, said Rufus. You don't have to wait here. Go on, Cyllius is probably waiting.

He was beautiful when he said that. He smiled and was beautiful. Yes, probably, I said. Thank you, Rufus.

I went, half ran, away from Red Rufus and the camp entrance, past the fires where the men stopped talking and watched me pass, up onto the worn path between the first and second row of tents, all black, all dark, all the way along to the end, then counted my way back, one, two, three, four tents. Everything smelled of bodies, of men. There were no fireflies here. I squinted. The fourth tent could be green. It was probably green.

Inside there was motion, and the sound of motion, of a body trying to move without making too much noise. I thought of Cyllius's crumpled lean, the careful careful way he pulled himself out of the water, from me. I put my hand carefully against the tent's wall, expecting cool, but it was warm, almost hot.

I shouldn't have spent so long with Rufus at the entrance. I should have taken the grey and gritty wrap off my feet and legs. I should have actually brought figs. I stood there, with my hand on the hot tent, catching the occasional ripple of movement, thinking, I should have, I should have, I should have, until, suddenly, an elbow or knee, hard and round and bodily, knocked my hand through the tent's skin, and without thinking, I pushed back against it, pushed it away.

The movement in the tent stopped.

Then a rustling.

Then a head pushed out through the flap door, looked around in the dark. I squinted, leaned towards it. Cyllius?

Oh! he said. His voice was mostly air, like he'd been running and had only just stopped, like I'd stopped him. He turned and saw me. Oh, he said again. Oh, Quiteria.

Marina, I said.

Oh, he said. Sorry. It's dark and I—

Inside the tent there was still movement. And, now, another voice, a rushed whisper, low and inaudible.

Cyllius pulled his head back into the tent and said something I didn't understand. I could run away, I thought. I should.

Cyllius pushed back out. Sorry, Marina, he said, his voice calmer now, closer to normal. Just give me a minute. I'll be out in a minute.

He disappeared again.

I should have run, but I didn't. I sat down on the dirt path and looked at my dirty feet and waited. I wanted to cry. Quiteria never cried. I always did. The voices of soldiers by the fire mixed with the sound of the crickets, constant, without meaning. I looked at my dirty feet. I didn't cry.

Cyllius came out again, this time all the way, pulling the flaps of the tent closed fully and firmly behind him. Your arms are bare, he said. You'll be eaten by bugs.

I swallowed, my throat thick and dense, clay. So are yours, I said, quiet as Liberata.

Inside the tent the other voice was humming. A song slow and low.

It's probably best if you don't come at night, said Cyllius. I mean, next time. I mean, I'm not sure this is the best place for you to be right now, or for me to be, now, with you.

I'm not sure you can tell me what to do, I said, still quiet. I looked at my feet. The voice in the tent hummed.

Cyllius didn't say anything.

Anyway, I said. I brought you something.

Cyllius reached over and pulled a bit of spiderweb out of my hair. Yeah? he said.

Yeah. I held the roll of cloth out to him, and stood to leave.

He didn't take it. Instead he said, Wait, Marina, wait. Sometimes, he said, when things are difficult, when everyone around you is broken, is falling, sometimes, he said, all you have is who you have, who you're with, sometimes—

In the dark of the night his hair was almost white, like his mother's, a halo.

Cyllius, I said, I—

Who is it? said the tent. Said the voice from the tent. It was low, gentle. Come back?

Cyllius looked away from me, looked towards it and took a step back,

and,

in that space,

I dropped the roll of tapestry where his feet had been, and turned and ran, back down the tents, back past the fire and the soldiers, back past Red Rufus, who stretched out a hand and said, Oh! Oh! Hey! Hey! Rocks and insects underfoot, I ran back past black pointed shapes of stones and bush, back past the gate and the grounds to the fountain, still full, flowing, even at night, always. I closed my eyes and pulled myself up and in.

That's where Basil found me the next morning. That's where she told me about a new God, the God of slaves and scorpions and stupid teenage girls.

And of commanders and kings, she said. Of everything.

Of water? I said.

Of water, she said. Everything, she said.

Of lemons? I said.

Everything, she said. Everything, everything, everything.

So I went with her. I went with her to meet the slaves and the stream and the God.

Julia's slave, Bea, was there, and ours, Claudia, and together they held me like a child and lowered me gentle into the muddy brown stream. They were careful with my head and dipped it under for only a second, not enough, not nearly long enough, so when they pulled me back up again, out, I said,

Put me back, put me back under.

So they did, and I lay there, with rocks bumped up under my back and the water just barely deep enough to flow over me, not pure and clean like the fountain, but murky and full of things, life, with light that swirled and changed, brown-green. They tried to pull me back up again, but I pulled their hands from me, pushed myself away, farther down. I lay there, watching the light, listening to it, for as long as it had things to say to me, and when I came up again the slaves and Basil were all there, watching me, waiting for me, and saying,

Not drowned! All that time, and she's not drowned!

And

Oh!

Oh!

Oh!

And

Miracle!

Miracle!

Miracle!

And

Hallelujah!

Hallelujah!

Oh

Hallelujah

No, no, I said. I laughed. It's just me. It's still me. I held out my arms, hoping Bea and Claudia would lift me, hold me again. Hoping they would help me up, but Claudia was crying and Bea was just staring and saying, Oh, miracle, oh, oh.

No, I said. Really, really, no, no. I turned to Basil, standing with the others, but she was saying it too, Miracle, Hallelujah, Oh, Oh, Oh.

So I didn't go back. Not yet. I went to the fountain alone and watched the underwater light there, waiting for Cyllius to come, waiting to not care that he didn't, alone. I went to Julia and worked on the looms and made things, made tapestries and cloth. I made more fish, I made a grove of trees, I made Julia and she smiled and looked like she was going to cry and said, I'll give it to your father, and I said,

No, don't, it's for you.

And Basil sometimes tried to talk to me about her new God again, to draw me aside in the evenings or in the mornings, but I pretended not to notice, I kept my eyes straight ahead and said, Thank you, and, Goodbye, and Claudia saw, I know, but she only did and said things that looked and seemed normal, like say, Good morning, Marina, and, See you later, Marina, or, See you at the looms, Marina, and, Yes, Marina, of course, yes, yes, yes.

And then, one day, our father, who had been home for almost a week, came to see Julia and me while we were working. He was carrying a large basket that he had to stretch his neck to see over. I couldn't see what was inside, but I could smell wool, freshly dyed and dried. It stank of sheep and piss. One of the slaves went to help him with the load but the commander shook her off and set it down himself.

I've brought you something, he said. He looked at Julia, and then at me. Where are the others? he said.

Julia looked at me, and then away. Tired, she said. They got too hot and it made them tired, so they went to lie down for a while.

The slaves looked at each other, then away.

I didn't know who to look at, so I looked at the giant basket. Yes, I said. They're tired.

Hm, said our father. He looked down, at the basket. Well, he said. I've brought you something. He nodded at one of the slaves, and she went over and lifted off the basket's wooden lid and the smell swelled up and caught my breath and I coughed.

Yellow, I said, when I'd found air again. It's yellow.

We'd never had yellow before. We'd had grey and red and blue and purple and brown, but never yellow.

Yes, said our father. He smiled.

But that's expensive, I said. I'd asked for yellow wool once before, for a picture I wanted to make of a line of nine suns, each one a bit bigger than the last, but Julia had said yellow cost too much and I had to use red instead.

It is expensive, but not too expensive, Quiteria, he said. Not for you and your sisters. Not for this.

It's Marina, said Julia.

Oh, said my father. Of course. Yes, Marina, Marina.

For this? I said. For what?

Is it? asked Julia.

It is, said our father. He smiled again, and the skin around his eyes creased and he was happy; he looked happy.

He left and nobody said anything, nobody moved. Then Bea, finally, stepped away from her place next to Julia, picked up the enormous basket, and brought it over to where we could reach. As she passed me she lowered her head to my ear, just briefly, just barely, and whispered, Veils, Marina. Wedding veils.

⁓

So we wove yellow. Yellow cloth as fine and soft as sun. Two days later, while we wove, Julia stopped humming mid-melody and said,

Your father loves you. He might not be around much, might not seem like he's paying much attention, but he does, he is. To your sisters, to you. He's loving and he's careful and he's paying attention. And he'll find the right boy, the right man, for each of you, the one who will make you happy. And who you will make happy.

I know it, Marina, she said. He will.

She had yellow thread wrapped around and around one hand that she held out in front of her, worked from. She unlooped one round and pulled it taut with the shuttle. She smiled.

I miswove a stitch, got tangled. Yes, I said. Yes, I know that.

I hadn't seen Cyllius since the night in the camp. Since the tent. Him, I said.

What? said Julia.

Nothing, I said. I mean, Yes, I said. I know.

Good, said Julia, and went back to her work.

I untangled my wool, working my way backwards until I was back at the start. Julia started to hum again, the song she'd left off, right from where she'd left it. It was gentle and measured and didn't fit with my new heartbeat at all.

Later, when our day was nearly done, I said,

You know Cyllia, the woman from my tapestry?

Of course, or I did, anyway, said Julia. When she was alive.

What about her son? I asked. The soldier? You've met him?

She unwound a loop. Yeah, she said. Sure. They've been around for a long time, that family, for longer than me, even.

Does my father know him?

Of course, she said. Of course he does.

And does he—

They were barbarians, you know, said Julia.

Her hand's wool was almost all used now, gone into cloth. Your father brought them here himself, she said. The soldier and his mother, when Cyllius was just tiny and the mother was still young, when they were both still wild. Totally wild, then.

She almost lost her way with the wool, almost knotted, but then carefully unwound a step and continued.

They found a home here, she said, once untangled. Found safety and peace, at last. Your father loved them, Marina, because of that, because he had helped them from wild to peace, from out there to here, to home. He still does, I think. The boy, anyway . . .

How long? I asked.

Were they wild? Or how long ago?

No, how long until the weddings? Do you think?

Julia had finished her wool now; she was tying off. Oh, she said. Not too soon, I don't think, because your father will want time to plan. And prepare the house. And all the rest. But not too long either, since we're hardly high society, out here. A few months, maybe. Assuming you like the fiancés and they like you, she said.

And he's really been watching? I said. He really knows?

Cyllius?

No, my father.

Oh, yes, said Julia. He does, he has. He's a good man, Marina, a good father.

Bea looked at her and raised her eyebrows. Assuming we get this cloth done on time, she said.

∼✦∼

I tried to tell Quiteria. I tried to tell her first, our hands both fountain cool, clean.

Yes, I said.

No, she said.

I tried to tell Quiteria at night, whispered in bed before sleep, but just heard her turn over, away.

I tried to tell Quiteria at the fountain, in bed, in the hall, at lunch, in the yard, in the morning, in the high sun, in the dark.

I tried to find Quiteria, I tried to tell her, to ask her.

But when she was there she would nod, maybe smile, sometimes smile, silent, fast, and then be gone again. And when she was gone, she was gone, lost.

∼✦∼

My heartbeat wouldn't calm down. I woke to it and I fought it to sleep. I spent the weeks weaving and weaving and weaving at a frantic new pace, just yellow, no pictures, just yellow.

I wove and I looked for Quiteria. Basil and Liberata were all right, I smiled at them and they smiled at me. I smiled at them and they smiled at me and I wove and looked for Quiteria and when I wasn't weaving or smiling or looking I was under the water, in the fountain, listening to my pulse counting down the days.

And I didn't think about the tent and the voice. Or I did, but when I did, I reminded myself that that was one thing and marriage was another, like the light of a candle and the light of day. I thought of what Julia had said. I thought of yellow.

～⋯～

If there is a water god, a god of everything, who is with everything and everyone, always, and good, wanting to help, wanting the best, like a father, quietly, desperately wanting the best always, like a father, then certainly, they would allow for time like water. For time that can flow back, sometimes, like when the rains are suddenly, unexpectedly, hard. It doesn't happen very often, almost never, but sometimes it does, and the rain comes fast and hard and thick as sand and the rivers, the streams, the water flows back, flows the other way, and at those times, as rare as those times, that god would be there, always there, and would let you ride back, dive in and flow back, unnatural back, summer to spring back, and let you try again. Just that once. Just as rare as a backwards river.

That's what I used to think, I used to believe.

But of course, he doesn't. He wouldn't.

That water god, that father god, he is so quiet, so desperate, because he knows. He knows everything. And because he knows everything, he knows that if he put you back there, back with the same options and the same feelings, the only option would always be the same, and always the one you take, the one you took. He knows that you'd make the same mistake and then beg to go back and then make the same mistake again, over and over and over. Back into a locked room with only one door, and you looking, over and over and over, for a fault in the wall, a crack in the ceiling, some other way out, something, over and over and over, and him watching, heartbroken, quiet, knowing, the whole time. That's what I know, now.

～⋯～

It was a full-sun day.

It was a brilliant bright day when Quiteria found me.

It was a beautiful day, a perfect day, when Quiteria found me, when she, finally, told me her plan. Their plan. My hands were yellow from the wool. I'd begun to worry that my hands would stay that way forever.

It's good, said Julia, whose hands were as yellow as mine. It sets you apart from the others.

It was a full-sun brilliant bright beautiful day when Quiteria found me at the fountain and walked with me down to the dry stream; our feet falling into time together, automatic. Everyone else was going off for naps or for slow indoor work; it was the time we used to escape to secret lives together as kids, and used now to escape to secret lives alone.

Marina, she said. Come with me? Please?

I walked with her across yard-stones shining with heat, out through the back wall window and down, into the scrub, down to where Basil and the slaves had said, Oh, Oh, Oh, except the stream was dry now, again, just a dusty bed of stones on stones.

Basil and Liberata were already there, each sat on a big smooth stone, the heat in the air between us making their faces twist and blur.

I sat with them.

Quiteria stood. Stayed standing, like I knew she would, about to say what I knew she was going to say. My stomach was heavy and hard, was the stone I sat on.

Come with us, she said.

Stay with me, I said.

I can't, she said.

I can't, I said.

But, she said.

But you, I said.

Please, she said. Please? She took a step, took a breath. She waited.

I looked at my feet. I'd pushed them down into the rocks where the water should be; the undersides of the stones were no cooler than the tops, no wetter.

This is it, said Quiteria.

I stayed quiet, looked at my feet. I thought of my father. Who will be the dog boy this time? I thought. Who will tell him his daughters are gone?

You'll break his heart, I said.

Quiteria looked up, almost smiled. I hope so, she said.

Will you come back? I said.

No, said Quiteria.

We'll try, said Basil, far away.

We didn't take hands and we didn't make promises, because no one had died, not really.

Liberata stood, and Basil stood too.

Bring water, I said, and they nodded.

Bring lots and lots and lots of water.

⁓

That night, after everyone else was asleep, Quiteria whispered my name, in the same smaller, quieter voice she'd used just the one other time, before. I was awake; I was always the last one awake, but I pretended to be asleep and not to hear. She waited, then whispered it once more, a bit louder. She waited and I waited. Our sleeping sisters breathed together in long night breaths, in time. I listened, held, and tucked away the sound.

Then Quiteria rolled over, away, and, in time, her breathing joined theirs.

When I woke I found a sword, short and shining and strong, that had been tucked into a pocket of my tunic, and I found my sisters gone and that I was alone.

I

QUITERIA

And so we ran. Again. Better. I led and Basil and Liberata followed, for Real and for Good, this time, through the nights, heading north, we ran.

~✂~

And ran.

~✂~

And ran.

~✂~

And sometimes, together, we three, running, escaping, laughing, sometimes we would catch each other's eyes or brush each other's arms or hands, moving, always moving, and we'd smile and we'd rise up, the brightness of it all would lift us right up, off the ground.

~✂~

Then, in the morning, once the sun was partway high, we'd stop. We'd eat grasshoppers and locusts and wild asparagus and young stonecrop and whatever else we'd find, along with small, measured bits of fig, date, and dried fish we'd taken from the house, and would drink exactly enough and no more water from the flasks and bladders we'd tied close to our bodies.

It's good? I asked Basil. Isn't this good?

It's good, she said, flask to her lips.

Isn't it good? I asked Liberata.

It is, Quiteria, she whispered back. It's good. The sweat on her forehead and neck shone golden in the early sun.

There were nine streams on Cyllius's map, all marked Probably Dry. Of the nine, six were dead dry and one was just wet mud, but two were living, alive. Basil ran down the bank and stuck her whole head in, under. Then Liberata. Then me. From there, underwater, I could see their hair free itself and float, wild. We drank and drank and drank. And then we refilled everything, and washed everything, then drank and drank and drank again, even though we'd cramp, even though we'd need to stop again and again to pee, still, we drank and drank.

But, usually, we had only the water we carried, or what we could squeeze from roots or leaves, and we'd drink just enough, and eat just enough. After that, we'd use sticks or rocks or our own fingers to draw Cyllius's map on the ground, with a pebble marker for where we thought we were just then, not looking at each other, at each other's. If they weren't all the same, exactly the same, we'd rub them out and start again.

The first night, Liberata drew only from where we were forwards, to the river.

You forgot the commander's house, said Basil. And the road and the path and the tree that looks like a person reaching and the pile of stones that are mostly but not all orange. And the village, you forgot the village.

I didn't forget, whispered Liberata. I left them out because we're past them now. We don't need those bits anymore.

I think we do, said Basil. They're important.

They're not.

They are.

They're not.

Basil turned to me. It's important, isn't it? she asked. It's important, right? To keep remembering where we came from? How to get back? She held her drawing stick in her hand like an extra finger.

Liberata's drawing rock was on the ground. She kicked it away. Looked at me.

It's probably important to know as much as we can, I said. About everything.

See? said Basil.

We can't know everything, mumbled Liberata. That's impossible. But she went and got her rock and drew in the rest.

We'd erase the maps with our feet and hands and, as the sun continued to climb, tuck ourselves away, hiding under thick brush or, after checking for snakes and spiders, in the shadowy spaces between big stones or, in Liberata's case, up in the tangled branches of high bushes and trees. Then we'd sleep, together and deep, through the brightest light of day. We'd sleep until the sun started to fall again; then we'd get up, wipe the dry day dust from where it had settled over our eyes, eat and drink just enough, and go, run again.

This was our work now, our job, our everything. Our legs were tired, our legs were strong. We woke in the mornings because they kicked out, restless, ready, knowing it was time to go. Needing to go.

We ran and ran and ran, and, sometimes, we flew.

⁓

We ate the last of the salt fish on the tenth night. Which we thought was fine, because we had lots of dried fruit, plenty still, and could generally catch and find enough other food; Basil even caught a snake, once.

But then, Basil got a cramp in her leg. A bad one, which meant we had to stop and wait and watch while she gasped and kneaded and gasped.

Then I got one too, in my side.

Then Liberata, in her stomach.

Then Basil's cramps spread to her side too, and mine to my stomach and Liberata's to her legs and sides.

Soon we were stopping every few hours to gasp, knead, gasp. Then every few minutes. Then every few steps.

It didn't make sense. We had everything we needed. I had made sure of that, always, was sure of that. It didn't make sense, we were fed and watered and strong and together. But, still, we were gasping, slowing, stopping.

Maybe we should stop? gasped Basil, whispered Liberata.

But we couldn't stop. We had enough food and water if we kept moving. Only if we kept moving. No, I said. We're fine. I'm fine, I said. Follow me. It will pass, keep going, keep moving. It will pass.

We gasped through two days and nights, sleeping in brief pointed scraps between the violence of muscle panic. Gasping, we went on moving wary and delicate, still moving, still going, across the nights, starting, stopping, gasping, going.

Then, on the third night, when the sky was still red with the memory of day, we passed a scraggly grove of trees with a tiny and faraway handful of houses scattered next to it, down in a valley on our right-hand side. Olives. I could feel the smooth roundness of the fruit in my mouth, could taste the bitterness of the skin, the sharpness of the green, the butter of the black, the salt.

The salt.

I stopped walking.

Basil stopped too, looked at me. She was holding her side.

Salt, I said. Stupid, stupid, stupid. Dangerous, childish stupid. Not water, not food. Salt.

Under cover of dark, we followed the tramped earth down to the vats. We knocked them open like the night sky over us; we brought the brine to our lips in cupped hands; we dumped our weapons and filled our pockets with salt-soft fruit, our tunics wet and stinking with them; we felt our cramps release and give way, a grudge forgiven.

Was that stealing? Liberata asked, later, after.

Of course it was stealing, said Basil. The olives belonged to someone else and we took them. That's stealing. That's what stealing means.

The stars were out now and were huge, were everywhere.

It was stealing, I said. But it wasn't bad. It wasn't wrong. We needed the olives more, so it was okay.

How do you know? asked Basil. How do you know we needed them more?

And anyway, I said. We didn't take them all. We left plenty.

Because we couldn't carry any more, said Basil.

Yes, I said. But still.

So we were criminals. Officially. It was uncertain whether running away from our father and his marriage plans was technically illegal, whether we were actually, already, technically criminals, but now, now that we had stolen, we were definitely, technically, criminals. It wasn't hard. It was as easy as stripping the flesh from an olive, as blowing dust off a dry rock.

We kept stealing. We didn't hurt anyone or anything, not yet anyway, and we didn't take more than houses could give, but we did steal, a lot. It was easy; it was so easy.

I waited for my mother to come, in my dreams, to do or say something, but my sleep stretched out clear and blank as breath, and she never did.

So we stole. We ate and drank our fill. We got to dry gorges and ravines and jumped right across, soared right over.

What about us? asked Basil one night, running. She could run and talk better than Liberata or me; she never sounded even a bit out of breath.

What about us? I said, panting.

Liberata didn't say anything, never did while running, but she sped up a little to catch us, to listen.

Were we stolen? asked Basil. And, if so, by who? From who? Did the village steal us from the commander, or did the commander steal us from the village?

I thought for a few strides, found my breath. I'm not sure you can steal people, I said.

Of course you can, said Basil. Especially children, babies.

The earth was soft here, you could feel the gentler plants of the north starting to gain ground underfoot. Well, I said. Both, then, I guess.

Who, then, do you think, she asked, needed us more? Most?

She ran off, ahead, before I had a chance to collect thoughts and breath, before I had a chance to say, We do. We need ourselves. Before I had a chance to say, That's why, Basil, we've stolen ourselves from both, from the village and from the commander, and why, even if we're criminals, it can't be wrong, it can't be bad.

And Liberata padded along beside me, slower, exhausted.

You're doing amazing, I said to her. You're almost there; we're almost there.

How many days has it been? Liberata asked after the sun was up and we'd stopped and were getting ready to sleep. She was unwinding her sandal straps, round and round and round her dirty ankles.

Since we left? I said. I was patting down the space under two spine bushes, considering it for my bed. It would be good, shaded, hidden, so long as I didn't move at all in my sleep.

Yes, she said.

Um, I said.

Twenty-two days, said Basil, lying down between dry tufts of grass, completely hidden.

That's what I thought, said Liberata. Twenty-two days. That means the commander will be getting home soon.

I guess so, I said. Soon or fairly soon.

Bet he'll be pretty mad when he arrives, said Basil's voice from the grass.

Poor Marina, said Liberata.

Bet he sends horses, says Basil. For us, I mean.

We've got to be close to the cave now, I said. Almost there.

I expected a crack like a crack in a wall, tall and thin, up the side of the rock face, but the entrance to the cave wasn't like that at all. It was low, a dug-out half-circle barely up from the ground, like a fox had made it. The same size as if a fox had made it too, tiny. If you looked away and then back again, your eyes would lose it against the night and you'd have to spend half a minute finding it again.

Basil kicked at it with her foot, which almost covered the whole opening. Wow, she said. Small.

I crouched down and put one hand through, in. The air was cooler, already, just that much inside. A scorpion crawled lazily out. We'll eat you, I said to it, but it didn't care, just kept crawling over to the shelter of another, smaller crack.

We don't eat scorpions, said Liberata. We can't.

I know, I said. I was just—

So this is it? said Basil. This is definitely it?

I looked up and along the rock. There was the bit to the right that jutted out like two hands begging; there was the hill to the left covered in ant mounds. This is definitely it, I said.

Are you scared? asked Liberata.

No, I said.

But no one moved.

Okay, then, said Basil. I guess I'll go first. She took the two sacks she was carrying, olives and dried horsemeat, both stolen, and threw them into the darkness. Then she untied the water bladders from around her waist and pushed those through too. Finally, she took off the fruit knife she kept strapped to her ankle and put it between her teeth. She got down on her belly, tilted her head so it would fit, and, down like that, like an animal, an insect, crawled through the hole, in.

Liberata went next, doing just as Basil had done, until, like Basil's, her head then legs then feet disappeared into the black.

I stood alone, looking at the hole, not letting myself look away, lose it. I knew my sisters were there, just a dusty dive away, but from what I could see and hear, they were gone. They were nothing. Crickets whirred. I breathed the open air in big deep drafts, one, two, three.

I crouched down. I closed my eyes.

And I followed.

There was nothing there.

Black is a colour, but there was no colour there, not even black, there was nothing. There was nothing, nothing but me. The only air was the air I breathed, the only motion was the motion I made. Every thing, everything, the whole of the universe was down to me. I was everything, and, so, I was nothing.

And because my air is the only air, I breathe shallower and shallower; and because my eyes are useless, I keep them closed; and because movement is so close to impossible, just pushing my things forward a finger's width, then myself, just a finger, then things, then me, again, and again and again and again and again, with nothing to show, to know, I'm moving at all, because I'm moving almost nothing amounts through nothing, it feels more worthwhile, most worthwhile, just to stop, to stay, to sleep, while my breath shallows and shallows until it's all dried up, gone, like a wave disappearing onto the sand shore; to let the emptiness hold me like a parent.

My mother is holding a baby, me, the baby me, and the baby, me, is sleeping and my mother is rocking it, me, and not smiling, but not upset either, just tired, both her and the baby are tired, really, really, tired.

I'm not even asleep, I say. Why are you here when I'm not even asleep?

But she doesn't respond, doesn't see me, because I can't be two of me at once, can't be the baby me and the me me and I'm surrounded by dark and dark and dark and nothing, because I'm nothing.

Sh, she says, not opening her eyes, rocking herself with the baby, both together, lulled.

But, I say.

Sh, she says. Sh, sh, sh, now, now, now.

I stop. I stopped. I listened. I listened to her. I stopped and it was the same, was nothing; I stopped and listened, just listened. Nothing. My mother. Nothing.

I listened. And I listened. And then, past my mother, past myself, past nothing, at the farthest reach of nothing, there was something, something else. There was the slow scratch and drag of something, something not me, outside of me. There, a still reach through the nothing, was the sound, quiet but constant, like the sound of a lemon seed sprouting, when you listen, when you really listen, there was the sound of Basil, of Liberata, of moving, of my sisters moving forward. I latched on to it, on to that sound, that seed, and followed. Pushed away my mother, myself, and followed my sisters. I kept moving. For hours and hours and hours and hours and hours. Forever and ever and ever.

A world before, a world of light and sun and air, Cyllius had said that he'd heard from another soldier who had heard from another soldier, this one a child, a boy soldier from some other place, a place with boy soldiers small enough to fit, that this cave went on and on like this, narrow and long, on and on and on, a rock snake, on and on, clenched and choked, until, suddenly, it didn't, until, suddenly, it uncoiled, unfolded, opened itself up like a temple, a giant, unexpected, breath-taking temple, with a moon-shaped hole in the roof through which the day could shine.

But he was wrong. It didn't open up like a temple. A temple is just a room, just four walls like anything else. This didn't open up like that. This opened up like being born. Alive, again. The moon and starlight shone down through the hole above us like rain.

We stopped there to eat and drink and rest. Liberata tried to get up to that hole, to get up and see out to what, it seemed, must be the view of the whole world it held. But it was too high, much too high, even for her, and she couldn't get anywhere close.

So we continued. Left the temple, back down, back into the dark, and, as the sun started to rise outside, we made our way on and on until, at last, Basil saw, and reported back to Liberata, who reported back to me, the almost certain sighting of a grain of light, up ahead. I couldn't see it, I couldn't see anything, but I gripped on to the promise of that grain and we moved forward finger by finger by finger as it grew to the size of a lemon, then a lamb, and then freedom.

The running, the stealing, everything was all easy after that, and the days passed fluid and fast, like us, almost there, almost there, free and fast and on the other side of a big stone wall to anyone trying to take us back, to claim us as not our own.

Then, one night when we'd been moving for only a few hours, maybe only two or three, Liberata stopped, one foot on a rosemary root, the other on stone. She caught her breath. We waited. Then she said:
Listen.
Basil and I listened. The smell of rosemary was heavy, everywhere.
Liberata closed her eyes, breathed in, then out. The river, she said. I can hear the river.
Then she ran again, and I, even Basil, had to work to keep up with her.

We came through a clump of resin-scented trees, and there it was. There it had always been. We felt the new cool breeze that blew across the water, and we watched it shine, run. I did it, I let myself think. We three alive, well; we three at the river, I did it.

When Cyllius had told me about the river, before, I had to stretch my imagination into picturing something more than the almost-always-dry stream near the village, something bigger, maybe even twice as big, as deep, as full.
But this river, this river with the smell of deep green all around, wasn't like the stream. Was nothing like it at all.
As children, in the village, we'd had winter storms, sometimes, rarely but sometimes, when, with a change in the air like a god changing their mind, clouds crowded the sun out of the sky and turned it to water, falling greedy over everything, light you could touch, could drink.
But then the god would change their mind again and the storm would end and the sun would return and all the puddles and streams would go dry again within a few days. The earth and sun would drink up the wet, desperate, and all we'd have would be what we'd caught in the pots and basins and bowls we'd rushed out with when the clouds were gathering, and soon enough, we wouldn't even have that anymore, the sky, the earth, the pots, the basins, the bowls, the trees, everything, dry again, for weeks, for months, for years, watching the sky.

This river was more like one of those storms than any stream. Except this water, this storm, wasn't in the sky, it was here, on the ground, with us. And it wasn't here and gone in an hour like the storms either, it flowed, on and on and on, always. This god didn't change their mind. It was constant, it was alive; which meant we were too.

Oh, Cyllius, I whispered too quiet for Basil to hear, too quiet, even, for Liberata. Thank you. Thank you thank you thank you.

I found a space thirty steps up from the bank, a space where the ground was dry underfoot and the trees were generous overhead. I rolled away pebbles and stones. I cut and cleared brush and used what I'd cut and cleared to build a wall, camouflage and shelter. I drew up imaginary lines and borders, places where we could be alone, places where we could be together. The only homes that are really homes are the ones you make yourself. No one can put you in a place and tell you it's home and have it be true. I made that place, that camp. I made my home, finally, finally.

The pine trees that surrounded us on three sides had strong, dense branches like ladders, like blankets. Liberata could climb up and disappear in one motion, one breath.

It's good, right? I said. It's good here?

It's good, she said, and her voice bounced down, amplified by the spread of the needles, loud as day, as any of the rest of us.

We learned to catch and eat raw fish, which the river had as much of as water. And we stole. I stole. There was a village close by, but not too close, and a town a bit farther along, but not too far, and farms and houses dotted all across the surrounding hills. We stole from all of them in rotation, though most from the town, since the town always blamed its problems on itself.

Lemons, said Basil, that first night after I'd set up camp. We were standing with Liberata in the river up to our knees, getting used to the pull of it, the fight, scary and wonderful.

We stole lemons, she said. All along, since we were tiny. We've been stealing all along. Doing this all along.

Exactly, I said. Which means it can't be bad. Can't be wrong, right?

No, she said. Which means it's natural. Human. Which means it can be forgiven, can be okay, I think.

So far, said Liberata, widening her stance a little against the current.

I think, said Basil, always. The water pulled and dragged her tunic, hanging loose. Liberata and I had left ours on the bank, dry.

Always, she said, looking up to the steadily lightening sky.

I was on my way home, once, in the cool of deep night, coming back to camp from a garum factory on the outskirts of town with my pockets full of salt that dripped through the seams a few grains at a time whenever I forgot to step lightly. The factory was always working, day and night, people packing down fish guts; people spreading salt; people filtering out the gold-orange sauce, sun and sea at once, for people like the commander, like Julia, for Marina, now; people potting up the grainy leftover allec for the villages, for everyone else. I stole garum for my sisters whenever I could, but that night I didn't, I hadn't, I had salt, just salt. We had our own fish to preserve. Liberata wanted to try making our own sauce. It was easy to pass as one of the workers; it stank so much that everyone kept their heads down, eyes low, hands busy. I slipped in, slipped out. I did it a lot. I assume everyone at that factory stole too, anyway, to make up for living, day and night, with that stink in their noses, their hair, their skin.

Pockets full, a mile away, I could still smell it. I was lifting a foot carefully, silently, over the low bush that led to the trees that led to our camp, when I saw, there, on the bush, on a little flower that looked white then, in the night, but was actually yellow in the truth of day, there, on that flower, I saw a bee. I stopped. I watched it. It was moving, wasn't dead. It's nothing to see a bee on a flower, yellow or white, in the day, of course, but it wasn't day, and to see a bee, moving, in the middle of the night, was different. Was something, meant something. I looked around, to other flowers, and, yes, yes, yes, they all had bees on them too, bees moving, working, fizz-whispering, busy from one night blossom to the next. A night bee on every flower. Hundreds of them. A bit of salt dripped through my pocket and landed on the back of one, and it sparkle-shone like a grounded star. Bees in the night, this many, and alive, moving, meant something. I ran back to the camp dripping salt, emptied what was left into one of the wood bowls Liberata had carved, then turned around and followed my own sparkling trail of spilled grains back.

When I got to the bees, I chose one and watched it. I watched it land on a flower, whisper-fizz, then alight and move to the next. I watched it do this seven times, and then, when it rose up higher and started to fly farther away, I followed it.

It flew fast, but I ran fast, it flew faster and I ran faster. We ran and flew together over the brush and flowers, the dust and thorn, until we stopped.

In front of us spread a stone wall full of little arched holes, each just big enough for a loaf of bread or a baby. The bee landed on the lip of one of the holes, climbed through it and then into a smaller hole inside, away. As soon as it came in, another came out and flew off. All along the wall bees were flying in and out of the arched holes. All along the wall, inside, bees were humming, singing, making gold, more precious than garum, even, more precious than gold, making honey.

Exactly in the middle of the wall there was a door, person-sized. I pushed on the warm wood of it and it gave way, easy, and let me into a big open courtyard. On one side there were two slaves, asleep, heads resting on arms swollen with stings. On the other side were two big vats, honey vats, with one big dog sleeping at the base of each. Bees crawled on their backs and between their ears. I breathed in, out, and the air was thick, sweet. I breathed and watched. Everything big was asleep, still, and everything small was alive, moving. I breathed and stepped to the right, towards the vats and the dogs, and when the animals smelled me and woke and rose it was together, exactly, like a team, like soldiers.

I know dogs. I've dealt with dogs many times before, in the village. We all have. We all know how to stand our ground, firm, how to look them in the eye and bark, loud, how to be dominant. How to quickly, and effectively, become master.

But I couldn't bark now, not without waking the slaves. And I couldn't run, not without the dogs giving chase, turning hunter.

I could have used my aim. I could have used the sword I had strapped to my wrist, could have got it out fast enough, aimed and thrown it like I'd practised with Cyllius, over and over, could have wounded one dog and distracted the other, aimed and thrown like with Cyllius, like with the cardoon, except these weren't plants. And they weren't people either. They were dogs, just dogs, who hadn't done anything wrong, not yet, maybe not ever.

So I didn't aim, I didn't throw. Instead, I pulled back my sleeve, got my sword, and walked right to the dogs. I reached slowly, gently, over the growl of the one who was missing a fist-sized patch of fur along its left haunch, reached right over him, and used the blade to pry off the top of the vat. Then I plunged my hands, both of them, into the smooth, deep syrup. The dogs growled, watched, but didn't move. They were letting themselves hope, were holding themselves back, just in case. I pulled my hands out and, dropping the sticky knife, I gave them what they wanted, all they'd ever wanted. I held my hands in front of me, one to each dog, and they stood and came, silent, and licked and licked and licked them clean as rings of bees buzzed in lazy circles above their heads.

I took two pots crusted with leftover salt out of my pockets and filled them as the dogs watched. I corked the pots and put them back in my pockets as the dogs watched. I turned around and walked back out of the courtyard, back through the door, back down the hills, back through the trees, and the dogs followed. Back in the camp, in the heavy dark before morning, I washed my hands in the river, put the pots by the salt in what would be shade, later, stepped past sleeping Basil, and curled myself into the shelter of a low pine canopy, my bed, and the dogs followed me, and I let them. We slept there, together, and when we woke, they stayed.

~

One night Basil, the fastest among us, came back from the village to the north with fire. She came along the sand-rock beach of the river with the lit branch held far out in front of her, keeping the sparks from her face and lighting her way. The dogs crouched, hid themselves back under my tree.

And nobody saw you? I asked. Shining all the way?

No, she said. No one. Everyone asleep, as always. And even if they did, it could have been fireflies.

Those would be big fireflies, said Liberata.

You're sure? I said.

Yes, she said. Yes, yes.

Like the virgins in the cities, the virgins our Julia used to talk about when talking about how messy we were and how much neater, cleaner others were, others could be, like those virgins, we kept our fire strong from then on. We tended the fire and the dogs, and the fire and the dogs tended us and we stole and we ate and we stood in the moving river and we washed and we drank and time pushed forward and ran in the current that pushed cool through the cracks between our fingers held down, still, waiting for fish, fish we didn't have to eat raw, anymore.

And waiting for Cyllius. He knew where I was and would come, I knew. Was coming. A month or a year or ten, someday, he would come. I tended the fire and the dogs and my sisters and waited.

It was autumn and there would soon be the possibility of colder nights. We were discussing the best way to steal blankets. It was tricky, since we usually stole things when people were asleep, but people tended to sleep with or near their blankets.

Fleece, maybe, said Liberata. There are looms in town and in big houses; we could use raw fleece, maybe.

Basil made a face. It stinks, she said.

Yes, but probably less than a horse or pig blanket, said Liberata.

Let's get both, I said. We might as well—

I stopped. The dogs had stopped licking each other and were looking upwind, alert.

Might as well what? said Basil.

Sh, I said.

Sh, said Liberata. Then, quieter. What?

I don't know, I whispered back. Something. Do you hear something?

We listened, tried to hear what the dogs smelled.

Just the river, whispered Basil.

And the dogs, whispered Liberata.

And the wind, whispered Basil. Pushing that one creaky tree.

And—whispered Liberata,

And that's when the dogs started to bark and I ran to get weapons, and, just as I was helping Basil get her knife free from her ankle, where it had been, unneeded, ignored, for months, then, just then, the heavy boughs we'd fixed around the camp, our protective wall, were pushed apart, aside, and someone stepped in, walked right in. A person with a long simple braid of hair running down her back like a trail. Liberata screamed. I jumped in front of her.

Sorry, said the person.

It wasn't Cyllius. Not yet. It was a stranger. A barbarian.

Then another person, with eyes almost shut, squinting like we were miles away, stepped in beside the first and said,

Yes, sorry, sorry to interrupt, to startle you, really sorry,

Sorry? said Liberata, poking her head around from behind me with a shield up in front of her face, only her eyes showing.

Yes, sorry, we realize this is pretty rude, said the first. Just barging in like this, I mean.

And scary. We acknowledge that it could be a bit scary also, said the second.

As they spoke, another barbarian, a third, in a tunic that was frayed around every edge and looked like it had once been red but was now just mud, stepped in around to join them.

Sorry, said the braided one, again.

But, well, said the squinter. There it is. We've done it. We've interrupted. It's done now.

And we need your help, said the braided one. Please. We really didn't want to disrupt you, don't want to, but we need help, now, this time.

They weren't carrying any weapons or even protection that I could see. Nothing but themselves. They looked over towards the stones and stump we used as chairs and we looked too and for a beat nothing else happened. Then Basil crossed one of her legs behind the other so her knife was hidden and lifted her hand palm up and said, Do you wanna come in?

They came in. They sat down. They'd spotted us many months before, the first one told us. We saw a ball of fire running across the night, they said, and we knew it wasn't carrying itself.

I looked at Basil. Basil looked at me, then away.

So we followed it, said the second, squinting all the time. And we saw you and saw that you seemed like no trouble to us. And you continued to be no trouble, to not disturb us, so we didn't see any need to disturb you.

Until today, said long braid.

Until today, said squinting eyes.

They stopped at that. The third one, who, up to that point, had been silent, stayed silent.

They looked at us. We looked at them. Basil pushed an old fish skull under a bush with her foot. The river pulled along.

Why? I said, finally.

They needed us because there was something they had to go and do, all of them, all together, something that would take two or three days at least, during which time they needed someone to keep their fire, someone else, one of us, hopefully. And then they'd come back and could return the favour, tend our fire, if we ever needed to go somewhere all at once.

But, whispered Liberata. How do we know you won't tell anyone where we are? For money or something like that? Or food? she added. Or whatever?

What? said the barbarians. Pardon?

I repeated what Liberata had said, louder.

Oh, said long braid. Well, because, if we did, then you could tell them where we are too.

And that would be bad? said Basil. That would be bad for you, people knowing where you are?

That would be bad. That would probably be death. For us, I mean, said the braid. Prison at least, but death most likely. So yeah, pretty bad.

But we don't know where you are, whispered Liberata.

What? said the barbarians. Pardon?

I repeated what Liberata had said.

Oh, said the squinter. We live out of these trees. Follow the goat path up the rise, go left at the spot where the ground cracks like a three-point fork, then up, up, up, until you get to the pox-marked wall of the upper mountain.

Liberata put a hand to her face.

In the stone? asked Basil. That's where you are?

In a little cavern in the stone, yes.

In the dark, I thought. In the terrible dark.

We've got food, said the braid. We've got lots of food you could eat while there. We've got fish.

Fish is good, but how do we know that after splitting us up, maybe letting us eat a bit of fish, you won't just kill us and take our things? I asked.

There was a beat while everyone looked around. We do have things, I added. We have a few things. And our camp is pretty nice too. And we've got dogs.

The dogs, seeing that no one was fighting anyone, had become bored long ago and were lying in a furry pile, licking each other.

We won't do that, the barbarians promised. We won't do anything to hurt or compromise you.

How do we know? I asked.

We won't.

But how?

Because we wouldn't. We couldn't.

How?

There was a beat, silence, the river. Then,

We'll leave something here, with you, in your trust, said the braided barbarian. Something precious.

A jewel? whispered Liberata. Gold?

Honey? I said.

No, said the barbarian with the braid down her back, the one whose name was Sarah. A child.

And the silent barbarian said nothing, just nodded.

They left. They said they'd give us some time to think about it and to discuss it, and that they'd come back the next day. They said it was nice to finally meet their neighbours.

Wow, said Basil, after they'd gone. They looked a lot like us. Didn't they look a lot like us?

But dirtier, I said.

About exactly as dirty, said Basil.

The child sat on one side of the fire and I sat on the other. He was three, they had told us. Old enough to do what he was told and not pee on our things. He was looking at me, through the fire. It makes your face crazy, he said. I like how it makes faces crazy.

Basil and Liberata were gone, at the barbarian camp, watching their fire. Do you eat normal food? I asked the boy.

I eat normal food, he said. I love normal food.

I went to the river, hunted us some fish. The boy was singing when I left,

Strength, praise, and glory,

And all the good things

amen amen amen

Strength, praise, and glory,

And all the good things

amen amen amen

He sang it around and around, while looking at the fire. He was still singing, around and around, when I got back. He managed, even, to keep humming while eating.

Is it good? I asked. Is it okay? I don't know what kind of food you guys eat.

Just normal food, he said. I love it.

He drank river water in big sputtering swallows, almost drowning with each gulp, peed on a little bush, then settled into sleep on Basil's blanket, the dogs curled around him.

—✂—

Bye, he said, two days later, when Basil and Liberata came back. Sarah with the braided hair had come with them to take him, her son, back to their camp with her.

Bye, Quiteria, he said. Those were the funnest days of my life, ever.

—✂—

It was quiet by the fire after he'd gone.

The squinting one didn't come back, said Basil. The other two did, and others with them, new people. But he didn't. The squinting one didn't come back. She raked her fingers through a pile of dry pine needles.

Their tunics were spattered with mud, whispered Liberata. And blood.

Who were the new people? I asked. Where did they come from?

Prisoners, said Liberata. Former prisoners.

Just people, said Basil. Sarah and Sufjian saved them.

Busted them out, said Liberata.

So, said Basil. She threw the needles into the fire, where they hissed and popped and smoked.

So?

So, said Basil. I told them we'd go with them, next time. I told them we'd help. The smoke from the needles swirled up right into her face, but she didn't back away, didn't move.

Are you saying you agreed to help break people out of jail? I said. Like, convicts? Bad guys? Just like that, because some strangers asked you to?

Prisoners, whispered Liberata. Not bad guys.

According to some barbarians, I said. You just took the barbarians' word for it? The blood-spattered barbarians?

They're just people, said Basil. Neighbours.

We know nothing about them, Basil, I said. They could be anything. Anyone. You trust them, knowing nothing about them? Think, Basil, I said. Think. If they want to help the convicts and criminals, it'll be because they're convicts themselves. Criminals. Think about it, Basil.

No, Quiteria, said Basil, you think about it. We stole lemons. Remember? We steal salt, we steal meat, we steal blankets. Honey, garum, olives, figs, fire. *We* run, *we* steal, Quiteria. *We* are the bad guys.

She stopped. Caught her breath, closed her eyes.

As much as they are, anyway, she said, quieter. Probably more.

Liberata stepped closer to her. No, she whispered. To Basil, not me.

If it comes down to choosing sides, Quiteria, said Basil, finishing, taking Liberata's hand, it's pretty clear which side we're already on, you're on. And yes, anyway, yes.

Yes?

Yes, I'd trust my neighbours, she said. Yes.

So we did. So I did.

~

The next time was the town jail. The big town, the big jail. Sarah and the others had been waiting to do that one until they had more bodies, more support, us. We'd have to walk through the night until morning, until the dirt turned to path turned to road and the brush turned to people turned to crowds.

You're sure? whispered Liberata.

Yes, we're sure, said Basil, catching my eye.

Yes, I said.

Liberata stayed at our camp to mind our fire and the silent one stayed at the other camp to mind their fire and their child, while Basil, the barbarian with the braid, and I walked towards town along the fold of the river as the buzzing bugs of night gave way to the buzzing bugs of day.

My name is Sarah, said the barbarian.

I'm Quiteria, I said.

Are you sure you want to do this again, so soon? asked Basil.

It's not so much want to as have to, said Sarah.

And you're not scared? I asked. After last time, after . . .

No, said Sarah. I'm not. I don't want to die, but I'm not afraid to. Because it's not really dying, is it? Not anymore. It's just finishing in one place and starting in another. And that time, when you start, it will be forever, that time it's starting and never finishing, never-ending.

Like a river? I said.

Exactly, said Sarah.

Basil nodded.

So you shouldn't be afraid either, said Sarah. None of us should be.

I'm not, I said. Of course I'm not. I had my shield tied with gut rope to my back under my tunic. I had the warm, familiar handle of a sword in my sleeve, the blade flat against the inside of my wrist. I'm excited, I said.

We moved with the haphazard crowd through the town gates and in, then on towards the centre with the natural flow of people, goats, carts, and flies, and no one paid us any attention, none at all.

There had been stories of prison breaks, of course, stories that had spread across the hills and down the river, curled and spiralled around and around in the whirlpools of villages and towns; there had been stories that had spread, certainly, certainly as far as that town. But those stories involved monsters of men, barbarians huge with muscles and weapons and dogs and, sometimes, lions. They didn't involve skinny girls and weary middle-aged women. They never did, even years later, even dozens, hundreds, of breakouts later. So these people, these guards didn't pay us any attention at all either.

The jail was a hole-in-the-ground type, with the convicts down in a sort of pit with walls too tall and slick to climb, a cheap and, generally, effective design, if you had the space and slave power to dig it. There were two soldiers, two guards. They looked like Cyllius, but they weren't Cyllius. One was outside the door, watching it. He had hair fair as sun-bleached grass, faraway hair. The other one was inside, watching the prisoners, making sure they didn't try to climb out, which they couldn't anyway, and lowering down water in pots or food in bags if any friends or family brought it for them, which, usually, they didn't. That soldier, the inside one, still had the delicate thinness of boyhood in the long pull of his legs and arms, skinny in his uniform; he had hair that was dark and short, hair like our adoptive brothers and sisters, like all the kids in the village. The two men leaned in and out, respectively, towards each other, whispering. They waved away flies with long, open hands. They didn't pay us any attention. They whispered, they waved, they laughed.

They were young and they were beautiful. Not Cyllius, I told myself, and gripped the handle of my sword.

We walked in. Just walked in. Friends of the freaks? asked the door soldier, pulling up straight when he finally saw us, pulling up, away from the door.

Yep, said Sarah.

Bringing food or water or just prayers?

Just prayers, said Sarah.

Ha, typical, he said. Their loss.

Ten minutes, said the inside soldier, leaning out. Tops. Your songs hurt my ears.

I kind of like them, said the door soldier. But yeah, still, ten minutes. Tops.

They both stepped aside and we stepped in, as easy as that. It wouldn't always be easy, but, often, it was. This part at least. Don't attack until you absolutely have to, I knew. Before you attack you're just a person; once your sword is out, you're a problem. Once your sword is out, their swords come out. The skinny boy-guard watched as Basil and I walked over to the hole in the ground. He was probably trying to figure out if we were actually the same, actually twins or not. He didn't seem worried. He watched us for a while and then leaned back out, back towards the door, the other soldier. He didn't notice Sarah as she walked around the other way, behind him; people rarely did, rarely do, notice women like her. She slipped her wooden baton out of one sleeve and a rope out of the other with a tiny flick of her wrists, practised, easy. Then, in a beat, in a breath, she whispered, Go, threw one end of the rope to Basil, and brought her baton down hard on the back of the soldier's head.

The soldier didn't shout; he didn't say anything, just took an abrupt intake of breath and then crumpled, down into Sarah's arms, waiting. She lowered him carefully onto the dark dirt floor and I thought of her child back there, in the camp, of lowering him down to sleep. The soldier didn't utter any sound, but the crack of wood against skull was enough to catch the ear of the door guard, who leaned farther in, and my chest clenched. Not Cyllius. Like Cyllius but not Cyllius. I flicked my own wrist and, sword out, half fell, half ran towards him.

I had him on the ground, under me, before he even blinked.

Basil and Sarah pulled prisoners out with the rope and I held him there, sword to his throat, shield heavy and hard against his chest, both our hearts going heavy, full, fast. He struggled and I pushed the sword slightly farther, down, and he smiled.

Once the prisoners were all up and Basil and Sarah had run with them, out, away into the moving camouflage of the crowd, I counted to thirty, then leaned in over my own sword and kissed the soldier.

Then I drove my full weight into the shield, into his chest, so his air was pushed out, so he gasped against the impact and I jumped and ran, out into the tangle of people, carts, noise, heat.

Basil and Sarah and the prisoners ran one way, and I ran the other. Again, my heart thumped, again, again, again.

Did he die? whispered Liberata, back at the camp. The first soldier, the boy? Did he die when she hit him?

I don't know, I said. We left before he woke up, or didn't.

Off to the side, facing the river, Basil and Sarah and the freed prisoners held hands and whispered songs and prayers.

The prisoners drank and drank and drank from the river, then washed their bodies and clothes, then used our knives and swords to cut their hair, to turn into different people, and then left. I thought they might stay, that they might join us, but they said, Thank you, whispered another short prayer with Basil, and left.

They'll have their own lives, their own people to find again, said Basil.

But surely it's too dangerous, going back? Surely it's not worth it?

It's always worth it, said Basil. For a lot of people, it's always worth it.

We did it again. And again and again. The Christians were saved, the Christians left. The soldiers crumpled, the soldiers smiled; I pressed my sword into their necks and my shield into their chests and the soldiers almost always kissed me back. The ones we'd tricked, beaten, would be replaced, and we'd do it all again with new boys, new men.

Things went like this, went on in days, weeks, months, running like our river, like us, on and on and on, moving and waiting at once, moving and waiting, moving and waiting, waiting, waiting.

One morning after a raid, Sarah and I left the freed prisoners to wash in the river with Basil and walked on to the barbarian camp. I needed to get some herbs they kept for healing and for sleep. My right wrist throbbed, broken and swollen bigger than my hand; Sarah had a dark bloom of blood soaking through her veil at the back of her head. We walked in silence for a while, and morning birdsong filled the space between us. Then, when we were halfway to her camp and halfway from ours, she said, Quiteria, can I ask you something?

The birds quieted down, not afraid of her voice so much as adjusting to it.

Yes, I said. Of course.

She stopped walking and turned to face me, though not quite full on because the sun was rising behind me and was too bright.

Are you . . . flying? she asked. With Basil, when you run? I've seen it, sometimes. I think I've seen it, seen you.

My left hand held my injured wrist and I could feel my heartbeat through it, steady, warm. Yes, I said. We are. Sort of. Just the smallest bit. Sometimes, only sometimes. And Liberata too, I said.

She breathed, in, out, and looked away from me, away from the sun. Then why, she said, do you bother? With the fighting? With running at all? Why don't you just fly the prisoners out, fly away, avoid the fighting, the injury, the damage?

It's not like that, I said. No. We can't. We couldn't. It wouldn't work like that. It doesn't.

Why not? The stain on her veil had dried, was brown-black and, I knew, would never come out, not even with hours and hours of soaking in the river, of scrubbing.

It just doesn't, I said. You can't force it, control it. We can't.

That's a bit pointless, then, isn't it?

Yes, I said. I guess, I guess it is.

And then, one day, Sarah got a slash across her face. We were all cut or bruised, all a bit broken, most of the time. Basil had a black eye and two sprained wrists at the same time, once. I had my ankle completely shattered by the blunt edge of a sword, once, and had scars like the stripes of river fish on my cheek, back, legs, hands. But this slash, this cut, meant that one of Sarah's eyes went forever dark. None of us had had that, anything quite like that, before.

If you close the other one, the good one, does the blackness feel the same, equal in the two? I asked.

No, she said. Not at all. The potential for light is a world apart from no light at all.

Because of that, that slash, that eye, her son, older but still a kid, asked her to stop, now, please, to stop and to take him home. And, even though he was too young to actually remember any other home, even though she had said she wasn't afraid, ever, she said, Yes. She said, Okay. She said goodbye and took him and left. The other one, the quiet one we never saw, was gone then too, lost.

She said she'd stay and fight til the end, I said to Basil after they'd left. I was scraping the more stubborn bits of flesh off a rabbit skin. If I could get them clean enough, which I rarely could, Liberata would make them into toys for the dogs or mittens for us, even though it was never cold enough to actually need mittens. Sarah said she wasn't afraid, that she was never afraid.

You can be not afraid for yourself and still afraid for other people, said Basil. She was slicing rabbit meat into little pieces, skewering the chunks on a blackened, sharpened stick.

Not if she believed, really believed in what she was saying, I said. In a life after life, in that life, that place, being better, safer, being forever. I scraped too hard and made a little rip in the hide. I tried to pull it back together and the rip got bigger. If she believed that, I said, really did, then she wouldn't be afraid at all, ever, for herself or for her kid.

But she was, said Basil. Because she's just a person. A mother.

A disappointment, I said.

Of course, said Basil. Sometimes, of course.

We stayed. And we kept freeing, fighting, and my blood rushed and my heart thumped, again, again, each time, every time, and the prisoners said thank you and thank you and thank you and prayers by the water and left, and with the dogs and my sisters and the river, I was happy, even though some nights, on the rare occasions when we'd sleep at night, when Basil and Liberata and the dogs, even, would all be asleep and it was just me and the dark, even the river gone dark, some nights I'd forget and I'd start to reach a hand out, just start, never farther than that, towards nothing, towards where Marina's bed was, would have been, even though, under it all, always, under the free the fight the river, I was waiting, still waiting, always waiting, though sometimes, a lot of the time, I'd forget for who.

~ⴟ~

And then, one morning after we'd freed them with only a broken toe on one, some torn-out hair on another, and a slashed-up ankle on the third, some prisoners told us that they knew us, that they knew our face. They told us they'd seen us already, our face, in Carthage. That our long-ago-lost sister, Vitoria, was there, and was one of them now. They called her a different name and said that her clothes were cleaner, that she was a bit taller than us, maybe, but that it was her, it was her face, our face.

And she's in trouble, they said, pulling fish off the bone with their teeth.

Everyone is talking about it, they said.

It's very big news, they said.

Well, not her, exactly, but people connected to her, they said. She's not the big news, but she's connected to the big news, at least.

And the big news is trouble? I asked.

Yes, they said, fingers dripping with hot fish oil.

But she's still a child, I wanted to say. But she's not even full grown.

Oh, whispered Liberata.

We need to go, said Basil.

So Basil and Liberata left, to Carthage, to find her, to find and get our now grown, somehow grown sister, maybe save her, and bring her back. I gave them a sword. One of the longer, more serious ones I'd stolen off a soldier knocked cold.

Don't fight without us, whispered Liberata. Don't go to the prisons alone.

I'll be fine, I said. I'm fine fighting alone.

Are you sure? asked Basil.

I always am, I said.

You'll have the prisoners, said Basil. Ask some of the prisoners to help you. To stay and fight with you.

They always go, I said. They'll always go.

Maybe, she said. Maybe eventually, but still, before they do, they might stay for a while, they could stay here, with you.

I won't force them, I said.

Of course, said Basil, of course not. But still. It's good here. There's water. There's food. It's a good place for them.

Do you think it's good?

Of course, she said.

Of course, whispered Liberata, her echo. They were both as thin, as mangy as the dogs.

Come back soon, I said.

We will, said Basil.

We will, whispered Liberata.

And they left.

~

That night the dark wrapped round as heavy as water and my mother was there, lying beside me. She was covered in sleeping children stretched and curled across and into every bit of her. Aren't you cold? she asked, and I could barely hear her because there was a baby's leg over her mouth. You must be so cold.

I'm not, I said. I'm fine.

Freezing, she said. Frozen. Her voice muffled and warm.

I'll be fine, I said, and I pulled a dog in closer, between us, pushed my forehead into its fur. Fine, I said.

⁂

You draw it, then. You do it, I'd said.

This was before we'd left the commander's, back in the rock-yard behind the army camp, when Cyllius was having me draw the map to the river over and over and over again in the dust-dry ground. I'd forgotten a little copse of stone pines just northeast of the trail, the tiniest detail, and he was erasing everything, again, making me start all the way over, again.

You do it, then, I said. You do it with no mistakes, absolutely perfect, every time. You try to do it.

He was down on his hands and knees, rubbing the lines out of the dirt. He stopped and looked up at me. No, Quiteria, he said. He stood and rubbed his hands together, and dust and tiny pebbles fell like dry rain. That's the point, he said. It's there, it's all there, in my head already.

The dirt under his fingernails was the same colour as the dirt under mine.

I don't have to draw your map, he said, because I already know it, Quiteria. Every single detail. By heart. The way you'll go, where you'll be, it's all there, he said. By heart. And I'll never forget. Never. Never, never, never.

⁂

My first morning alone at the camp I walked away into the denser growth, everything green and soft, until, on the dark side of a fallen tree, I found two small mottle-brown mushrooms. I picked them and brought them back to camp. There, careful not to touch my face, I crumbled them into pieces and stirred these into the last of my honey, in my smallest pot, until they were invisible, gone. Then I washed my hands in the river, built up the fire in the mud stove with just enough stones, not so few that it wouldn't keep, not so many that it would smother, and walked alone for two hours to one of the smaller, nearer towns.

It was still early, but the streets were full. The streets were always full. It was hot with bodies before it was hot with sun. I moved, ignored, through them, to a small jail, a holding pen for the bigger ones, really, where I knew there would be only one guard, where there was usually only one, anyway.

He was new but old. Maybe the father or grandfather of the actual soldier who should have been there but had overslept. The armour pressed into the ample flesh of his upper arms and belly. He looked miserable until he saw me, anxious after.

Oh, he said. No. No, no, see, I'm not supposed to let anyone in, no visitors. You can visit him later, in a couple of days, when there's room at the main one in the city and they move him there. You'll have to wait until then. You have to.

I waved my hand casually and felt the sword pull under my sleeve. Oh, no, I said. I'm not here to visit. Visit him? No, I don't think so. No way. I'm here to visit you, I said. Of course.

Oh, said the old soldier. Oh? He stood up straighter at the same time as looking at me a bit more closely: my torn, stained tunic, face a bit bruised, beat up, hair in no particular order, but still, a girl. Something.

I'm nothing special, I said. I mean, I'm just a peasant girl from the farms, so I know it doesn't mean much, but I wanted to come and see you. To say thank you.

Thank you? he said.

For what you do, I said. Keeping us all safe. Keeping me safe. I touched my face where a sword had caught it a few weeks ago.

He stepped back, then forwards. Did they? he asked. Did the Christians . . . ?

Yes, I said. I lowered my eyes.

And . . . he said. He stepped forward again, just a tiny bit. I could reach him now. I could slip the sword down into my hand, easy, and reach him, easy. But I didn't. Instead I just breathed deep, raised my shoulders, and then let them slump.

So, I said, anyway, that's why I wanted to drop by. To say thanks and, oh. I fumbled in my pocket and brought out the pot, the honey, To give you this, I said. To say thanks.

For me? he said.

Yep, I said. Of course.

It's honey, I said, even though he'd already unstopped it, could already see, already smell for himself.

He looked from the pot to me and back again. Oh! he said. I never. I mean, they never give us . . . Oh, thank you, he said. Thank you. Then he caught himself. Oh, he said, again. Do you want to? I mean, we could both . . .

It's for you, I said. From my father's bees. Just for you. But I can come back, maybe, in an hour or so to collect the pot. If you don't mind.

I don't mind, he said. I'd like that. I'd like that a lot, actually. He smiled, finally, for the first time. What's your name? he asked. Who's your husband?

My name is Julia, I said. And I don't have a husband.

I walked around town being nobody, being everybody. The hot hard stone paving hurt my feet. The river, I promised myself. After this was finished, I could stand as long as I wanted in the river. I watched women on slave-hoisted litters going into the baths, I watched women on slave-hoisted litters coming out of the baths. The river, I promised. I watched two slaves wait until their charge was gone, disappeared into the steam, who then sat down immediately and started comparing the indentations and bruises on their hands and shoulders in a language I didn't know. I watched a child all decked out in her engagement jewellery trying and failing to keep up with two other children between and around columns white and straight and unmoving as dead trees. I watched and waited and walked and then, when the sun had moved high enough in the sky that people were starting to divert their paths, seek out shade, I circled back to the jail, to the soft soldier. He was sitting down, leaning against the wall of the building. He was smiling and crying at the same time.

Hello, I said. Maybe you should stand up?

He looked up at me, then kept looking up, higher and higher, neck stretched like a turtle reaching for food. I never knew, he whispered, that you were a goddess. He whisper-laughed, little puffs of air out his nose. I should have known! he said. Just look. Look at you!

He wasn't looking at me; he was looking far, far above my head.

Demigoddess, I said. But yes, exactly.

Yes, he whispered. Exactly.

I think you should stand up, I said. People will notice. People will be concerned.

Oh! he whispered. Of course! Oh, geez! It's disrespectful, isn't it? Sitting at the feet of a goddess! He tried to stand up on his own but had too many legs, too many feet, so I had to help him, half lift him.

There, I said. Okay, I'm going in now.

Okay, he whispered, crying.

There was just one prisoner inside. I took the key from where the guard had dropped it, in the middle of the floor, unlocked his shackles, and walked out with him, right passed the guard, who was, at that point, lying on the ground. Noble goddess, he said.

Demigoddess, I said. And you should stand up.

Okay, he said, but didn't move.

Bye, I said.

Bye, he said.

The prisoner and I walked, casually, down the street and around the corner, and then ran all the way out of town, down the road, to the path, into the scrub, into the trees, to the river.

We stood in it together, the water beautifully, warmingly cold. Are you a Christian, a barbarian, a criminal, or some combination? I asked.

The prisoner wiggled his toes in the water, slowly nodded.

I've got weapons, I said. And poisons. And I know how to use all of them, okay? I'm not stupid, weak, or slow, okay?

He nodded again, wiggled again.

I need you to stay, I said. I need you to help me, stay with me, okay? Even if only for a few days, a week, I need you to stay.

His language, his home, was far away from there, from me, but he nodded. He stayed. He fought.

Until he left. But by then, we'd freed others, found others who them-selves stayed and fought and found others, freed others who stayed and left and stayed and left and stayed and left, swords in sleeves by my side in the towns, bodies warm and close in the camp, singing, praying, eating, drinking, pulling close in the night, sometimes to each other, sometimes to me.

Some stayed for weeks, some months, some just days. One stayed, one boy, for one year, five months, and six days. His hands were just the same size as mine, but softer, years softer. When our fingers folded together it was like two versions of my hand, one that could have been and one that was.

You could, he said, you could come. Come home with me.

No, I said, his skin silk on mine. I can't. I have to watch. I have to wait.

Not long after that, not too long, a group of freed Christians who had been with me for two weeks went up the water to look for river mussels. They were the only other ones with me then. See you soon, they said.

Okay, I said, see you soon.

They left and never came back, and I was alone, again.

I'd wait a few days, I told myself. A few days to nurse the dog whose eye was infected and weeping all over its face and anything it touched, and to gather up what I needed, new supplies and plans, and then, at one of the smaller jails, one of the private ones, maybe, at the back of a villa, one of the ones for uncooperative slaves, somewhere small like that, somewhere manageable, I'd try another solo venture. I'd done it before and I could do it again. In a couple of days. I was alone, I was tired. I just needed a couple of days.

And then I got sick. Like Gema and Germana and Liberata had been sick before. The prisoners were gone, the boy was gone, Liberata was gone, Basil was gone, Marina and Cyllius were gone, gone, and I was alone, and the tiredness grew and the dark crept in, crept back again, and I lay down and closed my eyes and there was my mother.

Winter babies always grow up saddest, she said, heavily pregnant, stirring water into porridge more chaff than grain a tiny bit at a time, not too much, not too much.

Like you? I said, standing near despite the heat of the fire, hoping for a splatter or drop I could lick up.

Yes, she said. And like you. A tiny bit more water in, not too much.

Aren't we more spring, really? I said. Early spring?

Hm. You could argue that, I guess, she said. I guess we'll see, she said, pulling the flask back, cap back on, not one drip, splatter, or splash.

I got sick and lay, interrupted, in thick dreams of mothers stirring and sisters with lemon crowns. Never, said Cyllius. Never, never, never, never.

I lay, in between home and away, waiting.

5

LIBERATA

When you're sick you can talk quietly. I don't want you to get sick, but if you do then try it, you'll see. When you're very sick, you can talk very quietly, as quietly as you want, because then, finally, people listen to you. They stop whatever else they're doing or thinking about and lean in and listen, really listen.

When I was sick and getting hotter and hotter and hotter, Basil, the sister who lived with me, ran to the stream and back, to the stream and back, bringing me cup after cup after cup of murky water. Still, I got hotter and hotter and hotter, night after night after night, until my skin, my face, bubbled and boiled and broke and I almost died, almost, almost, but then didn't. Just because. Because of the dream I had of the sun saying, Sh. Of the fish, cool and silver and coiled. Because sometimes you die and sometimes you don't.

I got better. My face didn't. My mother, Basil's and mine, suggested making a mask for me, out of an extra bit of cloth, but there never was an extra bit of cloth, so there never was a mask.

I spent a lot of time in trees, up high as much as possible. From up high you can see everything, and nothing can see you.

I looked out from trees in the village orchard, where the hunger made us brittle and bold. I looked out from the tree at our childhood camp, where the thirst made us stunned and slow. I looked out from the taller, stronger trees that gave shade to the commander's yard, where the ease made us fat, made us forget.

I looked out from the strange new trees of everywhere, everywhere we ran after that, when we ran once we ran. So many, many different trees, trees with sap that stuck fingers together, trees with perfume that made my head spin, trees with fruit that made a bird fat and a person sick for three days. I climbed up and looked out from them all, and years passed like blossoms, like birds overhead, up too high to reach, too high to catch more of than a fuzzy, passing blur.

And then I was grown, almost, adult, almost. Even though it didn't make sense, I'd survived, quietly grown strong, and was looking out from the tall pines of the riverside home Quiteria made for us. We had food, tied into sacs and hidden up with me in the top branches, and we had water, flowing fuller and faster, almost, than Basil. And we had weapons, real ones, from real soldiers, some gifts, some stolen. Same-same, said Quiteria.

We didn't have Marina. She stayed with the commander, with the idea of marriage. The day before we left she sat beside me at the looms, the last time I sat at a loom, felt the soft-rough spin of the wool.

You could stay, she said. You could stay with me. I could ask our father if instead of marrying you off, he would just let you come with me. Come live with me. It would save him a lot of money. It would make sense, be easy. You could, she said.

I promised Basil, I whispered.

And Quiteria? she said.

And Quiteria. I can't stay, Marina. I'm sorry, I whispered.

I had one small knife I used for food, for gutting and cutting birds and squirrels, and one rusty hand axe I used for firewood, cutting, splitting. I never went with Basil and Quiteria and the Christians on their raids.

I was afraid. Afraid of the blood and the pain and my own weak body. Afraid that if I went and something happened, something bad, if I hurt someone, killed someone, even, maybe, that I would fall down, that that would be that, and I would never float or fly again.

So I stayed in, stayed up. They fought and I waited, watched, whispered prayers through the branches for them to come home, for no one to have hurt anyone.

I was up in one of those night-green needle trees when the dogs, who had been asleep, were usually asleep, woke and stood, ready. They smelled Quiteria, whom they loved more than anyone because she loved them more than anyone, and were preparing to meet and greet her and lick down her wounds as necessary. I squinted until I saw the swords my sisters carried shining like grounded stars, until I could recognize my sisters carrying them, coming home. There were three other figures too, walking just behind. Freed prisoners. There were more all the time. Quiteria had a strict policy. One day and one night here, with us, then they had to go. The prisoners could go wherever they wanted, towards or away from where they came, towards or away from each other, just could not stay with us anymore. We'd give them each a flank of salt-dried rabbit and send them on their way. I tallied in my head: food, dressing, space. We should have enough for three today. But not three every day. We would have to tell Basil, again.

Usually eating was the first thing everybody did once they got back to the camp, the fighters hungry from all the running and fighting and the prisoners hungry from having been prisoners, but not this time. This time the first thing they did, Basil did, was shout in the direction of the trees, where she knew I was, though she couldn't see me. She shouted up,

Liberata! Liberata!

She shouted at the wrong tree.

They found her! she shouted. Liberata! Liberata!

Who? I whispered, and the needles magnified and carried my voice down and everyone, including the prisoners, turned around, away from the wrong tree, and looked up again, towards the right one.

Vitoria! shouted Basil. Our sister!

Vitoria, I repeated, too quiet even for the needles to hear; my lips just making the shape. Our sister.

Come down! shouted Basil. So we can talk without shouting!

And so we can eat! shouted a prisoner, a woman.

The other prisoners nodded. Two men. Quiteria nodded too.

Okay, I said, and came down.

We sat by the fire eating fish like we almost always did, which was boring but definitely better than locust or lizard. The sun had set and the night air wrapped cool around us, damp, heavy with nightbird song.

She looked just like you, said the young man prisoner, to no one in particular, to all of us.

The woman prisoner nodded.

They're chasing us down, said the older man prisoner. Hunting us all down, even the important ones like your sister. Stamping us out like rats. They'll get to her soon, if they haven't already.

The woman nodded. Like rats, she said, mouth full.

How long do you think we have? asked Basil.

No idea, said the old man. Then he spat a fish bone into the fire.

Not long, said the woman. Not long at all, I'd say.

The young man nodded. Thoughtful. He hadn't eaten anything, just drunk five cups of river water, one after the other after the other, as soon as they'd gotten into camp.

And you're sure it was her? One of us?

Mostly sure, said the man. Pretty sure.

The young man nodded.

Absolutely sure, said the woman. She'd cut off all her hair, or had it cut off for her, and what remained stood thick and spiky off the top of her head, as if she was always surprised, always caught off guard. I remember a face, she said. Yes, she said. I'm sure. Absolutely.

Carthage? said Quiteria.

The woman pointed off, away, east, south. Carthage, she said.

Carthage. The word stretched out in my mind, filled the whole thing. A word, a place, so big it could fit hundreds and hundreds of people inside. Thousands. More people than water in the river. And if it had that many people, it would have many, many different kinds of people. Every kind of person. No one would look different because everyone would be different. Everyone would be the same in the bursting river of different.

I'll go, I said.

Quiteria turned away from the prisoners, over to me and Basil on the other side of the smoke.

No, she said. No, Basil should go, of course. She's quickest. I think Basil should go.

Basil looked at me, next to her; looked over to Quiteria, smudged and blurred by smoke. We should both go, she said. Two is safer than one.

And slower, said Quiteria. She was missing teeth in two new places, her mouth was all swollen on one side.

But safer, said Basil. We two can go and get Vitoria, and you can stay and keep freeing prisoners, get help from the prisoners until we get back. Until we're all back.

And then we'll all meet back here? said Quiteria. Then you'll bring Vitoria and we'll meet back here?

Yes, said Basil. Exactly.

And if not, if something happens, then Carthage, I said, quietly. Go there, look there.

Yes, said Basil. Exactly. But it won't. We'll take swords and water and we'll be okay, and we'll both be back here within the year.

Not both, all three, said Quiteria.

Yes, said Basil. Exactly.

Yes? Quiteria.

Yes, said Basil.

Yes, I whispered.

And the prisoners and dogs chewed little bones and watched us, quiet.

—⁂—

Quiteria swapped knives with me, gave me her sharper, better one. But I don't know how to use it, I said. Not really.

Exactly, she said. That's why you need it.

We'll see you soon, said Basil.

And Quiteria repeated it back, We'll see you soon.

Who will watch out for you? I whispered. If I'm not here? Who will take care of you?

And Quiteria smiled, and even with her face bruised and big, she looked lovely, like she always did when she smiled. I will, she whispered back. I've been taking care of all of you for seventeen years, I can take care of just myself. I will. I promise.

We were seventeen years old.

We took plenty of water. We left.

~⚬~

We stole horses to ride, something Basil and Quiteria did all the time; something I'd never done.

But, I said, I don't know what to do. How to control an animal like that.

You're not controlling it, said Basil. You're talking to it.

With your legs?

Yes. As easy as talking.

Talking isn't easy. Not always.

You haven't tried this kind. Maybe you should.

Maybe.

So we stole two horses, and I learned to ride, and, as long as I remembered to listen as well as talk with my legs, my body, it was easy.

We rode the way the Christians had pointed us, east and south, sleeping across the heat-stretched days and riding across dark-full nights that pulled on and on and on, overwhelmingly empty. Sometimes Basil sang or prayed, but mostly we rode quietly, becoming experts on the tiredness of a horse based on the feel of its breathing, on the tiredness of each other based on the shape of our silence. We rode towards the sea.

~⚬~

We were in between when he came. Not here or there, not camp or Carthage, in between. Basil and the horses were all having running dreams, asleep, and I was up above, in the moving shade of an umbrella pine's top branches, the sun hitting my face in thin flashes through the branches.

There was only me and the tree and the sun and the dreams and the tree and the sun and the dreams and me, just me, until there was a flash that wasn't soft sun through tree. There was a flash of new light that sliced across my face, sudden, acute, harsh.

No, I whispered. Go. Go away. Whatever it was, whoever. No, I whispered. Not yet.

I looked to Basil first, but she was fine, asleep. Then I looked to the horses and they were the same too, fine. Then another flash cut across and I closed my eyes for a second, just one.

And then I opened them, turned away from Basil and the animals, and looked towards it.

And there he was. A soldier, a man. Walking with a shining, flashing sword out before him, a man who was walking towards us.

If I killed I'd fall down, I knew. I wouldn't fly again. But if I lost Basil, let her be lost, falling down wouldn't matter. Flying wouldn't matter. Nothing would matter, ever again. There weren't enough leather strips in the empire, not in the whole world.

I reached up my sleeve and freed the knife strapped there, Quiteria's knife. I stayed still, frozen, waiting for the man to come close, come to me, and then, when he was close enough, I let myself go, dropped down onto the ground behind him, reached up, and put the knife, Quiteria's knife, to his throat.

Go away, I whispered. There's nothing for you here.

He inhaled, sharp, fast, and with one hand, just one, thrust up, flicked my knife away, and twisted me around by the arm so I was in front of him. No, he said. I'm not—

Then he stopped and looked at me. Looked at my face.

I'll kill you, I whispered. Even though my knife was on the ground and he was holding me. Stop looking, stop staring, I whispered. I'll kill you.

He looked down. I'm not, he said. Then he looked up again. You're, he said, you're—

I got better, I said. I'm not sick anymore. I'm not, I'm not contagious.

No, he said. No, I mean.

I'm not, I said.

No, Liberata, he said. It's you. You're Liberata. You're Quiteria's sister.

I blinked.

He blinked. Aren't you? he said.

Yes, I said.

He let go of my arm. Put his sword away, in his belt. He put his hands over his eyes and rubbed them like he was waking up, or like he'd been crying. Is she here? he asked.

Quiteria?

Yes, Quiteria.

No, I said. She's far away, miles and miles and miles.

You're—

I'm sure, I said, rubbing my wrist where he'd been holding it. Are you her coach, from before? Out by the big stones? Her fighting teacher?

I'm her friend, he said. I'm Cyllius.

He was in the army, our father's. But he was also a Christian, he told me. Even though those things didn't go together, of course. Couldn't. There were a few of them, just a few, and they hid it well. They had secret symbols. And using those symbols, they would hear things, sometimes, about others they could help wherever they happened to be stationed. Others living out in hills and caves, or pilgriming through. There are lots of little camps, lots of hidden people, he said. We slip away from camp when we can, bring them bits of food and wine. Weapons sometimes, when we can get away with it, whatever we can. And they tell us things, he said. Stories where we might find more people to help, who might be hiding or passing through, where, when. And, he said, that's how I heard.

You heard?

I heard two sisters were coming. Two Christian sisters, wild sisters who look just the same, almost exactly the same, who might be here just when we would be here and who might need help, and I thought, Maybe, maybe . . . His hands were still up, he was holding them just in front of his throat. He was missing two fingers, I saw, two from the same hand.

I've been out here every morning since we arrived, he said. I've been looking and looking, Liberata, every day, whenever I can slip away, slip out. Every day.

He finally let his hands drop, then walked over to where my knife had landed, picked it up, walked back, and handed it to me.

This is yours, he said. Here, sorry.

It's not, I said. It's hers.

Quiteria's?

Yes, I said. Quiteria's.

But you said she's not here. Is she, Liberata? He looked at me and his eyes were the sky. You're sure? he said. That you're here alone?

Fifteen paces behind us, under a bush more thorn than green, Basil slept.

She's not here, I said. I'm sure. I'm alone.

His good hand held his bad one, covered it. We move on the day after tomorrow, he said. North, east, away. The commander hasn't stopped looking for you, he said. I don't think he'll ever stop.

Our father? I said.

The commander, he said. He has us always moving, always looking, back and forth, round and round. Again and again and again.

She's not here, I said. And I'm not here either. None of us, nobody is here.

Cyllius let his hands go. And me, he said, I'm not here either, right? Nobody was.

Exactly, I whispered. Nobody saw anybody.

Something, some kind of bird, flew across the sky and we both watched it.

I almost forgot, said Cyllius. He reached up and untied a bit of cloth he had around his shoulders. Bundled inside was a small loaf of bread, a child-sized pot of wine, and a coin with a fish on it. These are for you, anyway, he said.

I bundled everything back up and tied the cloth around myself. Thank you, I said.

Is Quiteria by the river, Liberata? he said. Still?

I can't, I said.

He adjusted his sword. Okay, he said. I know.

The place on his tunic where the sword rubbed was thin, was lighter-coloured than the rest.

Would you tell her, though, when you see her, he said, that you saw me? That I was here, actually here? That, that I'm on her side, still? On your side?

Okay, I said. I still had the knife in my hand.

They'll notice I'm gone soon, he said. I have to go.

Okay, I said.

He leaned forward like he might kiss or embrace me, but then leaned back again. Goodbye, Liberata, he said. Thank you.

Goodbye, I said.

He walked five paces, then turned around.

Liberata, he called back, God is love. You know that, right?

Sure, I mouthed. Goodbye.

Goodbye, he said, then straightened up, back into his full height, back rigid, and walked away in the direction he'd come.

I climbed back up into the tree. When Basil woke I would give her the coin, she would like it. I would tell her I found it hung in the tree, bundled in the cloth with the bread and wine. I would tell her that was all I found, that they were all just there, alone.

We rode and rode and rode.

And then, eventually, we came to the sea, water forever. And ever and ever and ever. We stood knee-deep, the hems of our tunics floating up and pulling back with it. Basil watched me. Taste the water, she said.

I made my hand round, cupped water, drank. Then I threw up.

Salt, I gasped.

Salt! she laughed. And water, together! All this water, and none of it to drink, not a drop! She laughed again and turned to face out towards the moving, living, salt-poisoned sea. She closed her eyes and prayed.

I knelt down so the water came up almost to my chin, and let the swell push-pull me, almost knocking me down each time, almost pulling me under, but not quite.

At the bottom of Carthage city, down, level with the sea, there was a circle, a giant circular military port full of men and ships and weapons of war. At the top, up a long bright slope of tall trees and honeyed buildings, was another circle, the Vestal temple. We climbed away from the port, up and up and up. We walked passed the guards and in and up, and like everyone else, we gave up a bit of being ourselves and, in return, became part of it, became the city, where the streets were cramped and full and noise flooded everything like sun.

We made it. I made it, I said, and Basil didn't hear, didn't even notice.

The next morning we wore white, the white cloaks and shawls and veils that Sossia and Maxima, two of the Vestals, had given us. And even though our tunics underneath were the same grimy grey-brown as ever, and even though we had weapons in them, tucked away, we looked Good. Like we could, actually, Be Good. Passably pure.

What happens if they catch you pretending to be a Vestal when you're not actually a Vestal? I whispered as we made our way through streets hot with people, animals, flies, noise. They parted before us like weeds for water, so it was a bit quieter and Basil could hear me.

They kill you, she said.

Oh, I said.

Hot lead down the throat, probably, said Basil.

Oh, I said.

But they can't kill an actual Vestal, said Basil, so Sossia and Maxima wouldn't get that for lending us clothes and doing our hair.

A cow was in the road in front of us. Its owner, frazzled and embarrassed, was trying to pull it out of the way, saying, COME, to the animal, then, Sorry sorry to us, then, COME ON, then, Sorry sorry sorry.

What they'd do to them, instead, continued Basil, is bury them alive. Which doesn't count as killing them, even though they'd die, definitely, eventually, from starvation or suffocation. It would just be indirect. And take longer. And be . . . darker.

Oh, I said.

The cow took a step backwards. The owner looked like he was going to cry.

Just remember to walk calmly and confidently, whispered Basil. Just remember we're visiting for the festival, the games. We're visiting from across the water.

Well, we are, I said. That's true. That's good.

Exactly, said Basil.

The owner gave up and let the cow go the way it wanted, backwards. He followed it saying, Sorry, sorry, sorry, and we walked on. This was Carthage, and it was beautiful.

Do you think we'll recognize her? I asked Basil, after the cow and its man had faded back into the crowd. So many years later?

We're identical, Basil said. All of us.

You are, I said. Not me.

Yes, you too, said Basil. We'll recognize her and she'll recognize us, she said, quietly, firmly.

How do you know?

I prayed.

And that means you know?

Yes. And it means she knows too. She will know.

A man selling rows and rows of little pots of oil held one out towards us, a gift, an offering. Basil waved him away.

I'm excited, she said. Are you excited?

We walked through the beautiful awesome chaos down towards the centre, the prison.

Yes, I said. Which was true, though I wasn't exactly sure about what.

─≈─

I tried to make Felicitas comfortable, said the soldier. We tried.

Two prisoners huddled in the corner of the cell where the door-light fell. Men. They watched us, eyes wide. I'm sorry, said the soldier. He looked up at me, my face, then away, back down to his hands. His sword was off, leaning against the wall, too far to reach. My weapons hung heavy against my chest and hips. I couldn't see our sister; the soldier must have been between us and her. Sorry, he said again, quieter.

I looked over to Basil, tried to catch her eye, but she looked straight ahead, straight at the soldier.

Thank you, I whispered. I'm sure you've done your best. It's not your fault.

Even though it was, said Basil's expression, her clenched hand. Even though men like this man were exactly whose fault it was.

You're here to collect her, I guess? said the soldier.

I tried to catch Basil's eye again. Nothing, straight ahead.

Yes, I said.

The soldier looked tired. Thank goodness, he said. I have no idea what to do with a baby. That's never happened before.

Basil broke, let her gaze shoot over to me, then away again, straight ahead.

Yes, I said. Of course.

Yes, she said.

Of course, said the soldier, more to himself than us.

He stepped aside, and there she was, our sister, just like us, just like always, curled, still, on the floor. Dark all around her. No straw, no mattress, just the hot hard dirt.

And on the floor beside her, naked and pressed into her side like a dog, was a baby.

New, tiny. A held breath of a baby.

There was a girl behind them, pregnant and young, very young, with her hands on Vitoria's side and head, protective, possessive. She was as still and open-eyed as the men in the corner.

She's had milk, said the girl. The baby has had milk.

But I didn't have anything to wrap it in, said the soldier, who, even though he didn't fit the picture, even though he shouldn't be, was still there. I'm sorry, he said. Her own clothes were too stained, too wet, and all my things too rough, too—

He took a step away from us, like he was afraid. I'm sorry, he said. You'll get the baby clean, I know. You'll get her somewhere clean and safe, I know.

Basil nodded.

The dark around Vitoria was blood. Blood and other body wet, other life wet, leaked from our sister and the baby. I'd seen it before, when Quiteria's mother died with the upside-down baby who wouldn't come, all of us running, bringing muddy silty water in, from the stream to the fire to the house, taking bloody things out, from the house to the stream to the sun, keeping the other babies away, out in the shade of the trees, out with the men. And when our neighbour died, on her first, as small as the baby, almost. And Quiteria's adoptive sister, alone in the orchard. And the woman who brought the sheep to be shorn every spring. And again, and again and again, women and water in, men and blood out, again. Dark spreading pools, again.

The cell door was open, the bar lifted. There was nothing keeping us out, or them in. Still, no one moved. For a heartbeat, no one moved.

Then Basil inhaled and stepped forward. She went to our sister, and I went to the child. I lifted it and it weighed nothing.

She's dead, isn't she? said Basil.

And the baby opened her eyes and looked up towards the voice, at her, at me, alive. I took off my veil and wrapped the child up and the white cloth bled red, bled pink, and she kicked her legs into my chest and opened her mouth and cried and the sound filled the stone circle of the jail, filled our ears, filled everything, alive, alive, alive.

Vitoria, our sister, was dead. She didn't move when we took the baby from her, didn't move when she screamed. One hand holding the child, I put my other one to her chest, bare where her tunic had been ripped. The skin was soft. Smooth and cool. Her hair was up, braided, like she had been looked after, like she had been important to someone. Basil kissed her forehead and I kissed her forehead and we made silent promises.

Before we left, I ripped Vitoria's tunic a tiny bit more, where it already was, and pulled off a thin strip of fabric, only as long as my smallest finger. I tucked it into my sleeve, away.

Bless you, said the girl from the shadow behind.

Bless you, said Basil. And then, looking up, to her, she said, I'm sorry. We can't—

It's fine, said the girl. I'll be fine. We'll be fine.

We took the baby, still screaming, still alive, and left. The soldier stood aside, stood back.

Thank you, he said, quickly, as we were leaving.

Basil nodded her head a little in response, and I did too. And that was all. We took the baby and left.

—⁂—

The baby cried as we walked out of the jail, cried as we walked back into the street, into the day, squinting and kicking at the shock of light.

Sh, sh, sh, said Basil, holding my arm, pulling us along. We walked as quickly as we could without causing alarm, eyes straight ahead. We had to figure out how to feed a baby and then we had to get back to the real Vestals, to the temple. And then, maybe, we could think about Vitoria. We could think about the sister we'd lost just before we found her. About how things might have been, could have been, if we hadn't slept one of the hours we did, hadn't stopped to eat, to drink, to look at the water, the port, the walls of the city, if we hadn't waited for that cow, that stupid cow. We walked through the endless twisting streets of the city, not thinking this, trying not to think this, and trying not to look at the people looking at us. We moved, eyes open minds closed, through the streets, the people, the crying and crying and crying of the baby.

I counted down in my head. Nine eight seven, then seven six five, then five four. Just four.

Just four, I whispered to Basil, eyes straight ahead.

Five, she whispered back. With this baby, now five.

The baby screamed.

The people stared.

We need to find a goat, I said.

We didn't even need to buy the goat. Our outfits were more powerful than swords. We've got this baby to purify, said Basil, to the market-stall woman. So we need a goat. A sacrifice.

The woman nodded.

A female goat, said Basil.

The woman nodded.

Lactating, said Basil.

The woman nodded, said nothing, went to go look through her goats. These outfits were so powerful they made people mute, other than the word sorry. Like swords.

The goat the market woman gave us was a colour partway between grey and brown, a non-colour. The woman gave it to us and we took it and left, just like that.

It had a rough rope lead and followed wherever we pulled it, managing to find things to pick up and chew without ever stopping.

Let's call it Julia, said Basil.

And even though I didn't feel like I ever wanted to smile again, I smiled.

Yes, I said. Good.

In the temple, the baby fed eagerly, almost frantically, from Julia the goat while I held her hot, straining body in place. She was still wrapped in the veil, she was still filthy. Food first, then washing. Always. The baby fed and the goat and I stared at the temple fire, glowing strong, even in this high heat. Always.

She changed her name, I said. The soldier called her Felicitas, not Vitoria. Somewhere between leaving and now, Vitoria changed her name.

I didn't notice that, said Basil, unwinding herself from the white cloth. Did he call her that?

He did, I said. Felicitas, not Vitoria. She drew a line between us, before, and her here, now. Changing your name is cutting something off, something you don't want anymore.

Not always, said Basil, her dirt-grey tunic starting to show again, starting to emerge like a butterfly going backwards.

Almost always, I whispered.

Seven days after getting the baby, we named it. We walked circles around her, like Sossia and Maxima and the other virgins at the temple wanted, and poured warm water over her head, like Basil wanted. The virgins' circles made her confused and Basil's water made her scream. We purified her like that and then named her.

Vitoria? said Basil.

No, I said. Felicitas.

Eight days after we got the baby, it was time to go. To say thank you thank you thank you to Maxima and Sossia, take the goat and the child, and go. Quiteria was back on the other side of the water, waiting. It was time to go.

I don't want to go, I whispered.

We have to go, whispered Basil.

On the floor, the baby slept. Beside it, the goat chewed. The fire cracked, glowed.

Well, said Sossia, who was feeding the fire dry olive leaves, dropping them in one at a time because she liked the way they snapped, if you don't want to, you don't have to go.

The oldest Vestal was retiring; in two weeks she'd be forty-one years old and her time would be served and she would be done. There was a man who sold pomegranates in the market who she wanted to marry. She wanted to wear colours other than white and take less than two hours to do her hair in the morning, and to marry the man who sold pomegranates in the market. So she was going. She was done.

So we'll need to replace her, said Sossia. Because then we'll be five and we have to be six, always. Except no fathers have offered their daughters, lately. They want them married instead.

To men who sell pomegranates in the market? said Basil.

Sure, said Sossia. And then, after considering, Actually, probably not. But still.

So . . . there's a vacancy, I said.

Yep, said Sossia, holding a leaf above the flame like she was teasing it, like torture, then dropping it in. Exactly. We could say, she said, that they heard, across the water, about our need, that they sent a replacement, since they had loads already, since fathers over there don't care as much about their daughters. About marriage.

But they do, said Basil.

Whatever, nobody will know, said Sossia. They think you all have eleven fingers and backwards feet anyway.

They do? said Basil.

And faces like this, I said.

No, said Sossia. They know faces like that here too. Every city does. Every city, everybody. They'll think it makes you all the holier, anyway, to have survived.

Yeah? I said.

They'll think that because it's true, said Basil.

Exactly, said Sossia. Yes, exactly. So. What do you think, Liberata? Do you want to stay? They'll probably have a parade or something like that, to officially welcome you, and you get pretty decent food and almost never have to pay for stuff.

I do, I want to stay, I said, looking at Basil, not Sossia.

Are you sure? asked Sossia. Once you're in, you're in, and that's it.

She is, said Basil, quietly, looking at me, not Sossia.

—❧—

I walked Basil to the city gates. I was still in white; she was back to normal, in her tunic with the pockets for weapons sewn in by Quiteria. There was a big crowd of people trying to get into the city and the gate wasn't very big, so we had to stop and wait in a small queue of others trying to get out.

You know what's weird? said Basil.

No, I said. What? A woman with a live chicken under each arm joined the line behind us.

They didn't ask us to pardon them, said Basil. The other prisoners in the cell with Vitoria. They could have asked us, we had that power, or they would have thought we did, but they didn't even ask.

A man with a big basket full of smaller baskets got in line behind the chickens.

Maybe they wanted to die, I said.

Nobody wants to die, says Basil.

Maybe, I said. Maybe nobody wants to die. But sometimes people want to stop living.

Basil turned so she was facing me instead of the front of the line. You'll be happy? she asked. Here?

Maybe, I said. I think I could be.

Someone near the front shouted something and they stopped letting

people in and started letting people out instead; the line suddenly pulling forward like the lead ropes Julia always wanted to chew on.

Maybe, said Basil, maybe it was that those prisoners knew something we didn't. Something about life after life. About better life.

The line pulled forward by two steps and us with it.

Maybe, I said.

Three steps.

Yeah? said Basil.

Yeah, I said. Maybe, yes.

Okay, said Basil. Okay. Good.

Bye, Basil, I said. For now.

For now, said Basil. I love you. God loves you.

I know, I said. I know, I know.

Then she was pulled forward again with the crowd, to the gate, and out.

~

The water we crossed was a border, life before and life after. Basil went
back across and I stayed.

~

The baby Felicitas stayed with me. Everyone knew about the child the
Vestals had saved, and everyone accepted that I, with my face, would
never have had a baby of my own, so it was okay to keep it without
shame or expulsion or death by being left alone underground. So Felicitas
stayed with me. She lived in the temple and grew and when she was too
old for Julia's milk she kept the goat as a pet, feeding her bits of her own
dinner and the olive leaves that were meant for the fire. And we never
had to think about eating her because there was always something else
to eat, always enough. Felicitas learned how to keep the flames happy
but not wild and how to count by listing the names of my sisters:

Quiteria, one
Marina, two

Gema, three
Germana, four
Liberata (mama), five
Basilissa, six
Felicitas (Vitoria; other mama), seven
Eumelia, eight
Genebra, nine

And Felicitas, you, ten. I'd add.
And Felicitas, me, ten, she'd say.

~

Sossia finished her thirty years of service, then retired and went to take care of her parents in their small town near the sea that stank of fish and dogs, and where the people, she said, even the ones who hated each other because someone's kid dyed someone else's sheep with beetroot water, or someone's fishing net came up empty every time someone else looked at their boat, all the people, even the ones who hated each other, came together in the morning to sit on the big rocks that faced that water to watch Aurora announce the new day, every day, no matter who hated who, no matter who loved who, no matter what, they all sat together to watch the sun that always rose up; they knew it wouldn't rise, Aurora wouldn't make it, unless they were all there. They watched quietly, together, and then those who hadn't started work for the day broke off to start their work, and those who had been out for hours already with nets or boats broke off to get back to their work, those who didn't hate each other chatting as they went, those who hated everyone going in silence, every day.

Are your parents chatting people or hating people? I asked.

It changes, said Sossia. Lately, I think, my father has been chatty and my mother has been hatey. But my father's too weak to walk down himself now, so my mother carries him. She's hatey, so she carries him down silently, with the help of a neighbour. He's pretty small and light now; I don't imagine it's very hard. I reckon I'll be strong enough to carry him unaided. And her too, if she ever gets to that point. In two separate trips, of course.

And will you be chatty or hatey?
I'll be happy.

~~

Maxima finished her thirty years, then retired and went to live with the girl who delivered the firewood, and who, after thirty years, wasn't a girl at all anymore, the girl who had a laugh as broad as her shoulders, as broad as Maxima's smile every Thursday when she knew she'd be coming. The girl would leave the wood in a pile just to the side of the door every week at just the same time as Maxima came back from the herb sellers, smelling wonderful. Maxima would have a sprig of rosemary poking out of her veil, tucked behind one ear. She'd give the girl lavender and the girl would wear it, there behind her own ear, all week, until she came round again, until Maxima slipped a hand in, into her veil, into the darkness of hair she never saw, only felt, and took the old lavender out and put a new sprig in. The girl, who was not a girl anymore, had had a husband, but he had died.

You'll be okay? another Vestal asked, while Maxima was folding the one spare tunic that was hers, not the temple's. You'll have enough?

Everything we need, said Maxima. We'll have everything.

~~

And what about you? I asked Felicitas, after they'd gone, after she'd grown from a goat-milk baby, screams bouncing off the walls like bells day and night, to a full-bellied child, bouncing off the walls like a bee kept inside, to a stretched and silent young adult, walking up and down the length of the temple walls like a prisoner. I held her and watched her grow, and held her and watched her and held her and held her and held her and, at the same time, held the question far away, out of reach of us both, for as long as I could, pushing it back, away, whenever it threatened to burst out. But now Felicitas was seventeen. She was as old as I was when I arrived. But now it wasn't fair, anymore, tucking it away. So one morning, after a same-as-every-morning goat-milk porridge, down with the fire and the wood, same as every morning, I opened the little door in the back of my mind and let the question tumble out:

And what about you? I asked, as full voiced as I could manage. Felicitas, do you want to stay or go?

I was thirty-four years old. Barely halfway through my service.

I'm allowed? she said.

We were preparing sticks for giving out fire to the neighbours. Choosing the proper-sized ones from our big and tangled general pile. Not too big or else we'd miss the firewood, not too small or else the flame wouldn't last. Felicitas was being very picky. Only two sticks in her pile, so far.

You didn't agree to any thirty-year bond, I said. And you're old enough, now. You could go, now, if you wanted. I pushed a too-small twig away from me, back into the safety of the big pile. My pile was almost finished, forty-eight sticks.

She took a branch, looked at it, put it back. Chose another, did the same thing. Well, she said, I didn't know that. I didn't know that was allowed.

It is, I said. You are. I looked at my pile, not at her. All my sticks looked wrong now, too small or too big. Allowed, I mean. You are allowed, I said. I'm not, but you are.

She looked at my pile too. Then at hers. Not at me. Oh, she said. Oh. I mean, she said. I don't know. I don't know what I want. I'll think about it, okay?

Okay, I said.

Even though we both knew, she and I, that she did know. She put her two sticks on my pile, then picked up the whole bunch and turned to take them to the fire.

She left before she was eighteen. She took Julia IV, her newest goat, and some rosemary and as many coins as I could fit in her purse and a little flask of wine.

And this? I said, my hand open with the grubby strip of fabric from my sister's, her mother's, tunic. Will you take this?

No, she said. I'll leave that here. I'll only lose it. I'll get it when I come back. You keep it safe here.

Bread? I said.

Yes, I'll take bread, she said, and took the loaf from my other hand.

She went to cross the water, to go back to where I came from, to try to find my sisters, the commander, the trees. I had drawn her a map. Still, after all those years, I could draw the map perfectly, no mistakes. She copied it out, stroke by stroke. I'll come back, she said. I'll remember.

Then she left and I stayed where I was, feet firmly on ground.

I finished my thirty years. I didn't want to retire. I didn't want to go.

So I stayed. I fed the fire and shared the fire and walked through crowds up and down spider-leg streets and waited.

I draped and folded white cloth over and over again and waited. I collected rosemary and pardoned prisoners and pardoned more prisoners and more and more and waited.

I got another goat and didn't eat it.

I waited.

And when I was old and the rest of my body buckled and puckered and matched my face, and I was laid on a mat dragged near the fire, where the heat was so full it was almost cool, almost Good, and the new Vestals, the young ones, leaned over me, beautiful in their white veils, like the sky, like the fire, and said, Sister? I said,

Give this to her.

And I opened my hand and lifted it, with the scrap of fabric on it, towards them, and the goat, Julia IX, tried to eat it, but a young Vestal pushed her away and said,

For Felicitas. Of course.

No, I said. The goat. I mean give it to the goat. She's been trying to get it for years. You can give it to her now.

So they did. The goat ate it and bleated for more, but there was no more, so she walked away, and the younger, newer Vestals watched to make sure she didn't try to jump in the fire or anything like that and then turned back to me, and when they did their faces weren't their faces, they were Basil's and Quiteria's and Vitoria's and Gema's and Germana's. They were Felicitas's. And their faces looked exactly like my face, which looked exactly like theirs, with no difference of time or place or plague.

And I closed my eyes and smiled
and the fire burned cool
and isn't the fire just like music?
isn't it?
and I was lifted up,
isn't it?
up
up.

6

BASIL

Imagine this:

Imagine a God who is everything, like, actually Everything. And because everything is enough, more than enough for everyone, this God wouldn't hold back. This God would give and give and give. The more It gave, the more It would Be. This God would be something, something existing, happening and happening and happening, this God about giving, living, being, happening. This God. This would be the Only God because if this God Was, then there could be no others, there'd be no Need. This God of Giving. Of Everything.

Some people can't imagine that. Because it's too big, it's too much. It's like trying to see every star in the whole sky at once. It's too True.

But try, if you can. Try thinking of the sun.

Try thinking of a mother, our mother, mine and Liberata's. She had twelve natural kids. And the four who died. And us. So that's eighteen. Eighteen lives she made. Lives she created, carried, nursed, arse-wiped.

If there was a God who was about living, about giving life, sharing life, about the Everything of Life, she could be like my mother. Or yours. Think of that.

Imagine that.

And then, instead of sacrifice, instead of death, we would exist to exist; we would be. We'd glory in the glory of being. We'd run, forever. We'd run not on food or water but on being, on happening, on the joy of happening, right now. We'd sing Right Now Right Now Right Now. We'd run on fire.

Like the sun.

Alive with, part of, Everything, bellies full of Life and fire, like a mother, like the sun.

Amen, amen, amen.

When we were sick, when the pox came and Gema, Germana, and Liberata were sick, were in between worlds, my mother and my adoptive sister Taga got sick too. Taga was just a baby, could only just sort of crawl, and only backwards, and had only three teeth. My mother was pregnant. Most of the people who had the pox were quiet-sick, whimpering and sleeping and burning up in a muted sort of a way, but not Taga. She was loud-sick, and cried and screamed full voice, scaring all the birds from the trees, all the spiders from our house. She would start to scream, angry-sick, blind-sick, and my mother, eyes closed, quiet-sick next to her, would reach over and pull her up, onto her bare chest, and Taga would scream and writhe until she found the nipple, and then she'd take it, take milk, and as she nursed, as she drank, the red would slowly drain away from her and she'd be cool, be quiet.

Isn't it bad for her? I asked. To have your milk now, when you're sick too? To have sick milk?

No, said my mother. It isn't. It isn't bad. It's the best thing; it's the only thing now. My body knows what she needs, and her body knows what I need.

So you're saving her and she's saving you? Round and round and round?

Yes.

And it doesn't hurt? Not even a bit?

It doesn't hurt, Basil, said my mother. It's the only thing that doesn't hurt.

Imagine a God like that.

The first time a soldier came to the orchard where we lived, he came alone, and he took me alone. I was scared, sure, okay, a bit. I was only eleven years old, not strong yet, or not sure of anything yet, so yes, I was scared, but I was also excited. I'd never seen anything beyond the struggle of our skinny trees, and the road he carried me up was longer and straighter than anything I'd known, his tunic a deeper colour, his armour hotter against my bare legs than anything.

Cyllia's ill, he whispered to me, up over his shoulder, as he ran down that road. I'm sorry, he whispered, but Cyllia's ill.

I didn't know who Cyllia was, but I knew about illness, so I said, I'm sorry. Will she die?

I don't know, he said. That's why I wanted to find you. I wanted to tell you. He twisted his head back to try to look at me while still running, although it was impossible, really. It is you? he asked. That I was meant to find, to tell? Is it you?

I could feel his heart beating through the back of his neck where my chest and belly were wrapped around, fast, strong. Yes, I said. Yes, yes.

That night, after my sisters had come to get me and we'd run back home together, I tried to turn my hand-locked head to my mother as she was braiding my hair for bed, like she always braided all our hair before bed, and even though it was impossible to turn properly like that, I tried, and asked,

When you met my almost-father, your husband, before he was your husband, did you feel it, did you know it not here,

I put my hand over my chest,

but here?

I moved it lower, low down on my belly.

There? Did it burn?

Oh, gods, she said. I should think so. Sixteen kids with the man later, I should think so. Maybe not always, she said. But in general, yes. She closed her eyes, then opened them again. We give each other what we can, your father and me. We give what we can. She reached out, batted a fly off my arm. What have we got if not that? she said. What have you got?

Her words rang in my head and came back again later, again and again, like the crash of a dropped pot echoing on and on between the listening mountains.

—∞—

No matter how far away we were, how far we ran, I could still hear her, not always but often, when I was bending over to examine a stone maybe sharp enough to use, when I was wrapping a tunic-torn bandage on a bloodied stranger, when I was pulling fish bones more clear and pure than anything, than anyone, from between my teeth. What else have you got? she'd say. It's the only thing, she'd say. The only thing that doesn't hurt.

I didn't know, yet, about Everything. About the God of fire and water and being and Everything. But I heard her voice, in stones and flies and blood and lemons, I heard her.

So I went back, a few years after that first soldier, when we were up in the mountains, me and the sisters who were still alive, all so hot and thirsty, when we had run away from the soldiers, more of them this time, run away from them and, therefore, also our home in the village, without saying goodbye to our families, without a chance to say goodbye or to bring anything of home with us. I told Quiteria I was going to look for water, for something to save us, and I did, I just went looking for it where I knew it would definitely be, with my mother, at home.

The thing is, I'm fast. Faster than any of them, faster than a soldier, certainly, by that point. I knew I could get home, get back, and get away from anything or anyone, if I had to.

So when my sisters and I were thirteen and out dying of thirst under a half-dead tree, I ran back down the mountain, back into the scrub of the valley, back down along the trail, back to the village. I went to the stream first and drank and drank and drank. Then I walked in the stream, right in it, all the way up to the huts, to my mother's house.

Everyone was out in the trees except two of my adoptive siblings, three-year-old Tagus and four-year-old Taga, too young for real work, too old to be carried along with our mother during hers. Taga was eating a lemon peel, scraping her teeth along the length of it again and again. She looked up when I came in.

Hi, she said.

Then she went back to scraping.

Hi, Basil, said Tagus. He was standing just outside of his sister's hitting range, watching her. Taga says I can have some of that when she's done, he said.

That's nice, I said. I bent down and kissed them on the head, first him, then her.

Ew, said Taga, scraping.

Ew, said Tagus, copying.

I'd been gone four days at that point. Is Mama far away? I asked.

Yes, said Taga.

Yes, said Tagus.

Do you know where? I asked.

No, said Taga.

No, said Tagus.

She's having another baby soon, said Taga.

I know, I said.

I know, said Tagus.

Okay, well, she is, said Taga.

Okay, said Tagus.

I found my water bladder slung on a hook in the clay wall where it always was, with all the others. There were two pots on the floor near it. I took one.

I bent down and kissed my brother and sister on their heads again. Take care of each other, I said. And of Mama. And the new baby.

Yep, okay, said Taga.

And Dada? said Tagus. And the big kids and everyone?

Yes, I said. Even Dada. Even everyone.

Okay, said Tagus.

Okay, said Taga.

Then I went back to the stream, filled the bladder and the pot with fresh, living water, and ran away, into the scrub of the valley, around and up, up the mountain, away.

I didn't tell Quiteria where I went, where the water came from. I couldn't. Going home was defeat to her. Was quitting. And was stupidly dangerous too. But she didn't know how fast I was, I could be; when you're that fast, nothing is quite so dangerous, or feels it anyway. So I didn't tell Quiteria. Not then, not later.

And I didn't tell Marina either, because she would tell Quiteria, almost certainly, since she was always looking for something, anything, to bring her closer to the brighter, fiercer flame of our first sister.

And I didn't tell Liberata, because she'd want to come too, with me, and she couldn't. She was too slow; it would be dangerous for her, for real. And I didn't want to have to tell her that.

So I went alone and told nobody after, shaking my hair out in the wind on the way back to get rid of the smell of lemon.

We had enough water, then. We survived, then, out there, and Marina braided my hair and hummed and Quiteria thought and planned and thought and planned and Liberata watched out, up in her tree, over us all, alone together.

Then the soldiers came, again, came back to get us. And I could have run fast enough to get away, but my sisters couldn't. What else? whispered my mother's voice, around Liberata's scarred legs, through Marina's tangled hair. What else have you got? So I stayed with them and let the soldiers, armour shining hot, take us away.

They took us to the big house again, which was too big, too too big to be a house, a real house anyway, but which was, in fact, our house, our real house, or that's what they said. They also said that as well as being our house, it would be our home, with food and water and wine and love, even, probably, so no need to leave, to go back to the village ever, please, they said. They locked the door to our room for the first few nights.

We are so grateful for what they have done, down there in the village, saving you and raising you so far, they said. We have sent gift baskets.

But we need you to stay here now, okay? said the slave with the long nose and the black-dark eyes. You ran once, you understand? she said. So we're just supposed to lock the door for the first few nights. The first little while.

Until you feel at home, said the other slave, the one with cheeks like raw dough. The one who would later push me underwater and pull me back out again.

Your father, she said. They said. Just that. Your father. Like that was reason and explanation all by itself. And for them, for most, it was.

Your father, said Julia, who was his wife but not our mother. She sighed and made a small patting motion, her fist over her heart.

So there we were. Not technically prisoners, but prisoners. But luckily, prisons never really posed much of a problem for me.

~

Even in the beginning they didn't lock the door during the day. It was five thousand eight hundred and eighty-one running steps from our new house back to my old house. People rarely noticed I was gone at all. Julia or a slave or a soldier would look around and see one of us down by the fountain, or one up in the olive trees, or one walking the dust paths just behind the house and think: Oh, good, there they are. All the same, even Liberata, from the back or far away. Our sameness meant we could be in lots of places at once, or could disappear. It meant we could be magic.

My mother was in the hut, on the floor, sitting, a screaming baby trying to scratch its way out of her arms and Tagus, crying, pulling on her sleeve. She fought the baby down and onto a breast, using an upper arm to deflect its kicks from her already rounding belly. She did it without looking at him. Her eyes were open but glazed over, there but not there.

Mom? I said, when the baby had finally latched and Tagus had stopped for breath.

She looked towards the door, towards me, but her expression didn't change. Her tunic was crooked, the collar stretched over her shoulder from Tagus's pulling. It wasn't a real door, not like at the commander's, a door that could open or shut, it was just a hole, a place to get in or out, a passage.

I brought you some things, I said.

Tagus let go of her and turned to me. Smiled.

Taga came up behind me, a half-brown lemon in her hand. She squeezed around me and walked over to our mother and gave it to her. Here, she said. And then, Hi, Basil.

Our mother bit the lemon in half and handed the more yellow part to Tagus, who made a face and threw it on the floor.

She picked it up and handed it back to him. It's what you wanted, she said. He threw it on the floor again.

And then again.

And then again.

Then she shrugged and held the fruit out, back to his sister.

NO! said Tagus. He grabbed the lemon and stuffed it into his mouth, peel and all.

For a beat nobody said or did anything, waiting to see if he'd choke, or if Taga would fight back, or if the baby would do anything, but he didn't and she didn't and it didn't. Silence. Tagus began chewing in heavy wet bites. My mother closed her eyes, opened them, looked at me and said,

Right. What did you want?

They knew where we'd gone, of course. They'd seen us marched past on the way to the commander's. And then they'd got the baskets.

A man taller than any other man brought them, said Tagus, after he'd swallowed the last bit of pith. A man in a hat made of gold.

A helmet? I asked.

No. A hat made of gold.

They gave us lemons, said Taga. They gave us back some of our lemons.

And a baby goat! said Tagus. He pointed out the door, towards the trees.

I looked. Sure enough, there was a small goat, head butted up against the side of a trunk.

A male goat, said my mother. They gave us a male baby goat to feed.

A silence. I watched the goat try to jump from one rock to another rock, stumble, scramble, fall, recover.

He's really sweet, said Taga.

You could kill it, I said. Eat it.

Kill a goat from the commander? My mother gave me a look.

It's not like he'd know, I said. Or care. I think maybe that was the—

No, said my mother. We don't kill the commander's goats. We feed them and let ourselves starve a bit more instead.

The goat tried his jump again. Stumbled. Fell. Recovered.

We also got oil, said Taga. In the bottom of the basket there was a nice little thing of oil.

Yes, said my mother. That was good. It's gone now.

So I brought them oil. Each time I came, if I could, I brought oil for my mother and our more decent food scraps for the kids and our less decent scraps for the goats. Taga had named theirs the Commander, and the other families liked that, so they were all called the Commander now. I brought as much as I could carry while running, in my pockets and bundled in cloth tied into my sleeves. After my first few visits, my mother gave me the emptied gift basket.

Here, she said. Do something useful with it.

Then I started using the basket and could carry twice as much. I strapped it to my back using strips of cloth, tests or scraps from the weaving women. Sometimes, when I noticed that Taga's tunic was ripped again or that there was another new baby, naked and red, I'd leave the strips and would run back home with the basket hooked around my neck like a piggybacking child, bouncing up and down with each step as I ran back up the hill, the path, the road.

We could do more, I said to Julia, who was not our mother. Maybe we should do more.

Yes . . . said Julia. But we also need to be careful, we don't want to overstep, we don't want to patronize. She was walking to the weaving room with a big basket of wool puffs; I was following to try to get more scraps long enough to use as basket ties. We walked together now, in step.

If we did it carefully, I said. Maybe no more goats.

Maybe, said Julia. Maybe. Aulus has an idea, anyway. A plan, for your birthday. A nice idea, something nice for those families. She shifted her basket, trying to redirect a bit of wool fluff that was brushing up against her chin. It and three other bits fell out. I bent to catch one that caught the wind and had started rolling away towards the chickens, the gate, freedom.

Our families, I said.

Your other families, said Julia. She was turned away, trying to get the other two bits of wool without upsetting the rest. She said it quietly, not really to me.

I almost caught my tuft; I thought I had it under my foot just before a little gust blew across the yard, lifting it away. I gave up and watched it go. Who's Aulus? I said.

Your father.

I'd never heard his name before. None of us had. Oh, I said. Right. Of course. What is it? The birthday thing?

A surprise, she said. She didn't look excited. But she never really did. She'd grabbed her two balls and was stuffing them back down deep into her basket, secure. Basil, she said, I've seen you run. You're really fast, aren't you? You're really good.

Oh, I said. I'm not—

Just around the yard, she added. Just up and down the road.

Oh, yeah, I said. Yes. Of course. Thanks.

We started walking again, past a chicken fighting with an olive pit. Aulus doesn't mind? I said. Me running?

He doesn't know, said Julia. He mostly stays inside when he's here, meeting with important people. Or way out in the back, with the soldiers, the other important people.

We passed another chicken, fast asleep, even when we stepped right by it, even though the dogs were out.

I wish I could run like that, said Julia, and I said nothing, because we both knew that was totally impossible. Not just Julia running as fast as me, but Julia running at all. Her clothes were beautiful, her hair was beautiful, her face, her movement, her steps, all too beautiful, too beautiful to run. We walked the rest of the way to the looms in silence.

When we arrived, the slaves looked up at me and then away again. They knew why I'd come, why I always came, and they knew that they probably weren't supposed to give me what I asked for, but still, they always did, handing over the extra bits of cloth, eyebrows raised, when Julia wasn't there.

Anyway, said Julia, setting down her basket and patting the wool gently into order, into place. I'm glad you came today, that you found me. I guess Marina told you what we've been up to; I'm guessing you're here to learn a bit of weaving with us, finally?

Without turning my head, I looked over at a slave. She nodded.

I nodded. Yes, I said. Even though Marina hadn't told me anything. Even though my mother was waiting, down in the village. Even though I'd promised her salt.

Julia smiled. Good, she said. I'm really glad. And your father will be too.

Aulus, I said.

Yes, Aulus, she said.

—⁕—

Five weeks later, at the Surprise Birthday Dinner, which followed the Surprise Birthday Parade, which was half made up of soldiers in full uniform and half made up of our families from the village holding flags they'd been given, smiling because they knew they were supposed to smile, even though they looked a bit like prisoners, in between the soldiers like that, after that, after the parade, in which Taga looked terrified and Tagus looked thrilled and my mother looked tired, the baby she was carrying awkwardly in the arm that wasn't carrying a flag not bothering to wake up for the event, even though there were bugles and drums, after all that, after the speech the commander gave, after everyone had paraded their way up to the front of the house, where he said:

I don't want to

and

Speak for very long

and

It's not about me

and

This, I mean, this isn't about me.

After that speech and everyone being unsure what to do when it finished, the families unsure if they were allowed to put down their flags and leave the soldiers and come to us, we unsure if we could go to them, or should, the slaves unsure who to lead in to dinner first, since normally it would be, should be, the commander, but his speech made it seem like maybe it should be the families instead, but then again it was our birthdays, so maybe it should be us, after that was sorted by some kid, one of Quiteria's little sisters, seeing a chicken inside the now open gates and running in to chase it, so that we all watched, horrified, and then Quiteria's old father shrugged and followed the kid in, and then everybody else did too, in no particular order, after that, at dinner, which was huge, much more huge than it needed to be, much more huge than any stomachs used to less than a meal and a half a day could handle, at dinner, my mother picked up a piece of meat bigger than her hand, bigger than any piece of food she'd ever had entirely to herself, examined it, and said, quietly, to me,

He must feel very guilty, the commander. He must be a very guilty man.

Or good? I said.

She took a bite. Closed her eyes and held it in her mouth, then gave a little nod and swallowed. She opened her eyes again. No, she said, not good. Men with power and money can't be good or bad. They can just be guilty or not guilty. She took another bite, chewed slowly, carefully.

We must have looked tiny, she said.

Where? When?

There, in the parade, in among the tall, shining soldiers, she said. We must have looked tiny. We must have looked so small.

No, I said.

She looked at the meat in her hand, still huge, two bites gone. She put it down.

No, no, I said, again.

Soldiers walked them home again, an envoy, for protection, since it was after dark.

Protection from who? asked Liberata. We never had protection, before.

From barbarians, said Marina.

From their neighbours, Quiteria said. They sent soldiers to protect them from their own neighbours. Who might smell the feast on them and rip them open like night birds to get at it.

They wouldn't! said Liberata. Of course they wouldn't!

Of course they wouldn't, I said. They're too busy taking care of the goats.

Time passed, ran, flew, days and then years. The commander left and he came back, then he left and then came back, left and came back; we had another birthday, and then another, with feasts and gifts but no more parades, no more villagers. We learned things, important and stupid, and ate things, so many things, and I ran and ran, back and forth and back and forth, and Tagus and Taga got bigger and ran with me, sometimes, when they were allowed to or when no one was watching. They always stopped at the big bank of scrub before the road up to the house, though, always stopped before they'd be visible to anyone up there. Then they'd turn and run back, racing and chasing each other, and I'd run on, up to the commander's, alone.

I was sixteen when I saw the slaves drowning each other and Everything Changed. I had a flask of oil and bundles of bread and salt fish in the basket on my back. I also had a pomegranate, harder to steal, a special treat, tucked up my sleeve where it would be safe. It was for my mother, since it was almost her birthday, it was something for her to sacrifice. I couldn't figure out how to steal and safely carry hidden any live animal without probably killing it in the process, so I got the closest thing, a fruit that would bleed.

It was winter now, or early spring, when I was running with the basket and the pomegranate. I was passing the upper bit of the same stream that ran through our orchard. It had often dried up by the time it got to proper spring, and was always totally dead by summer, but there was still water then, almost knee-deep. In winter, I often stopped for a drink on my way, alone on the way down, and with Tagus and Taga splashing and slurping on the way back up. I stopped now, alone, and saw that, actually, I wasn't alone.

There were four of them. Claudia, the round-cheeked slave, and the kid from the kitchen and one of the horse men and Bea, Julia's woman, who gave me the wool scraps. They were standing, all of them, in the water, farther upstream than me, facing away, back towards the house. Bea and the horse man were holding the round slave, one on either side, and were pushing her down, into the water, while the kitchen kid, who was maybe her son, watched.

He didn't try to stop them. Instead, he took a handful of water and dumped it down over his maybe mother's head.

Her eyes were closed. She wasn't struggling. She's already dead, I thought. Oh oh oh, she's already dead.

I didn't know what to do. Round slave wasn't ever particularly nice to me, but I still didn't want her dead. And I didn't want other slaves thinking they could just go and kill whoever they wanted, whenever they wanted, by drowning if it was winter, or some other, drier way in summer.

But there were three of them, not counting the drownee, and only one of me.

But they were slaves and I was not. And I could run. I knew these trails and I could run.

I stepped forward, towards them, and shouted,

WHAT?! HEY!

Which didn't really make sense but did the job. They stopped. They all turned around, to me, even round slave, who opened her eyes and found her footing on the creek bed and steadied herself and stood and wasn't dead. They all looked very pale, very scared. Except the kitchen kid, who said, Oh, hi, Marina!

I'm Basil, I said.

Sorry. Hi, Basil!

He started walking down the creek towards me, smiling, but round slave, who almost definitely was his mother, lunged forward and grabbed him back. I'm sorry, she said. I'm really, really, really sorry, Miss Basil.

You're sorry? I said. Not the others?

Oh! said Bea. Us too! We're sorry!

Yes! said the horse man. Us too! Sorry too!

Then, because I wasn't sure what was going on, or what to say, and because they were all looking at me, all pale like that, I said, No, I'm sorry. I'm sorry.

Then no one said anything and everyone just looked at everyone else, except the kitchen boy, who looked up at his mother, confused.

So because no one was doing or saying anything, and because I was still thirsty, I bent down and took some water in my hands, drank. They watched me. The water was good, clean, cold.

Okay, I said, when I'd finished. I looked at Bea and the horse man. Were you trying to drown her?

No, said Bea.

No! said the horse man.

Ha! said the kid.

I turned to round slave. Were they trying to drown you? Or . . . otherwise kill you? I asked.

No, she said. No, Miss Basil, just the opposite. Exactly the opposite.

Although, said Bea, I can see how it might look like that. We don't blame you for thinking that.

But we weren't, said horse man.

No, they weren't, said round slave.

The kid just watched them. He'd sat down in the water so it came right up over his bare chest, right up to his neck.

Okay, good, I said. Then I wasn't sure what to do again, because even if they weren't drowning each other, they still shouldn't have been out here, all together, like that. But I wasn't really supposed to be out that far either. And I had stolen oil and food strapped to my back and a precious pomegranate up my sleeve.

They watched me, unsure.

I watched them, unsure.

What do you mean? I finally asked. The opposite? What do you mean they were doing the opposite?

The horse man looked at Bea and the round slave looked at the horse man and Bea looked at the round slave and the kid looked at me and said,

Simple. They weren't killing her, they were making it so she can never be killed. They were helping her go on forever. He smiled.

Everyone else was quiet.

What have we got if not that? whispered a sunken stone in my mother's voice. What have we got? I bent down and picked it up.

Forever? I said.

The kid half submerged a fist and squeezed it. It made a little fountain.

Yep, he said. And I'm next.

His mother didn't look happy, exactly, with what he was saying, but she didn't stop or correct him either.

Forever? I said. Like a god?

Yeah, said the kid. Exactly. He squeezed again and another little jet of water jumped up and out of his hand.

Well, said the horse man. Not exactly.

But kind of, said Bea. Basically . . .

But not like a god, said round slave.

But not *not* like a god, said Bea.

No, not not not like, said horse man, because—

Jesus died for us, said the kid. For *us*. For, like, you and me and slaves and commanders and normals and everybody. Everything. To make everything like a god, forever . . .

Who? I said.

Died, said the kid. Like, sacrificed *himself* so that we could, so that you and I and everyone—

His mother slapped a hand over his mouth. Not here, she whisper-hissed. Not now.

But, said the kid, muffled through her hand. He looked up at his mother, then back to me. I thought you said—

Then he stopped, craned his head forward and looked at me closer. Hey, he said, you're bleeding. He pointed.

Everyone, including me, looked at my right arm. Thick sticky rivers of red were running down from the end of my sleeve to my wrist, onto my palm and my fingers, then falling in bright drips into the water, swirling and being swept away. Oh, I said. Oh no.

What have you got? asked the sunken stone.

I need to go, I said. Will you be here again, at the same time, tomorrow?

We could be, said Bea, if you wanted us to be.

I do, I said.

Then we will be, said Bea.

Yes, said the horse man.

Yes, said the round slave.

The kid didn't say anything, his mother's hand still over his mouth. He just looked, worried, at my arm. I dipped it into the water and red bloomed out all around like fire. Then I lifted it out, clean, and ran away, down the hill, through the scrub, down to the village, discarding the cracked and crushed pomegranate farther along, out of sight.

—⁓—

It's about running, I told Marina, two days later.

Running? she said.

We were in the fountain behind the commander's house, legs hanging out and over the hot stone side.

Yep, running forever. Being able to run and run forever and never being tired at all.

Even after you die? Marina asked. She lifted her legs and pulled her feet up over the lip, into the water.

Especially after you die, I said. Except you don't really die. That's the thing. You keep running. Dying just makes you free so you don't have to do or think about anything else, never have to worry about food or water or sleep again. Never stop again. You run as free and easy as down the mountain at night.

I pulled one of my legs up and in, but left the other out so the one would feel even cooler in comparison to the other.

But how much do you have to sacrifice? she asked. How many goats, lambs, bulls? How can the slaves afford it?

That's the thing, I said. It's about life, about living. Nothing dies. Nothing has to. Not anymore.

Not even a chick or a scorpion or a spider?

No, nothing, I said. I pulled my other foot in. We were tight now, squished. Marina squeezed her legs together, made herself smaller, made space. She tucked her face into her knees. Then how? she asked, slightly muffled. How do you do it?

With water, I said.

She lifted her head. Looked at me. Water? she asked.

Water, I said.

The God of Everything? she said.

Everything.

Everything everything?

Everything.

~⁂~

I told Liberata.

Everything? she asked. Trees? she asked.

~⁂~

I told Quiteria.

Mothers? she asked.

~⁂~

I told Taga.

Kids? she asked.

~⁂~

Goats? asked Tagus.

~⁂~

Laundry? asked my mother.

~⁂~

Everything, everything, everything, I said.

~∞~

I wanted to tell Julia, I even went along to the looms, pretended to enjoy spinning and weaving for a few days beforehand, but Bea took me aside the morning before I'd planned to tell her, when Julia had gone to use the toilets.

Don't tell her, she said.

But it's good, I said. It's nothing to be ashamed of, afraid of, right? It's good.

It is good, said Bea. But some people don't think so. Some powerful people. You're okay, you'll be okay; you're who you are. But I'm a slave, remember. Remember that, Basil.

But she's Julia, I said. She's just Julia.

She's married to the commander, said Bea. She's the commander's Julia. Please, Basil, please don't tell her.

So I didn't tell Julia, nobody told Julia, and I didn't go back to weaving. I sang songs with Bea and Claudia and the others, songs that were like running, songs that ran from and between us like the water around our ankles, and I ran home to the village and back and home to the village and back, and the more I sang, the faster I ran and the faster I ran, the more I sang, and I sang and ran and ran until I could pass spooked rabbits, flat-footed lizards, sky-hung birds; until the brush and the sun and everything was a blur of song and air.

~∞~

I ran home to the village one last time. Before Quiteria and Liberata and I all ran away together, I ran home.

I had asked Bea, Will my fiancé be the new kind of man or the old kind?

She closed her eyes and shook her head and I knew that meant the Old Kind, even though all she said, eventually, was, The commander will pick. He'll choose with love.

I ran home one last time, with another pomegranate, held more carefully, and oil and salt and two clay whistles in the shape of fish, one for Taga and one for Tagus.

You can change the notes like this, I said. I moved my fingers on and off the holes. You can play a little song, I told them.

My mother looked up at me from where she was sorting lemons by colour with one hand, keeping a toddler away from the piles with the other.

But only play it outside, I said. And not too close to anyone's ear, or any sleeping babies.

I gave the oil and salt and fruit to my mother, making a little pile beside the lemon piles.

Goodbye, I said. For real this time, I think.

But you said goodbye before and then came back, said Tagus. So I'm not sad. You'll be back.

I'm not sure, I said. I'm not so sure this time.

I am, said Tagus.

Me too, said Taga.

Yeah? I said.

Yeah, they said.

We'll see, said my mother, holding up an in-between lemon, too brown to be yellow, too yellow to be brown. Goodbye for now, she said. She decided on yellow, put the lemon down. I love you, she said.

The kids didn't run with me anymore, not very far at least; I was too fast. But I could hear them, playing loud held notes on their fish whistles long after I'd left them by a pair of purple-blossomed bushes.

~❦~

So I ran away, with Quiteria and Liberata, away from our father and the proverbial fiancés and Marina, poor Marina, over hills and through fences and into and out of cracks and caves until we were Really and Truly Free. Safe and Free. But camp, once we got to it, was boring as porridge. We had enough water and we had enough food and we were free to do whatever we wanted and time dragged on and on and I was bored, very, very bored. I missed Bea and Claudia and the others. I

WE SHOULD NOT BE AFRAID OF THE SKY

missed Taga and Tagus and the village. I missed Marina. And I was bored. Which is what can happen, it turns out, when you finally have everything you need, but not everyone.

It was too far to run home; it was days and days and days and days and days away, even for me. And it wasn't safe now. It was even less safe than before. Barbarians and soldiers were one thing; a husband you didn't want was another.

So I didn't run home. I stayed there, in our new camp home, and caught and ate fish from the river with Liberata. I practised holding a sword and running with a sword and jumping with a sword and hiding with a sword with Quiteria. I sang songs by the river, to the river, to the living god of the everything of the river by myself, even though that's not how they were meant to be sung, even though the best way to sing is never alone.

And then, one day, out of the kindness of the trees, Sarah, Afulay, and Sufjian showed up. I could have kissed them. I did kiss Sufjian, later.

～

It's because they're like us, he said. We were between their camp and ours, halfway, in the place where we would meet, in the place where the wind caught the dust and drew it up into the sun like ghosts. We were on the ground, the ground that held every ant and flower and rock and root, that connected them all, us all. Our eyes were closed. We'd been singing together, Glory, Glory, Glory, letting the light of the word echo off and away, along the river to the farms and villages and towns it fed, across the hills and between the trees and over the rocks and cliffs and through the ants and dust and sun beating and pulsing and spreading all the way home. To my home and his. My head and heart swelled warm and full. We were holding hands. He stopped singing, and said,
   They're like us.
   The ants? I said, since there were some crawling over my foot. The ants are like us?

No, said Sufjian. Although yes. But no. The people they're taking away, the ones we rescue. That's why they're taking them away. They're like us.

Locking them up, you mean, I said. I opened my eyes. Killing them, you mean.

Yeah, said Sufjian. That's what I mean. Because the soldiers and things, the commanders, are afraid of them. Isn't that insane? Isn't that crazy?

Well, we do attack them. Or Sarah and Quiteria do, anyway.

Only to get our people back. Only as much as we have to. And that's not what they're afraid of, anyway.

No, I said. I know. They're afraid of the Everything. That it's big, it's huge.

And beautiful, said Sufjian. Beauty that could crush them, he said. Crush anyone, if they're not careful.

Even though it was already hot, already sun-full, my face went hot, hotter.

People are afraid of all sorts of things, I said. My father was afraid of bugs. And Quiteria's afraid of the dark. And Liberata's afraid of the light.

What are you afraid of? he asked.

I thought. Other people dying, I said. And you?

He thought. Being alone, he said. Same thing.

Until you die yourself. Then you're not alone anymore, right?

No, he said. Never again. He held my hand tighter, pulled it closer to him. I followed. And farther. And then our bodies were together with our clasped hands pressed between like dried flowers between stones.

God is Love, I said, and kissed his mouth.

God is Love, he said, and kissed mine.

~

There was a raid on their camp. Sarah heard the soldiers coming and took her little boy and hid with him in the reeds in the river, where she could stand but he couldn't, where she held him just high enough to breathe but not high enough to be seen or see, and they prayed for their heartbeats to stay quieter than the water.

Sufjian stayed and fought and they beat him with their fists, not even bothering to unsheathe their swords, until he fell. Who else? they shouted at him. No one else, he said to them. Who else? they shouted. No one, no one, no one, he said. No one, no one, no one. Then they hit and kicked him some more, taking it in turns to step aside and wipe their hands on some bundled rags, the beds, when they got too bloody, too slippery. They could have used the water, the river would have washed and soothed their hot tired fists, but they didn't, they just used the rags, the beds, over and over and over again, until, finally, exhausted, one of them sat down on the rags, and the others noticed and decided that was probably enough. They were tired, they were all tired. So they lifted Sufjian, who, at this point, was down on the ground, was not so different to the now-red bundles of rags, they lifted him up and tied him to them, and although his legs buckled when they made him stand, they made him walk away with them, bound, slumped, propping and propelling him along like a puppet, like a sad sleepy child. Sarah held her son high enough to breathe but too low to see but she could see, just, through stripes of brown-green leaf, thick and lush and healthy.

She slipped on the way back out, up the bank, she slipped and a sword-sharp reed caught her, cut her, all the way smooth across one cheek, all the way dark across one eye.

She came to tell us. And to tell us that she was finished fighting. That she was going home.

Where's that? asked Liberata.

I don't know yet, said Sarah. Somewhere else. Somewhere quieter, she said, even though the only sound for miles was the river and the flies.

How old was he? I asked.

Sufjian?

Yes.

I don't know that either, she said.

Maybe ninety? said the boy.

Maybe sixteen, said Sarah. Maybe seventeen.

We held their hands. We didn't sing. We said goodbye.

That night, Quiteria sharpened her sword on a wet river stone, and I watched, and she said, This is good, Basil. They'll think they've found us. They'll think they've won. They'll let their guard down.

I didn't say anything. I watched the grey of the metal against the grey of the stone.

She looked up, at me. I'm sorry, she said. You know I'm sorry too, Basil. But it's not all bad. There are ways we can make it good, ways we can win from this, still.

And I said, Teach me how to sharpen my sword.

I didn't run so much then, after that, during our raids. I stayed and I fought. I used my sword. I wasn't afraid of getting killed, not at all. I didn't care. And that made it harder for them to do it, so that I didn't die then or there at all.

I did die, eventually, of course, but not until later.

First, Liberata and I crossed a nightmare's worth of water and lost a sister we thought we'd found and found a baby we didn't know we were looking for and lost each other, left each other, she and the baby a glow of clean white in the middle of the throbbing filth of a city, me the same as always, grubby, grey, running away, back. We needed each other but needed other things more.

Bye, Basil, she said. For now.

For now, I said.

And I left, back out the city gate and onto the road, the trail, back towards home, finally, finally.

I didn't die until after that, until after I met Lucius, our lost sister's prison guard, for the second time, until we stood, facing each other, and he said, Really? And I said,

Really.

And anyway, I couldn't die, not really. Not forever. Not like dying before. Right?

Your sister isn't afraid of cows, he'd said, earlier, out of breath. He'd pushed through the crowd on the road, had, apparently, run to get to me. Wasn't afraid, I mean, he said. She wanted you to know that.

You're the guard, I said.

Yes, he said. Though technically I'm just a soldier. Not a guard by trade. Not trained . . .

From before, I said. From the jail. From Vitoria—

Felicitas?

Felicitas's jail.

Yes, he said. Yes. I'm Lucius.

My sword was strapped to my wrist, like always, ready with one flick, like always. I took a step back. How did you find me? I asked. Did you follow me?

Yes and no, he said. Well, yes. Just yes. I saw you walking with your sister, just now, it's hard not to see a Vestal, and then, yes, I followed you.

Why? I asked.

To tell you, he said. To tell you she wasn't afraid of cows, to—

I already knew that, I said. That's not something you run to tell people. That's stupid.

But, he said. She said you haven't seen each other since you were seven or—

Nine, I said. Still, I said.

He tried to give me a book of tablets with lines scribbled both ways across them all, up and down and back and forth, tight with scribbles, but I told him it was pointless, I couldn't read a word.

I could read it to you, then, he said. I'd started up again, walking down the road away from the gates, the city. He was running, almost, to keep up with me.

Don't you have to go back? I said. To your job guarding or stabbing or whatever?

No, he said. I've got a break. They give you a break, sometimes, when a prisoner dies.

I kept walking, faster.

I know you want to get to wherever, he said. But I'd like to read it to you. It's not for me, I mean, it's not about me. It's your sister's. It's

Felicitas's words, story. I've got some wine you could drink while you listen . . .

I stopped walking and turned to him. He almost smashed into me, then pulled back and pretended to wipe something off his uniform. Okay, I said. I'll listen. If you promise to go away after, to leave me alone.

Okay, he said. He held out his hand, but I didn't take it.

Can I have that wine? I asked.

We sat in some shade off to the side of the road. It stank, but the whole city radiated stink and it was less potent here than inside the walls at least. All around us hawkers shook things at the mass of people moving up and down the road: toys, baskets, idols, incense, fruit, flasks, animals, anything that could be carried or piled onto a cart. I took a drink of wine. Lucius watched me, cleared his throat.

I'm not afraid of cows, he said, he began, he read. Vitoria, renamed Felicitas, is not afraid of cows.

And there she was, back.

7

VITORIA

I'm not afraid of cows.

Vitoria, renamed Felicitas, is not afraid of cows.

Write that down. Please.

Who's afraid of cows? No one I grew up with. Not my sisters, not my neighbours, not anyone in the village. Rich people are afraid of cows, that's who. Like they're afraid of the sun, or of us.

Oh.

That stings. That hurts.

Oh, wow, ow, oh.

Stop. You should stop. You really, ow. Please, ow, please stop. You really don't need to bother. Don't clean it, don't bind it, don't bother. Really, really.

Really?

It's pointless, right? We both know it's pointless, right? It's a nice idea, making it look like you tried, like you tried to save me, but we both know that this little bandage and that little jar of wine aren't going to make a difference. And it hurts. Hurts more than it already hurts. Look, instead, how about you go and see if you can find something bigger to write on? Something proper, something a bit more durable. How about that? Could you do that? You can lock up, of course, not that I could run if I wanted, not now, and everyone else is dead already. Just me in here, nice and roomy, right? But anyway, feel free to lock up if you want, while you go. I won't be offended. Go. Please.

I'll wait.

That was fast. Thank you.

No, wine will just put me to sleep and that would be it, wouldn't it? Then your whole errand would be pointless. You can have the wine; keep yourself warm. Have the wine, and while you do, write this down on your new tablet, the big one, write everything I already said. Write: I was not afraid of that cow.

A herd, or a bull, or a mother with calf, sure, that can be trouble. But one cow, all on her own? She's got no desire, no reason to harm you. That's the difference between her and a territorial bull or a hungry lion or whatever else they might throw at the men.

They think women are so delicate that we expire in the face of a single confused cow. Poor waste of an animal.

The crowd spooked her. They shouted and waved things at her, but she didn't want to hurt us, she just wanted to get away. That she didn't kill us both, that wasn't a miracle. That was common sense. Listen, are you listening? That wasn't a miracle. Write that down. Write: It wasn't a miracle. No God, not one, not many, was involved with that. None. We probably don't have long, so if that's all you get, get that.

Well, I'm bleeding, aren't I? I'm dying, aren't I? It's okay, it's okay, it's not your fault. I'm not happy about it either, no, but I know it's not your fault. Not your fault and not the cow's fault. If anything, it's Perpetua's fault. I'm going to be dead soon and she already is, so I think I'm okay to say that. So I'm saying it. It's her fault she's dead and her fault I almost am. I'm not angry at her, but that's the truth of it. We might as well admit it.

Do you think you'll be able to get that, that writing you're doing, once it's finished, to my sisters, somehow? Eventually? No rush, obviously, but eventually, somehow?

Oh, ow.

Oh, wow.

That still stings. That still.

Oh, wow.

But anyway, you might end up coming across them, someday. So if you do, if you somehow manage to, eventually, tell them these things, okay? And tell them to tell the baby. My baby.

Just give them the tablets. Or, if they're too expensive to give away, and I understand if they are, you could use them as notes, so you remember what I've said, what to tell them.

No, it'll be easy. Because they'll look like me. Just like me. Maybe with different scars. Still, they won't be hard to recognize. Just look for me, again.

So. Write that down about the cows and I'm going to rest now, for a bit. I need to rest now, I think. And if wake up and am not dead then maybe you can write some more. Okay? Okay. Thank you. You rest too. You look tired.

Okay. I'm back. I'm awake, mostly, and not dead yet, surprisingly, so I'm going to keep talking, and you might as well keep writing. Okay? You've got the important bit, but I might as well tell you the rest, so it's not awkward, just me dying here and you watching, too polite to leave. I mean, I don't even know you, but I know you're nice. I know you're polite. A good man, a good boy. So I'll tell you more, and you can write more or just pretend, because, really, I won't know either way. But I'd like it if you did write, for real. Okay, okay.

After Gema and Germana died of the sleeping pox—don't worry, they'll know who that was, just write the names, however you want to spell them, or just the first letters, G and G, if you want to save space—my father, my adoptive father, got scared. It wasn't very clean, our village, he said. The air was bad, he said, too dry, too hot, and there weren't doctors or priests around or anything like that. Maybe there were some at the big house, but none that would come down to us. Children were dropping like overripe lemons. Our father was scared. He started asking questions, looking for networks, for ways to get us, me and his four natural, non-adopted children, out. We didn't know he was doing it, of course, but he was. I spent most of my time in the trees and hills with my sisters, five of us, still, then, spent most of my time running wild, not listening to whispered conversations from father to father to father. Not paying them any attention at all.

It took almost a year for anything to come of it. He lost one more child, my brother Gummus, three years old, before he secured our escape.

I held my real sisters' hands, all five of us in a circle, all holding hands, at the top of this one hill we liked. Write that. Write that I remember that. That we held hands at the top of the hill, in a circle, facing each other, and I said, I won't go.

And they said, We won't let you go.

But I did go, of course. And they couldn't do anything about it. I was nine years old.

My father had spoken to a slave from the big house who passed in and out of our village. That slave had spoken to another slave who was visiting as part of the entourage of a visiting general, and that slave had gone all the way back to Carthage with that general and had spoken to a slave from another house while their two masters were soaking together in the public baths, and that slave had spoken to a more important slave from their same house who had spoken to an even more important slave who had spoken, carefully, quietly, to the master himself, who had said, Yes, he probably did know of a family in need of some help.

A Good Family? my father had asked, back through all the same people, once this news had finally made it to him.

A Good Family, came the word.

Okay. Said my father. And he sent back word asking how to proceed next, what to do next.

It would probably have been faster just to write a letter, but my father didn't know how to write.

He cried the day they came to take us away. His three remaining natural children and me. He cried and we couldn't tell if he was happy or sad and, anyway, he was sick again and crying a lot those days.

So we four children walked away, just walked out of the village and away, following the man who had been sent to get us. We walked and walked and walked. We slept under trees and in the little rounded-out bits of ground left once we rolled big rocks away. At night we curled together, we four, for warmth and so that we, together, would be bigger than him, the stranger who was leading us, just in case. We were five, seven, nine, and ten years old. We ate bugs off the ground.

He had us tied together with rope that grew softer the longer it rubbed against our wrists. It held us so we wouldn't get lost and so we wouldn't run away and so we could walk with our eyes closed, if we wanted, just trusting the tug of it to lead us in the right direction, to know we were together, still. The sun made everything blurry, everything white. We sucked water off the base of aloe and aeonium leaves and ate bugs and kept walking.

Some of the grasshoppers were big, as big as my fingers spread. Once we'd sucked out the soft bits, we would chew and chew on the shells and the wings for hours and hours.

I thought about my real sisters. I repeated their names in my head to the rhythm of my chewing, again and again, even the dead ones, so that I wouldn't forget and, somehow, I hoped, so they wouldn't forget me.

You don't have to hold my hand.

Okay, but still.

Okay, you can, but you don't have to. But you can.

We walked for eleven hot suns. We walked and walked and walked and then we stopped, because we hit a wall. Not a wall up, like the walls we'd had round our house, but a wall down, down and down and down. It was the highest wall I'd seen and it went down instead of up. And then, there, at the bottom of it, was another wall, this one not up or down, but out. Water out and out and out, huge and moving and animal. For the first time in eleven days, the man opened his mouth to speak to us, but the water wall, way down below us, was roaring, so we couldn't hear what he said.

He said it will eat us, whispered Artur, my adoptive brother, before we tried to sleep that night. He said he needs to sacrifice us to it or it will eat him too. We stayed at the top of the tall-down wall, curled with our backs against a newly fierce wind.

It will eat us, we all agreed. This was okay with us. To be a sacrifice would be noble and easy at the same time. It would mean a stop to the walking and the sun. We kissed each other goodbye and fell asleep.

We woke, ready to be eaten. The man had another man with him now, to help with all that, and that man had a basket and a long rope. They put Lia in the basket first, because she was the smallest, I guess, the tester. They untied her from us and put her in it and said something that wasn't as loud as the wind and lay down on their bellies, on the ground, and lowered the basket down, down, down the wall. When they pulled the basket back up it was empty. They put the next biggest, Sabela, in it. She disappeared down too. Down to be eaten.

I was next.

The basket came up empty, no more Sabela. They untied me from Artur and I climbed into it. I smiled at Artur and he smiled at me. Then they started lowering it down. It wasn't very big. My knees stuck out over the edges and I had to lean to one side and then the other, back and forth, to stop it from tipping. It dropped down in jerks, sometimes banging the side of the wall, sometimes farther from it than I could reach. Down and down, and the roar of the water god got louder and louder.

But I didn't land in its mouth. And neither had the other two who'd gone first. I landed, clunky, sideways, on some rocks, with the roaring water fifty or more steps away. Lia and Sabela were there too, standing on the rocks, beside a woman dressed in the clothes of a man. She bent and pulled me out of the basket and tied me back up to the other two. I looked at Sabela. She shrugged. I looked at Lia, she shrugged too. The basket went back up, empty, and we waited. And then, eventually, it came down again, with Artur in it.

He saw us. We shrugged. The woman lifted him out and tied him to us and the basket went back up again.

The next time it came down, and the last time, it had the man in it. The man who we'd followed already, so far. His legs and arms stuck out and banged into the rocks even more than mine had, even more than Artur's.

The woman let him get himself out, which he did, brushing bits of grit off his legs. Then he nodded at her, took the end of the rope, our rope, and pulled us forward, on.

We all would have preferred to be eaten by the water god than to have to keep walking, but we had to keep walking. As the sun moved round, the water god crawled closer and closer and closer and the rocks got smaller and smaller until we were walking on stones so small they were almost dirt and the water pushed into our toes with each of its breaths.

He got a boat from a woman who squinted at us like we were too loud for her even though we were completely quiet. She touched Lia's hair, just once, pushing it behind her ear. The man lifted us into the boat and then pushed it out onto the water until he was wet to his knees, then jumped in himself and started rowing and the woman stood and watched, getting smaller and smaller.

Maybe he's bringing us right to the mouth, right to the middle of this water god, where the mouth is, whispered Artur, and we all nodded. There was a bucket of shining, wriggling fish in the boat that we stole from when the man wasn't looking. We bit off the heads and tails and tasted salt. We swallowed the skulls whole, making no sound at all. We waited.

There was no mouth. The water god didn't want us after all, our lives too little to be worth it. We were lifted out again on the rocks on the other side of the water, were given a small flask of wine to share, to wash the salt from our tongues, from our teeth and the roofs of our mouths, and we walked some more, walked and walked and walked, the skin on the bottom of our feet hard and black.

Lia died. She was too small, too young. Not fast enough at catching bugs, not smart enough yet to tell us when she lost another one, went hungry again. The new man untied the rope that bound us to her and we tried to dig her a bed between a flat black rock and a bush with small yellow flowers, but the ground was too hard, was too dry to dig. We broke off some branches and flowers to lay her on. We kept walking.

I don't know how long. Just forever. Lia's forever. Almost ours. I imagine you've done walks like that, with the army. Just forever, so that walking is breathing and steps are time, moving, rolling, always moving. We walked and walked and walked.

And then: the city. This city.

You could hear it before you could see it. You could hear it for miles. Smell it too.

And then we were in among so many people, more people than we knew were possible. And we were walking on stone, suddenly, not earth, which was hotter on our feet, which seemed like a stupid idea, since it was so hot, but most people were in sandals, not bare like us, so I guess they didn't notice. There were buildings everywhere and people in and out of them everywhere, and some of the people looked like us but a lot of them didn't, and some were even in white, in bright white, and I couldn't stop looking at that, at them. There was a lot of dirt, a lot of bad in our world, but now, there was also this bright white, this cleanness, like these people had somehow caught and skinned the sun. Like they were wearing the sun. And I looked and looked and looked and soaked it up, knowing there could be real clean, real pure, real good.

They didn't keep us together the way they told my father they would, the way he told us they would. The man untied me first. He took my hand and placed it in the hand of a boy with no hair, took some coins from him, and continued on with the others, still tied together, off through all the people, through all the grey and colour and white. I didn't see them again, there or anywhere. I don't know where they went. They were called Artur and Sabela, and I don't know if they got to stay together or not.

Hi, said the boy. His accent was new, high and light. His head, where the hair should be, was very round and a little bit fuzzy, like a new boar. I wondered if that was what my head looked like too, under my hair.

Hi, I said.

It's not far, he said. To go. To walk.

I nodded. I didn't remember what far and not far meant anymore.

You want water?

I nodded.

He pointed to a person made of stone ten steps or so in front of us. There was water shooting out of the person's mouth, splashing into a basin at their feet. I stared at it.

Go on, he said. I'll wait here.

I didn't move. I looked at the boy. I looked at the person. What . . . ? I whispered. What's wrong with them?

Huh?

Are they cursed?

Who? We don't have much time, if you're thirsty you should—

I didn't ask any more questions. I went to the water. I stuck my head into the basin, underwater, where the person's stone feet were, and felt a coolness I'd never felt before in my whole short life. I drank and drank.

My head was still wet, my hair still dripping, when we got to my big new house. It was bigger than the whole orchard at home, the whole village. There were people of stone all up the path leading to it and there was a basin of water, like in the city, around the back, by the door the boy told me I had to use, if I wanted to come and go, but there was no need telling me that, I knew, because I knew I would never leave, never ever want to leave again.

And then a fat woman opened the back door to us. She was the first fat person I'd seen, other than pregnant ones. The boy ran off, behind her and away. I love you, I said after him. Goodbye, I love you.

The fat woman looked at me and raised her eyebrows. My hair dripped down. The drips made dark marks on the hot stone I was standing on. All right, she said. Into the basin with you. Off with your clothes, and into the basin.

All of me?

All of you.

I loved her too.

They burned my clothes and cut my hair short, like the boy's. They scrubbed my scalp and body with oil and it felt wonderful and I felt as pure and as bright as the togas I'd seen in the square. I felt Good.

Oh. Yes, I guess I will, okay.

Yes, thank you. If you could lift the flask to my mouth, I, yes. Oh.

Oh.

Oh.

Thank you, soldier. Thank you.

And then, and then after that first bath and scrubbing and haircut, the fat woman put me in a grey tunic and handed me a pair of soft dust-brown sandals that felt like they were always about to fall off my feet but never did. She cleaned me and groomed me and dressed me and then, when she'd done all she could do, she said, Okay, good enough, I guess.

She took my hand and walked me down sun-full corridors until we came to a room where a girl, a girl my age, not exactly, but close enough, was pushing a chair towards a far wall, away from another chair, the only other thing in the room.

The girl saw us. She stopped. The chair fell over. The woman let go of my hand and went to put it back, upright.

No, said the girl, quietly, calmly. No, Vibipuella, I will do it. The chair was bigger than her. Dark wood and heavy. Vibipuella and I watched the girl struggle it up onto two legs, watched it fall again, watched her duck out of the way so as not to get squashed by it, watched her try again to push it up, watched it wobble, watched it settle, back, up. Then the girl continued to push it. She pushed it right up to the far wall. Then she stopped and stood for a few heartbeats, getting her breath back. Then she climbed up, onto the chair. She sat with her legs dangling over the front and looked very small and I wondered if I looked that small when I sat on chairs.

She looked at me. Felicitas, she said. That's your chair. You go sit over there. She pointed across the room, to the chair pushed against the other wall, the farthest point from her and her chair.

Nobody moved. I looked up at the woman, who had come back to stand beside me.

Fe-li-ci-tas, said that girl. Do you understand me? Go, there, to your chair.

I kept looking at the woman, whose name seemed to be Vibipuella and Felicitas at once. I was hot. The new tunic didn't have any holes in it.

The woman looked down, back at me. Then she looked at the far-away chair. Then at me again. Then the chair. Then me. I loved her and wanted her to love me, so even though I didn't feel like smiling, I did anyway. I smiled as big as I could, with teeth. She smiled back, a little. Go, she said. Go to the chair. And then she left.

So I did. I walked over and climbed up onto the faraway chair. The girl, in hers, looked straight ahead now, not at me. I looked at her. Who's Felicitas? I said.

You are, said the girl.

I'm Vitoria, I said.

No, you're not, said the girl.

Yes, I—

Not anymore, said the girl. Now you're Felicitas. You're my sister Felicitas.

～

The next day the girl, Perpetua, had pushed the chairs a little bit closer together, about ten steps apart. You mustn't talk about your old sisters anymore, she said.

Why not?

Just don't.

There wasn't too much we could do, sitting apart like that, now that I couldn't tell stories from home anymore like I had the day before. We sat quietly for a while. I watched a fly trying to find a way out of the room until it did find a way out and then I said, We could play What Thing Am I?

But you can't be your sisters.

They're not a thing.

Still.

Okay. I won't. I'll be something else. Ready?

Okay, I guess. Ready.

We played What Thing Am I for the three days, from after my morning chores and Perpetua's breakfast until her lessons and my guts-taking-out time. I was:

A Stone
A Bug

A Bush with Small Yellow Flowers
and
A Hill.

She was:

A Crown of Olive Branches
A Small White Mouse
A Sunset Over the Southern Hills
A Room Bigger Than This One
and
Any Other Game.

By the third day, she had the chairs pushed up so the arms were touching.

Okay, I said. Fine. Let's play a different game, then.

Which one?

Well, we could play a game that's not just sitting, I said.

I don't think you're allowed to run around, she said.

Says who?

My father.

Perpetua talked about her father a lot. Mostly in terms of rules. Mostly rules I wasn't allowed to break. I'd never seen him. I wasn't sure he existed.

I bet I'd be allowed to run around if you were running around too. If I was following you.

She thought about this. Well, she said.

And then she jumped off her chair and ran out of the room. I ran after her.

We only returned to the chairs and to What Thing Am I on the few days that it was too hot to run, too hot to move, or when the locusts were swarming and would get into our eyes and our mouths if we went out. Which was funny, because I used to try to get bugs into my mouth. But now they were giving me real, actual food. Bread and fish and olives too. And I was growing a little bit fat, like them, and I started closing my eyes and mouth to the bugs, like them. And Perpetua and I ran up and down her family's garden chasing each other or the animals or the animals boy and soon my hair grew longer again, and soon my tunic and my sandals were too small. And,

And,

What?

Who?

Oh, yes, yes, he is.

Her father, yes.

Yes, the most important man I've met, I guess, but I've barely met him. At the end, when he and Perpetua weren't speaking, he would sometimes send messages through Vibipuella to me for his daughter, and once or twice he caught me in the garden or hall and whispered a few words directly to me to bring her, but I didn't know him, not really; he didn't speak to me, not really. A bit at the end, but still, not much. Not really. Sorry.

But I'm sure he'd appreciate your reverence. He liked that sort of thing. Still does, I imagine.

I didn't see him there today, in the podium, not in his regular seat, anyway, so I doubt you'll have the opportunity to speak to him in person. I don't think he came today.

No, it wouldn't be very nice, given the circumstances.

No, I wouldn't have either.

Do you know what happened to her? Or to her baby?

No, it's okay, it's okay.

Maybe I'll lie down now. Is it okay if I lie down now?

Here is fine. No, it's fine. I don't mind a bit of dirt, a bit of blood, some milk too, if I'm honest. That's the smell, the milk, mostly. Sorry. I'm just, I'm just getting tired.

More water maybe, yes.

Thank you.

Thank you.

Are you still writing? Show me.

Okay, good. Thank you. Thank you.

Perpetua was my age. Not exactly, like my sisters, but close enough for her parents, the bosses of the house. She was their daughter, their only daughter.

No others? I asked her.

No, she said.

Not even two or three?

No, she said.

A tiny one? A tiny baby somewhere?

No, Felicitas, she said. No, no, no. No. None. And I'm glad about it. She crossed her arms. Looked at me with her eyes made tiny. But I do have one brother, she said.

Just one?

I used to have two. Now I have one. Just one.

Okay, I said. That's okay.

Except you, said Perpetua. No sisters except for you.

Do you have sisters, soldier? You must. I think you must.

Well, I'm surprised to hear it. I would have thought. I would have sworn.

Oh.

Oh. I'm sorry. Both at once?

Both at once. That's not better or worse. That's just, that just is. I'm sorry. I'm sorry, soldier.

We played together, like real sisters, when Perpetua wanted to. And when she didn't want to, or when she was off eating fancy food or in lessons, I helped in the kitchen gathering up the animal bones and guts and grape stems and olive pits and old dry bread and carrying them out to the pig. At first, if no one was around or looking, I would hide the olive pits in my pockets to suck on later, or would dip the old bread in the fountain to make it soft again and eat it with the animal guts spread on top before I got to the pig. Sometimes it made me throw up, but sometimes it didn't. But then I got used to not feeling hungry. I trusted not being hungry, and eventually, I stopped. I also stopped taking a drink from the fountain every time I passed. I finally knew, finally trusted it was going to be there, always, and always with water in it. Even on the very hottest days, it was always, still, there, flowing like winter, like it didn't, couldn't, know thirst.

If the kitchen didn't need me and Perpetua didn't want me or was busy, I would help the bald-headed boy, the animals boy. Together we cleaned the pig's house and gathered eggs from the chickens and got them to stop pecking each other and took turns milking the cow and goats. Neither of us liked milking the goats, because they were mean and kicked, and we both liked milking the cow, because she was calm and gentle and didn't even notice us there, really. She also gave more milk, so the fat woman was less likely to notice if some went missing, warm and rich with cream that coated your tongue so you could taste and remember it for three hours afterwards. So we took turns milking the cow and the goats, getting kicked and getting cream.

But that was just sometimes. When I was with Perpetua the boy had to milk the cow and the goats. I'd see him later, at the slaves' table in back of the kitchen, and he'd have a film of cream around his mouth or a fresh bruise on his arm or shoulder and he'd smile, either way, he'd smile at me.

It's very hot in here, isn't it? It's really really hot. You must be totally boiled in your armour. You can take off your helmet, at least. I mean, I'm not about to punch you in the head. Hm. Imagine that. But I won't. Don't worry, I can't, and even if I could I wouldn't, let's say.

That's a nice smile.

Yes.

Yes.

And nice hair too, probably. If anyone could see it. Take the helmet off, for heaven's sake. It looks like it weighs a ton. A ton of hot gold. I can't think of anything—

There.

That's better, isn't it? You look more comfortable. And you do have nice hair. Lovely, sweaty hair.

And what about that ridiculous huge sword halter? You keep bumping it when you write, is that comfortable? Sure, I might die right away and then you can stop and stretch out a bit, but I might not, maybe not for hours, in which case, you might as well get comfortable.

There, better?

Good, good.

The animals boy asked me to get married about one and a half years after my first bleed. I don't know exactly how old I was, because no one was keeping track, but I do know that my feet weren't quite finished growing, that I went through another two sizes of sandals afterwards. We were with the goats. I remember there weren't too many flies yet, so it must have been just early spring. The goat he was milking, the one we called Old Bastard, got bored, like she often did, and kicked out, like she often did, while the animals boy's head was down, watching the milk, and hit him straight on, in the side of the face, just under his eye. I laughed, because we knew, we both knew, that you don't lower your head with her, we both knew that. I laughed, he swore. If the kick had landed slightly higher he'd have been half-blinded. We both knew that too. He was bleeding. I pulled the pot out from under my goat so she wouldn't knock it over and waste the milk, and I went to the house, to the kitchen. I stole some vinegar and a clean-looking cloth and brought them back to him. I cleaned the wound, had him hold the cloth to it. You're lucky, I said. Back with my sisters, we didn't have vinegar, we just had piss. He didn't respond, just kept opening and closing his mouth to check that it was all still holding together. I gave him a tiny bit of my cow's milk to drink to stop him doing it for a while. He got the very top, the warmest bit. He held it in his mouth for a few seconds. Then he swallowed, open and closed his mouth again twice, and said,

Let's get married, Vitoria, you and me.

He said it like that. With my old name. My real name.

I watched his mouth open-close. I watched the blood bloom through the cloth. Okay, I said. Let's.

I don't know how old he was then either. He had grown since my arrival; his tunic falling higher against his legs, square with muscle from carrying, lifting, running into town and back, his legs now soft with hair, like mine.

My hands were sweating. I wiped them on my tunic and took my bucket from him and put it back under my goat. Okay, I said. Sure.

The animals boy stopped opening and closing his mouth and, half-hidden behind the blood-pink vinegar cloth, smiled.

I told Vibipuella in the kitchen, as she was scrapping meat slop into a pail. Will you share a bed? she asked. Will you not need yours anymore?

I don't know, I said.

A bit of slop, a purple-red clump of whisker and skin, fell away from her knife. She wiped the blade on her tunic. You know where the wild carrot grows? she asked.

No. We didn't eat them; Perpetua hated them. They were too tough, too bland.

You want a fish swimming around in your belly?

No. I don't think—

Then you need to know where the wild carrot grows. I'll show you after lunch. She scraped at a bit of skin that had become stuck to the counter, digging her knife in a little harder with each go until it finally came loose and skidded away from her, towards me.

Okay, I said, picking up the skin and putting it in with the other scraps. Thank you.

And let me know about the beds, she said.

I was lucky. I'd been lucky. I didn't know it, didn't even think of it, then, but I was. My proximity to Perpetua came with some advantages, some protection. The others, Vibipuella, the cleaning girls, all the others knew where the wild carrot grew. I was lucky; I was naive.

I told Perpetua that evening, the evening of the day the animals boy had asked me. We were up in a tree, seeing who could stomach more raw olives picked from it.

You're not chewing, she said. You're just swallowing them whole. That doesn't count.

I bit down. The bitterness rushed through me, cold. My lips went numb. There, I said. Also, I'm getting married.

She bit down too. But she always did. That's why she usually lost. She made a face. To who? she said.

The animals boy, I said.

The animals boy? She made another face.

Yes, I said.

Doesn't count, she said. Marriage between slaves doesn't count. And then she said, Anyway, it doesn't matter. I'm already married.

Which I knew was a lie, because a girl like her doesn't just get married without anyone noticing, without the whole house taking part. Marriage, for a girl like her, isn't between two people at all, it's between two whole working households, two colonies, like ants. But I didn't say that. Because she knew that. And she knew I knew that. Instead I said, Oh. To who?

You don't know him yet, she said. You weren't there, she said. It was in lessons.

Is he another student? Or one of your tutor's sons?

I didn't think her father, her father with all his rules, would like that very much. I didn't think he would like that at all.

No, she said, although my tutor did introduce us. It's not a normal marriage, Felicitas, it's better.

Because you're rich?

No. Not different like that. It's better than a normal marriage. And easier. You should consider it.

Do you still get to sleep in your own bed? I asked. What about wild carrot?

What about it? It's gross.

Yes, but, I said.

It's not a normal marriage, Felicitas, she said. I told you. She reached up over our heads and picked two sun-green olives.

What's his name? I asked.

Jesus, she said, and handed me one of the fruits. It was as hard as the stone it protected. His name is Jesus.

Perpetua's marriage involved getting to take a sort of bath in front of lots of people and in clothes.

Mine involved the animals boy saving a chick that had come out of its egg already dead to take to the house's second-best altar. It didn't bleed much at all. It had only as much blood in it as when Perpetua poked her finger on a spike-plant once and squeezed and squeezed to get some drops out to try to prove that she was injured. The chick's eyes didn't even look like eyes yet, still sealed up and covered over in feathers like fur. My marriage involved Vibipuella from the kitchen lending me an orange band to tie around my tunic and knot in a special way that she washed her hands to do, and that the animals boy and I took ages to try to get undone, later. It involved me seeing his cell, dark and warm in back of the barn, between lots of others, between the sound of bodies and grunting and breath, some animal, some human, his space not as big as mine, not as clean, not as close to the house. It involved us taking off our tunics and seeing the lines where the sun and dirt stopped and the flesh underneath continued softer up and up and his reaching up to pull me down to him, my stepping back, not to step away but to stretch things out, to have more time to look at him, to watch him looking at me, it involved waiting for the pain Vibipuella warned me of but there being no pain, just animal flashes of how I'd see the cow and bull, the goats, the dogs, the horses, of how this was so much bigger, so different but was also the same, the same, the same.

It involved him telling me his name, Vibipor, which I already knew, and his real name, Danel, which I did not. I told him my real name too, repeated it, even though he already knew it.

Danel and Vitoria. We said them out loud under the noise of bodies, grunts, breath.

He rolled away before the end, just before, and made an animal sound and curled into himself. It was dark. I couldn't feel him anymore, so I couldn't see him. I heard his breath catch and stop and then gradually pull back to slow, back to normal.

What? I asked.

If there's a child they can take it away, he said. They can have it. And you might die.

So this is what we did, after we were married.

Perpetua did things differently.

Don't be embarrassed.

Sorry. But, I mean, this isn't the worst thing you've heard, surely. You're a soldier, after all. Right?

We were married, for heaven's sake.

For heaven's sake.

Are you married?

Oh yeah, of course, you're a soldier. Of course. That's okay. You have time, you have time. Lots and lots and lots of time.

Yes, I would.

I'd recommend it, yes, yes, yes. I, I,

I found new colours when I married Danel. That's what it was like. Now they're gone.

Now my eyes are tired. Too much light, too much white. I, I'd like to take a break, just a

. . .

. . .

No.

No!

I mean no, that can't, no, you can't let me. I'm fine I'm fine I'm just getting warm. Really warm. I'd really like to sleep. To take a break. But I can't sleep. Not anymore, not yet.

I don't know.

I don't know.

I just know: Not yet.

I'm just getting to the good part anyway, the best part. I want to talk about that part, those colours, keep talking.

And you keep writing. And if I stop talking for more than a few seconds I need you to throw that water at me. At my face. Okay? And if there's no water left I need you to use your hand. Slap my face. Okay?

No one will see. No one will care, even if they do see. Will you do it? Will you?

You are good. You will get married. Or not. You will get what you want. You can have my ring. You—

No. He's dead. Danel is dead.

Don't be sorry, you didn't kill him.

I did. But later. That all happened later.

You can be married to Jesus and also married to a normal man at the same time, Perpetua said to me one day. I was braiding her hair. She liked it up now, tucked up and away, most of the time. She wouldn't let me fold flowers into the braids either. We hadn't talked about her marriage, her strange man-not-man husband, in a while. I thought, maybe, she'd moved on, or forgot.

You can?

Yes. We had to stop talking about all that, she said. Me and my tutor, while Father was home and started unexpectedly dropping in on our lessons. Sometimes he would just sit there, in the corner, for the whole afternoon, even though he already knows all about poetry and numbers and whatever other normal, boring things I'd be learning about that day. But now he's gone back to the borders with my brother and his armies, and I've been learning more, again, more of the good stuff. I've learned that . . . are you ready for this?

For what?

For this news?

Oh, yes.

Okay, good. I've learned that my mother is married to Jesus too. That she was the one who told him about it.

Told Jesus?

No. Told my tutor. That she was the one who gave him a holy bath, so now he's married too. She did!

I tried to imagine Perpetua's mother giving Perpetua's tutor a bath. I couldn't.

That's horrible, I said. That must be heartbreaking. And weird. I'm sorry, I'm sorry, Perpetua.

No, it's wonderful!

To be married to the same person as your mother? And . . . your tutor? Is that even allowed? Wonderful? Is your father married twice too? Does he know?

It's not a person we're married to, Felicitas, remember. Not a normal one, anyway, so it's okay. And anyway, it's not something we discuss with my father. Not yet. And you don't either.

I never discuss anything with him.

Still.

And he's miles away. In Rome or wherever.

He's not in Rome. He's in the wilds. Like always. And I'm not kidding, Felicitas, I'm serious. My tutor says it's dangerous, it can be very dangerous, to talk about this to other people, people who aren't us. That there are people who hate love.

I don't hate love, I said.

I love love, said Perpetua.

Me too, I said. Me too. We were silent then, for a while, while I finished her hair. How do you like it? I said, once I'd finished. One boring braid across the top. No flowers.

I love it, said Perpetua.

One night Danel came to bed walking strange. One leg normal, one leg pulling around in stiff circles. He had a cut on his face, just under the eye, the same place the goat had kicked him, before. He saw me looking. It will heal, he said. They're just afraid, he said. He tried to lower himself down to the bed, to me, but pain caught him and he straightened back up again. The people out there, he said. The people in the city are afraid. He tried again to sit down, a different approach, a clumsy one that was basically leaning to one side, the good side, until he fell and then letting his arms catch him and lowering himself the rest of the way down. He winced as he did it, but made it, this time, down to me. The barbarians are getting closer, he said. You don't go out much, to the city, so maybe you haven't heard what people are saying. They're saying they're ambushing now, killing travellers on the outskirts, they're saying the barbarians are worse than ever before. And worse than the ambushes, worse than the possibility of attack, people are getting sick again. People are getting sick because, they say, the barbarians have brought the sickness back. Intentionally, some people say, unintentionally, other people say, the same result either way, people say. People are afraid, Vitoria, so . . . he tried to turn towards me, but the pain caught him and sent him back, so he stayed on his back, as he had been, looking straight up to the barn's rafters, not at me. So anyway, he said. All we know for sure is that some people are sick and the barbarians are closer, getting closer. That's why the commander and his son have gone again, so soon. And that's why people are afraid. He sighed.

Then, on top of that, you have Perpetua and her mother, he said. And the tutor and all their lot acting weird, speaking in secret symbols, holding themselves apart. People see these things, Vitoria, barbarians getting closer and some people getting sick and rich people acting weird and they think: These things could be related. They are afraid and they think: Here's something, something probably related, something real and local that we can pin our fear to so it can turn to anger, so we can do something about it.

So your leg? And face?

It's not my place, out there, to say what I think. It's my place to defend this household.

So you did?

So I am trying.

We didn't sleep together that night. Instead we slept side by side, sharing warmth but not touch. I was afraid touching him would hurt him. He needed his legs, he needed his eyes, he needed them for work and he needed them for me. In the morning he got up slowly and carefully, like our oldest goat.

Be careful, I said. Out there.

It's you, Vitoria, he said. The thing you need to understand is that it's you who needs to be careful. With Perpetua and her tutor and their ideas. In here.

Some nights I stayed with him and some nights Perpetua had me stay with her, just as she always did when she felt lonely or scared or bored of sleep. Vibipuella had given my old bed away to a new slave who prepared baths, mostly.

The thing you need to know, said Perpetua, the next night, blanket up to her chin, is that the thing that makes it different, that makes it amazing, that makes it all make sense where other things don't make sense, is that he was just a person. Not different from us, not above, just a person. A god, but small, like men. Just a man, she said. Like the tutor.

Like Vibipor, the animals boy, I said.

Sure, she said.

She told me about her engagement to the tutor six months later. I tried not to make a face when she told me. He was old. He was serious, all the time serious.

Are you happy? she asked. Glad for me?

Yes, I said. I had wool wrapped round and round my hands, was spinning it. All the women there spun and wove at least from time to time, even the ones, like me, who were no good at it, even Perpetua. It was boring, but it was expected.

Felicitas, she said. I want you to be happy. You need to be happy. You're my sister.

But also a slave, I said. So it doesn't really matter. Anyway, yes, I'm happy. Happy for you.

No, she said, stopping my hands, stopping the spinning. No, Felicitas, she said. No, you're not.

Not happy?

Not a slave. Not just a slave. We're all the same, Felicitas. Slave, Roman, God. We're all weak, we're all great.

My fingers itched. Even the animals boy? I said.

Even him, said Perpetua. Even my father.

He's not going to let you marry the tutor, you know, I said.

I know.

So?

So. I'll figure something out. We will. Right?

I stretched my fingers out, back, trying to move the wool up and down, trying to scratch the itch with the same thing that was causing it in the first place. Yes, I said. Right.

First, we heard the crowd. It was later, a few days, maybe a week, maybe two. I was in bed, in Danel's cell, and we heard them, maybe ten, maybe twenty, maybe fifty people, talking to the house's gatekeeper. First talking, then shouting. We heard him first talking and then shouting back; we heard lots of voices trying to say or shout things at the same time, over top of each other, louder and louder, and then the animals starting to wake and get upset and make their own noise, so Danel and I had to get up and calm them, and then, soon, it was all quiet again and we went back to bed and Danel said, whispered,

There was fighting with the barbarians today, just outside the city walls. Some people say they were just looking for food, some say medicine, some say blood. We killed five of theirs, he whispered, and they killed three of ours. Our people from outside, farmers, traders, have been pouring in, into the tense, sick safety of the city. People are all afraid. Spooked, like animals.

Our people?

The ones who, you know, you know what I mean.

Yes. Yes, I do.

We lay in silence. We lay and listened as the rest of the house came awake, as people started walking around, lighting lamps, talking, running. We heard the accountant in the cell next to Danel's get up and go to the house. We heard him come back. He knocked on the ground and then came in to us.

Just so you know, he said, our gatekeeper is dead. They hung him up. They put dead fish in his pockets, and then they hung him up.

Then the accountant went back to his cell and closed the curtain door.

You think I'm callous. That I'm being callous, and impious, telling you all this, just like this, when I'm about to die, when I should be praying, probably, or at least thinking good thoughts about people and things, that it doesn't make much sense, when one's about to die, to be callous and impious.

But that's it. Things don't make sense. That's why. That's why I am, maybe, callous. Definitely impious. Two of my sisters died before even being alive. That doesn't make sense. Two more died before their new teeth had even finished coming in. What's the point? What's the point of bothering with new teeth at all, then? Danel is dead because of me, the only one who really, really, wanted him to live. You, you're barely older than a boy. You're younger than he was, younger than me. But your life is already about death. Causing it, preventing it. Causing it to prevent it. I'm cut here and here and here, but I don't hurt there; the only place I hurt is here. Just here.

What's your name?

Lucius. That's a very normal name. That's a good name.

The only place I hurt is just here, Lucius.

We didn't know about temples or care about gods or the One God back in the lemon trees, growing up, Lucius. But everything was the same. Everything was pointless there, just like it's pointless here.

When I'm dead it would be good if you gave my body to those wild animals, the ones they put in with the men in the games, if you gave it to them to eat. They're only trying to protect themselves and to eat, those animals, and yet they always take the bodies away, once the animals have killed them. I know you're not allowed, so you won't, but, Lucius, that would be good, wouldn't it, if they could have my body to eat? That would make sense. Animals, the ones that aren't us, at least, at least they try to make sense.

Nobody slept that night. Not the accountant, not the animals, not Danel, not me, and not Perpetua either. After the accountant had gone, we lay there, looking at the beams of the ceiling, listening to the animals' worried breath, and then listening to more footsteps coming towards us, to another knock on the floor.

Felicitas? Are you there?

Perpetua stayed there, on the other side of our curtain door. She'd never actually been down to the cells herself, as far as I knew. Usually, if she wanted me, she would send someone.

Yes, I said.

She paused. Exhaled. Her breath was as heavy as the animals'.

Will you come with me? she said. Will you please come sleep in my room tonight?

Yes, I said.

She took my hand as we walked across the garden, back to the main house. She ignored the people running around us. She ignored the lamps, the talk, the questions. She held my hand and she said,

You're my real sister, Felicitas. You are.

We got to her room and got into bed and she still held my hand and she asked,

Will you let me baptize you? Before it's too late, will you?

And I loved her, so I said, Yes.

She wasn't my real sister, but I said, Yes.

They built taller walls around the house after that. They replaced the gatekeeper, the one who was now dead. He had been an old man, thin and friendly, but the new one was the largest slave in the house, large and young and mean. Turned mean. They burned the dead fish. I would have given them to the dogs, at least, but they burned them. They made sure we had food enough to last us all as long as we needed and told us it would be best for us all to stay in, in the house or within the walls, at least, until Perpetua's father got back and could decide what to do, so we stayed in, we waited, and Perpetua and her mother and her tutor prayed.

My baptism happened in the garden fountain. Perpetua would have preferred it to be in living, moving water, like hers had been, but there was none of that within the house's walls. Within safety. So we used the fountain. I had to fast for two days before, and so did Perpetua.

But we have food, I said. But we have enough food for us, and everyone, to eat. Why make ourselves weak if there's no need? That doesn't seem holy. That doesn't seem right.

You've got to empty yourself, said Perpetua. We were walking, slowly, up and down the garden path, up and down. So the purity can get in. So the good can get in. You need to feel the need.

She had never needed food when she couldn't have it, so this made sense for her. I had, so it did not for me. Being hungry made me panic. It made her pure.

Perpetua, her mother, and her tutor were all there. I wore a white tunic borrowed from her mother. It was the first and last time I'd ever wear white. Perpetua asked me questions and I said, Yes, Yes, Yes. She was wearing white too. I sat in the fountain, almost too small to hold me, and she held my head and lowered me down, carefully, until I was all the way underwater. I opened my eyes and saw only moving light. I opened my ears and heard only my heart.

I'd been hot and dirty my entire life. The baptism and the time I stuck my head in the city basin when I first arrived, back when the animals boy was just the animals boy, were the only times I haven't been.

When I sat up again, up out of the water, Perpetua, her mother, and her tutor were singing.

You look the same, Danel whispered as we milked the animals, me a goat, he the cow.

Yes, I feel the same, I whispered back. Which was mostly true.

They didn't tattoo you, mark you somehow?

No, of course not.

Okay, good, good.

He still checked me over that night, checked my whole body in the dull, inconsistent light of one borrowed lamp. Okay, okay, he said, fingers up and down my back, my legs, my neck, the parting in my hair. That night he didn't roll away at the end of sex. That night he stayed with me. And the next, and the next.

The night before her father came home, Perpetua said, I don't care if he kills me. She was getting undressed. Taking off her sandals and jewellery. I used to do this for her, but now she did it for herself.

He won't kill you, I said.

Maybe he will, maybe he won't, but I don't care if he does, she said.

The next day we all lined up in front of the house, everyone, slaves and soldiers and Perpetua and her mother and her tutor, and waited for her father to arrive home. It was hot. We waited. There were flies. We waited. There was dust, there was no water, we waited. And then, at last, surrounded by the noise and the smells and the colours of his own soldiers and slaves and animals, he arrived, at last.

He brought gifts. New strange fruit for the household, for everyone, even Danel, even me; heavy, deep-coloured cloth and shining earrings and necklaces for his wife; and an animal for Perpetua. A tiny lioness. With a lioness's colour and shape and movement, but small, small enough to pick up with just one hand, even fully grown. He handed it to her in a basket, which the lioness immediately jumped out of and ran away from, into the shade under the wheels of a cart. One of the new slaves went to get it. It scratched him on the arm. He put it back in the basket and brought it back to Perpetua. It jumped out again. The slave looked to the general, who shook his head. So the slave let the animal stay there, under the cart, and handed Perpetua the empty basket instead.

Everyone waited. Perpetua's father, surrounded by soldiers and slaves and riches, all waiting, didn't look glorious. He looked sad. He waved a hand, dismissing us, and walked, alone, into his house. His wife and daughter followed. The lioness, probably eager for the shade of inside, followed them.

Once the cat was all the way in, gone, and the family too, we slaves and soldiers all moved towards the two large baskets of new fruit left there for us. Danel and I waited in the queue and, when it was our turn, took one each. I watched a soldier eat his, pulling off and discarding the skin first, then biting into the flesh underneath. I did the same. It was soft and slimy at once. It was sweet like something half rotten. The smell was overpowering. Everyone was talking about the fruit, saying what it did and did not taste like, how much they liked it or did not like it, comparing sizes, textures, opening their mouths to let others inspect the chewed version, looking into other people's mouths to see it chewed. I pulled Danel to the edge, faced away from everyone else, and said,

Perpetua will tell him tonight. About the tutor, the engagement.

Tell or ask? said Danel.

Tell, I said.

People will already have told him about the gatekeeper, said Danel. The fish in his pockets. He won't be happy.

No, I said. But he won't kill her.

No, said Danel, probably not. But maybe the tutor.

Maybe.

We'd finished our fruit. The milk-sweet film of it coated my tongue, my teeth. I needed water. Danel, I said, I have a fish too. I have a fish in my belly.

He stopped chewing. Leaned in. There was a small smear of fruit up the side of his mouth. Really? he said.

Really, I said.

I don't see it, he said.

No, I said. Not yet. But I feel it.

How much time do we have?

Still months, I said. Months and months.

Only that, only months, said Danel.

That night:

Perpetua told her father.

Danel started to plan.

The mob, knowing the general was back, returned. Came back to the house's gate and demanded to speak with him. Demanded him now, now, now.

I bent down beside the fountain and threw up all the new fruit I'd eaten and my lunch and dinner too and the lioness watched me, curling around my legs, then came and slept with Danel and me, with the warmth and safety of other animals.

That night, the general, Perpetua's father, had gone out, out to the crowd. He took wine and bread for the people and had the new gatekeeper distribute it as peacefully, as placatingly as possible. The general spoke. The general made jokes, one about barbarians, one about women. The people chewed bread and drank wine and listened. They laughed. They respected him, still. Or they wanted more wine. Or some of each. Either way, they listened as he joked and listened as he said to them: This is a Good House, a Holy House, as it always has been. If there is trouble with secrets and witchcraft and cults, it is nothing to do with me, with this house.

He said, I've come home now, early, to find the traitor and have found him and now I give him to you. He knows that he is no longer a part of this house.

He motioned and a slave, another of the new ones, brought out the tutor. He walked free, the slave didn't need to use force. He walked through the opened gate to the crowd. Then the general, the slave, and the gatekeeper turned and walked back inside the house's wall, locking the gate behind them, so that they, and we, were on one side, and the tutor and the crowd were on the other.

The tutor didn't come back. We never saw him again. The baths slave said maybe they sent him to Rome, to trial there. Vibipuella, in the kitchen, said, Of course they didn't. Don't be stupid, of course they didn't.

They wanted to be safe, Lucius, you know that, right? The people wanted to feel safe. They needed to, like hunger.

People were sick and people were dying and we were very very far from Rome, from protection or guidance. The terror swirled around them and they just needed something, someone to grab on to to feel safe again, to feel secure. They just needed to feel safe, just like you, just like everyone.

The next night I slept in Perpetua's room. She unbraided her hair. We're already married, she said. The tutor and I. We already did it. Under God. She showed me a ring. Simple, but gold, real gold. She wore it on a leather string around her neck, under her clothes.

Did you have Vibipuella tie the knot for you? I asked. Did you have witnesses?

No, she said. But we are married. I would have liked you to be there, I would have liked to tell you, but it was fast, it had to be fast, and quiet, she said.

And, she said, doing her hair herself, back up into another braid, her night braid, and I'm pregnant, Felicitas. So he's still with me. The tutor's still here. He's with me, so neither of us need to be afraid, she said.

She looked afraid.

She was a month further along than me. She was, now that I knew to look, already starting to show.

They're rounding them up, said Danel. All over the empire, they're rounding them up and asking them to prove their fidelity, their loyalty, to the empire, to the emperor, to not being traitors, and, he said, and if they don't, when they don't, that's it. That's it for them.

They'll come here soon, he said. Wait and see. Not just the mobs, but the soldiers too, soon. The general can't keep them away forever; they'll come here soon.

So? I said. So I'll tell them I'm loyal. I'm not a traitor. Simple.

And if Perpetua asks you not to? he asked.

I was showing now too. Though the cut of my tunic made it possible to hide, sometimes.

We both have to leave, said Danel.

Run away? I said.

Escape, said Danel.

Desert? I said.

Save ourselves, he said.

We'll have to leave the city, I said.

Yes.

Barbarians, I said.

Yes.

You're not afraid?

Look at me, Vitoria, he said. Do I look Roman? Where do you think I come from?

I looked at him. Oh, I said. I never, I said.

It's okay, he said. People never do.

And a midwife? I said.

You think barbarians don't have babies?

Oh, I said. Of course. Of course. Danel always thought in straight lines.

If we go, I said, we can't come back. We can never come back.

If we go, we can be free, he said.

Free to eat grasshoppers and suck water from roots, I said.

Yes, he said.

I love Perpetua, I said.

I know, he said.

Okay, I said. I'll go. Let's go.

Normally, you'd run away at night. That makes the most sense. But the house and the city locked down double at night, with gatekeepers and soldiers everywhere. So we ran away during the day, in the bright, easy morning light.

We took some blood from the kitchen scraps and rubbed it all over the belly of a young goat. A terrible rash. We showed the house's daytime gatekeeper; he was big but not as big as the night-time one. A new type of rash, explained Danel, one he hadn't seen before. And so, we told him, we need to go, need to go ask the veterinary specialist about it. In case it is contagious. In case other animals of the house, or people, even, are at risk from it.

Look at her, said Danel, look at how she suffers.

The goat stood there, looking at nothing. It lifted one leg to scratch another. The gatekeeper took a step back. And her? He said, pointing at me. Why does she need to go?

We need to check her too, said Danel. And me too. Since we both work with her. Need to see if we're affected.

Or, I added, the cause.

The gatekeeper leaned into the fence, away from us. Straight there, straight back, he said.

Straight there, straight back, we said.

He opened the gate.

Danel picked up the goat, up and onto his shoulders.

We left.

At the city gate we told the same story, only now it was herbs we needed, she needed, from the west side of the hills just outside the walls. A place people went all the time for those sorts of things, or used to. Our master sent us, I said.

The general, said Danel.

The general? said the soldier.

Yes, we both said.

Be careful, said the soldier.

Yes, we said.

Very careful.

Yes, we said.

Because I don't want your blood on my hands.

No, no, of course not.

I don't want my own blood either. I'm not coming to find you if I hear screams, right?

Right.

Straight there, straight back, said the soldier.

Straight there, straight back, we said.

He opened the gate.

Danel picked up the goat.

We left.

We followed the road to where it curled around behind a shelf of rock, away from the city view, then put the goat down. We put her on a lead. And then we ran, pulling her along.

We ran and ran and ran.

We stopped. I threw up. We milked the goat and drank the milk. We let her eat wide purple flowers off a bush that was mostly thorns, and then we ran again.

Night started to pull in and bring cold, so while there was still sun, we made a fire using a mirror I'd brought, stolen from Perpetua. And just like that, just as easy as me bringing the mirror, or the mirror bringing fire, the fire brought the barbarians.

Two of them, just two, at first. Danel heard them coming. I heard nothing but the fire and the goat. He called out to them in words I didn't know. They called back. He called back again. They called back again. Then they appeared, from behind, from the dark, one with something sharp to the goat's throat, one to mine.

Danel laughed and raised his hands into the air. He patted his tunic down. Said some words.

The barbarians laughed and put down their knives. They sat down. Okay, then, one said, in Latin. Okay, said the other. They were women.

I barely remember how to speak to them, Danel said to me that night, before sleep. But I guess I do, enough. Enough to say we're not soldiers. To say, Look at us! We're clearly not soldiers!

And please don't kill us?

Why would they want to kill us?

Well, they—

They wanted to be sure we didn't kill them, Vitoria. Most of the time people are trying to kill them.

Or . . . they're trying to kill people?

Generally it's both at the same time. Chicken and egg.

And now it's neither.

Exactly. Now it's neither. No chicken, no egg. All sorted. Just us and a goat.

And now?

And now they want to watch us to be sure it's not a trap and make you some tea to make the sickness go away.

Why would they do that?

Because they say you look miserable. More miserable than the goat.

I felt more exhausted than miserable. More than anything. I was parched for sleep, but once we lay down, all four of us, quiet, I couldn't reach it.

My double hearts beat beat beat beat and I stayed awake and watched the women, who stayed awake and watched me.

They didn't kill us. And we didn't kill them. We stayed there for two more nights, together. They got water from somewhere, herbs from somewhere, and made me the tea. I drank the tea, I felt better. They didn't kill us and we didn't kill them.

After that, after two more days of nobody killing anybody, they asked Danel if we wanted to go to where the water was, and he said yes. So they took us, led us three hours along and down to the water, to the banks of an enormous lake, enormous like the sea had been, but calm, gentle, and there, camped up all around it, were their people, the barbarians.

We put the goat with their goats. She was easy to tell apart from them, since her belly was still red, but the other goats didn't seem to care. They sniffed her and then went right back to kicking dirt and chewing thorns and flowers and jumping onto rocks and jumping off again.

Danel and I stayed. We helped care for the goats, all of them, milking them, distributing the milk. We drank water from the lake and milk from the goats. If a goat died in a way that wasn't sickly, we drank the goat's blood too, and ate goat meat. We caught fish in the lake and ate them. At night we sang songs I didn't understand but learned anyway. I sang. I grew big.

I wasn't sick anymore. I was heavy, I was hungry, I was happy. I think I was happy.

Danel's hair grew, thick and full and out. Mine grew long, down and down. He combed the wind's dust and tangle out of mine with his fingers and I did the same to his. He remembered more of his early words. He remembered songs. He held his hand to me and felt the fish. He sang to the fish. He laughed. He started to build a house. We started to build a house.

The soldiers were just looking for water, is what I think. They looked so thirsty, so tired, when they arrived. So young. Like you, Lucius. And they looked surprised, surprised to find us there. And then, when they realized what they'd found, terrified. They screamed, they drew swords. The people around us, the barbarians, were terrified. They screamed, they drew their own swords. Danel and I ran to our half a house. We covered our ears. We sang songs quietly to the fish and to each other.

The soldier who found us had a cut along his neck. He won't live, I thought. Look at him, look at his beautiful young face. He opened his mouth and shouted and wasn't beautiful anymore. Captive! he said. I've found a captive! A Roman! A woman!

I put my arm out, in front of Danel. No, no, I said. No, no, no. He is mine, I said. He is my husband. Not my captor. He is the animals boy of General Vivius of Carthage. He has no sword. He is his, he is mine.

They tied our hands behind our backs, to be safe, but mine not very tight, and they let me ride in the cart with the extra swords they'd collected, and with the dead soldier bodies. The soldier who found us was on my left. He wasn't dead yet, but close enough. Close enough to get a ride. He put his hand on my belly. Danel and the others who were not dead, both captives and soldiers, walked. Back, back to the city.

We left the goat behind. We didn't have time to get her.

Danel and I had one more chance to speak, after that. Only one more.

When the cart got to the gate of the city the soldiers there recognized the soldiers with us and let us in right away, with no trouble. When it got to the gate of the house, Perpetua's house, Perpetua's father's house, however, there was confusion. The gatekeeper was afraid they were there to round up people, Christians, anyone, from inside, that they were there to take people away, not bring people back. The soldiers were afraid that the general would be angry, because he was angry, a lot of the time, about a lot of things. The other captives were confused because they didn't know if they were going to be killed or not. There was a lot of talking, of shouting and crying, of stomping back and forth, for those not tied up, anyway.

In the confusion, Danel stretched his ropes as far as they would go

towards the cart, towards me, bringing two other barbarians he was
bound to with him.

Tell them I forced you, he said. Vitoria, you need to tell them I
forced you to go. You need to tell them that.

I don't, I said.

You do, he said.

I don't, I said.

You do, he said. You do, you do, you do.

And that was all. Things were sorted with the gatekeeper and they
pulled Danel and the two other captives back, away, and we all rolled
and walked and stumbled through the gate. The soldier next to me in
the cart was dead now. His face was beautiful again.

I didn't see Danel after that. They took us to different cells and guarded
them. Or that's what I assume they did with him, at first, anyway, since
that's what they did with me. My guard was the bathwater woman.
The one who had taken my bed. She looked at me and shook her head
and brought me water. She shook her head and cut my hair. She shook
her head and brought me bread, oil, meat. I don't know if she was supposed to or not. She shook her head and brought me Perpetua.

Perpetua's face was red. Her belly was huge. She had been crying but
was not crying now. Everyone is going, she said. Everyone is going or
gone. Not loud, not accusatory, just fact. Just that. And I'm still here, she
said. Alone, though I'm not alone, not with the baby, not with Christ.
Still, alone. I'm alone, Felicitas, she said. She was sat down in the straw
like me, like an animal, and bits of it were stuck to her tunic, in her hair.

Danel forced me, I said, and the lioness, who had followed Perpetua,
sat down in the straw, between us.

Danel forced me.

I looked down, at the cat. I didn't look up.

Danel—

I know, said Perpetua. I know.

The lioness looked at me. I looked at it.

Did you hear that, water woman? asked Perpetua. Did you witness
that?

Yes, said the water woman.

You will witness that? asked Perpetua.

Yes, said the water woman.

Another day and night went by and then the water woman said, Okay, you can go now.

Go where? I said.

I went to Danel's cell, but he wasn't there.

I went to Perpetua's room and she was there. She was praying. She saw me and stood. I walked to her. My tunic was dirty and ripped along the bottom and under one arm. It was the same one I'd been wearing since Danel and I had left. Even so, even though I smelled like goat and blood and fish and barbarian, she put her arms around me. She cried. I folded into her. We were both huge. We were both tiny. I cried.

Sh, sh, sh, she said.

I cried.

Let's go look at the sea, she said.

The gatekeeper let me out because I was with her and they let her out because of who she was, still, even if she was, maybe, probably, a traitor.

Some people crossed the street when they saw us; some ignored us, some shouted things. Perpetua ignored the insults and awkwardness and greeted them like normal, by name if she knew them, generally and politely if not. I ignored them all completely, and we kept walking down, to where the city met the water.

I hadn't been to the sea since my crossing with the slave trader and my fake sisters and brother. It was the same. More boats and dogs and people, but the same. The same moving god-wall, loud and animal and huge. Awesome. We stood back a ways, on some smooth grey rocks, warm and round like our bellies.

Jesus walked on that, said Perpetua. And it didn't eat him or pull him down, she said. He tamed it. Imagine.

I tried to imagine. I couldn't. I didn't want to. I didn't want it to be tamed.

We were both heavy, tired, so we sat down on the rocks. We played What Thing Am I? And she was The Sea and I was The Sea.

Perpetua had her daughter five days after that. My first thought was that she'd wet the bed, then that I had. Then I thought my waters had gone, a month too soon. Then, after waking up enough to think for real, to see for real, I looked over to Perpetua and saw the whiteness of her face and knew that of course it was her. It was her turn, her time.

I'll go tell someone, I said. Find the midwife, find your mother.

First, pray, said Perpetua. For me.

For you, I said. And I did.

She didn't die and neither did the baby. People thought she would, a lot of people thought she definitely would, as punishment, retribution, but she didn't. She waited, was bored, waited, and groaned and waited and groaned and waited and groaned and screamed and pushed, screamed, pushed, screamed and screamed and pushed and pushed and then there was a baby, alive, and she was a new mother, also alive.

It took a day and a half, and it was during that day and a half that the soldiers came. Not her father's soldiers, but other, bigger ones, with more armour, more shine. Soldiers all the way from Rome. We have orders, they said. We're to gather them all up. Every one. Even Romans. Even wives and daughters of generals.

Listen, said the gatekeeper. Not as big as the night-time one. Just shut up and listen, will you.

So the soldiers listened. And they heard, through windows and walls and through everything, really, Perpetua's screaming.

Oh, they said.

Come back, said the gatekeeper. Come back later.

Then Perpetua had her baby on the outside while I still had mine on the inside, and she lay in bed and nursed it and looked at it looking at her and smiled in a new, soft, kind of stupid way, and I brought food and wine and things back and forth to her as quickly and as much as my belly would let me and watched them and wondered if that would happen to me too, if I would get that stupid smile.

You can hold him, Felicitas, said Perpetua.

I did. And realized it wasn't stupid, she hadn't gone stupid, just slow. That holding the baby made everything slow. It was sort of the opposite of stupid, really, this almost perfect, warm slowness. The almost perfect wisdom of it. Almost perfect, but not quite, because he wasn't mine. Because he was wonderful, but the baby I held wasn't mine, yet.

The soldiers came back two weeks later. This time with stonier faces; this time with stricter orders.

Is there anyone in this house who calls themselves Christian? Who chooses this over the name of Roman? asked a small one with a big voice. Announced more than asked, really. You probably know him, you probably know the one. He asked this even though he, they all, already knew the answer. Even though they'd come to this house specifically. It was a formality. The gatekeeper wasn't sure how to respond.

Um, he said. Not me, he said.

Perpetua came out of the house with her baby, her mother, and me. One of the soldiers stepped forward to meet us. Just say no, he said, quietly. Just say, No, there's not. Not us, not anybody. And then we can go and leave you. Leave you alone.

But Perpetua didn't, wouldn't. She looked over him, not at him, and said, over him, Yes, yes, I do.

And her mother said, Yes, I do.

And I didn't say anything.

The soldier sighed and got rope to bind our hands, to walk us to the prison with the others, already tied, waiting just outside the gate. I recognized most of them from baptisms and things Perpetua and her mother had hosted. Some were slaves, some were not slaves, all were tied together, the same.

There was an issue with the baby. Perpetua wanted to bring him with her. And the soldiers wanted to let her. But she couldn't carry him with her hands bound. And she couldn't be a proper prisoner without being bound. And they didn't want to carry him. So they tied her around the waist instead. Her hands would be occupied in holding her son, so she probably wouldn't be able to grab a knife and start stabbing anyone or cutting anyone free. Not without dropping the baby, anyway.

They tied Perpetua's mother and me normally, by the hands.

Perpetua's father came out of the house only at the end, only as we were leaving. He didn't seem to know what to do. To command or shout or cry or stand stern, firm. He waved. It was unclear whether he was waving at the soldiers or at us. The small one with the big voice waved back.

We were in the cell, in this cell, for four days before the trial. But you know that. I don't know why we were there, here, for those four days. Maybe you do. Maybe they wanted to give us a chance to think, to repent. Maybe they were waiting for someone important to get into town. Maybe they were waiting for Perpetua's father to do something, say something. I don't know. But I do know that Perpetua was still bleeding, then. That they had to send the water woman back and forth and back and forth with fresh rags for her. The baby nursed and nursed and didn't look like the tutor or Perpetua, just looked like a baby. He didn't sleep at night and neither did we. Groups of captives prayed. Perpetua prayed. She held my hand and I held her hand and I held her baby but I didn't pray. I just felt hungry and tired and hot. I rocked the baby back and forth and back and forth and whispered, Sleep, dammit, sleep.

The evening before the day of the trial, Perpetua's father came. He must have known when it was going to be, must have known more than us. The jailer let Perpetua out to speak with him. They went to a different cell in a different part of the prison. We couldn't hear anything of what they said.

Then he brought her back and left with his wife.

Then he brought his wife back and asked for me.

The cell we went to was empty. It was so much cooler than ours. I pressed my back up against the stone wall. I was so big. So hot, all the time, hot, boiling. A soldier stood politely, awkwardly, just outside the door. Not you, someone else. He didn't lock it.

She won't change her mind, said Perpetua's father. She won't even pretend to have changed her mind.

I don't care, he said. I honestly don't care what she believes, who she puts first or doesn't. I don't care, I don't care, Felicitas, she can do whatever she wants, back at my house. But here, she just needs to pretend. You understand? She needs to. She needs to.

Yes, I said. I know, I said. But she won't.

Please, he said. Talk to her, Felicitas. She listens to you.

She doesn't, I said.

She respects you, he said.

She loves you, I said.

She doesn't, he said. She loves everyone now. Which means she loves no one. Not really. Not anymore. Not me. Not me anymore. But she listens to you, at least. She will. If you talk to her, if you convince her, you can both go free.

I know.

I love her.

I know.

I didn't talk to Perpetua. I didn't tell her what her father asked me to. I didn't even try. I knew there was no point. That it would just make her sad, angry. That it wouldn't change anything in any good way. At least that's what I thought then. I don't know what I think now, so I don't think about it. I didn't say anything to her about that meeting with her father, and she didn't say anything to me about it either.

And then it was the trial.

The governor was tired, already, by the time we were led in. He kept running his fingers over the skin around his eyes, which was red, already, making it redder. By the time we finished it was practically purple.

There was testimony by people I recognized and by people I didn't. Normal people, free people. Talk of cults, talk of secrets, talk of cannibalism, of barbarians, of mercy. The people in the gallery shouted encouragement, contradictions, insults. The governor rubbed his eyes.

My belly squeezed, pulled, pressed down heavy. I needed to sit down. I couldn't sit down.

The trial went on, and on, and then, after all the testimonies, after the calming of the crowd, again, and again, after the squeezing pulling pressing pressing pressing, the governor rubbed his eyes and said, Okay, let's do this. Let's do it, then.

One at a time, we were called up. There were eight of us in total, not counting Perpetua's baby, not counting mine. There was nothing tricky or difficult about it. One at a time, we went up and were asked:

Do you?

And if you said no, they'd hand you a cup of wine and you could pour it on a little altar as proof. As sacrifice, as loyalty. To prove it. If you did that, you were free.

But if you said yes, the governor would sigh and walk towards you and hold out his hands and explain, again, what it meant to say yes. Then he'd ask again,

Do you?

And if you said,

Yes,

again,

well, that was that.

Two of the others said no. Poured the wine.

One said yes, and then no, and then poured the wine.

Two said yes, and then yes. They were both men. One a slave, one a soldier.

Perpetua, her mother, and I were last. The two of them because they were the most prestigious prisoners present, the stars of the show, and me because, I think, they forgot I was there until then, forgot I wasn't just accompanying Perpetua in my official duties.

And this is where, Lucius, I'd like you to start writing carefully again, at least the main points. If you can. If there's space, anywhere, on the tablet. Maybe up the side, or across the other words, against their grain. If there's space anywhere, please write this:

Perpetua's mother went first, of the three of us. They called her and untied her hands and she walked up to the front. People shouted things, the soldiers calmed them. You calmed them, Lucius. Thank you. The general was there, in the gallery, with the people. He looked at his wife. She looked at him. The governor asked his question. Perpetua's mother looked at her husband.

He looked at her.

She looked at him.

He looked at her.

No, she said.

She poured the wine.

They called Perpetua. She handed me her child. My belly squeezed and pressed and pulled and I saw white, I saw black. She walked up to the front. People shouted things, the soldiers calmed them. You did, Lucius. The general looked at his daughter. She didn't look at him. She looked up at the sky through the ceiling, the cracks of sky shining through the cracks of ceiling. The governor asked his question. Perpetua looked at the sky. Her father looked at her.

Yes, she said.

And then,

Yes, she said

again.

It took a long time, after that, for them to calm the crowd. For you to. It was my turn, but everyone had forgotten, was wild among themselves in the crowd. The general slipped out, left. You tried, Lucius, you tried and tried to calm them.

Then they remembered me. The governor did. He called me up. He called me Perpetua's girl.

Felicitas, said Perpetua, even though she wasn't supposed to talk.

Felicitas, said the governor. Felicitas, then. He rubbed his eyes. He was almost done.

Perpetua's hands were tied now. Her mother was untied, but in a different section, across from us. I didn't know what else to do, so I handed the baby across to her, to Perpetua's mother, which made him cry and made my belly press white, press black into my eyes and I leaned into the soldier who led me up to the governor. It wasn't you, Lucius, another solider. I leaned into him and the white, the black pressed and pressed and then stopped. I stepped forward.

Okay, Felicitas, said the governor.

Half the crowd had gone, now that the good bit was done. Half were in the process of leaving.

Felicitas, he said. Do you?

Nobody shouted anything. The general was gone. Danel was gone. My sisters were gone. My hair was gone. Vitoria was gone. I looked at Perpetua. Perpetua looked at the sky. I looked at the sky. I didn't say anything.

Just say no, said the governor, and nobody was paying attention anymore, so nobody cared that he did.

Just say no and pour the wine and we can go, we can all go, he said.

Go where? I thought. And I stayed silent.

I leaned on the soldier again on the way back to the cell. He let me. Not you, but still good. He let me.

They chanted and sang around me, that night in the cell. Made a little circle around me and chanted and sang and everything pressed white and everything pressed black and everything pressed and pressed and pressed and pressed. You brought water. You sat looking and then looking away. Perpetua held my hand.

The ceiling cracked and pulled and I saw the sky pouring in, the white of everything in that sky. I saw the black of everything.

I wasn't awake to feed my baby when it came, so Perpetua fed it instead. She had milk. She wasn't my real sister, but she fed it. When I finally woke again, she told me. And she told me how two angels had come to collect it. Two angels just like each other, just like me, my angels, who had more milk, good milk, and clean cloth and took it away all wrapped up safe and white and pure as cloud, and that the soldier, that you, Lucius, let them. That they took it away and I never heard it cry, not once.

Vestals, you whispered, even though you weren't supposed to talk, not to us.

They thought you were dead, Perpetua said. So they saved the baby. They knew that you were dead, that we were all already dead, but that they could save the baby. A mist that appears for a little while and then vanishes, she said.

Us or them? I said.

Both, she said.

That morning Perpetua gave me her ring. Her tunic was wet with unused milk. Marriage is how people who aren't family become family, she said. Take it, she said.

That was the games day. I couldn't walk. Perpetua, the others, helped me. She dripped milk, I dripped blood. I leaned on her, I leaned on them. They chanted and sang as we were led out of the cell and down the street and they chanted and sang as we were led into the arena. A parade. The crowds shouted and they sang and there were drums and horns and we were joined in a line by the gladiators, the animals, and the governor, that same tired governor, leading us all in a slow circle. They chanted and they sang and my chest throbbed with the drums and I leaned and we walked in one big circle, all together, and it was beautiful, in a way.

I saw Perpetua break her skyward gaze just once to look into the crowd, into the higher stalls where her father would have been, where he was not.

Then it was the men's turn. The governor went up to his seat, and the gladiators went to warm up, and the musicians went to their safely-out-of-the-way spot, and we women were led away to wait our turn, which would be after the men. They led us off to the side, where we were, mostly, safe, guarded, but could still see, could still watch. The men, one former slave and one former soldier, were pushed out to the middle of the arena. They were praying, chanting, singing.

There was one lion and one hyena. I'd never seen either in real life before. The lion was a female; it looked just like Perpetua's pet made big. It looked beautiful. It looked exhausted. The hyena looked nervous. They both looked starving. I remembered enough of life before Perpetua, the long hot dry summers of goats and sheep chewing hopelessly on withered lemon skins, to recognize a starving animal. An animal made crazy by it.

And then these animals were presented with something. With something that could be food, could be salvation. With the men. So the lion and the hyena hunted. They hunted because that's what they do, what they had to do.

The former slave and the former soldier ran, because that's what they had to do.

The lion was beautiful when she ran. People say horses run beautiful, but she was more beautiful than that. Perpetua didn't watch, her eyes fixed upwards, but I did, I watched her run beautiful. The hyena ran like a dog, away from the lion. Away from the noise. And then back towards the men. And then away from the lion running towards the men. The lion in straight lines, the hyena in every direction, back and forth, stopping-starting, crazy.

The whole thing took maybe thirty heartbeats, maybe twenty. Then the men were caught and that was that. First the slave, by the lion, then the soldier, by the hyena. The animals got as much as they could and were dragged away. What was left of the men was dragged away.

And then it was our turn.

Perpetua held my hand. They let her. I leaned on her. They let me.

She kept her eyes up, fixed, as we walked to the centre of the arena, as we crossed the wet red dirt. I don't know how she didn't trip, didn't fall.

I'm happy, she said, quiet, to me.

What? I said. The crowd was loud.

I am happy, she said.

The men had a lion and a hyena, both hungry. We had a cow, frightened. Not a bull, not angry, just a cow, just frightened, panicked. I am not afraid of cows, Lucius.

It ran this way, it ran that way. If it ran too far, a soldier would spear it a little, redirect it towards us, keep it spooked. The audience clapped and shouted, and that spooked it too. The drummers drummed, the horns blared.

I think we were supposed to run too. But we didn't run. Perpetua was happy and I wasn't afraid. She was singing now, and I was whispering, calling to the cow, calm words, cool words like water, Sh, sh, sh, now, now, now, like anyone would to calm an animal, like you would to calm a baby.

Eventually, we were in the cow's path, and it struck us. Accidentally; not her fault, not ours.

Eventually, accidentally, the cow struck us. Perpetua in the chest, with its head, then me, here and here, with its horn, and here and here and here.

We both fell.

It stopped and looked at us, at what it had done, confused, its foot on me, here.

Sh, sh, sh, I whispered, now, now, now.

It blinked. It looked at me.

Then it walked away, to the far side of the arena, the bit the farthest away from the drums. It stopped. Confused, tired. It folded its legs the way cows do and sat down.

The crowd roared.

I think they thought we were dead.

I looked at the sky, the open sky over the arena. Open and huge and white and black. One hand on my still-big belly, I whispered, Sh, sh, sh, now, now, now, under the crowd, under the sky.

Perpetua rolled over, looked at me, and screamed. I think she thought I was dead. She grabbed my hand and then let it go. She got up and walked, whole and strong, to the nearest soldier. It wasn't you, Lucius, but it could have been you. It could have been any of you.

She whispered something and took his sword and put it to her neck and looked to the sky. He whispered something back. She nodded, just a bit because of where the sword was, where she was holding it. He didn't move. She whispered again. He nodded and looked up, to the sky. He put his hand over hers and pressed, and then they both pulled the sword, in and across, together.

He held her. For a moment. Held her so that she was still up, so that she seemed the same. Then he let her fall. And the crowd roared.

And then you came, you and two others, to get me, to get us. You were shaking, a bit, maybe from the crowd, maybe from my weight, when you lifted me. Sh, sh, sh, I said to you. I'm not dead, I said. And then the brightness of the noise blocked out the sky and I fell asleep.

When I woke I was here. You were here. I'm not afraid of cows, I told you.

I'm not afraid of cows, Lucius.
Write that, Lucius.
I am not afraid of animals. Write that.
And I am not afraid of the sky. We should not be afraid of the sky. Write that.

Are you happy? asked Lucius.
He stopped writing and looked at me. He looked at my eyes, which were closed, and at my chest, which was bare and soaked with blood and milk and breath and beating and breath and beating and then not. And then nothing. Like Perpetua.
Vitoria? he asked. Can I write that you were happy? Can I?
And I said, or I thought, one hand on my belly,
Sh sh sh
and
now now now
and
sh sh sh
and
now now now now now.

6

BASIL

The soldier was shivering, shaking. You fell in love with her, I said.

He didn't respond. Just kept looking down at the book of tablets in his hands. He'd had to rotate it round and round to read all the text, to get it all.

Aren't you sad? he said, finally. For your sister? For yourself?

I'll see her soon, I said. I'm not sad, I'm excited.

I'd finished his wine, but I wasn't drunk; it was mostly water. He set the book down carefully on the side of him farthest from all the people, all the feet. He looked at me.

I'm not her, I said. I know I look like her, but I'm not her.

I know, he said. Anyway, you don't look just like her; you're a bit older, for one.

I'm not older, I said. I'm exactly the same—

Right, he said. Sorry. Of course. I mean, I just mean—

I've spent a lot of time outside, I said. Running. And fighting. And—

Me too, he said. Me too. He scuffed his toe in the dirt, more like a child than a soldier. So, he said. You're not really a Vestal, are you?

No, I said. Did you really think I was?

No, he said. But it was a good excuse. For both of us. A good reason to let you rescue the baby.

Thanks, I said. I thought so.

We sat in silence for a while and watched the feet go by, some in sandals, some bare, some so dirty you couldn't tell if they were in sandals or not, until, finally, he said, Aren't you afraid I'll turn you in? That you'll be imprisoned yourself, or buried alive, or just plain killed?

I looked at him. His eyes were still red from crying. No, I said. I'm not.

He looked down, nodded slowly. I might have to, he said. Did you think of that? To save my own self.

Well, I said. We'll see.

He nodded again, still looking down. Where'd your sister go then? he asked. The other one? And the baby?

Vestals, I said. For real.

Yeah?

Yeah.

I didn't know babies could do that.

They don't let them tend the fire until they're at least three, I said.

Probably smart, he said.

She's very smart, my sister, I said. Liberata. They all are, but her especially.

He nodded. Sure, he said. I bet.

And your sister, soldier? I asked.

She died last year, he said. A baby that wouldn't come. They cut her to get it, to try to save it, at least, but it had gone too. It really didn't want to be apart from her, I guess, they said.

Oh, I'm sorry, soldier.

Lucius.

Lucius.

More feet, more sandals went by. Someone dropped a goat and it wailed and they scooped it back up and held it over their shoulders like a child. Someone else tripped on a stone and spilled a sack of dried peas; they rolled down the road behind her like a small river. One rolled out as far as we were sitting and I picked it up and put it in my mouth, sucked it. I offered another to Lucius. You'll see her again, I said to him.

Yeah?

Yes. I'm sure of it, I said. I stood up, picked up my things. I need to go now, to keep going.

Can I come with you? Just for a while, an hour or so?

You promised, I said. You said—

I know, he said. But. Just for an hour.

I'm not sharing my food.

I know.

You won't be able to keep up.

I'll try my best, he said. We'll see.

We left the book with Vitoria's story there, by the road. He'd memorized it anyway and I couldn't read it and hardly needed anything else to carry, to weigh me down.

I slowed myself. I ran only as fast as Lucius could manage. And then, that night, even though I'd usually run on, through the night, and sleep in the morning, I stopped. I found a soft and hidden place where we could lie, and when he leaned in to kiss my mouth, to pull me to him, I didn't pull away, I let him.

The god of everything? he asked. Even soldiers?

Even soldiers, I said.

It's stupid to move in the day, in the full light, when the sun is hot and everyone is awake. And it's stupid to move slow if you can move quick. It's stupid, when you've practised your whole life being small, being unseen, being quick, to partner yourself with someone as visible, as glaring, and as slow as an imperial solider. We give what we can, said a grasshopper we passed, in my mother's voice. What have we got if not that?

What have we got? echoed a small yellow flower.

It took less than a day for another soldier to spot us, and less than a couple of hours for him to tell his camp prefect and less than another day for them to get around to sending a small but horsebacked crew out for us, less than a couple of hours for them to find us.

There were ten of them. They waited until we were in a relatively open area, just a few small and lonely trees, too far apart to hide anything or anyone, the tufts of brown grass short and dry and crunching underfoot. They made a circle around us, up on their horses. The animals were blinkered so they couldn't see each other, couldn't conspire. Hello, soldier, said a soldier, up on a grass-brown mare. Where were you off to?

Unless they knew me, knew the things I'd done, which I didn't think, don't think, they did, I was innocent. I was just a poor work girl out for a long walk with a soldier. Maybe a bit immodest, but nothing illegal, nothing worth chasing. A soldier, on the other hand, run off, away, for three days, was a deserter, a problem.

I stiffened. I readied my wrist and kept my other hand in my pocket, where my backup knife was. I waited.

Yes, sir! said Lucius. I mean, hello, sir. He saluted. I didn't.

Well? said the man. Some of the other soldiers looked at each other, looked at me, gave each other sharp little smiles.

Lucius looked at me. I looked at him. Raised my eyebrows just a tiny bit. Now? I meant. Ten was a lot, and all with horses too. Still, I'd been in situations almost this bad. Still, I knew what to do. Lucius nodded the tiniest, tiniest bit. Now.

I jerked my arm and the sword slid out and up, into my left hand, and instead of pulling out a knife with the right, I used it to reach for Lucius; there was a gap, just big enough, between a black and a near-black horse, I was going to grab Lucius and drag him, if necessary, I was going to run through that gap as fast as I could and get us away, disappear, like I'd done before and before, like I knew I could. All he had to do was hold on. Give himself over and hold on.

But he didn't. But he wouldn't.

But, when I brought out my sword, when I reached for him, Lucius didn't take my hand, but instead he drew his own sword, and, with one practised, professional blow, knocked my sword away, into the dirt, and brought his arm down and around my chest. He brought his sword up, to my neck. His arm shook, his body, his breath, his voice shook.

I got her, he said. She is a killer of soldiers. An impersonator of Vestal Virgins. A defender of Christians and barbarians. She's wanted across four cities. I was getting her. Bringing her to you.

The man on the brown horse looked unconvinced. Yeah? he said. Isn't it strange, then, soldier, that you were running with her, away, for so long? Days and, ahem, nights away? Not back, to us?

There are others, said Lucius, tightening his arm around me so its tremor vibrated against my chest, my heart, like music. A gang of them, he said. All criminals, all the same. She was leading me to them. He looked straight ahead. Not at me, but not at the man on the brown horse either, somewhere out over the soldiers' heads, out into the trees.

I looked at him.

Yeah? said the man.

Yes, said Lucius. Yes, sir. And he shook, and we shook, shook, shook.

What's the punishment for desertion, soldier? asked the man.

Death, usually, said Lucius, to the trees.

Lucius, I said. Lucius.

Specifically? said the man.

Um, death by stoning or stabbing or beating, said Lucius.

Lucius, I said.

Beating with? said the man.

With clubs, usually. Clubs with spikes. Cudgels.

Good, said the man. That's right. So. I guess we have to find a way to determine whether what you say is true, whether we should arrest this girl and congratulate you, or let the poor thing go and get out the cudgels for you, soldier. Don't we?

No, I said. Not a poor thing. But nobody, except maybe the horses, maybe the trees, was listening.

Yes, we do, sir, said Lucius. I guess so. I mean, yes, you do, you. Not me.

The soldier next to the man on the brown horse, a soldier on a beautiful sunlight-gold stallion, leaned over and whispered something. The first man thought, then nodded.

Okay, he said. Here's what we'll do. We'll let you decide. We'll make it simple. If you really want us to believe that what you're saying is true, and you really were running just to catch these incredibly, rather unbelievably, dangerous girls and bring them back to us, then you can demonstrate that to us and save us the trouble by just finishing what you've started there, by just running your sword along that incredibly criminal throat, killing the girl, and coming back with us now. Or if you'd rather not do that, if you'd rather not kill this perhaps quite innocent, if a little dirty, girl you've spent the last three days, and nights, with, then you can drop your sword and we'll let her go and take you back with us.

To the cudgels, said the soldier beside him, on the golden horse.

To the cudgels, he repeated.

We give each other what we can, said the horse. What have we got, if not that?

Lucius shook. I could feel the heat of his blade kiss my skin and then pull away and then again and then again. He didn't say anything back to the soldier or the horse. He didn't look at them, he didn't look at me.

Even liars? he said, to the trees, and his breath, his words shook like song. Even scum?

Even liars, I said. Even scum.

Really? he said.

Really, I said.

Lucius closed his eyes and pressed in. Warm, solid, still. And he cut.

It doesn't hurt, said bits of dust floating in the sun. It's the only thing.

Amen, I said, or thought.

Amen, he said.

I

QUITERIA

And I lay, sick, outside of time, and listened to the endless river-god-water-whisper.

2

MARINA

Even though I didn't need to anymore

even though we only needed enough cloth for one veil
    now

not four

after my sisters left I went to the looms each day

still

I sat next to Julia

and we both wove.
    They'll be back soon, I said.
    Of course, she said.
    And we wove.

And then, not so much later, the commander, my father, came home, bringing with him trumpets and drums and banners and, all up on their own horses, some like ours and some new and different, four fiancés and four sets of fiancés' parents, clean and shining and smiling, bright and beautiful and happy.

Because we didn't know what else to do, we lined up in greeting as usual, first the slaves, then the soldiers who had stayed, then the dogs, then us, Julia and me.

Stay with us, here, I asked Bea; I asked Claudia.

I can't, said Claudia.

You know we can't, said Bea.

And they broke away to go stand with the other slaves, between the soldiers and dogs.

The first slave along, the first person the parade would meet, was Claudia's son Tichus. He was drawing fish in the white dust of the ground with a stick, round body, triangle tail. He didn't run out to greet them. Nobody did.

Eventually they got close enough for the trumpeters, at the front, to see the issue, the problem, which was me, or the fact that it was just me, just me and Julia and no one else. No one who mattered, and they stopped playing. This made the drummers, behind them, stop too, confused. The marching soldiers started exchanging looks with the soldiers lined up with us, looking for a signal or direction. Stop or continue or . . . fight? Who with? Cyllius was marching, nine soldiers along in the first row. He looked at no one, his eyes firmly ahead, fixed on the soldier in front.

The whole group moved forward but more slowly, awkwardly, now, while I counted the families and fiancés again. Four. Why, with Cyllius, would there need to be four? The young men and their parents were still smiling, if with slightly less shiny confidence than before.

My father, on his tallest-of-all horse, looked to the trumpeters, then to the drummers, then to the soldiers, then to the boy with the stick, then, finally, to Julia and to me. Our hands were clasped, together.

For a beat, just one beat, his face went soft, fragile, unsure, then it set again, hard, sure, and he continued on, and he and his horse and everything and everyone behind him passed us and continued on, through the gates and to the house, and only our dogs broke ranks, chasing at his horse's heels.

Four? I tried to whisper to Julia. Why are there four?

But she kept her face as forward and set as his.

After the fiancés and families arrived and were tucked away, I went to the fountain and sank myself under. I was getting taller, still, and it was more difficult to fit my whole self in, even with my knees up, but I could manage. I knew it would be dinner soon and I'd have to be out, be dry, be presentable and be presented. I knew I'd have to have my hair rebraided and my clothes changed and knots retied, and would have to be there and say I don't know and I don't know and I don't know and I'm sorry, I'm sorry, I'm sorry, while the parents stared furious into their wine and the sons, none of them Cyllius, stared sad at their spoons in their soup.

The hands that reached down into the water and guided me back up were careful, almost kind.

Is it? I said.

Yes, said my father. Yes, it's me. Just me.

He helped me up, his sleeves soaked, his face blank, and I said,

I don't know. I don't know. I don't know where they are. And I'm sorry. I'm sorry, I'm sorry.

His sleeves dripped down onto the dry stones. A soldier said you'd be here, he said.

Cyllius, I said. My tunic stuck and clung wet to me, ridiculous.

Yes, Cyllius, he said.

I'm not marrying him, am I? I said.

He reached over and pulled a dead fly, drowned, out of my hair. He dropped it on the ground and said, I'm sorry.

We both watched the fly, but it didn't do anything, was dead. It looks like we're both disappointed today, doesn't it? he said.

I didn't say anything. I wanted him to reach over again and lift me all the way out, to lift me up, to carry me.

He wiped his wet hands on his tunic. Come to dinner? he asked.

I will, I said.

Back in our room, which was just my room, now, I was sitting in the straight-backed chair with Claudia retwisting and repinning my hair when we heard the soldiers marching out and away. So soon, said

Claudia under her breath, to herself more than me. So so soon. They were marching out to find Quiteria. To find my sisters and get them back. They had horses, swords, shields, and orders.

God bless them, whispered Claudia, and I didn't know who she meant.

God bless them, I whispered too.

Then we heard Julia coming down the hall towards us, the sound of Julia in sandals, and we were both quiet again.

The door was unlocked, despite everything, but, still, Julia knocked.

Yes? said Claudia. I said nothing.

They'll be gentle, said Julia, from the other side. The soldiers, I mean. They'll be kind, she said. And they won't be long, she said. She was sure, they were sure.

Do you want to come in? I asked.

Okay, she said. Thanks.

Claudia left my hair and went and opened the door, and Julia came in and looked at the beds, all the beds, for just a second, and then sat down on one, Liberata's, and said,

But in the meantime, since you're here, and the families are here, and Basil, Liberata, and Quiteria are not, yet, back here, you can choose your fiancé, and family, from the four. Whichever you like best. How about that? A pretty good deal, I'd say, said Julia. Right?

It has to be one of those four? I asked.

Yes, she said. Of course. She smoothed Liberata's blanket, even though it already was smooth, undisturbed. I think you'll like them, Marina, I do. At least one of them, she said. She found a tiny wrinkle and ran her hand over and over it until it was gone. They are good-hearted boys, she said. Men. You will grow into each other, you will. Trust me. One of them is an almost-general, she said. And one of them can sing.

I looked at Bea, who had come with Julia and was now standing just behind her.

She looked at me.

When? I asked. When do I have to choose?

Not right away, said Julia. Of course. You'll have a few days, a week, even. And then the others will be back and the real preparations will start, the real fun.

I stood. Took a step towards the door. Okay, I said.

Julia stood too. See you at dinner, soon? she said. She took a step towards the door too. Bea got out of the way, then followed her. There's going to be goat, said Julia. Lots and lots of it.

Okay, I said.

After she left Claudia lifted a mirror to show me the back of my own head and said, Do you know, Marina? Do you actually know where they are? Where Basil is?

I'm sorry, I said. I don't know. I'm sorry.

Over the next four days I met with each boy, some of whom were actually men, one at a time, each morning. My afternoons were my own, for me and the water, while everyone else slept and prepared to eat more meat. I took each boy on the same walk, out past the fountain, through the courtyard and the back wall window, sharp turn away from the army camp path, up into the hills, up and up, to the point with the best, longest view. We generally did all this in silence; most of the boys were out of breath by the time we got to the top anyway, with nothing left for talking. Once at the top I climbed up onto a high flattish stone and got each boy to climb up with me. Together we looked out and around, trying to catch any movement, any sign of the soldiers, and my sisters, returning.

Then I'd sit down on the stone, and the boy would too, and I'd ask: Where would we live?

The one with dark hair and skin, who'd chosen to wear his full military garb for that whole thing, the whole walk, answered,

In a house?

Like that. A question back to me.

Yes, I said. I'd already assumed that. But where? A house where?

Oh, he said. Little rivers of sweat trickled out of his helmet, down his jawline. Carthage? he said.

The one with no extra flesh on him at all, skinny as a dog back in the village, stayed standing up on the stone after I'd sat down again. He picked a pebble out from where it had got stuck between his long thin feet and his long thin sandals, looked at it as though trying to determine why it had wanted to hurt him, then threw it, far, down into the valley. An impressive throw.

Where? I asked him.

He sat down next to me and said,

As far as we possibly can from my parents.

The one with a triangle of freckles that scattered from between his eyes down onto his pale cheeks, making him look like a child, even though he was the furthest from a child of the four, wrinkled his nose slightly, crumpling the spots, and said,

Rome.

All the way out there? I said. All the way to Rome?

There is nowhere else, he said.

And then he tried to kiss me, his breath heavy with goat and heat.

The one with eyes brown-yellow like the end of summer hummed all the way through the courtyard, all the way up the mountain, all the time we were up on the stone, and, when I asked,

Where would we live?

he stopped humming just long enough to say,

By the sea.

The sea? I said.

Yes, he said. It would have to be by the sea.

Yes, I said. It would.

The tunes he hummed were the same as the ones from before, long before, were the tunes from the village.

We waited another week after that, but the soldiers didn't come back. So we waited another week, and then another, and then my father sent three of the families back home again. When the soldiers did come back, finally, three months later, it was without fanfare, without my sisters, and without Cyllius.

Where is he? Julia whispered to me as we stood by the gates, watching them file back in. She was standing straight and still and holding my hand, as always, but her eyes darted quick and anxious up and down the moving line of men.

I don't know, I said.

Oh, she said. Oh, oh, oh.

We had the wedding after that, smaller, quieter than planned, and then the boy with the brown-yellow eyes and I moved, along with Claudia, Claudia's son, four horses, twelve donkeys, one loom, and one dog, down south, down

down

down

to the sea.

It was so much more spacious than the fountain. Instead of lying squished and still, I could move in the water, I could swim, circle, flip, dart, fly. And I could see. I could look down as well as up and see that there was, as I'd always suspected there was, a whole other, better, world down there, between sun and earth.

And for a while, I forgot to pray, down there in the water, I didn't need to pray, didn't think I needed to, anymore.

I spent the first two months in the sea, almost always in the sea. I didn't touch my loom at all. I was on my own at first, then, sometimes, Felix, my husband, started to join me, when he wasn't busy with meetings. I couldn't hear his humming underwater, but I knew the shape of his mouth, so I knew he was still doing it. He had to surface more than me, but then he'd come back down, find me again, swim on, still humming.

Two months after that, I was pregnant.

A little fish, I said.

Our little fish, he said.

And even though, as a child, I wouldn't have said it was possible, the days felt hotter, heavier, than they ever had before, and Claudia complained every day because I'd started taking my lunch in the sea, and that meant she had to bring it out to me, eggs and rice, every day, eggs and rice, her feet and ankles caked in wet sand. She tried flavouring the rice with lemon, once, and it made me sick for the whole day. Just eggs and rice, I said, nothing else. Nothing.

Claudia gave up on fixing my hair every night. She complained but she stayed with me, sat in the surf with the water splashing up onto her belly, fuller and rounder than mine, even now. Her son worked for Felix, running messages back and forth to other houses or the town two miles inland. When he wasn't working, when he was free, he'd come and stand on the beach, close enough to keep an eye on his mother, but far enough that his feet never risked getting wet. He was older now; he was getting older.

When there were only a few days left—according to Claudia and to the doctor who came by from time to time, mostly to eat salt sardines, but also to look me over and smear oil onto my belly, and according to the midwife who had only recently come, for whom Claudia had prepared two rooms, one with a bed and one with oil, basins, sponges, a neatly folded stack of white cloth, and a chair with most of the seat missing, a chair that was only half a chair, when the midwife had come, and, according to her, to them, there were only a few days left—Julia arrived.

It's good to see you, I said.

It's good to see you, she said.

Am I going to die? I said.

I don't know, she said. Maybe.

The time for the baby came, the time for the baby went, and still I floated in the salt of the sea, and still no baby came.

It's late, I said.

Are you sure? asked Julia.

I'm sure, I said.

Are you sure? asked the midwife.

I'm sure, I said.

I waited, I floated, I waited, until, twelve days late, I swam back to where Claudia was standing waist-deep, watching. I surfaced and asked,

Is it too late?

Too late?

Too late to ask your God? I asked. To ask your God to take care of me? To help me?

She wiped the water from her face, from where I'd splashed her coming up, and said,

Never. It's never too late. That's the wonder of it.

One of them, I said.

Yes, just one of them, she said, and the drips ran down her neck, down her body under her sticky wet tunic, and back into the sea again, back into water.

~

Usually the dogs had many babies. Like it or not, prudent or not, back in the village, back when there had been dogs not owned by anyone but themselves, dogs that had babies as and when they pleased and with whatever other dogs they pleased, back then, the dogs, usually, had many babies, puppies. Three or four or six. Writhing, chirping, crying in soft furry heaps by their mothers in the unfaithful shade under carts, behind broken half-houses; you'd stumble uninvited onto them, moving and noisy and hot.

Usually the dogs had many babies, but not always. Once, just once, there was a dog, an old dog, older, anyway, than most, since hunger or thirst or anger or adventure got most of them before age could, once there was a dog, grey and brown and white and yellow and no colour, a dog who was old but not actually old, was quite young, really, who was pregnant, and got bigger and bigger and bigger, was pregnant for ages, forever, until, one night when the moon and stars were finally soft, kind, when she left the others and burrowed her way under a pile of pruned branches, still fresh, still smelling of fruit.

And, there, moon, stars, fruit, she had her baby. Just one. Just perfect. Just one. Perfectly small, perfectly still, perfectly quiet. Just the night and her and her perfect one, she licked it and licked it, until the tired moon dropped away and the sun came up and we, come to clean and clear the yard, found her there, under the branches, still licking, licking, licking, her one baby perfectly still, perfectly quiet. Despite that, and despite us being there, despite the sun, despite everything, she licked and licked and licked. She tried and tried and tried. She tried and tried and tried and tried and tried.

~

Despite everything, the midwife washed my baby, perfectly quiet, perfectly still, in her basin, the special little basin she'd brought with her, and it was quiet and still and perfect, perfect, perfect.

They bundled it in cloth and took it away and it could have been anything, could have been nothing, and I worried it would be too hot, all wrapped up like that, I worried; it can't see like that, I worried, I said, I said over and over and over, It can't see, it can't see, I can't see, he won't see, Felix won't see that it's perfect, now. How will he see? How will he know? He can't see he can't see he can't, and Claudia said, Sh, sh, sh, and because I am human, not animal, flesh not fur, because I couldn't lick and lick and lick, I folded into myself and said, Oh. Quieter and quieter said, Oh, oh, oh, oh, oh, oh, oh, all the way down, all the way to nothing.

Because I am flesh and not fur, they took it away. Before Felix came home, even,

they bundled it up

they covered its eyes,

    never opened

they took it away.

Despite that, despite everything, the bleeding and the milk went on and on and on. Claudia stood beside me, stood between the bed and the door, and watched and waited while I didn't talk to her, while I talked to no one. Claudia stood beside me and Julia came and went and came and went and the god of water stayed inside me as silent inside as I was outside.

It's because of you, Julia told me, one morning, or afternoon, or evening, or night. You can't keep track of day and night when there is only night.

One morning or afternoon or evening, Julia said, It's because of you that the commander's army's tents are coloured, are vibrant and beautiful, you know.

It's totally pointless, she said. Detrimental, even, in terms of military function. And also much more expensive than they should have been, too expensive.

I watched her mouth while she talked. I thought about how ridiculous it was that such a small, soft, vulnerable thing should be given so many key tasks to survival. Eating, drinking, breathing, communicating. Her lips were dry and chapped. Had they always been dry and chapped?

It was a dark time, a hard time in the commander's life, said Julia, said her mouth. After he came home and heard that you'd died, and that his first wife had died too, he needed something. Anything. Many things, to pull him back up after that. He needed colour. He needed something to make joy, find joy, again, said Julia, said Julia's mouth. He's not a bad man, Marina.

And her eyes, I thought. Julia's eyes were integral to everything she did, her weaving, her direction of the whole house, but they were just two soft tiny balls. As fragile as that. Dull grey and fragile as newborn babies.

Could you do that? she asked. Could you find some colour again? Could I help you?

Julia came and went and Claudia stood, Claudia stood by.

And time slid away, meaningless, like a bundle of cloth; it might have been a long time. Or maybe not.

Julia went home and Claudia stood by.

And, then, I got a letter.

And it wasn't real light and it wasn't real day, but it was the first idea of light, the first admission of the possibility of light, possible day, maybe pink and maybe warm on the inside of your still-shut eyes.

I got a letter
and the first thing I said was
Where?
Where did you get this?

The courier was a city slave, unknown to me. He looked at Claudia, afraid.

Claudia nodded.

Just from another slave, ma'am, he said. Another city slave. Rebekah, with the pet rats in her pockets, you know?

No, I said. I don't know. Do you know where Rebekah got it? From who? Did she say?

No, he said. She never does. That's why she's so popular, so busy. She never says. And the rats don't either.

Then he left, relieved, ran back to the city.

—

The letter was from Cyllius.

I think of you,
It said.
and your sisters, a lot. Fondly. Especially Quiteria, God help her,
God help us!
Here is a map,
It said.
I should have told you before, but I couldn't.
It said.
You understand?
It said.
You always understand, Marina.
I know you do.
So you understand, now, that I couldn't tell you earlier. I couldn't.
And I probably shouldn't now either. But, well, some things are

bigger than other things. More important. So I am. Now. Here is a
map. I don't know for sure if they'll still be there, or if they ever
even made it there, but I know this is where they were headed.
Here is a map to your sisters, Marina. Maybe.
I'm well. Tell Julia, if you see her, that I'm well. Tell Quiteria.
C

The map was hand-drawn, the same scribbly hand as the script. I'd
learned to read and write only since marriage—Felix had found me a
tutor once he realized, with slight embarrassed horror, that I'd never
learned—but already my hand was neater, more refined than this.
Marina.
He'd written my name,
You always understand
like a child.

I was still in bed. Julia had gone home to my father, but Claudia
was by the door, there, like always. I sent her to get some water, then
spread and smoothed the map out on my lap. I walked my fingers
across it, three steps, here to there. One two three, here to there. Not to
him, but to them. Maybe.

Then Claudia came back. I rolled the map back up and I drank the
water she brought even though I wasn't thirsty, even though it hurt
to pee.

Good? she said.

Good, I said.

She bent to take the glass back from me and the softness of her veil
almost brushed my hand, almost but not quite. He's saved, she whispered, still there, down close enough that her breath was like a kiss.
And his mother too, she said. Both were, both are. The new kind of
people. Like us, she said. They hid it because they had to, but they
were, they are. Then she straightened up again, back into herself.

Yes? I said.

Yes, she said, and took the glass away to fill again.

I hid the letter and the map. Tucked them away where they wouldn't be
seen by Felix or Claudia or me for twelve months. Twelve months of
water and salt and my husband, humming, still, always, even when we

were together, even in the hot nights made cool by each other, a year of days like smoke.

Then, twelve months later, I lost another child. This time before it had even grown into its own shape, this time just blood and blood and blood.

And then I lost Felix too, to the same sweating sickness that had taken half our village half a life ago.

I think it's good, he said, lying in the bed where he would die, shortly before he did die, his head propped up a bit sideways on too many pillows. I think it's good, he said, that the babies didn't live longer. That they didn't live long enough for us to fully love them, only to then have this pox take them. Don't you think it's for the best, Marina? Don't you think it's good?

And, at that moment, anything I'd grown to feel for him, for his voice and his hands and hair, his breath in the water and in the night, anything I'd felt, slow and careful, for and around him, pulled out, back, and away, into those children, those two babies, who were already full of so much love, who I didn't think could hold any more, being only what they were, memories of weight and smoke, and

at that moment
I let go of him

just for that one moment.
I said,
No.

and then he was gone.

Then, after the second child went and Felix went, but before the horses arrived, the two horses that would have been sent, I knew, I was sure, with riders, with Julia again, maybe, with soldiers, maybe, with my father, maybe, even, horses that would have been sent to get me, to bundle me up and bring me back to my father's house, experiment failed, try again, try again, try again, maybe the boy who hated his parents, maybe the man who needed the city, before that, any of that could happen, I bound my milkless chest. I took off my long red and blue and white clothes and put on a simple dark tunic like the one I'd worn as a girl. I took a horse and supplies from Felix's house and kissed Claudia's veiled head, asleep in my doorway. Goodbye, I whispered.

You have to go? she whispered back, because she wasn't actually asleep, she never was, just resting, or pretending, or praying. She kept her eyes closed.

I do, I said.

I'll miss you, she said.

I'll miss you, I said.

I'll think of you, she said, which meant, I'll pray for you.

I'll think of you, I said, which meant, I'll think of you.

Say hello to your sisters, for me, she said. To all of them.

I will, I said. I will.

And, I said, Claudia?

Yes? she said, opening one eye halfway.

Thank you, I said.

You're welcome, she said, and closed her eye all the way again.

I found the map just where I'd left it, not touched, not forgotten. I followed it.

The first I saw of my sister were some feet, stuck out from the otherwise complete cover of a pine tree's low boughs. They were dirt-dark and cracked. They were bare. At the camp, her camp, there was a mud stove with the fire long dead inside, some blankets hung up in trees, a few old chipped cups, plates and pots stacked against a rock, three roasting sticks stuck into the dirt like a tiny fence, two logs, one big stone, and flies everywhere. There was no one else there, just me, the flies, and those feet. Everything was a bit broken, a bit dirty. I picked up a pot and put it back down. It had the stamp of our father's house on it, faded but there. The feet, and person attached to them, didn't move. I went closer, looked closer. They were covered in little cuts and scars, even on the inner arch, the most protected, most vulnerable part. Quiteria's, I knew, then. Sleeping or dead. I could have found out which by reaching over and pulling the branches away to see the rest of her, to see her face, watch for breath, but I didn't. I didn't want to. Not right away, not yet. I just looked and kept looking at those feet, listening to the river and looking at those feet.

I stood there, in between not knowing and knowing, for minutes, maybe hours. And then I batted the flies away from my face and from the feet, took a big breath, leaned down, and pushed the boughs aside.

It was the white pox, of course. It was the same white pox, wrapping itself back around again. It had come round one more time, just to remind me it could.

She wasn't dead, though. Not yet. She was sick, deep-sick, but not dead. Two dogs curled into her sides. They growled, long and low, when I reached over to pour water through Quiteria's cracked lips, water that mostly spilled out again, making trails like tears through the dirt and grime of her face and neck, but they didn't stir, didn't twitch.

I ate fish from the river and stale bread that one of the dogs eventually brought to me and fed small bits of water-softened bread to Quiteria, who slept, heavy and deep as a river stone, through everything. While she slept, I told her about Julia and about our father and about my marriage and my husband and about sex and about babies, while she slept I told her about the sea, Like your river, I said, but stretched out huge, stretched and slow and forever. Stretched so huge the salt of the earth leaks in, I told her. So huge the water and the earth and the sky are all one, all the same.

You have to see it, I said.

You have to, Quiteria.

I reached into the very bottom of my pocket and found what was there, what had always been there: a small, matte medallion with a fish printed on both sides. I stood. The two dogs woke but didn't move. I placed the medallion on Quiteria's burning forehead and pushed.

I

QUITERIA

Then Marina came. Marina came back.

I knew you would, I said. I couldn't sit up. I couldn't make the word sounds, but I made the shapes with my lips and she understood.

Liar, she said, not making any sound either, and her breath smelled of lemons.

I couldn't cry because I'd sweated out all my salt, so she cried for me, instead; she cried and because she was up, knelt over me, some of her tears fell on me, on my face and hair and rolled down my cheeks and into my mouth until I had enough salt, again, enough water, and I could cry too, and my tears rolled down into the dirt-soft fur of the dogs next to me, who didn't move, didn't make a sound.

She waited there, for me, with me, her hand heavy and warm on my shoulder; flies buzzing around and around our heads. When she did, eventually, get up to get us fresh water and cloth, she stepped back, huge in silhouette against the sun, against the pine boughs, and I found my voice again, I found my breath.

You look fat, I said. You look great.

She never told me why she came back and I never asked. You were married? I said.

Yes, she said. But I'm not anymore.

You had children? I asked.

No, she said. No.

I got better and better until I could run again, could hunt and fish again, and she ran with me and rose up with me, sometimes, and fell down with me, sometimes, and hunted and fished with me, and within a few weeks, a few months, her tunic and her face were as dirty as mine, even if the dogs were always a little bit wary, a little bit afraid of her.

—⚬—

I kept fighting, kept trying to free prisoners on my own while Marina stayed with the fire. I didn't ask the Christians to help me fight anymore; I didn't ask them to stay. Marina was there; Marina was enough; anyone else, anyone new, could threaten that, could change things again. So I didn't ask; so I fought alone.

Twice I lost prisoners, recaptured. Once I lost one, actually lost him, a soldier's sword through the pathetic thin fabric at the back of his tunic, blood brighter than any dye. And, once, I almost lost myself. Hand twisted behind my back, sword knocked aside, away, a soldier held me fast, close, Next time, Quiteria, he said. Take the horse now, this time, this time, but not next time.

I threw my head back and knocked out two of his teeth. I took the horse and flew.

Then, for those weeks, those months, everything was everything. Was enough. And I forgot to consider, to remember, that everything, even everything, changes, ends. For those weeks, those months, there were two of us, again, and we were we and that was all, and that was everything. Even Cyllius was forgotten, or muted, at least. Even Cyllius didn't matter, not really, anymore.

Or that's what I thought; that's what I felt. Marina felt differently. She was watching, always watching, my scratches, my bruises, my limps, the fire, the smoke, the sky. I came home one day, one day that was just like all the others, that had nothing to mark it, no rooster call, no coins or kiss or smoke, one day, indistinguishable, I came home, to her, to the camp, and went down to the water to wash the blood and dirt away and Marina was already there, ankle-deep, braiding her hair. One day, out of nothing, out of the water, Marina said,

We need to go. One dark strand over another, over and over and over. We need to go.

Go? I said. The water was shock-cold on my legs.

Yes, she said. Strand over strand over strand.

Where? I said.

Back, she said. Home to the commander.

But, I said. No, I said. This is—

They're *killing* you, Quiteria, she said. You're fast, you're strong, but you're not fast enough, not strong enough, not by yourself. They're going to kill you. Soon. Soon. And then I'll be alone. Again.

No, I said. No, Marina, no, I said. I'll ask more prisoners for help; I can, we can, right here, we can be enough.

Marina finished her braid; tied it with a little piece of wool. She looked up, to me. We need to go back, she said. We need to go home.

My hair was short; I'd cut most of it off years ago, just after Liberata and Basil and I made it to the river. Marina had tried to braid it once, but it wouldn't hold. No, I said. We don't. Of course we don't. We already are. Marina, we already are—

Who do you think is the one locking up those prisoners? she asked. Giving the soldiers their orders? Telling them to arrest Christians? To kill them?

No, I said. No.

The commander, said Marina. Our father. She finished her braid, finished her speech, but still stood there, just stood there, in the river. My feet were freezing; but she was always able to stay in water longest, to not even notice it.

I thought you loved him? I said.

I do. And he loves us.

Loves you.

Loves us. And that's why he'll listen to us. That's why we should go talk to him. Just go ask him to stop.

So he can arrest us or lock us up again and force us to get married.

He won't.

Marina, of course he will, of course he will.

If he does, then you can kill him.

I thought you loved him.

I love you more, she said.

She was upstream of me. The water hitting her was even colder than the water hitting me.

I'm not afraid to, you know, I said. To kill him.

I know, she said.

And I'm not marrying, ever.

I know, I know.

It had been more than two years since Basil and Liberata left. I think. Had it been? Had it been three? Maybe it had. Longer than the commander had been away, ever. Longer than Cyllius had been away, back there, back then. It had been more than five years since I left there, left him. Five years, and he hadn't come. He had been marched far away, or had died, or had forgotten. Or was never going to, was never anything. I knew this now, I mostly knew this. I bent low, scooping water up and over my face, letting it run down, drips red and brown. I had been alone, for years. For years and years. Okay, I said.

And Basil and Liberata will know, when they come back, said Marina. If they come back, while we're away. They'll know where we've gone.

Okay, I said.

And we'll come back here after, she said as the drips ran down my shoulders and chest, little rivers. We'll come back and wait.

Okay, I said. Yes.

Tonight, she said.

Tonight?

Yes, tonight, she said.

2

MARINA

When I found her
   found her again
Quiteria was sick.
   Like Felix.
   Like Gema, like Germana.
   Like Liberata.
   Like sisters, long ago.
But she got better. They didn't, but she did. She was Quiteria, bigger
than mountains, fuller than rivers, she was Quiteria, and she did, she
had to.

She was eating normal food again within a week, able to walk down to
the river in two, and back with a sword in her hand in four.

They're blaming Basil's people, she said, one wilting hot afternoon
while we picked burrs out of the dogs' fur. For the pox, she said. They're
blaming them and they're locking them up. Then killing them, usually.
Starvation, strangulation, this or that.
   Basil's people? I asked.
   Christians, she said. You know.
   Oh, I said. Claudia's people. The god of everything. The god of
water. Why? Most of the burrs I'd got off the dog were now on me,
stuck to my tunic or in my hair.

She shrugged. It always helps to lock someone up, I guess, she said. Or seems like it helps. Could help. She pulled off a burr and blew it away, off her finger with a single, violent breath.

No, I said. Not the soldiers, or whoever is doing the locking. Basil's people. Why would they do that? Why would they bring the pox? I thought of them by the stream at the commander's house. Lifting me, holding me. I thought of Claudia, one eye half-open.

Marina, said Quiteria, it has nothing to do with Basil's people. Or the barbarians. Or anyone.

How do you know? I said. How can you be sure?

Quiteria dropped a burr and lifted her hands, held them between us, palms out, blocking her face from mine, scars on them like a dozen round white suns. I know, she said. These things, she said, these hold-your-breath-and-close-your-eyes terrible horrible things happen, sometimes, to some people. And that's all. They happen. They just happen. Not because of a god or a lack of a god. Or a passion or a curse or the stars or the moon or people like you or people not like you, she said. Like the wind blows or it doesn't, they happen. They just happen. Or they don't.

She lowered her hands again, back into the dog's coat.

So what do we do? I asked. What can we do?

We catch fish to eat from the river, she said. We tend the fire. We take care of the dogs and each other, we watch, we wait for the others to come back, and we fight, said Quiteria. We find things that do have a cause, an enemy, and we fight them. There's always something, someone, worth fighting.

Claudia would say something else, I said.

Who?

Claudia, I said. She wouldn't say fight. She'd say we pray, we hope.

Well, Claudia's not here.

No, no, she's not.

It was just us. Just me and Quiteria. First two born, twins. She would go to fight and steal and I would watch the fire and each time I told myself this could be the time she doesn't come back, it's very likely, it's very likely this time. The knife that just slipped past her neck last week won't slip tonight. The hand that had her ankle but lost grip would hold. The watchman she assumed asleep wouldn't be. The dogs she assumed friendly wouldn't be. The swords the spears the trips the falls the hands the anger the men the the the.

Still, she always came home. Bleeding, limping, smiling, she always came home.

Do you think you're protected? I asked, handing her a bandage I'd smeared with honey to wrap around her knee.

She pressed it onto her leg and wrapped it around. Blood and honey leaked out from the sides and she wiped them up with a finger. By who? she asked. By what?

I don't know. Luck? God?

She licked her finger. I don't know, she said. Maybe. But it's not something I'd count on.

What do you count on?

Myself.

And?

Just that. Myself.

One of her dogs, the skinnier of the two very skinny dogs, sniffed at her bandage, looked up at her, then folded itself down into a bony ball at her feet.

It wasn't quite home, but it wasn't not home. It was all there was.

And

sometimes
    when we slept
    if the air was cool enough to sleep close, if the dogs weren't between us
sometimes
    just before sleep, when we were close and safe and together, there, like that
sometimes
    the ground would push away, gentle, and we would rise above it, clean, cool
together.

Just a finger's width, almost nothing, but something, something wonderful.

The first time it happened, I turned to wake Quiteria, to tell her about it, ask her about it, but it stopped as soon as I turned and we fell back, down.

〜

I didn't like the stealing. I tried to eat mostly fish and rock samphire and other things I could get for myself. Quiteria liked honey and figs and dates, so she stole. I was in the water one hot afternoon, hands gripping tufts of well-rooted water grass to keep me from pulling away with the current, when she came back from some fig-getting and stood over me. Her face and body were blurred with wet and sun, and, for a second, I didn't see her, I saw Cyllia. Then I sat up, out of the water, and saw my sister.

I don't want any figs, I said.

I know, she said. Anyway, I already ate them. But I saw something else you might actually like, might want. Little fish were gathering around her toes, taking turns darting in to peck off bits of dead skin. She kicked them away.

Hm, I said.

No, she said. I think you would, really. Listen, Marina, she said. She sat down in the water, beside me. Every time I go to this house, this one house, I pass the same thing on my way to the pantry; every time, I pass a loom. A small but not broken loom. And there's never anything on it. No wool, no linen, no thread, nothing, ever. No one uses it, Marina. For years, no one's used it. But you could.

The fish were gathering around her again. It's small enough to carry? I said.

For two people to carry, yes, she said.

I tried to remember the feel of a shuttle, of thread, of creation. Okay, I said.

She smiled, and more fish came.

And thanks, Quiteria, I said. For thinking of me.

Always, she said, and stood up, and fish radiated away from where she'd been like rays of the sun.

We stole the loom first, awkward, clumsy, but without confrontation, and then the thread, luxuriously already spun, afterwards, from a different house. It gave me something to do apart from watch the fire and worry while Quiteria was out stealing, fighting, running. It had been a long time and my fingers had forgotten a lot. I often had to undo and go back, pull back and start again, but eventually, as I ran the little shuttle back and forth and back and forth, my fingers started to remember and could work without me having to watch them again, and I worked and hummed Julia's songs and worked until the portraits, one, two, three, four, five, six, seven, eight, nine, side by side, started to appear, as the sun washed the thread into the true, muted colours of life.

<hr />

Quiteria was away. I was working at the loom, the top of our heads, all the same height, our hair, all the same colour, when he came. I was humming in time to the shuttle's rhythm; I was bent close. He came along the water, not through the pine bough door. The first I heard of him was the sound of feet lifting through shallows, the sound of water. I looked up and, through the cage of my thread, saw the sun as it moved on the ripples all around him.

Cyllius, I said.

Quiteria, he said. Finally.

My words knotted together like the thread between us and all I said, all I could say was,

Yes.

I said yes and I stepped around the loom and walked towards him. He was the same as ever and I was all the emptiness of lives grown and gone, I was the burning emptiness of the water around our ankles, so I said yes. I put my arms around him and pulled him in and kissed his dirt-smeared face and pulled off his armour, the cloth underneath.

And he said, Quiteria, Quiteria,

And I said, Yes.

Afterwards, he picked up his sword and belt from where they'd fallen on the riverbank stones. He put everything back on and tried to brush the mud off his tunic, but it just smeared. You need to go, he said. They know where you are. You need to go, you need to run.

But, I said.

Tonight, he said.

You've got distinguishing characteristics, he said, the first time he pulled himself into the water with me, back, years ago, back at the house. He came back, he found me through the water. He must have known, he must have known.

He was gone hours before Quiteria got back. She brought half a pocket of almonds. There was dried blood under her nose and one of her eyes was swollen mostly shut.

We need to go, I said.

Go? she said.

Yes, I said.

Where? she said.

Back, I told her. Home to the commander.

But, she said, this is—

Tonight, I said.

Tonight? she asked.

Yes, tonight, I said.

I

QUITERIA

Before we left, I carved a striped rectangle on the trunks of all the camp trees big enough. I scratched it into the face of every stone. If you came into the camp, then, and maybe now, still, you'd see nothing but that symbol, over and over and over and over. It was the symbol from Cyllius's map, his symbol, our symbol, for the commander's house, over and over and over.

I kissed the dogs and told them that they were free, that they didn't have to stay, to wait, for me to come back, that they could run and hunt and do anything, everything, that dogs love to do, and they looked up at me, heads on their paws, and didn't move.

2

MARINA

My tapestry wasn't done; the tops of our heads were still missing, but I cast off, I bound it, and I cut it off the warp with the sword. I rolled it and folded it and put it in my pocket and when Quiteria asked, Ready? I said, Ready.

She held out her hand and helped me up from where I was sitting and kept hold for a beat, both of us facing the river.

You've packed enough water?

Yes. You?

Yes.

And then

as fast as we ever could

we ran.

I

QUITERIA

We ran. Marina, who, before, usually dragged along at the back, took my hand and pulled ahead. Should we get horses? she asked.

We're quieter without them, I said.

We're faster with them, she said.

The next day, as the sun was setting and we were getting ready to go, I saw smoke coming from behind us, from back where our camp had been.

We put out our fire? Marina asked.

We put out our fire, I said.

We stole horses from the next stables we passed and rode them hard all the way to the caves.

Where'd you learn to ride? Marina asked.

Cyllius, I said. I leaned my weight closer into the animal's sweat-damp back, pushed it faster.

At the cave mouth we gave the horses as much water as we could spare and set them loose. They walked for a few steps, confused, then realized they were free and bolted, back towards the ropes we'd cut them from.

Maybe we should have killed them, eaten them, I said.

Too late now, said Marina.

And then we slipped back into that cold, closed dark.

And, even though it was black one way or the other, I closed my eyes and kept them closed. I held my breath and the sound of Marina, in front, moving, still moving, the whole way. Make it through this, I told myself, just through this. Each inch an inch closer to light.

On the other side, in the full bright sun, eyes open, we stood, stretched tall, and I looked at Marina's face, which was my face.

Okay? she said.

And I said, Okay.

And, on our feet again, we ran.

There were no more horses to steal. They'd all been locked up, warned. So it was just us, just our legs, our bodies, each other, running, just running.

2

MARINA

I knew the soldiers would notice we'd gone, that they'd follow us, but I didn't think it would be so soon. But they did, and it was, and soon there was smoke, smoke, everywhere we looked.

Campfires, I said to Quiteria. Because they're not afraid to be seen, to be known. Because they have nothing to hide.

So many, she said. For us? They can't all be for us . . . Because she didn't know, even at that point, that the smaller something is, the more angry it can make big things.

We had no fire, now. We ate our meat, when we caught it, raw.

Do you think it's better, I asked, to live in a straight line, someone else's line, and eat cooked food every day and never have to hide?

All the best food is raw, said Quiteria.

We took turns sleeping, and when it was her turn, I watched the smoke on the skyline and my sister's face in equal amounts. Her face peaceful and open and trusting, like there was nothing, nothing that mattered, to burden her. We don't have the same face, I thought. Not really. Not at all. I shooed flies away from her hair and tried to pair my breathing with hers, tried to make us match again.

When it was my turn to sleep I stayed awake as long as I could and, with my eyes closed and body still, prayed to Claudia's God, to Basil's God, to the God of water. With my eyes closed and Quiteria watching out over me, I prayed to the God of everything, even her.

Most of the time, we ran. And, sometimes, while running, Quiteria would look over to me and smile, and I would smile back like a prayer, and we'd rise up just enough, enough to keep us ahead, keep us going.

I

QUITERIA

We were only two nights' run from the commander's when we saw smoke in the hills in front of us. In front as well as behind. It rose in searching, lonely ribbons until it met the smoke behind, until they pushed, pulled, fought, danced together. Do we divert or stay true? asked Marina.

We're almost there, I said. Stay true.

We ran. We ran and ran and ran. We ran as the soldiers behind us drew up. The cave had bought us time; that time had slipped away under the faster, fresher feet of their cavalry.

We ran as the soldiers in front drew in. As they pushed and pulled and danced us off course after all, south. Just a detour, said Marina. We'll divert this way then come back around the other side. Just a tangent, a loop. We threw away our broken sandals and ran, away from the smoke, the soldiers, the house, the lemons, the village, as the land under our feet pulsed with sun and rocks and thorns. We ran, like before, like when we were girls, through broken brush, dust hot and dry in our eyes and mouths and hair.

We ran, like before, except now there were just two of us, not nine, not seven, not five, not four. If they caught us they would kill us, I knew, we knew. Still, we smiled at each other, for each other. We'd catch each other's eyes and smile, and our feet pushed off and over the weeds and rocks and dirt, and our steps were steps of clean, pure air.

We would have kept running forever, I think, if we hadn't come to the edge of the world.

2

MARINA

It was the soldiers

and their smoke

and drums

and shields

and swords

reflecting the sun

shining

even from away.

It was the soldiers who decided where we would go

in the end

who directed us south

it was

it wasn't

wasn't us.

Wasn't me.

It was the soldiers

and the smoke

that cornered and corralled us like sheep, like fish, away from the path that led to the road that led to our father's house; it was the soldiers, the smoke, that pushed us, instead, to the cliff overlooking the sea.

I laughed.

The sea, I said to Quiteria. We were so close to the sea, all that time. The waves roared and I wanted to laugh and laugh.

Quiteria looked down at the water. She kicked a stone over the edge. I took her hand.

I

QUITERIA

Water and nothing, nothing else. Not water that cut through things, like our river, but water that cut everything else away. The end of the world, of everything. It was louder, even, than our hearts.

The sea, said Marina. We were so close, all that time.

We looked down, at the white birds floating between us and it, easy. I kicked a fist-sized stone and we watched it spin and roll down, through the empty space of air, away. It was too far to see it splash. I pulled a sword, dented, rusty, out of my sleeve and Marina pulled one out of hers. You have a sword? I said.

Of course, she said. From you, she said.

I looked closer. The sword had a ridge down the middle and a dark, soft handle. Oh, I said, of course, of course.

We turned around, away from the water, and there they were, the soldiers, the boys facing us, curled all around like a lover's arms.

2

MARINA

Swords out, we turned around and faced the men facing us,

I

QUITERIA

And there he was.

2

MARINA

and

there he was.

I

QUITERIA

And there he was. Again. After years and years and years and years. There he was, in the back row of a three-deep net of men. There he was, to my left, our left. He looked at me and then at Marina, at me and then at Marina, and his face was the face of my mother when all the babies were sick, when there was something big, too big all around. Oh, said my chest, my blood, my everything, Oh, oh, oh, oh, oh, oh, oh, oh, oh

2

MARINA

Oh,

there he was

my Cyllius.

He looked at Quiteria, he looked at me.

He looked at me.

He blinked. He looked at Quiteria.

and

I

QUITERIA

and he looked at me. He blinked like he'd never seen the sun.

And he put his hand to his sword.

He looked at me and he blinked at the sun and he put his hand on his sword and, the very very smallest bit, he nodded, at me.

2

MARINA

and

I

QUITERIA

I feel bigger. I am bigger. And sometimes this is helpful and sometimes it's not. Sometimes it means I have to carry more; it's a given, expected. It means when someone says, What next? Now what do we do? that everyone turns to me, everyone else is quiet.

I shook my head. No.

I gripped Marina's hand tighter. And I looked at Cyllius, my Cyllius, perfect, broken Cyllius. And I shook my head. No.

2

MARINA

and then he looked down and the soldiers pulled in close, radiant in
their armour and excitement and heat,

I

QUITERIA

And one of them, not Cyllius, lunged forward and knocked Marina's sword away, while another, not Cyllius, lunged for me, for mine, and I let it drop before he even made contact.

Then three more, not Cyllius, not Cyllius, not Cyllius, lunged in after them, with them, and, in the perfect motion of one body, one beast, pushed into the single hand's width of space that had been between our weapons and ourselves, pushed through it easy, like water, up, and, in that motion, that pure, synchronized sweep, they held their swords to our filthy, sticky necks, these swords like their own arms their own hands, and, as they did, the weapons caught the light and

2

MARINA

the tapestry was still in my pocket. Nine sisters

not quite finished.

I closed my eyes.

I

QUITERIA

and the cliff and the sun and the men and the weapons and the water were my prayer, were our prayer.

We were twenty years old.

We were alive.

2

MARINA

And we were holding hands, Quiteria and I.

It'll look like flying, she said. It will feel like flying.

And she counted

One two three four five six seven eight

nine:

and then both

together

we jumped,

my sister and I

up and up

into the rolling

roaring

Everything of sea.

THANK YOU:

Nicole, for the enduring ardor through thick and thin,
cocktails, and school closures.

Cathryn, for the same; we are tired, we are true of heart*.

Ian B. and Ian R., for patiently and thoroughly
answering questions about tunics and pockets.

Janice W., for trudging through a quagmire of commas.

Villa Lugara and, with it, Fiona and Steve (and all the others),
for the pool and the cake and the stable and the sun
and the writing it all added up to.

And Kit, who interrupted it all with joy.
And Aubrey, asking the bigger questions.
And Charlie, my forever first reader.
And Ione and Rick and Chris, of course.
And Erin, for the blood-harmonies all along.

* with credit to D. Eggers.

© Charlie Williams

Raised in Alberta, **EMMA HOOPER** is a musician and writer. Her debut novel, *Etta and Otto and Russell and James*, was an international bestseller and was published in twenty-four countries. *Our Homesick Songs*, her second novel, was longlisted for the Scotiabank Giller Prize and named a *Globe and Mail* Best Book of 2018. As a musician she performs as solo artist Waitress for the Bees, a project which earned her a Finnish Cultural Knighthood. She has also performed with Peter Gabriel, The Heavy, her string quartet Red Carousel, and numerous others. She now lives in the soft green of England's South-West, but comes home to Canada to cross-country ski as much as she can.